# contention

Also by Aaron T. Brownell

*Reflection*

# contention

## a sara grey tale

## a novel

## aaron t. brownell

iuniverse, inc.
new york  bloomington

**Contention**
**A Sara Grey Tale**

*iUniverse books may be ordered through booksellers or by contacting:*

*iUniverse*
*1663 Liberty Drive*
*Bloomington, IN 47403*
*www.iuniverse.com*
*1-800-Authors (1-800-288-4677)*

*Because of the dynamic nature of the Internet, any Web addresses or links contained in this book may have changed since publication and may no longer be valid. The views expressed in this work are solely those of the author and do not necessarily reflect the views of the publisher, and the publisher hereby disclaims any responsibility for them.*

*ISBN: 978-1-4502-1373-8 (sc)*
*ISBN: 978-1-4502-1372-1 (dj)*
*ISBN: 978-1-4502-1371-4 (ebk)*

*Printed in the United States of America*

*iUniverse rev. date: 4/12/2010*

I would like to sincerely thank Betsy Baker of Potsdam, New York, for suffering through my atrocious use of the English language.

The second journal chronicling
the life of
Lady Sara Anne Grey


Born: London, England
June 21, 1633


Died: London, England
July 2, 1651


Current Age: 376 years


Penned in New York, USA
July 2009

# chapter 1

The quiet beauty of a clear midnight sky and the gentle breeze gave way to the crashing of Adriatic waves against the rocky shoreline with a steady cadence that made me calm and then happy in equal measure. Though the breeze from the west was cold enough to box the local human inhabitants up in their homes, it did not shake my mood in the slightest.

In retrospect, it's interesting to note that these two things had become the physical contrast of my mood. I loved them both, because they told me things about myself.

The Adriatic's cold wind and steady tides told me that I was a child of the sea. It also told me that, no matter how surrounded by humanity I was, I was actually alone. I knew this, for I was the only one who had no feeling for weather.

Crete had become my home, and I loved her dearly. But she was not England. The Thames had no waves and few tidal problems. Before you find me suffering from some sort of melancholy, that is as far as it went. On the days and nights that the cold wind blew, I would go out to the cliffs and look toward the Mediterranean Sea, wondering about England. The remainder of the time, I was quite content to be on Crete. Over the decades that I had resided on the island, I had become fond of its many attractions.

First, unlike England, Crete is warm the vast majority of the year. The cold winds and snow came rarely to the island. The majority of the days, I basked in the radiant warmth of my island home. Many nights, I walked along the beaches and absorbed the heat that emanated from the sand. It was a wonderful sensation to be baked by the sand at night.

Second, food was easy to come by. The port city of Heraklion had such a large transient population of sailors that all I needed to do was walk out the doors of my office building and pick the one I wanted to hunt. With all the language barriers among the dock workers and sailors, no one really paid any attention to people looking for the missing. All I really needed to do was act with some discretion, and life went along nicely, much the same as the docks of the Thames. The killing was easy there.

Interestingly, I seemed to need less blood in those days. I needed to hunt less on the island because of the amulet I wore. The amulet had an inexplicable habit of absorbing energy from the sun and giving it to me as life force. I assume that the sun's brightness had a lot to do with it; the sun in Crete seemed to give me more energy than it had in England, much like the crops that grow better closer to the equator. Whatever the reason, I found that one good hunt a month put me in a perfectly acceptable mood. Economy is good for the vampire. Attracting less attention increases one's margin of safety.

As far as my business went, the move to Crete was a mixed blessing. I had moved the main office of my shipping company, known as Grey Cargo, from London to Crete. Moving got me away from the turmoil of Europe, but it never really shifted my company's power base out of London as I had intended. One of my older confidants, Christopher Wyndell, continued with the clients of our London office as always. My new confidant, Christopher's son John Francis, managed a second and highly efficient central business office in Crete. In the end, the move gave me a company with two points of command—two heads, as it were. In a word, it was chaos. Oh, everything ran smoothly enough; there just always seemed to be some kind of management-level friction. The final say was mine, so it was all fine; it just all seemed quite daft.

So there you have it, me standing on the cliffs of Crete, looking into the December winds and reflecting on my life. The year was 1760, and many things had come along to mark that year as a good place to take up my tale of adventure. After all, one's life—especially a life like mine—is an adventure, if you look at it the right way.

Let's see. The Seven Years' War rumbled along and saw the British making a good show of it. That's all things considered. They defeated the French in what would turn out to be the last naval battle for New France. It was the Battle of Ristigouche. The English commander, Lord Granby, gave what can only be called a heroic performance when the Anglo-Hanoverian Army, led by Ferdinand of Brunswick, stormed Warburg.

In the spring of the same year, the great fire of Boston in the colony of Massachusetts destroyed 349 buildings. Unfortunately, my office buildings and storehouses were among them. Fortunately, none of my more valuable assets or personnel were lost, as they were in the office buildings on the other side of the city proper. All that was truly lost was the unloading facility at the Boston harbor.

That year saw the birth of the German poet Johann Hebel, the Italian composer Luigi Cherubini, and the priest who would one day become Pope Leo XII. It saw the deaths of Nicolaus Zinzendorf, the German religious and social reformer; the French historian Jean LeBeuf; and Alaungpaya, the King of Burma.

It also presented the English with a change through the death of King George II and the ascension of King George III.

Now, change can be difficult to judge at first glance. It can look good, be bad, and then turn out for the best. All one really needs to do to prove that that is true is look to the history of the French. Do that, and you really could waffle. As for me, it turned out to be okay, I think.

The warmth of the morning sun on the large stones of the manor's terraced, cathedral-like entrance made the stones friendly to my touch. It wasn't long before I was ready to begin what seemed like an arduous task. The stones' warmth gave me strength, and the solid luminous glow of my amulet reassured me that all would be fine.

I stood and took in the sun as the stableman brought around a jet-black mare named Eloise. She was my primary mode of transport in those days. In London, transport had been a carriage, but in Crete, everything had a decidedly country pace to it. There were many carts and wagons but few carriages. Everyone rode where they wanted to go, or they walked if they had no horse to ride. It was good. I loved to ride through the hills of my island home and take in the barricade that the ocean provided me.

The great cliffs north past Kaliviani gave great views of the sea. The sea gave me comfort. It may seem counterintuitive, but the vastness of the sea can be helpful to a lady of my station. The rigors of sea travel slowed the spread of wild stories by sailors and travelers. Where one might assume the sea to be an obstacle, I saw it as a defensive barrier. As long as the natives didn't get restless because of my presence, the world was none the wiser. And that was the way I liked it.

I spent days riding the cliffs and crags of Crete's northwestern coastline, as the weather permitted. Being dead as I am, the weather didn't actually bother me much, but Eloise didn't like the gale winds that came in. She also didn't like the driving rain that sometimes followed the winds.

Eloise was a wonderful animal. I had raised her from a colt, and she was well into adulthood by then. We were creatures of a similar mood. She liked the open and somewhat unbridled life she led and did not seem to mind that her handler was a deadly predator.

By virtue of their instincts, animals knew full well what I was. I could not hide my true nature from them the way I could from humans. I just needed to find animals that accepted me. It became very much a bonding experience. I would talk to them a great deal to build up their confidence levels. Bonding is the reason that vampires keep trustworthy animals right up until the end of their days and then miss them like an old friend when they're gone. Animals give a certain kind of acceptance that a vampire can not readily get from humans. To the horse, I was just another one of the world's many creatures, I guess.

This being said, one usually finds vampires in the company of male horses. The large stallions, or the stout steeds trained for war, are the best. War horses tend not to scare when their intuition tells them to be scared. This is a nice quality. I had numerous war horses in my day. They were all good and true.

However, at that time I found myself taken with a mare. I was there when she was born. She seemed quite unafraid of me. I found this instantaneous brashness a good thing. Looking into her eyes, I could see that she knew I was dangerous, but she did not object. After that day, we became fast friends.

That particular morning, Eloise was in fine spirits. She seemed happy to be out in the bright sun. I was as well. The dull grey-black view of the landscape I saw through my heavy black glasses was in stark contrast to the way Eloise saw the world. She saw bright colors and shapes; I did not. Well, I did—but at dusk and dawn, when my friend the sun was not quite so luminous.

I had discovered quite by accident many years ago that a vampire does not need to shun the bright light of day. It seemed that they just did. The knowledge came to me in the journal of an ancient vampire who lived in what is now Siberia. It came to me along with the amulet that I wore.

The amulet and the information in the journal pushed me into the light of day. It was a wonderful transformation. However, it did have one minor consequence. My keen night vision could not bear the brash light of day. The vampire was designed to hunt at night. The opaque black glasses that I wore eased that problem. They turned the brightness to a dull grey. It was an easy concession to make so I might be able to walk around in the daytime.

You might think that every vampire would know this, but none seem to. The knowledge had apparently been lost in antiquity. Now, the other vampires are held back by myth and fear. I have told few others of my secret knowledge. That way it would not spread. Secrecy had been decided upon at the time by my circle of human friends.

Walking in the daytime was the prefect disguise for moving about in society. Everyone knows, to this day, that vampires do not come out during the day, lest they perish in some horrible manner. This little misconception has been a wondrous blessing to me, ever since I took my first step out onto the sunlit patio of my London estate.

I mounted Eloise and settled onto the English saddle she had cinched to her back. Then, like lightning, we were off. We rode the hillsides and cliff faces past Cape Spandra and roamed the beach and coast east to Hania. From there, we turned inland and made our way past Episkopi and on toward the metropolis of Heraklion, where the Venetian lion of St. Mark still stood resplendent on the fort wall. The buzz of activity was a drastic change from the solitude of my stately manor on the hill above Plantanos. Ships coming and going with a rush of urgency filled the harbor space not taken up by the Greek caiques on their way in from the fishing areas past the port.

I made my way through the streets to the stables next to my city house. I handed Eloise over to the stable boy to be washed and brushed down. The young lad always looked at me with the longing that Greek men possess for beautiful women. If he only knew that I was older than his great-grandfather.

I walked down the cobblestone side streets and out into the wide main area of the port. The Venetian architecture of the buildings surrounding the dock area always took me back to Venice. It is still such a wonderful city, even now that it has been overrun with day-tripping tourists who have no appreciation for its true soul.

Down toward the end of the large semicircular conglomeration of boats and load wagons sat a group of buildings with a decidedly Turkish influence. The sign that hung out in front of them spelled out Grey Cargo in both Greek and English. I found that bilingual signs helped the locals give foreigners directions.

As I approached the entrance to my offices, the bustling activity of the ships being off-loaded suddenly came to a stop; the local men all shifted their gazes my way. They smiled and waved and said many nice things. I smiled and waved in return. Then I continued on my way toward the office.

Greek men are an interesting enigma. They chase after every beautiful girl who comes along but then happily go home to their wives at the end of the day. The thing I liked most, though, was that even an old man smiled when he greeted me, as if I were the first love of his life. They were a truly wonderful people to live among.

I shrugged off the interests of the men as I walked into the large, open front room of the office. That was where people gathered to discuss generalities before going off to a side room for negotiation. Bion, the manager of the shop, came hurriedly across the floor and took my hand. Bion was from a well-established, old Crete family, and he knew the shipping trade, along the Adriatic and Mediterranean coasts, better than most men.

"Lady Grey, it's most pleasant to see you here today. You have become bored with the country life and have returned to the city to spend more time with us." Bion had a happy chuckle in his voice as he said it.

"Yes and no, Bion. I was wondering if you could send out word on the wind and discover the whereabouts of *The Summer Storm* and have it return this way."

"Certainly. Are you going on vacation? I hear that Alexandria is quite pleasant this time of year."

"No, Bion, I am going back to London. Lady Grey is going home for a while."

# chapter 2

As it always did in those days, matters took time. It was the better end of three weeks before the flags of *The Summer Storm* could be seen flying in the dockyards of Crete. The members of her crew had become used to being by themselves on the sea, and only her captain seemed in tune with my presence on board. Obviously, no one actually said anything about a woman on board, but I could feel the unease.

Unease, or no, I had set my sights on a journey, and a journey there would be. The tension dissipated quickly enough as the ship was loaded for transport. In the time it took to find my ship and return her to me, Bion had acquired proper cargo for her holds. Rugs from Constantinople, I think. I, apparently, was just along for the ride.

John Francis, my well-mannered, human confidant, did not seem overly pleased by the notion of travel. He said it was too soon to return to the British Isles. People would remember my face, he said, and my reappearance would undo the effects of my earlier disappearing act.

"You really need to give things at least another decade before you go charging back into town," John Francis muttered as he sat his teacup down on the study table.

"I have the desire to return to England now," I said with mock annoyance.

"I was not aware that you gave in to your desires."

John Francis turned and stared at the books along the shelf next to him. He wanted a moment to reflect on the situation at hand.

"John, you have no idea how many times that actually happens."

"Let the ship go. Give me some time to put together an alternative plan. You know that planning is always better than charging off. Besides, if you are going to do this, there are people who need to be warned."

"For a young man, you always seem to make sense. I can only assume that you get that from you father."

"Wisdom is only what you make of it, and I am not as young as I was when we started out together."

"Once again, I hear Christopher in your voice. How is he? Well, I hope. He only sends me business communications. He says nothing of his personal state."

John Francis moved slowly back and forth along the stack of books next to him. He removed a book and gave it a casual inspection. After a few seconds of thought, he continued in a low tone.

"He is fine. He sent me a personal communication last week. The family is well. All of my aunts sent me greetings. If I had to guess, I would say that being away from you has made his days all business and not so much fantasy."

"Where your days are more fantasy and less business?" It came out in a somber tone that I had mastered over the centuries.

"It is good enough. I'm pleased with the way my life has been, as I am sure he is with his."

I sat staring at John Francis for a second. People have a tendency to change. Sometimes, it happens as you are looking at them. Right there and then, he had found the Wyndell gift of measured review. That was what made wisdom grow. All the men of his family were wise.

"You are correct, John. Let *The Summer Storm* depart. I'll stay out of the British Isles for at least another decade. We don't want to ruin well-made plans. I, however, would like to go somewhere. What would you suggest?"

John Francis returned to the table and retrieved his coat. As he turned to head toward the door of the study, he paused.

"We should go to Boston in the colonies, or maybe New York. William and Amber are heading back to England with my wife for schooling, and I would like to see the colonies." He paused by the door and smiled. "I need to return to the docks and handle the disposition of your vessel. Have a lovely day, Sara."

Then, as sure as the seasons change, he was gone. I looked down at the table and the book about the American colonies that he had placed there. I was sure that it wasn't part of my library. He must have really wanted to go. He rarely called me Sara. Come to think of it, no one ever really called me Sara. That is the problem with a title; everyone wants to use it. I seldom heard anyone voice my name in those days. My father always called me Sara—well, unless he was really mad.

In those days, about the only one who called me Sara was Antonio. My fiancé, my dark lord, and the one who made me what I am. For all of our assumed closeness, I had not seen him in many years. In a sense, his absence was a good thing. Two vampires on an island the size of Crete would be bad, both for the human population and for our own safety. He had been there at the beginning and then moved along, tending to his own business.

One might think he would come around more as the only reason I had been transformed into a creature of death was for the continued future of his business interests. Apparently, I was doing a wonderful job at my own business, because he did not see fit to check on how I was handling his affairs.

Oh, I would imagine that at least part of his actions were predatory. Vampires are solitary creatures. They tend to give one another a wide berth so as not to raise human suspicion. Too many of my kind have died over the millennia for the sake of spending time together. It is much easier to stay on your own and concealed from the outside human world.

I could feel a small wave of melancholy sweep over me. I reached into my gown and rubbed the amulet that lay next to my breast. The amulet could sense my mood, for it began to glow ever so slightly brighter. It took only seconds of the luminous glow before my festering state retreated. The power of the friendly stones had made me warm all over, warm and content.

I knew that, one day, I would need to investigate whatever form of mysticism was used to conjure my amulet into being. I felt sure back then that it must be the work of evil men. Sorcerers, or some sort like that must have been responsible for harnessing the powers of the world. I was sure. However, by that point, I had also learned that rushing to judgment is a bad thing.

After all my studying and searching, I had no evidence that anything special actually ran the world. Father Josh used to tell me that I was proof enough of that. As nearly as I could tell, I was not special. I was not the first—nor would I be the last—vampire to walk the earth. I was among a small population of different creatures. We were like other creatures but not the same.

There seemed to be no proof of a grand design. In over a hundred years of being undead, I had managed to find neither the signs of a benevolent creator nor those of his antithesis. Things in the world just were what they were. The plants continued to grow so the animals could eat them, then those animals get eaten by other animals. Then we could eat them, so that they could go back to the earth and make new plants. This cycle went on and on and on. Over all of this, the sun gave its warmth to the earth to help it along. The whole thing seemed pretty straightforward.

But buried in the simplicity were things like the amulet, which made me question such childish beliefs. The warm embrace of the jewel's power gave me the feeling that I should move on toward happier thoughts. Thoughts of Antonio. Yes, thoughts of my tall, dark-skinned Spanish lord were always nice.

I walked over to a small desk, which was stationed next to a large bay of windows that overlooked the distant seashore, and retrieved a bundle used for correspondence. I quickly scribbled down a note to have Antonio meet me in Boston in about two years' time. I folded the parchment and stamped the Grey family seal into the hot wax.

Rising from the chair, I collected the letter and headed for the stables. I wandered in, looking for the stable boy, but I happened upon a young girl named Elpis, who was tending the animals. Elpis was around thirteen years of age. She possessed the smooth, deep-toned skin that Mediterranean women are famous for. Her long, dark hair and pleasant smile helped to smooth her features. While these womanly features would help to land her a good husband one day, her youth held remnants of a childish, open curiosity. This gave her insights that she could not explain.

She was the only one of the staff who had any clue as to the otherworldly nature of their employer. I could just tell every time she looked at me; somewhere in the back of her head was a glimmer that told her I was different. Her advance toward adulthood had clouded over most of her natural intuition.

Numerous people had speculated that children possess a better view of the world than do adults. Not a better one per se, but probably a truer one. Children, as a rule, seldom try to organize their visions into boxes based upon what they have learned. This is what adults do. Children see what they see and accept it, because they see it.

As time marches on, the human adaptation for learning obscures everyday sights that one sees. Knowledge tells adults what things are real or not real and what to believe. Some say that sorcerers and witches are just people who have managed to keep hold of their childish sight of the world. They still see the things that are right in front of them and use that sight to their advantages. I don't know if that is bollocks or not, but it sounds right to me.

Fifty years ago, I would have let her in on my little secret. Fifty years ago, I did it a lot. Those little indiscretions were what had caused my move to Crete. I had been naively willing to share my secret life with too many people in England. I had done so thinking that they would not look down on my shortcomings. For the most part, this was true. It had just proceeded along to the point where my willingness to share was about to unravel on me. Too many people knew my secret.

Taking this into account, I did what any self-respecting predator would do. I reduced the number of people who knew of my situation and left the British Isles so the remainder of them could die in peace. I decided that I would return when the only human who knew of my vampirism was John Francis's son William, my then new confidant. That was my plan. A Wyndell man had been my confidant since William's great-grandfather had taken the original position. That family of men possessed two distinct gifts. They maintained a solid aptitude for business affairs, and they held a predisposition toward the occult.

Looking back to the beginning, I had made a promise to the first Wyndell man in my life that I would look after all the other ones who might follow. I would look after his family. I have been doing so ever since, although I confess it sometimes feels as though they are looking after me.

As I stood in the doorway lost in my myriad of thoughts, Elpis came over with her trademark smile and childlike glow to see if I required any assistance. That snapped me back to the present.

I gently handed the parchment over to her and asked if she knew the location of the stable boy. I wished him to deliver it to John Francis at the shipping office. I hoped for it to catch the outgoing tide.

The young girl gathered up the correspondence and stated that she would be happy to handle the task herself. The truth of it was that she secretly had a fancy for John Francis. Most young women on the island had a fancy for John Francis. The thought of it made me chuckle as I watched young Elpis skip off down the street toward the docks.

# chapter 3

The chatter of the rain against the large ornate windows of the ballroom made my thoughts drift. The January rain was a nice neighbor to have, I thought.

The winter weather could have been much fiercer than it was that particular night. It had only been some years back that the golden horn had frozen over completely. That had altered my business plans for months. It had also been a general nuisance.

However, the rain was nice that night. It was not as nice as the sun or the full moon, but it was nice. I don't particularly like being out in the rain, so being inside gave me time to think (as it does even today). As they usually did in those days, my thoughts revolved around my dark lord.

I had been told that the correspondence I had sent out on the tide had been delivered without incident. He had not sent a response. I had been waiting for the better part of two years. During that time, I had been making plans for travel. I had expected him to respond by that point.

Thinking about him generally produced melancholy. During that period, it had had the opposite effect. It had made me jump with anticipation. The thought of his hard embrace made my blood run warm. The power he exuded was wondrous to soak in.

The rain fell, and I stood transfixed in the ballroom. I quietly thought about Antonio. Looking back on it now, it felt a lot like being inside that Eurhythmics song, "Here Comes the Rain Again."

Truth be told, Antonio wasn't the only thing on my mind those days. Since it had been decided—mostly by my confidant and traveling companion John Francis—that we were going to the colonies, I had been on the lookout for information about what we were getting into. I had trading vessels that went to the American colonies on a regular basis, but they brought back much more gossip than useful information.

I learned that some silly chap named Benjamin Franklin was experimenting with electricity. Apparently, he was flying a kite in a lightning storm and the lightning gave him a shock. At the time, I found him quite odd indeed. Since then, I have revised my opinion of him. I saw an episode of *Mythbusters* on the Discovery Channel, and the team had some interesting times trying to reproduce the event.

I learned that the British had taken control of French Canada a couple of years past, when it fell in the Battle of the Plains of Abraham outside Quebec City. I had known we were doing quite well, but it was always nice to hear about conquest.

Interestingly, as we set out for the new world, that was pretty much all I knew. Oh, I knew there were cities and lots of people. I knew there were Indians and many slaves who had been transported from Africa. I knew there was much to be had for the taking. I really didn't know what I was getting into.

I was happy I spoke the language. It had been many years since we had come to Crete, and I still struggled with the language of the Greeks. I had learned enough Greek to get by and appear polite. As far as business went, rich ladies employed interpreters for such things.

John Francis spoke several languages well. As had his father. Having grown up on the island, young William and Amber both spoke Greek fluently. They were completely bilingual. That was a trait that I lacked. Bugger all, I had spent decades living in Bristol, and I had trouble with regional differences in English. Truth be told, I still do to this day. Today, it produces fond remembrances of earlier days; back then, it was simply a hindrance.

John Francis informed me that young William was going to learn a few additional languages so he would be better suited to take over one day. He was also being extensively schooled in the ways of the occult. William appeared to enjoy the mythology very much. He was a quick study with the darker side of life, as the rest of the men in his family had been. All the Wyndell men possessed the trait of absorbing knowledge. I find it amazing, even today.

I remember asking John Francis if William was capable of making the transition from fantasy to reality. After all, not knowing what he was getting into earlier on had made the transition almost impossible for his great-grandfather. John Francis smiled and said that one's true nature never comes out until it's tested. How true that was.

I felt sure then, looking out into the rain, that reality was about to bring out my true nature again. While I stood in front of the window, my mind was brought back to the now (or then, as it were) by the clacking sound of boots on stone floors. Making the assumption that it was John Francis, since only he and the stablemen wore boots, I kept my pose.

Then, as if scripted, Mr. Wyndell walked through the doors of the ballroom and directly toward my station. He took up his customary position to my left and asked about my day. I told him that it lacked hostility and then asked how he felt. He said he was in fair enough shape to take a beating from me, if that was required. That was what I had had in mind.

He followed up my assumption with a hearty laugh. I smiled. I had no choice. I had no intention of actually hurting him, even though it would be quite easy to kill him. I was wearing a floor-length gown and shawl and could kill him before he drew a breath. However, I didn't want that; I just wanted to let off a little bit of steam.

Once in the beginning, when he was younger, there was need for the surgeon. He was always willing to go at things full speed, which led to him being badly beaten. He possessed a streetfighter's sense for violence, even though he was a well-trained boxer and martial artist. He was proficient in numerous weapons as well, though he preferred bare knuckles on most occasions. Above all, he lacked restraint. Some of his forebears had fought with me as if they were fighting a girl. He fought as if he were fighting for his life. He had no compunction about throwing me against walls and beating me in the skull repeatedly with heavy objects. On one occasion, he stood on my neck until he thought me unconscious. Needless to say, he required the surgeon that day. My lack of need for air just gave me time to become really hostile.

I think he fought that way because he was one of the ones who really understood what I was. The others knew on an intimate level what I was capable of, but John Francis could actually see the other side of my personality. To him, I was a killer. All the other things were window dressings to cover up the fact that I was a ruthless, cold-blooded sociopath and killer.

In a strange way, I sensed that that knowledge was what made him truly happy to be working for me. It gave him an odd sense of security for his family. What could overcome a guardian such as me?

Men are said to be the stronger sex. They are mostly the ones who wage war. They are the ones who enslave the vanquished. Yet they would work for a woman if it meant protecting their own possessions. Men are strange creatures.

While thinking these thoughts, I slid my arm inside his and slowly turned him round. Then as calmly as an old couple headed to church, we started out toward the basement.

My large Crete estate had been professionally constructed for my needs. Mostly, it was like any other manor. It contained all the usual quarters and large rooms with ornate windows and walls of paintings. It had all the outer trappings of wealth. It also contained a room in the basement set apart from the remainder by a hidden door and stairs. That space was completely for me. It contained no windows and was lit only by candelabras. The walls were stone, as was the floor. The door was made from heavy timbers and sealed out all noise. The space stayed a constant cool temperature and never lost its earthy smell.

The space was open all around. There were plush settees and thick carpets in one corner by the door. There was a small chest, which resided on a rickety, wooden table. Blocking the chest from the other furnishings was an intricately styled, oriental screen. The screen had been a present from Antonio when we had first come to Crete. The chest and stand were common and old. John Francis had procured them from one of the ships in port.

John Francis sat on the settee or paced to and fro, looking at weapons, while I slipped into my secluded space and changed from pretty attire into the shirt and trousers that the trunk contained. There was also a dark-colored chemise in the chest for those occasions when I needed to practice fighting like a lady. I could kill quite efficiently in the fancy dresses and heeled boots of the day, but I always preferred to train in pants. The trousers offered greater speed and mobility and gave me less to think about.

I had learned to wear trousers back in Bristol, when I was but a newborn vampire. My original confidant and trainer, the first Charles Wyndell, had thought it best to train in something that lacked the confusion of women's fashion. I did such until I was able to do my bidding without making a mess of my victim.

It took practice and training to bleed someone out without spotting up my wardrobe in the process. I needed to know how to feed without getting blood all over me or on whatever well-crafted camouflage I had manufactured. This was especially true for me as a woman, since changing on the run was not an option in those days.

I changed and hung my dress and throw on an elegant iron hook set into the stone. Once changed, I stepped out from behind the screen. At that point, it was go.

When I emerged, John Francis was able to attack. Sometimes he would wait until I was out in the room before he attacked; sometimes he would not. There were also times, such as this one, when I would leap from behind the screen and take the fight to him. I could tell that he was always prepared for such a plan. He did not flinch but always went directly to a combat footing and defended himself.

He was very good at defending himself. He could hold his own most confidently with the best of men. With a hundred-plus-year-old vampire, however, it was a different thing. He could escalate his aggression to a whole new level and become truly violent. I often wondered if he were bipolar, once I learned what bipolar was.

Bipolar or not, he sprang into action that day with all the courage he could muster and a six-foot, wooden staff. As I plunged at him with full attack speed, I focused on the ends of the staff. Waiting for that parry, I missed the shift in his stance and the forthcoming kick. The kick impacted the lower part of my jaw. The pain it created was searing. The impact threw me sideways against the wall, where my head slapped against the well-crafted vertical stones. The gobsmack I received from the stone almost knocked me senseless.

I was just beginning to refocus when John Francis dropped the staff and struck me with a heavy Italian mace. I hadn't noticed the mace, which had been hanging against his leg. The mace's eight-flanged head, which had been designed to smash its way through the plate armor worn by the chivalrous knights of old, impacted my temple midway from eye to ear. The strike ripped a gouge of my flesh completely out of place. The blood and flesh spraying from my head did nothing to slow my opponent's attack. He pulled back and began swinging the bloody weapon with all the anger he could summon. Again and again, the head of the mace smashed into my forearm. I had barely managed to get my arm up in the defense of my skull before the barrage had begun.

John Francis must have come around with the weapon some fifteen times before he paused to draw breath. The head of the mace was soaked in blood and covered with severed chunks of my flesh. My arm, for that matter, had basically been reduced to a semihard mush. The bones were broken in numerous places, and much of the flesh was torn or missing.

I was losing blood from my wounds at a pace that disturbed me greatly. I was worried about succumbing to it all. It is a little known fact that vampires can actually bleed out. Oh, we won't actually die (I think?), but we will lose all our power and eventually become catatonic. This state only comes on after a massive loss of blood.

John Francis, likely sensing my fear of my own doom, attacked again. This time it was all for naught. With my good arm, I deflected the incoming blow from the mace. The impact of the steel mace's head against the adjacent stone wall threw sparks all about and produced a noise inside the room that echoed off all the walls.

Using a page from John Francis's playbook, I attacked. I rolled up on my back and kicked John Francis in the chest with both feet. The impact lifted him from the floor and threw him several feet back into the room. His connection with the floor produced an audible thud.

The contact between my feet and his chest produced a shock wave that traveled through my feet and legs halfway to my buttocks. Minimizing the experience, I leapt to my feet and closed the distance between us as John Francis pulled himself off the floor.

The damage to my skull had almost healed by that point in the battle, which had lasted long enough for my initial confusion to turn into outright rage. I could not believe I had been bested so easily. John Francis could sense my change in mood, as he tried to remove himself from my path. Adjusting for his movements, I rammed my good forearm into his chest, so I could wind him. The force produced the same shock wave that my feet had experienced.

The ripping of buttons on John Francis's shirt showed the front portion of a cuirass, which he had inserted under his shirt with a small bit of leather padding. The pain that the impact with the metal shield had produced was hearty. John Francis used my instant of confusion to produce a short, one-handed, Swiss bastard sword and thrust it firmly into my midsection. My face curled up in anger as a burning pain from the two-foot blade punched its way through my midsection. I recoiled instinctively. I pushed back with such force that I landed halfway across the room. Fortunately, I landed on my feet. Blood gushed from the two large wounds that the sword had made. A black veil of pain and hate started to overtake my senses, and my vision narrowed at the edges.

I lowered my stance, as years of killing automatically overcame my reasoning. I stretched my jaws open, exposing large, white enamel fangs. I was going into killing mode. The sight of my fangs produced a look of genuine fear on the face of my enemy. It was the image of his face that snapped me back to reality. Things were getting seriously out of hand.

It took all the willpower I could muster to grab control of my senses. I had to get them back in check fast. Getting a firm grip on myself before the killing started in earnest, I stood and backed up several steps. I wanted to show a truce.

John Francis readied the bastard sword, but he did not advance.

I slowly closed my jaw and attempted to garner a sincere expression to my bruised and battered face. It had restructured itself to the point of being only very black and blue. My arm was a different matter. It would require much more time to reach that state. I knew the large sword wounds would require bandages and lots of blood, but they would otherwise heal fine.

I attempted to straighten my shirt, and then I looked at John Francis. He was still fully ready to pounce. He had the look of a man who truly wanted to kill me. That was worrisome.

"I think that will probably be enough for today, John. Any more of this, and you might actually need to find new employment." I did my best not to sound shaky as I said it.

John Francis instantly relaxed his stance and placed the bloodied sword on the ground.

"You didn't seem to be yourself, so I thought it best to fully protect myself." As he talked, he walked to the settee and slowly sat down.

I lay down upon the cold, smooth, stone floor and let the blood slowly seep out under me. John Francis was correct; my mood had been strange as of late. It must be the leaving; I was never really good at leaving. The new and unexplored left me apprehensive, even though I had done this very thing many times before.

"No, John, you were right to do so. Good show on besting me today. Now, if you would be so kind, I could use some bandages and a large goblet of blood. I should start to heal the damage you have inflicted sooner rather than later. And more directly, could you fetch my amulet? It's hanging on the hook behind the screen."

John Francis stood and slid the metal plate out from underneath his shirt. He retrieved the amulet and placed it gently upon my chest. Then, quietly, he removed himself from the room to find further supplies.

I closed my eyes and rested on the cold stone floor. The warmth of the amulet's power slowly soaked into me and made me feel at peace.

As I lay there feeling the chain of the amulet against my breast, I realized that I wasn't breathing. It struck me funny at the time that I had forgotten, though I just forgot about those things from time to time. It reminded me that I was not actually human.

I put the thought from my head and went back to lying numbly on the floor.

# chapter 4

Time passed by, as it always does, and I was myself again. The goblet of blood turned out to be a bucket by the time I was back together. I heal expeditiously; still, I am sure I would not have wanted to let things go much farther.

I assumed I would cease to be if I had bled out. I admit I still don't know for sure. I don't know any vampire who has perished in that way, but it seemed quite logical. I needed blood to survive, so no blood, no survival. Well, you know what I mean.

To be honest, I only know of one vampire who has died. I killed him. It was all right; he had it coming. Creatures can be so presumptuous. Some vampires seem to think that they are better than humans, because humans are their food. They seem to have forgotten that they had once been humans.

I kill to live—usually the older or weaker members of society. Not because it's easy, but because it's better for the species. At the end of the day, I am no better than they are, just different is all.

Needless to say from the buckets of blood, the interaction between John Francis and me was stiff at best. It was that way for weeks afterward. He had a tendency to assume that I had the same emotional range that he did. This is actually not true. By their very nature, vampires are much more cause-and-effect creatures. Most shed their human emotions early on, which has the tendency to make them ruthless. I found that came pretty much naturally.

I am one of the few vampires I have met who have made a conscious effort to hold on to the trappings of humanity. It has served me well over the years. I believe that knowing the intricacies of one's adversary makes you stronger in the end. If human emotions weren't useful, then humans wouldn't have them.

Now, my emotions aren't nearly as in tune as those of the average human. Mine are more of a guideline. I was able to hold on to the basic framework. I know when I should be mad or happy or sad. I just lack the high and low fluctuations. Mine is more of a monotone system. I run into a situation, and my emotional framework tells me that I am supposed to be upset. I think about it a moment and decide if I'm going to be or not. Then I respond however I want to.

This ability to respond to the situation coldly if necessary is a great way to control people. It manipulates them to do what I want them to do, whether that is to step into a dark alley or sign a business agreement.

Having my emotions locked away does leave me at a loss at times. People can become so irrational, usually when driven by their emotions. I still don't get that. People just feel more, I guess.

Such was the case with John Francis. He apparently felt bad about the damage he had inflicted on me. Deep down, I knew that it was not true, but closer to the surface, I think he was worried about me being worried. I knew full well that he had done what was asked of him and that the fault was mine. He didn't seem so sure about the whole thing.

It mostly did not matter to me; it was cause and effect. There was one part of it, however, that did cause me concern. He had been ready. He had been armed. And he had caused me great pain, even though I had known he was coming. I have faced larger men who were armed and ready more times than I care to count, and in all these encounters, I have barely received a scratch. I just engaged, killed, and then fed or fled, depending upon the situation. John Francis, however, had really gotten past my defenses and inflicted some major damage. If that had been a true life-or-death altercation, I would not have fared well. I would not have lost, but I would have received serious injury. That could be a big problem.

I pondered this dilemma for some time. I had obviously become out of practice at combat. I was good at killing, but I had apparently become lax at the important part. I needed to improve my combat skills. I needed to return them to where they had once been.

In years past, I would have dominated the event. He would not have gotten the sword back to swing it. I was obviously getting soft. I wandered if that was what getting old must be like. The realization that I was not as good as I once had been was unpleasant. The difference, I thought, was that I could retrain myself. I could become proficient again.

Yes sir, that was what I needed to do. When we got to the colonies, I would go back into training. I had always enjoyed combat. I could practice in a whole new setting. Maybe I could stalk some Indians. People wouldn't really notice missing Indians. Well, that's what I thought before we left Greece.

I would get to ponder Indians for a while, as it would be nearly June before all would be said and done. *The Summer Storm* would need to make her rounds back to Crete. Suitable cargo would need to be procured for us to sail out. I was not going all that way unless it was profitable. I was and am a businesswoman, after all.

There was also a need for proper lodging in Boston. John Francis found a wonderful property just outside the city in a place called Cambridge. For a while, I had thought it too close to Salem for my taste. But in the end, it seemed nice. John Francis had a manor house and stables built for our needs. The manor befitted the times, but it was modest compared to the stone and finery that I had grown used to. He assured me that it would meet my needs. I reminded him several times that a lady from the House of Grey had a certain level of expectation to live up to. He continued to reassure me that it would be fine.

John Francis's planning came and went, and toward the end of May 1762, *The Summer Storm,* with the Grey family flag flying high on the head mast, slipped out of the harbor and turned her bow west toward His Majesty's colonies in the new world. The trip was long but uneventful, because most of the spring storms that plagued those waters had blown themselves out.

The trip had three planned stops, and with good winds, it took a mere fourteen months to reach the port of Boston. I spent the majority of the voyage by the lead railing on deck, looking at the nothingness of the open ocean. It made me wonder about existence, and I had other deep flowing thoughts as well. The remainder of the time I spent belowdecks in my cabin.

The bright sun that the top decks offered was good to me. It kept my amulet fully charged and kept the thirst at bay. I could pass the long hours on the open ocean with little effort. I coasted along nicely until we reached a port of call. While in port, I gorged myself upon the local population. The blood and the sun helped me ride out the next stretch of the voyage.

My time sequestered belowdecks was usually spent reading and resting. I had purchased a volume of *The Arabian Nights* sometime before and had not yet found time to enjoy it. I read the book completely twice and was on a third go-around by the time we managed to find the Americas. I found myself impressed with the young princess, Scheherazade. I wondered if she had really ever existed or was a construct for someone's ideas. I hoped she had lived.

I also became drawn to the stories of the flying carpet. It seemed so fantastical a thing to be able to fly from one spot to another, to go aloft like the birds and soar. It didn't seem possible; it just seemed like a work of most excellent fiction. I still carry that volume with me whenever I travel. You can imagine the workings of my ironic sense of humor when I first carried it onto an airplane. Apparently, science and magick aren't that different after all. Ha!

It really is a great collection of tales. I held it firmly in hand as I stood on the deck by the wind rail and took my first look at my new home. The ship sailed smoothly on the calm sea. The sails were all but drawn, and the city of Boston spread out before us as though we had wandered into a landscape painting. Boston in 1763 was a strange creature to behold from the sea. The city stood out from the surrounding wilderness like a stronghold of reason in the midst of chaos. It appeared quite anomalous in its surroundings.

Functionally, Boston was an interesting place. Compared to the other places in the world I had seen, it was much younger. It contained no large stone buildings, no grand villas, and no cathedrals. The whole city was apparently made of wood and stone but not like the European cities of old were. This was a place of hand-hewn lumber and fieldstone not one of cut marble and fine detailing. Its youth gave it charm and promise, a sense of the growth to come. At least the place was clean.

*The Summer Storm* glided gracefully into an appropriate space and came to a gentle stop against the loading docks. Looking down on it all, I could see that the timbers showed age and hard use. That was a good sign. It agreed with the reports that Boston was a commercial city with great business. The people who handled the Grey company office in Boston had said as much, but it was always nice to be shown right.

The harbor personnel and deckhands scurried about like rats as the gangways were laid so we could disembark. In the midst of the scurrying, I noticed a well-dressed, rotund fellow standing off to one side by the corner of a large building that resembled a storeroom. You could tell his life consisted of too much food and not nearly enough work.

I was pondering his existence, when John Francis appeared and pointed to him. He said that he should be the man named Paul Renaldo. He was the man who ran my Boston company office.

I turned to John Francis, who was obviously overwhelmed with the adventure of it all, and said, "He had better run my affairs better than he runs his own."

John Francis turned to see my unimpressed expression.

"The colonies do well, Lady Grey. I am to understand that we have steady and profitable traffic from the port, or as much as the currents will tolerate."

"I'm sure that you're right, John. I just have an aversion to sloth. And gluttony, come to think of it."

"Let it go, ma'am. All people are different. As long as he does well by us, it would seem that he could be any way he chooses."

"As usual, you are wiser than your years, John."

With that, I turned slowly and took his arm so that he might escort me down the gangway. As we moved from the ship to the shore, I took the time to notice the bystanders who had gathered to view the excitement we had created. New ships always produced excitement. The bystanders inspected two of us exiting the ship with a look of either curiosity as to what might have brought us here or a strange awe. I could tell that some wondered if I were ill, or possessed of a well-dispensed sadness—the kind of sadness nuns have for children with an illness. I guessed this because of my opaque spectacles. That was fine. My well-trimmed white dress made the men of the docks look on in a completely different fashion.

John Francis walked along next to me, unflinching in his wonder at it all. The people had become lost on him. He was taken up by the experience. It was there that I noticed that he had some of his Uncle Jimmy in him. His uncle had been a good and seasoned traveler. I could tell from his look that John Francis would head down that path if chance would allow.

It seemed my life suited him. I'd been dragging him around on my exploits for some time by then. I hadn't really paid much attention to how he had come to embrace it all. I wondered if his exploits caused friction within his family. If it did, he did not show it on the outside. I wondered for a moment if that was why his whole family had gone back to London for schooling. They had parted ways so he could travel again. That would be an interesting conversation to have at a later date.

John Francis was easy to talk to. He had acquired that quality from his father. Christopher was the one I enjoyed talking to lately. He possessed a genuinely open personality. Almost all of the men in the Wyndell family had that trait. It was one of the things that made me want to keep them close to me. They were also a good challenge to my intellect. Unlike the solitary nature of other vampires, I had been born and raised to be intellectually curious and socially outgoing. That is the core of my personality. I refuse to yield to the want of the night, to give in to cries from the hunter within.

The Wyndell men all helped me keep that sense of social connection. We tended to talk at length about the issues of the days, whatever they happened to be.

As we moved along, John Francis continued his visual festival. While doing so, he managed to lead me directly to the rotund fellow, Renaldo. He introduced himself and made pleasantries in the fashion of the day. Then he showed us around the corner to a splendid carriage. He stated that the driver would convey us to our new manor house. Then once we were rested, he would be honored to go over all aspects of the colonial trade with John Francis.

I explained to him that I would be the one he was educating, because I was the owner of the company. The confusion was fine. It was normal in those days for men to assume that men were in charge. I explained to Renaldo that I would be happy to hear his presentation in the morning at our colonial office. John Francis stayed quiet during my retort. That made me happy.

I confessed that I was curious about the new colonial business and manor house that I had come to. I asked Renaldo if he knew of the manor house. He stated that he did. Interestingly, he didn't seem put upon by the interrogation I was giving him. At least, he didn't play me the prat.

Mr. Renaldo explained that he had supervised the construction of the manor, and it was on par with the best of the residences in the city. As far as business was concerned, he assured me that I would be pleased with the state of affairs. Then he helped me up into the carriage.

As he turned and quietly strolled off to where the captain was supervising the off-loading, I realized that John Francis was correct yet again. One should not judge a book by its cover. After all, I was an old girl in a new world myself—a strange kind of book.

# chapter 5

A succession of years passed by as I attempted to adjust to my new home. I tried, but strange things seemed to be afoot all around me. I had no more than made landfall in America when turmoil appeared to be heating up the times.

In May of 1764, a chap named Otis, who was apparently a Boston lawyer, denounced the British tax laws. He was unhappy that the colonies had no say in their monetary system. On the heels of Otis's denunciation, the next years brought the Stamp Act to the colonies. This bit of business required revenue stamps on any goods purchased by the colonies. Then, as if the stamps weren't bad enough, the Currency Act came along and threatened to undermine the colonial economy.

There was some good news, I guess. A man named James Watt patented the steam engine in 1769. The steam engine would lead to the rapid expansion of railroads across the world. Railroads had already been around for a while by that date, but they were simple carts rolling on wooden, grooved tracks. They had no real reliability. It would take both the steam engine and the invention of steel rail to really push railroads into the forefront of travel. In time, two vast rail systems would develop out of those two ideas. The one in Europe would come to be a model for moving people efficiently, which was nice because traveling by train always made for a better journey. The other one would come to dominate the later, free America, and it would move trade. Goods would move across the vast country in an endless wave. I liked that system more. I equated it to watching little boxes of money going past.

I am getting way ahead of myself. Bringing things back to 1769, there was also a certain amount of travesty afoot. On the far side of the world in the country of Bengal, a horseman from the apocalypse inflicted a famine on the Indian population. It would consume the lives of some ten million inhabitants and become known as the worst famine in recorded history.

All of these stories filtered into the port of Boston with the trade and added disquiet to an already tense city population. Really, the larger part of Boston didn't seem to care much. The large immigrant population of the American colonies was merely happy to survive. They replaced despair in other places with jobs, food, and relief from disease. That thought was the same everywhere, I guess. People just wanted a better life is all.

The people in my new social circle were a completely different matter. They were all well-to-do businesspeople, heads of state, or diplomats of some sort. They understood economic interest, war, famine, trade, taxes, and the like. Those outside topics, combined with the local array of issues that seemed ever constant, like the Indians, created great tension.

The calmer businesspeople did their best to pacify the fears of their counterparts. My adversary (the church), for its part, did nothing to calm the fears of the masses. They were sure that everyone should repent—now!

I wasn't really helping the situation either. With my decision to sharpen my combat skills, I had taken a small, warlike stance against the local Indian population. The Indians did not enjoy the experience.

I had settled into my new country manor life and quietly gone about inserting myself into my empire in the colonies. When I had come here, I had thought that I would stay in this new land of plenty for some time, the same as I had thought when I had landed in Greece. That would turn out not to be. The colonies were too unstable for a creature like me.

The needs of my empire were actually an illusion. The real power base of my company had never really left London. The whole thing ran itself from there, and I just looked about the scene from wherever I was at the time. That trick was easy from Greece. Crete was on the close end of the trade routes and a short run from the docks of the Thames. Boston was not close at all.

In 1765, I established a route directly from Boston to London. It brought much more news and business information than it did trade dollars, but that was the purpose. The route was given to a merchant ship named *The Boston Gale*. Her keel was laid down in the Bristol mooring, and they built her to be fast. They also produced her fairly quickly. The problem was that even a fast ship like *The Gale* took twice as long to make the turn from Boston as *The Summer Storm* took to get there from Crete.

My being out of touch with command gave Christopher new sweeping power over my company. It didn't worry me terribly, as Christopher was a great businessman. His fortunes were intertwined with mine by that point, so it served him to serve me well. The worry was that he was no longer a young man. That bothered me greatly. I dispatched numerous inquiries about the state of his health and the need to return John Francis to him. All responses urged me to worry not. Sadly, they did not settle my concerns. I could feel change coming. It was in the air all around me and seemed close to eruption at most moments.

I knew John Francis had to take over soon. I knew I needed to return to my roots. Somehow, I just wasn't sure about it all. It was still too early for me to return to London. That was plain. I had to wait until no one knew me again. That time was getting close. I really needed to stay in the colonies a tad longer.

My unconscious wish to leave was compounded by the unsophisticated nature of my surroundings. Boston was too new for me.

The fancy manor house built for me in Cambridge was about the size of my stable house at the Grey Estate. I mean the bloody thing was small. It was sturdy and fine in comparison to the surrounding houses. The colonial post and beam timber houses surrounding mine were nice and all, but the solid stone, German colonial that had been built for me did somehow seem a bit nicer.

Engineering wise, it was stout as well—two-feet-thick stone walls, reinforced stone arches over the first-floor windows and doors, flared eaves, and a massive wishbone chimney. The exposed, interior, half timbers were fashioned in the style of the day.

The real problem did seem to be the size. It was just not big enough for a creature with my habits. It also lacked any completely private spaces. It left me nowhere to hide away from the world at large when I wanted to be alone. That was a dilemma. It caused me a buildup of anxiety, melancholy, and rage. That buildup was relieved on the local Indian population. (I knew I was going to make it back to the Indians.)

The Native American population was a much better target for my aggression than the local white people. The Indians were much more tuned into the world around them. They believed in ghosts, shape-shifters, succubae, and other bad things. They also believed in me.

I was not some demonic evil sent to earth to punish the sinners (also known as white people). I was just one more element in the shaman's universe. So, to the Indians, I simply needed to be put down or dispelled, if possible.

I liked that they accepted me openly. It gave me a certain comfort around them. I was only around them for the killing, but it was still satisfying. I was like wolves or bears.

Another good aspect of the local tribes was their ability to fight. I was not a lady to them; I was an enemy who needed killing. The Indians fought very well. They did so because they were fighting for their lives. Because of this, they did not cower; they attacked. Our interactions became a great training ground for me. It allowed me to, once again, sharpen my combat skills to a razor edge.

The better I became at combat, the more I came to appreciate the local tribesmen. The local Indians were very good warriors. They were a proud people and had a long heritage.

I made myself learn about their culture as I went. That helped me find a place among them. In a metaphorical sense, anyway. I really didn't want to become the story of a white apparition to them. I also didn't want stories about me to become widespread. That type of thing had bad consequences. I wanted to become something that the Indians already had an explanation for. That way, I wouldn't stand out as stories were passed along. Handed-down stories last forever; it's that way in every culture. I did my best to blend in with their world like a wraith.

I did my best to blend into Boston as well. The social scene in Boston was fine. It lacked the depth of London or the scope of the Adriatic, but the types of people were the same. That made everything predictable.

As a buffer, I had John Francis. He was steady, English company. That fellow Renaldo came to be quite pleasant as the years passed. He was an excellent businessman and a good judge of people's character. He also possessed an ability to spin a fine tale of adventure. It reminded me of all the sea captains I had known. That little thing alone made me like him. He seemed a good man to leave at the helm of my colonial affairs, even if I did not approve of his gluttony or his sloth.

The two of them, John Francis and Renaldo, helped me to blend in as much as possible. I had had a much easier time blending into Bristol society. The unknown layers of society in Crete were a cause of consternation that Boston did not possess.

Boston, as a place, was not as in tune with the ways of old money and nobility as Europe was. The Americas were just too new. They lacked the age of Europe. The age that Europe possessed made it much easier for me to move around and be myself. The youth of America made that movement much more difficult. People were moving to America to make themselves new. Because of that, there was no old establishment to settle in with. I had to become accepted on my own merits. That wasn't an issue, because I had money and taste. I was taken into the fold in much the same way as a retired army officer or a deposed head of state would be.

The interesting thing about it all was that I was not hiding anymore. All right, I was hiding, but only from some old people in England. I was sort of hiding my real life, and the other people in Boston were reshaping their own. The Indians were trying to hold on to their old lives amidst changing times. We were all just doing what we were doing.

I bonded well enough with the Boston social scene. As I said, they were mostly well-to-do businessmen or diplomats. They were the standard midsociety people of Europe. They knew the ways of money, which gave me common ground with them. I had shiploads of money. I had everything they wanted. I had quid to spare and a title to wear about. I held the reins to a vast shipping business that everyone just assumed was owned by my husband, who traveled too much.

For many reasons, they took me in. I embraced them the best that I could. Boston society came to conversation with an obvious need for knowledge. This in and of itself was a problem of sorts.

In Europe, society gatherings were filled with conversations of philosophy, religion, the politics of the day, and world affairs. Business, when it was conducted, was done quietly and out of the way or behind closed doors.

In this new society of Boston, people discussed business openly. And not only business, but trade and conflict in business in the colonies and Europe. Talking about business in common company distressed me greatly. It showed a lack of both manners and professionalism.

These people seemed to gravitate toward me because my business was a grand success. They obviously assumed that they could glean information from me. Either they wanted to make money from my business, or they wanted to use that information to make money of their own. Sadly, they all found themselves mistaken in the end. I was not the type of lady to tell tales about deals made with others. It was always in bad taste.

I tended to fall back on Ms. Palmer's gifts of social awareness. My nanny and primary educator when I was a young girl had taught me the gift of social grace. She had taught me to leave their questions unanswered and spin the conversation toward topics of my choosing— the philosophy of the day or some new bit of science or maybe even international politics at times. I liked to talk about the Indians as well. People would always talk about the Indians. After all, no one in Europe had any Indians.

It seemed that no matter what I talked about, people were always polite. I think the fact that I did not discuss any business only tended to make me somewhat more desirable. At least, it did to the people who wanted a leg up. And since I am no one's ladder that was highly unlikely.

On numerous occasions, I was approached for liaisons. I was always uninterested in them. They had nothing to offer me in return for my virtue. I just listened politely and then rolled the ring around my finger as I responded with something akin to "It would be impossible."

Now, the plain truth be known, I did greatly desire human contact. I longed to be touched by another. To be pleasurably touched by another was always welcome. To be touched by my dark lord once more was a long-held wish of mine. But vampire or human, I would stay alone rather than lower my standards to those of the people around me. They had the stink of want, and that was always unpleasant.

For his own part, my dark lord Antonio had not crossed my path since midway into my stay on Crete. It had been many years since I had been properly embraced by another. I would have been happy to let him conquer me completely at that point. I would just have to wait. I knew that we would embrace again. I also had an eternity in which to do it, so for eternity, I would wait for Antonio. All I needed to do was fill the time.

That is what the early American years were— filling time. I talked politics at parties, hunted Indians, and haunted my business offices along with Renaldo. I spent many hours talking to both John Francis and Renaldo. They possessed a depth of knowledge that was satisfying. But I will say that knowledge can give you pause as well.

That pause came during one of my warm intellectual exchanges with Renaldo when I was forced to examine the concept of time. The exchange was unintentional and, to be perfectly honest, unnerving. I am not talking about Einstein's idea of time or Dante's, for that matter. I am talking about the passage of time—my existence in the stream of time, to be precise.

Renaldo had asked me if I was as beautiful as my mother had been during her youth. He said that I must be, because the Lady Sara Grey who had pushed her way into the business of men had been reported to be a very beautiful woman.

"Is your mother still alive, Lady Grey? It seems odd that you and your mother would have the same name. That must have caused your father confusion."

He had meant it all in the nicest way, but it was a wake-up punch that I hadn't seen coming. It took several moments for the words to sit and fester like a bug's bite before the words really stung me. What was I to say? At the time, I didn't even know how to respond. I think I started to turn colors as well, because I tried to formulate a response for some time.

"My apologies, Lady Grey, I did not intend to intrude upon your feelings."

"It's fine, Mr. Renaldo, I just haven't talked about my parents in a long time is all."

"You certainly need not do it here if it causes you discomfort."

"No, it's fine. My mother and I possessed the same qualities when she was around the age I am now. My father always remarked on her beauty. They were both very much in love."

"She must be pleased that you chose to continue on in her footsteps, as it were."

"She passed on some years ago. I took control of the business so it would stay in family possession. Even though I am married to Signor Boca, the company retains the Grey family name, as it always will."

"My condolences on your loss. It was not my intention to make you melancholy."

"Relax, my friend. The passing of years makes us all melancholy at times. Let us go out into the sun for a walk. It should change the mood. One day, I will tell you a story of my family, but not this day."

"As you request. I would be happy to escort you about the town. Let me get your throw and my top hat."

We turned out into the Boston air and made our way around town. The conversation turned to the affairs of the day. I was happy for that. Earlier, I had been faced with a dilemma. I would need to ponder that problem and get it sorted.

The days when Charles had made up lies for me had apparently long passed. It seemed I needed to make up some lies of my own. The lies would need to be a set of suitable tales. Obviously, I had lived too long as Sara Anne Grey. Fortunately, people who lived inside a set life span also assumed that I did. Therefore, I must be Sara Anne Grey's daughter, Sara Anne Grey. I was not sure if that was good or bad. I was sure that it did require thought.

As we walked and talked, I pondered what Antonio's solution to all of this must have been. He had obviously lived many lifetimes. It would have been nice to talk to him then.

Renaldo and I walked and talked. I thought and conversed and wondered where on the seven seas Antonio was when I wanted him.

# chapter 6

*What to do? What to do?* I quietly pondered this singular thought for some time. All right, more like for a year. The one thing that vampires can do well is waste time thinking.

I was pulled away from my thoughts finally by the news of the day. It was March of 1770. British troops had fired on a mob that had been harassing them. The troops killed three men, and two more would later succumb to death. Six more were merely injured. Considering that only five people died during the exchange, it's odd that it would become known as the Boston Massacre.

The British captain, a man named Preston, was arrested, along with some of his men. They were tried and found to be not guilty. The verdict didn't seem to make anyone happy. Personally, for so little loss of life, I found the whole affair anticlimactic.

The new tension was the deciding factor for me. It was time to return to civilization. I had tried to assimilate myself into that backwater of a colony. All I had really accomplished was an increase in my own misery.

I liked the Indians well enough. They seemed to have some pride and sense of heritage. They understood the passage of time and their ancestry. In many ways, they were more civilized than the Europeans who were replacing them.

I had managed to find a place among them. The Wampanoag tribe that resided in the area around Boston spoke a language called Algonquian. They referred to me as Mishquèsand, which means blood spirit in their language.

They accepted me and knew of my kind. I tried not to kill too many of them. I made sure that all of their deaths were honorable ones. That way they could make their way to Kautàntowwit once they died. Kautàntowwit is the house where all the souls go.

The Indians had honor. The Europeans, on the other hand, seemed so removed from the Europeans I was used to. They had no sense of time or ancestry. They only cared about the now and what was to come along. I didn't approve of any of it.

The whole situation in the colonies seemed to create a separation between them and the rest of Europe. I could vaguely sense that "pick a side" time was coming. It seemed that each new decision made by either side moved them both farther apart. There were going to be big problems ahead. I was sure that I did not want to be part of it. As the massacre showed, whatever the conflict was going to be, it most certainly would be bloody.

What to do? Then it was what not to do. Not to get caught up in a territorial war of principles was one thing. Distancing myself from the questions of history was another.

I took the well-worn path the stable boy walked the horses on. I needed to pad about to think properly. I could barely break stride in the tiny cottage they called my manor house, so most of my good thinking was done walking the horse path or the streets of Boston.

I decided that I had to leave. I did not just want to leave; I needed to. That place was done with me. But it wasn't a leaving to be accomplished immediately. *The Summer Storm* was out to sea and would not be back until the fall.

I was pretty sure that I could make it until the fall. Fortunately, most of the summer was taken up with the turmoil surrounding the Boston Massacre or was otherwise quiet. The time to think was good. It made me realize that I actually needed to talk to Christopher again.

The conversation would not be a luxury. I actually needed to transfer my whole business and noble life to someone else—not a new owner, but a new me. Sara Anne Grey needed to die her natural death and, in doing so, let her daughter take over. To do that, I needed Christopher. He was the one in a position to make it all happen. John Francis could actually have done it all, but it would have looked messy. I needed it to look clean and neat. I required a transition that my competition would not question or examine closely.

I could cover up my old life to most people. There was one set of eyes, however, that I could not escape from, no matter how quiet my transition was. I could not slip past the gaze of the House of Shadows. The custodians of the dark would surely watch it all happen and document the whole affair. Not directly, of course, but they would find enough information to figure it out eventually. They certainly wouldn't do anything with their information; that wasn't what they did. Still, I didn't like them knowing so much about me or my kind.

I knew there was a solution to it all out there somewhere. I knew this had been done by others of my kind throughout the centuries. They must have done it several times. The problem was that I had not. Where the hell was Antonio when I needed him to teach me something?

As usual and once again, I would do it myself. Ever since my first confidant and truest friend Charles Wyndell had died, I had been doing it myself. The rest of my confidants had been window dressings compared to Charles. They hadn't really taught me anything. An exception to that could be made for Christopher Wyndell. He was there to guide my judgment at important times. The rest of them were nice to look at and to argue with, but they never really taught me anything much.

I actually preferred to act with self-reliance. I never have been one to ask permission to do things. My vampire nature also makes acts of submission a difficult thing. Vampires seldom yield to anyone about anything. I am not obstinate, just singular of mind.

My mind had become set on a new me. Who would I have myself become? I was a woman. I was sure that if I was Sara Anne Grey's legitimate daughter, then my new last name could not be Grey. I thought that would be the hardest part; I had been Lady Grey for a very long time. I couldn't just become someone else completely. I had to have a backstory, or my situation would be unbelievable.

Now, I kept seeing a way out of all of the conflict. I just wasn't sure if I wanted to take it. I had actually always had a plan in place. My mother (me) had always been engaged and presumably married to a fine Spanish gentleman, who just happened to travel all the time. If I had actually consummated that marriage with a child, that child's last name would be Boca. I found a deep-seated irony in that thought. I would reinvent myself to become … Spanish? I just wasn't sure about that. I was a good English girl for god's sake. It seemed a clash of cultures.

Knowing that I had until *The Summer Storm* reappeared, I decided to do something to get my mind off the problem and think about the other problems associated with changing business owners. I needed to sit and think about it.

Secretly, I had been missing my own image ever since I had arrived in the colonies, so I decided that sitting for a portrait would give me time in which to ponder. One thing that a dead person can do is sit still and think. I explored the idea for a time and ended up at the door of the painter, Singleton Copley.

As with everyone else I tend to gravitate toward, my choice in painter, one Singleton Copley, was something of an oddity. He was an absolutely wonderful painter and had developed a reputation in Boston that put him on an equal social footing with the patrons for whom he worked. His skill and fame had led him into an opulent lifestyle or as opulent as one could have in the Boston of 1770.

It was not a big thing to talk him into painting me. It took the utterance of two little words—seminude. That was unheard of during those times. I didn't care. I had secretly always wanted a nude portrait. I had just never been in a position to commission one. That seemed like the right time.

It wasn't nude as in without clothing, mind you. I am not sure why. I had lost all of my human inhibitions by that point in my life. It was just seminude. I had a sheer, almost translucent throw across my thighs as I sat semierect on the sofa. The painting was absolutely obscene for the time, even though it is only mildly risqué by today's standards.

I sat for Mr. Copley and quietly did my thinking. Separating one thing from the other wasn't difficult. The painting part of my task was merely sitting still. Staying still is easy for the dead. The thinking was the work. Fortunately, Mr. Copley did not talk a lot, which made my thinking easier. He spent most of his time furiously scratching and painting—most of the time, with a look of unabashed desire.

Desire or not, the quiet was nice. It allowed me to concentrate. The more that I thought, the more I couldn't get around the fact that

I would have to change my name. I would need to become Boca. It had the entire backstory that my transition required, and it was already useable. It also seemed logical to become my own daughter. I married Antonio, and we had a daughter—a daughter who was now me.

It would probably complicate my relationship with Antonio. He was my lover and would now be my father. As I sat there pondering it, the tale of Oedipus Rex kept popping into my head. I finally decided that Antonio had gotten me into this, so he would just have to get over it. I thought of it as a leveling of the pegging. I kind of liked that.

I would need a new name to go with Boca. It didn't seem prudent to be Sara Anne Boca. That was too close to real for the population at large. I wanted a whole new name. A brand-new name for a brand-new me. I had always liked the names Abbigail and Emily. I decided that my new name would be Abbigail Emily Boca. Yes, that was good; Lady Abbigail Emily Boca of London. I would not change the London part. It was also good that Antonio had a manor there. That was nice and neat.

I would keep my London roots, and I would keep Bristol. Bristol held my title, so in reality, I had to keep them both. My English fortune was actually split between the two places. I was not giving up my fortune for anyone.

I had found a new name for myself. Then there were other problems to solve. I needed documentation that transferred Grey Cargo and the estates from the old me to the new me. I decided that that task would fall to Christopher. One last little gift of charity that he could give me.

I also needed a level of security. I would be developing a paper trail. It was a paper trail that would definitely come back to haunt me if it saw the light of day. It was the paper trail that reinforced a need to have only one person know of its existence. Yes, there would be one man in the entire world who would know that I was not actually human, one man to know I was a vampire. This was the need for Christopher to make it happen. He had all the skills, and he was old. Soon he would die a natural death, and the only man to know of me would be John Francis.

John Francis would bear all of my collective identity. He would also get to wield incredible amounts of power in my world. He would get to run my company. He would be the only one to know he didn't own it, unless someone wanted to check that. I would own it, and he would run it. He would also be my confidant.

There would be no one else—well, save for Antonio and the other guests of the gala. The little invitation-only parties hosted for the pleasure of my vampire family. They were undead; they wouldn't tell a soul. And there were those damned people in the House of Shadows. They weren't likely to tell anyone either.

All that seemed like a good plan. I had developed a new me and had a painting of her too. The painting was grand, an absolute likeness of me. I was sure I would keep it always. As I looked at it again and again, I came to realize that it looked the same as the ones from Venice. It looked the same, or I looked the same in it. If I hung them all together, it would be confusing.

This led me to believe that I needed a new look. I might need an alteration to my appearance. Not a fake nose or anything of that sort, but maybe something subtle that would make me different in other people's eyes. I could slowly work the small change up in their minds as we conversed, and soon no one would really know that I was the same person as before. So I really didn't need to change much.

I stared at the painting for a while before it came to me. The change would be my hair. Not the color or the style, but the length of it. My hair had always been way down my bum. I would make it shorter. Not a lot, just a couple of feet, up to the midback or shoulders. I would also change my fashion to a degree. Since I had been in the colonies, I had been fond of the riding costume that was in style. It consisted of a coat with a tight waist worn over a low-cut bodice and a skirt with full petticoats. A masculine tricornered hat usually completed the ensemble. I liked it considerably better than the standard of the day, which was known as the sacque. It was a loose, full gown that hung unceremoniously from the shoulders and spread out over a hooped petticoat. It usually had short, ruffled sleeves that stopped at the elbow. It was not a good look, even then.

My new riding fashion and soon-to-be shorter hair would make me much less obvious. To make the look real, I would play myself as if I had grown up in the Americas. Renaldo already thought I was my mother's daughter. He would become an unwitting accomplice. I would have been schooled in Greece. That would explain my recent travels. I would have been at those places learning my mother's business.

Soon I would be back in England. I liked the plan. I liked the plan a lot. It seemed that the only people I needed to let in on my plan were John Francis and Christopher. John Francis would be next.

John Francis and I had been running down different roads pretty much since our disembarkation. I had been playing with the Indians or sitting for Mr. Copley. John Francis had been with Renaldo doing business. He seemed to enjoy the business. He liked studying and absorbing information about the new trade and the routing of ships. Normally, I would be the one doing those things, but he liked it, and it didn't really fit in with my plans.

Shortly after the painting and the thinking, we spent time together again. It was always nice to see John Francis. He was English. Everyone else who had made the trip had been in the Americas long enough to become American. He stayed English, like me. It was nice to have someone to talk to who was like me.

One night, John Francis and I had dinner, and I explained my plan. I told him about the reasons for it, the how, the why, and most importantly, the when. I explained that I needed to see Christopher again and why it was important.

As was his nature, he listened to the whole affair without saying a word. He pondered all I had said and then did the most unexpected thing.

"If you are going to go, then let's go. There is really no need to send out correspondence that we will most likely need to track down and destroy later on. Most everyone that we were avoiding has passed away at this point. This would seem as good a time as any, I suppose. I also like the idea of running everything in your empire as if it were my own." After the statement, John sat back in his chair, pleased with himself. I liked it all very much. He wanted to take power. That was good.

"Well, I guess the only things left are to find *The Summer Storm* and cut my hair." Then I sat back, pleased with myself as well.

# chapter 7

Harbor lights in the form of liquid yellow flame shone in waves from the tops of the mooring poles. The bolts of flame greeted us as *The Summer Storm* slid silently into the docking channel section of the Thames.

Even in 1770, it was not customary to anchor ships at night. Ships would wait at the mouth of the Thames and then glide gracefully into its embrace once the sun rose. The Thames could be wicked past nightfall.

My captain and crew were not afraid. They had managed ports trickier than this without incident. So we slid into London, quiet as the night. Truth be known, it was not actually quiet as the night; it was more so. Our arrival date was December 25, 1770. It was Christmas. In those days, it was also Yule and the first day of the Twelve Days of Christmas.

There was nighttime mass at every church. The bells of midnight could be heard clearly out in the Thames. I could hear the carol singers about the city praising and passing the Yule tidings.

Seeing the whole city stretched out before us made me feel young, as when I had first gotten around to pantomime and Father Christmas. Father would take me. He always said it was for me, but he seemed genuinely happier upon the leaving.

As we disembarked *The Summer Storm* a ways downstream from her usual stop, I imagined that the time for ghost stories and game playing or divinations was about to come upon us. John Francis and I made our way to a carriage that had been waiting for us and started our journey toward the Grey Estate. Fortunately, there was no one left at the Grey Estate who had known either one of us. It too was new again. It was the right place to start over.

Several small inquiries led to the knowledge that there were also only two people left at Brimme House, my mother's family estate in Bristol. The only person at the company office was Christopher. John Francis had three or four aunts who were still alive, but they lived away from London.

As the line of questioning produced results, it turned out that there was one other person I knew who was still alive. As chance would have it, he was a priest. My friend, young Father Josh of Westminster, had become Vicar Josh of St. Matthew's Church. He was long in years, like Christopher. They had also apparently become friends of a sort after I left. They were two people with the same secret to keep.

Vicar Josh was my only friend from the opposite side of the lines. He was a nice man. We had corresponded on numerous occasions over the years. I was happy to see he was doing well for himself. He was also happy to hear that I continued to live.

I needed to contact the vicar, but I needed to deal with Christopher first. I thought about these things as my carriage transported me down fairy-lit streets wrapped by decorated shop windows. No matter how it happened, it was right proper to be home.

The ride from the city was shorter than I remembered. London had apparently grown during my absence. We arrived at the Grey Estate around two in the morning. The whole estate glowed with the warmth of the season. It had been decorated in a fine fashion.

John Francis and I had timed our arrival just right; the house was just returning from midnight mass. They all seemed a lovely bunch as we introduced ourselves. John Francis had notified them that the new lady of the house, Lady Abbigail Emily Boca, would be arriving in London at Christmas. They were informed that no special treatment would be needed, just that the estate be in order. I decided that no matter what state my home was in, it would be leagues removed from that awful manor I had haunted in the Americas.

Our entrance and theirs seemed well-timed, so we all made our way to the ballroom where the usual Christmas traditions were observed. We sat—John Francis, the staff, and I—and became acquainted with each other. They asked many questions about my past and my travels, as well as about my time spent learning in Greece and working in the Americas.

I told them grand tales of my young adventures throughout the world. I explained to them that I was happy to have come to my ancestral home to reestablish my roots. I had obviously not been in England since I was very young.

They listened intently to the stories. They understood it all well enough. People in the eighteenth century were not as put off by strangers as people generally are today. Then, people could come seemingly out of nowhere, and all was well. As we talked, I began to feel very comfortable once again. It was nice to be home.

As the spirited conversation finally wore down, the sun tipped its head above the horizon. A new day was dawning. A new face had been put upon the world, and I had a new home to explore that world from.

I believe it was John Francis who wore out first. The rest of the humans followed suit. They had been going a long time. I was escorted to my bedchamber and directed to notify the staff with any requests that I might have. I stepped into my bedchamber and, once the door was shut, reveled in the darkness of the room. It was exactly as I had remembered it. I lay down across the middle of my bed and wondered what they all thought of me. I hoped it was good, because they all seemed to be nice-enough people. This would all turn out for the best.

I wanted to request some blood. I knew better, of course, so I closed my eyes and tried to rest. As I lay there with my eyes closed, all I could think about was the Mari LWYD and the times when that old grey mare used to visit my house in Bristol. I was sure that it was happening again that year. I loved the customs of it all; from the old grey mare to the Calenigg in the window of my Bristol home to the pantomime, the carol singing, and the kissing bough of the Grey Estate. The thoughts filled my head as I tried to rest, just as they had when I was a little girl and Father had still been alive.

The afternoon came full upon the house as I rose from where I had lain across my bed. I decided to wander about the estate as I had when I was young. The halls of my home were quiet still, even after midday.

All the humans were still abed or quietly doing the things that needed to be done.

I silently made my way to the study, which had always been the room where the Grey family had conducted its business. It was slowly becoming a room full of ghosts. The dust particles floating in the air twinkled from the light of the half-drawn draperies and gave the room an eerie quality. It was a fine place for ghosts.

I took up station in the robust, red leather chair where I had conducted so much of my earlier business with Charles, Charlie, and Christopher. A long line of Wyndell men had filled the sturdy chair that sat behind my large wooden desk. Now, it seemed that John Francis would get to follow in their footsteps.

As I sat there looking at the scene in my head, I could see Charles Wyndell sitting in the chair as surely as I was sitting in my own. The vision made my heart warm. I oftentimes missed my best friend. He was the one who had taught me about being a vampire. He had been a kind and gentle man.

As I stared at his apparition, he seemed to be content. I watched my old friend intently. It was like watching a play that you thought you had seen before, even though you didn't know what would come next.

Charles's ghost nodded in the direction of the windows. I followed the swing of his head to the spot by the window where my father was standing. It had been his favorite spot. Father had spent many days thinking as he looked out over the meadows. He had been a man made for quiet reflection and deliberation. He had also been decisive in his decision-making. It had made him a good businessman. He had also been a good father. He had always liked the holiday season. It brought him great joy. I noticed that Father seemed content as well.

My gaze drifted from my father and landed on the outline of another man. He was long in years and dressed in the style of a period long past. Goblet in hand, he seemed to be pondering which book to read. As my focus adjusted on him, he stopped deliberating and looked toward me. The man looked strikingly like Father. The old man possessed that genuinely honest sense of joy that was apparently a Grey trademark. He seemed to fit into his surroundings as the first two apparitions had done.

I wondered if this man was my grandfather. I had never met any of my grandparents. I decided that he must be. Quite quietly, I said, "Happy Christmas" to them all. They responded with smiles and nods all around as they faded into shadow.

I sat in the eerie silence for some time uninterrupted. Finally, the doors of the study opened. John Francis gracefully made his way in from the hallway and took up station in a chair next to mine.

"It's been a long time since I have been in this room. I can almost feel everyone else in here with me."

John Francis turned slowly to look at me.

"You look as if you have seen a ghost."

"Three of them, actually."

"I didn't know that ghosts really existed."

"Apparently, a great many things really exist. If you had been but minutes sooner, you could have wished 'Happy Christmas' to your great-grandfather."

"That's not funny."

"No comedy intended." I had a melancholy tone in my voice. John Francis reached over and took my hand in the way friends do at a funeral.

"From what I have been told, you two were the best of friends. So it would follow that if there really are ghosts, he wanted to wish you a merry Christmas. Or maybe wish you a happy return to your home?"

"There's that Wyndell common sense at work again."

"Maybe it's just observation."

John Francis turned his head and looked out the windows. A light blanket of snow had fallen to cover the meadow. I could see the chill of winter in the frosted glass. It was a painting of winter. I looked at the beauty of the landscape as I tried to shake the melancholy from my voice.

"Do me a favor, John? Fetch me my heavy boots and winter coat, please."

"Why, are you planning a trip in the snow?"

"I'm going to take a walk. I would like to talk to some old friends."

Young Master Wyndell did as I requested, and soon enough, we were out the door. Our walk out to the family cemetery was as I had remembered. It seemed an age since I had made the journey. The years had not helped it to lose any of its foreboding.

I stopped at the entrance and knelt on the marble slab to pray for the dead. It had been customary in more superstitious times to do such things. I had had the marble stone placed there so I did not have to kneel on the hallowed ground. Apparently, John Francis had never seen a vampire praying before, though he said not a word.

I rose from the ground and brushed the snow from my dress. Reaching deep into the folds of my clothing, I retrieved the amulet from its resting place next to my breast and removed it from my neck. It did not want to depart from my touch, but I calmed its anxiety with a small kiss on the jewels.

I handed it to John Francis and asked if he might hang it on a tree limb nearby, where the sun could shine directly on it. He, like every other human who had handled it, didn't like the idea of having to touch it, but he did as he was asked. I could instantly feel its absence. I felt tired. I was somehow sure that the amulet felt the same. We both needed recharging.

John Francis found a suitable spot for the jewel and moved back toward my location to keep guard on us both. I smiled and headed off into the cemetery. The first stop was Father's grave. I paid him my respects. He seemed pleased to see me once more. I made my pleasantries and moved on to the headstone located behind and to the right of my own. The name on the stone was Samuel Tyne Grey, and he was my grandfather.

"Hello. I believe we met only an hour past. My name is Sara, and I am your granddaughter."

A warm response came from the hallowed ground below. I had been right in my assumptions. I wished him a happy Yule, as I was not sure if he was religious, and moved on toward the resting place of my best friend. Charles and his wife, Susan, were pleased that I stopped to see them. I reported on the status of their family and wished them both a happy Christmas.

Once the pleasantries of the season had been dispensed with, I headed for the tombstone for which I had actually made the trip. Passing the footsteps that I had made while talking to Father, I sat down in the snow before my mother's headstone and pulled my heavy winter coat about me. I greeted Mum in the custom of the day and apologized for my absence. She understood; a woman had to do what was in her best interest.

I started to talk as fast as I could; I was happy I didn't need to breathe. As I went along, I told Mum about all of my adventures since I had left for Greece. I tried to speak loud enough so that all the dead could hear. It seemed polite, because they were all listening anyway. Besides, that way I didn't have to repeat myself later on. I talked to my mother for a long time. She seemed, well, giddy that I had stopped to share my time with her. I felt the same. I talked and talked and talked and talked as the sun slowly drifted off the far end of the earth.

Finally, it was dusk. I could tell, because I could see the amulet's glow from where I sat. The glow was a sign to leave, so I stood and bid farewell to all the souls in attendance. As I made my way out of the cemetery, I stopped at the headstone of young Sara Anne Grey and gave it a small kiss.

"Happy Christmas, Sara Grey," I said quietly to myself as I left the graveyard. Making my way toward the glow in the tree, I retrieved the amulet and returned it to its usual hiding place.

"I thought your name was Abbigail Emily now."

"Never lie to the dead, John Francis Wyndell. They already know all of your secrets."

I smiled nostalgically as I said it. That made him smile as well. We made our way down the path and back to the manor. It was necessary, as John Francis's all-to-human repugnance for the cold was long past its limits. Sometimes, I forgot that he felt things, because he never complained.

I was ready to make my way directly to the large glowing hearth in the study when John Francis diverted us to the house's rear entrance. I didn't offer resistance as he led us down the back hallways and past the doors leading to the main living area. Another quick turn or two and we were descending to the dungeon. This was another place where I had not been in many years.

I took up station on the settee, as was customary. John Francis requested that I make myself comfortable and stated that he would return shortly. I made myself comfortable, as I was instructed to do, and waited patiently. I removed my glasses and found the gloom of the windowless dungeon quite refreshing. My night vision was still intact and functioning. I had come to like the black of night very much, though I actually spent the majority of my time in the light of day.

Once I discovered that I could move about in the sunlight and that the sun's evil, destroying rays were actually a myth, I had quickly gone back to the standard human clock. This brought a life in the sun. I embraced it, as I had always been a child of the sun. I lived in the light, but I went back to the safety of the black night quite regularly.

I continued to wait patiently, even though it was not my way. I could smell John Francis long before he appeared in the doorway. The deep iron smell announced his return better than any drummer could have. The large pitcher he carried was the source of the newfound fragrance. As the smell became stronger, I became more excited.

"Happy Christmas, Abbigail." A broad smile came across his face as he said it. He seemed happy. I was definitely happy.

He handed me the large pitcher of blood and took up a comfortable station next to me. He continued his impromptu dinner show as he retrieved two glasses and a dusty bottle of wine from his overcoat. Then he removed his overcoat and loosened the cork. I poured a glass of blood as he did wine, and then we chinked glasses and drank.

The rush of life that came as the blood ran down my throat was an amazing gift. I had not realized how long it had actually been since I had fed last. I had not drunk any amount of human blood since I had been in Boston, and apparently, it had been too long. The feeling was grand. I made sure not to waste a drop as I consumed the contents of the pitcher.

"Is your wine good?" I asked through red-stained teeth.

"It's quite fine. I was unaware that your cellar was so well stocked."

"It is good to be rich."

"I agree indeed."

"Happy Christmas, John Francis, and thank you for your present."

"Thank you as well, Abbigail. I hadn't realized I missed London until we returned."

"We are all that way, John. London also missed us."

"That's nice."

"I agree."

# chapter 8

By Twelfth Night (January 5, 1771), my constant wandering about the estate had developed a somewhat rhythmic quality. The chefs had baked the Twelfth Night pie with both the pea and bean inside. But before the king and queen could be crowned, there was a new dynasty to be created. That new dynasty would be my own. A new age of the Grey Empire was about to begin, and it would be reigned over by Lady Abbigail Emily Boca.

The work to be done in the creation of my new dynasty was the literal invention of the person named Abbigail Emily Boca, the new lady of Brimme House and mistress of the Grey Estate. Most importantly, she would be the owner of Grey Cargo.

The running of my shipping empire would not, however, be the domain of Lady Abbigail. I decided that the Wyndell boys would quietly take over the day-to-day running of the shipping business. It seemed the best idea. In reality, the Wyndells had been running the company for some time by then.

The eleven-day wait to see the man responsible for my new life was a somewhat necessary step. I needed John Francis to meet with his father first and make sure that he could do what I was asking. I knew that Christopher was quite capable of preparing the necessary documents. I just didn't want him to feel pushed into it was all. I wanted him to do it because he wanted to do it.

In the end, he wanted to do it. He seemed almost relieved by the mention of it. He would get to put Sara Anne Grey in the grave and create Abbigail Emily Boca. It would be his final corporate action on my behalf. He would literally pass the company on.

I think that, in his own way, he looked at it as being able to exorcise some kind of ghost—a ghost named Sara who haunted him. It was not a literal exorcism, mind you, just a small bit of mental cleansing.

Christopher was the one who knew all about me. He had been there for the transitions in my life and watched as I had moved away from the darkness into light and back again. He had also been involved in decisions of mine that had far-reaching and lethal consequences. Basically, he knew too much, and it bothered him greatly. He wanted to put some of it behind him. It seemed a strange way for me, but it worked for him, so I was fine with it all.

The meeting between Christopher and me took place in the study of the Grey Estate. It was the first time since I had left London for Crete that we had been in the same place at the same time. I had missed the conversations that we used to have. The deep conversations had been handed off to his son, but they were not the same. The better ones were not forgotten.

The conversation held that day was not as I had remembered others. Christopher had aged well, but he had become melancholy. His spirit was quiet now. He seemed to have moved on to a life of ledgers and papers rather than one of adventure and business. For him, time had passed.

Our reunion seemed to make him both happy and sad. It had the same effect on me. Time truly had passed.

Christopher and I sat in our old, well-established positions. We talked about all that had passed us by. The tales of business were grand, and I let him continue for a time. The personal tales were short and guarded. It seemed he no longer wanted to reveal himself to the darkness. He was preparing himself for eternity, I guess.

After the better part of the day, we finally came around to the topic of the moment: the new me. Christopher had been thinking about it ever since John Francis had approached him some days earlier. The problem, it appeared, was how to keep ownership and control of the company without being in control of the company. The company could easily be taken away from me if I were unscrupulous in choosing the person to run it. Looking from the outside in, John Francis Wyndell would be Grey Cargo, just as Master Grey had been so many years before.

My ownership needed to be able to be proven if any problems arose. How to do that was the sticky bit. Christopher decided to handle the transfer of ownership the same way I would handle the transfer of title—a simple matter in which Lady Sara Anne Grey's last will and testament would bequeath ownership of her company to her daughter, Lady Abbigail Emily Boca. Direct ownership would be passed on the same way a title could be handed down from mother to daughter.

The whole thing seemed direct and airtight enough. The problem was that it was also traceable. If someone got hold of the documents and studied them closely—two or three sets side by side—they would discover a problem that could not be easily explained. Now, this one set was fine. But as other sets eventually got added, the problems could arise.

Christopher came to realize that I needed to keep them, and I needed to keep them secreted away. I needed a place to store the documents that would be secure and, more importantly, inconspicuous.

In Christopher's usual fashion he came up with a marvelous idea—a safe-deposit box at the Child's Bank. The vault boxes at the bank were old and well secured. The heads of every major house stored items in them. It was even rumored that the King's family possessed a vault box. The service was absolutely discreet, which helped with anonymity. It also helped with longevity. The institution had been around for a great many years and had a secure future.

Lady Abbigail Boca, Lady of Brimme House, had acquired a correctly sized vault box and would apparently be making a deposit after the holidays had passed. Christopher was a smart one. He had apparently figured out the tough bit first. The remainder, letting John Francis run operations, was a simpler matter. I would just give him a letter letting him run my affairs as necessary. The company would continue on about its business as if nothing had happened. John Francis would run my family business, and I would just blend into the shadows of London society. There I would happily go about my existence. The two of us would meet regularly to discuss my affairs, and I would gain anonymity as he gained power. He would be the only one to know that I was eternal.

I liked the plan. I liked it very much. Both the old and the new me liked it. I concurred with Christopher's ideas and proceeded along on the new path. As I had predicted, Christopher had brought the necessary papers with him. All they required were signatures and seals. That was my part of the project. John Francis seemed amused as Christopher presented me with my new identity. Apparently, he had not figured his father for such preparation. I had. I knew him well.

I signed and sealed the documents and placed them in a secure cabinet next to the journal of Kairynkutho for the time being. Christopher locked his gaze upon the journal as I placed the documents inside. He seemed to be reliving past events. As he regained his focus, he shifted his gaze to my breast and the long golden chain round my neck. Yes, the amulet was still with me as well. He drifted back to earlier times once more and then finally back to the present.

I smiled and told him that I had had the same thoughts earlier on. Returning to London had brought me to times past as well. It was nice to live in the world of memory once in a while. He agreed with my thought and asked if there was time for a stroll through the meadows with an old man. *There is always time for friends,* I thought, so out the door we went to take in the afternoon air.

The walk with Christopher was quite nice, but it was short lived. The brisk January air was tough on old lungs. To relieve his stress, I asked if he would accompany me on a carriage ride. A trip to East London would give us time to converse properly.

"Where would you be going in East London on Twelfth Night?"

"St. Matthew's Church."

"The one in Bethnal Green, located on St. Matthew's Row?"

"That's the spot," I said eagerly.

"Apparently, I'm not the only ghost you plan on stirring up this day."

"Sadly, he, like you, doesn't have many summers left on this earth. I would like confession and a little détente."

"You may want to skip over confession."

"I see your point, but I would just like to visit with one other old friend."

"I would be happy to escort you to Bethnal Green, but let us take my carriage. It is easier on my old bones."

I accepted his coach to convey us across the city to its eastern outskirts. The ride was pleasant. We talked about old times—no business, no money, no darkness, just silliness and joy and the happy memories of youth.

It is my own determination that the old remember only good things, because they can. They pick the pleasant times to usher them out. It is a good idea. There is a point at which you should be able to forget the bad.

The ride out to St. Matthew's Church did not take as long as I had planned, and we reached our destination about an hour after evensong. Because it was Twelfth Night, there would be a midnight mass. That meant I had a couple of hours before the church began to fill once more.

As we pulled up to the church, I noticed that the pace of the day had begun to take its toll on Christopher. Apparently, one really could have too much of a good thing. Upon exiting the carriage, I gave my host a warm embrace and a kiss on each cheek. He was unprepared for the embrace, as I had never randomly touched humans. That was a safety mechanism that his grandfather had taught me many years ago. Once he collected himself, he seemed genuinely pleased.

I thanked him for the ride and all his kindness. I could see the sparkle return to his eyes as I spoke. Apparently, there was something to this new me after all. I said that he looked worn down and that it would probably be better if he headed on home. I had kept him from his hearth for far too long. He laughed and agreed. I told him that I would make my own way home. He looked concerned. I told him that I would have the vicar fetch me a conveyance. He laughed and climbed back into his carriage. Before I could turn to leave, he held out a small parchment and then spoke in low tones.

"At some point of quiet when you are alone, please read this. It would seem that the House also knows that you have returned to the Isles."

I nodded and slowly pocketed the slip in a ladylike fashion, and then I slowly turned and strolled off. *Damn!* I thought to myself. I had temporarily forgotten about the House of Shadows. That earlier concern about someone seeing several copies of documents rushed in as clearly as a new day. I wondered if I could just kill them all, and then I put that thought from my head as well.

I tried to focus on the task at hand. I hoped the vicar would be in that night. The problem with gaining status is that others start to do your work for you. I had assumed that, because this was the last night of the Christmas holiday proper, he would be in attendance. It seemed a logical assumption to make at the time.

I looked over the edifice that was St. Matthew's Church as I walked up to the small guarded entrance. Compared to the grandeur of Westminster Abbey, St. Matthew's was a perfectly ghastly little structure. I guessed that advancement had come with a price attached to it.

I hoped that this move to the country had been good for the father; from all outside perspectives it seemed a step backward. Fortunately, I think the move came with the thought that I would return someday. The scroll above the doors had a Latin inscription that read, "Enter all ye, and be blessed in thy father's house."

It was an open-ended invitation that seemed to cover acceptance of creatures like myself. The old chap was a thinker. I liked a man who could use his noggin, so I entered his new house with my head down, as seemed appropriate.

The interior of the church was well lit and sparsely populated. That pleased me. I walked to the first row of pews and sat quietly. The space was adorned as was customary. It radiated a sense of piety that the grandeur of Westminster did not. I would imagine that all the dead monarchs got in the way of piety. Interestingly, this new sense did not seem threatening, as one might expect. To the contrary, it was actually somewhat calming.

While I adjusted to the pleasantness of the new space, I almost missed the two men who entered from a front side door by the altar. *Daft woman! Pay attention to your surroundings*, I thought to myself. I had let down my guard again. One day, someone was going to make such a thing turn out to be the end of me.

As I chastised myself, the two men paused at the altar to converse. They were a contrast in ages. One of them was young, maybe as young as I appeared to be, and the other was long in years. Their styles of dress were in contrast as well. The younger wore the robes of a father while the older man wore an ensemble that denoted a man of rank. It was a more elegant arrangement, though it still seemed completely religious. I had been right that the vicar was in attendance that night.

I sat quietly as the two men made their way toward the middle of the altar. In larger churches, there was an open area in front of the main altar. The space helped to shuttle the people to and fro. It also made a good place to converse when times were quiet.

They carried on their conversation for several minutes before the older man turned toward the pews. The difference between Vicar Josh's initial greeting and that of Christopher earlier on was amazing. The old theologian stopped his conversation and fixed his gaze on what could only be an apparition. He focused several times to make sure his vision was correct, and then he beamed widely. He was happy to see me. He was happy the way someone is happy to see a long-gone loved one or a child. *That is the difference that faith brings*, I thought.

Standing daintily, I made my way slowly toward the altar where the two men stood. The young priest saw a beautiful woman; the old priest saw an old friend. The two expressions could not have been any more different. They almost made me chuckle.

As I approached, there was a quiet exchange between the two, and the young priest shuffled off slowly to a point by the doors. The vicar greeted me in an uncustomary and warm manner for church. It was strange and comforting, all at the same time. He smiled broadly and then spoke quietly.

"You look remarkably like a young lady that I knew some years past."

"Lady Sara Anne Grey of Brimme House?"

"That would be the one."

"She was my mother. My name is Lady Abbigail Emily Boca of Brimme House and the Grey Manor."

"You look remarkably like your mother." The wry smile slowly covered his face as he spoke.

"Thank you, sir. I have heard that she was a beautiful woman."

He laughed and then caught himself. The vicar looked about to make sure that the good people of the community were not alarmed. All was fine, so he resumed.

"Come, my girl, your mother liked to view the stained glass. St. Matthew's is not as adorned as Westminster Abbey, but the three pieces we possess are quite grand."

"You are very kind."

We headed off toward the ambulatory that wrapped around the back of the high altar. Several smaller chapels recessed off the walkway to house individual family chapels or prayer stops for respected saints. At the apex of the turn, three large, stained glass panels appeared. As promised, they were grand.

"You've aged well?"

"I've lived a good life. And you? Time doesn't seem to have been unkind."

"I have made my way through the world. I would like to think that I haven't done too much damage."

"If your correspondence was correct, I would say that you are fine on that front. However, if it were not, I would say that it isn't wise to lie to your confessor."

We both laughed quietly. He had lost none of his wit over the years.

"I approve of your change in names. It is a prudent move."

"Thank you. I seemed to be gaining onlookers, as it were."

"They have been set on a new path?"

"I don't think so. An old friend gave me some notice not long ago."

"Your other 'old friend' would probably be correct. The House off Shadows would seem hard to fool."

I turned to look him in the eye. A quiet, deep, and steady gaze gave him the look of an older, yet somehow much wiser man.

"Over the years, I have come to understand and believe in many things. And if knowledge is power, I like to think I stay here because I choose to."

I was quietly shocked. He was a good man. In the world of men, there was a good man.

"You choose wisely, my friend. You choose wisely."

"I have few summers left, Abbigail. If I may be so bold, I would like to introduce you to someone. He is a quiet and unassuming priest who happens to view the world much the same way I do."

"Much the same way, or the same way?"

"It is good to be cautious. You have come a long way since the day that we met."

"I've learned a great deal about the world since then. I'm not sure how many priests such as you actually exist."

"Oh, two or three, I would suppose."

We both laughed quietly once more. He seemed happy to be doing this private business.

"For now, I'll think about it. That's the best I can do. I'm actually trying to remove myself from the eyes of men."

"That would also seem prudent." As he said it, he reached out and slid a small piece of parchment into my hand.

"If you choose yes, then so be it. Now on a more priestly matter, would you like confession while you are here?"

"I am quite sure, Vicar, that you would not like to hear of the things that I have done, since last we met. Besides, I'm not sure you have the time."

"Fair enough, but you know I had to ask," he said with his best priestly smile. I had to give him points for trying.

We went back to the glass, and he told me the story of Christ's Passion as it played out over the panels. It was a story that we both knew well enough. His storytelling made it all new once more. He still possessed the ability to move people.

We talked quietly and reminisced the time away. Soon enough, time for mass came. The moon had made its way high into the sky, and my leaving was at hand. We slowly made our way back to the entrance at the other end of the building, where, as one would expect, the vicar had a carriage waiting to take me home.

I discreetly embraced him one last time and whispered in his ear that I would return. He smiled, and I slid out into the cold night air, happy to be home and among old friends.

As a side note, if you are going to St. Matthew's Church to view the glass, don't bother. The church designed by George Dance the Elder was rebuilt after a fire in 1859. It also had facelifts after severe damage sustained during World War II blitz bombing. The church that now occupies a space on St. Matthew's Row is a remnant of the one that existed in 1771. It is sad, but the march of time continues.

# chapter 9

Abbigail Boca had a good life. She appeared to be a pleasant young lady. People in society liked her well enough and paid little mind to her dark spectacles or odd habits. After all, all the affluent were odd in some way.

At times, I completely forgot that this person was not really me. I am not sure why. Maybe, it was because everyone seemed to like her so. I believed that was because they knew nothing about her dark side.

I had become so adept at changing that I had almost become two distinct people. The vampire almost never appeared when I was human, and the human almost never came out when I was a vampire. Time was lopsided; when the vampire came out, she really came out.

I kept my hunting the dark places. I liked the woodlands of the estate. They were calming and held ample game. I also like the old ten footers and abandoned sections of the city. They were a source of ready meals. I was adept at hunting in both of these places, so the choice of meals bothered me not.

Now, it's true that, most days, I would physically eat something at mealtime. This was a convenience to keep up appearances. I found out early that I got on better with all the people of the estate when all the trappings of humanity were honored. As a rule, vampires gain no satisfaction from solid food once they have completely turned. The food just passes through the system unchanged. I would eat and then I would go out and feed in the dark places. It was the feeding that gave me strength and power. It gave me warmth and a sense of life. The feeding was good. It was almost primitive, but it was always good.

In the interim, I stayed my course as a human. I only needed to feed once a month or so. I tried to keep it to the time around the new moon. A full meal would last longer than that if necessary, but I tried to stay satisfied. I used the amulet to buffer the time in between feedings. I let the amulet out into the sun to feed, and in return, it gave some of that strength to me. It seemed a good arrangement. Both of us came out ahead.

I confess I did spend varying amounts of time pondering the existence of the amulet. What was it really, and where did it come from? These were two of my favorite questions, along with who made it, or was it natural like I was. I realize I am not natural, as someone made me, and then someone else made me what I am. By natural, I just meant that it could be rightly occurring in the world.

I would think about such things and then put them away in the back of my mind. A lady can be fickle, if she chooses. It was nice to have something to think about and not be confined to business or survival. It allowed me new time to be philosophical and gave me time to come and go as I chose.

In those days, I was splitting my time pretty evenly between Bristol and London. I had managed to wait just long enough before returning to my Bristol home, so I was anonymous again. The feeling it gave me to return was always the same.

During one of my trips to the west, I had taken one of my Venice portraits out and hung it in the grand ballroom with the rest of my family. Not having the use of a mirror, I had not noticed my own facial features. With my portrait hanging next to those of my relatives in the grand ballroom, I was surprised to finally notice that I possessed the qualities of the Brimme women. This fact gave me comfort. I really did belong there. I am not sure why I had never noticed it before. It must have just escaped my sight.

I would be happy at Brimme House for a while, and then I would return to London for a time. I would be happy in London for a while, and then I would return to Brimme House. Every now and again, when someone inquired, I would wonder where my fiancé, or husband, or—actually now father—Signor Boca had gotten off to. He was always one to travel his own road. Usually, our roads intersected much more regularly than they had recently. I had not seen him in a long time. His constant absence left me uncomfortably curious.

The cycle went on for some time. Lady Abbigail flitted about the world happily, and all was fine. Then came the winter of 1775 and those damned colonials. The first real problems actually occurred when I was still in Boston. They, in a sense, were some of the things that had prompted my leaving. Such things had been occurring ever since then.

The first big event was the burning of the HMS *Gaspee* in 1772. Colonials attacked it and burned it. Then the Crown put out a reward for the men. It said they would be taken back to London for trial. That point—that the trial would take place in London—infuriated the people in the colonies even more than the thought of the reward had.

In the spring of 1773, the American colonies received the Tea Act. In the fall, the colonials mounted opposition to the act and to the East India agents to whom it gave a monopoly. In the winter, the Boston Tea Party took place. Colonials dressed as Indians boarded merchant vessels and dumped the tea into the waters of the harbor.

As things continued into the spring of 1774, Bostonians called for a boycott of all English imports. This was the thing that really got my attention, as it had a direct effect on my business. It also got the attention of the Crown. General Thomas Gage was sent to replace the royal governor and to put Boston under the military thumb.

The English Parliament then enacted a whole series of new acts designed to draw the colonials back into line. The effect was the creation of the first Continental Congress in the fall of that year. That, in turn, led to the Continental Association.

The Continental Association decided that enough was enough and affected a full boycott of English imports, as well as an embargo of exports. The association also put an end to the slave trade. That little bit of opposition actually didn't hurt my feelings. The rest, however, was a major blow to my business.

In the spring of 1775, Parliament declared that Boston was in rebellion. Over the course of spring and summer, a whole series of armed squabbles occurred. King George refused to yield to the colonial petitions for reasonable negotiation. The whole thing went sideways, and from Bunker Hill on, open conflict took the place of sober politics.

Of course, if bad was not bad enough, I stood in the sunlit study of the Grey Estate looking out over its snow-tinged meadows and watching the rain fall. In my hand was a copy of a royal proclamation from King George III stating that the American colonies would be closed to all commercial and trade ventures as of March 1776.

In three months, I would lose the majority of my business in the Atlantic. It seemed that the damned colonials were forcing me to go back to work. I really didn't want to return to the docks. It would restart a whole cycle of life for me that I had happily put to rest. The immediacy of the situation seemed to warrant it.

I was pretty sure that John Francis would not be put out if I stuck my nose in his daily affairs. He was a good man. The ripple it would cause was what I wondered about. I had been out of the head seat for a long time; remounting it would draw attention to me.

Oh, well. Like the winter rain melting the snow always told me, petty diversions don't really last all that long. Nature does what it wants. It would seem that, as business is my nature, back to business I would go.

Now, the news about life in the colonies was not the only thing in the world for those five years or so. Poland was carved out between Russia and Austria. Some English chap named Day built a submersible ship with heavy stones that could be cast off to make it come back up again. In France, Louise XV died, and his grandson Louise XVI assumed the throne. In England, the rules for cricket were lain down. A couple of weeks farther on, Pius VI would become the new pope. Change, change, and more change—sometimes it all seemed never ending.

I turned my mind toward business and realized something else. John Francis was long in the tooth as well those days. I would need to gain a new confidant and adapt the business to a new Wyndell. Oh, joy!

So on a nice winter morning at an hour proper for a lady to be traveling, I hopped into my coach and headed for the Thames. Happily, the business was right where I had left it. That made me feel good.

I quietly entered the building and headed directly for the head office of John Francis Wyndell. It was located next to the one that my father used to occupy. Everyone was nicely busy, so my movements were not noticed.

As expected, the head of Grey Cargo was hard about his tasks. I entered quietly and sat in one of the chairs at the side of his desk. He stopped and smiled over a significant stack of parchment. He seemed pleased that I had stopped in.

"Good morning, Abbigail."

"Top of the morning to you, John Francis."

"Pleasure or business?" he said with that mischievous look he'd always used to have as a child. It made my heart warm.

I handed him the proclamation with a woeful look on my face. He read it quickly and returned it to me, the mischievous look still firmly intact.

"That old thing. Not to worry. It should have little impact on our affairs."

"The colonies are well more than a third of our routes."

"That was true five years ago. We have been slowly moving away from the colonies since their troubles started. Now, it's mostly outgoing business, which that proclamation does not address. There is a small amount to the southern coast, but that is mostly cotton and produce grains, which can be shifted to other places. The businessmen that we service are happy to be accommodated by the arrangements we make."

"Apparently, I lack foresight."

"It's fine. We have discussed it with all our clients. Those affected by the ban were found new markets for obtaining and selling their goods. We have been mostly unbothered by the whole thing. The rest of our competition was not as forward thinking, since they seem to be falling behind and finding our new markets already filled."

"I guess I should not have overreacted to the whole situation."

"You come back to right your ship?" He beamed a bright smile that only one of the Wyndell boys could produce.

"That's not funny. I worry about things."

"Relax, old mum, it's all sorted."

"It's not funny. I don't want a piece of our business nicked by independents, or those damned East India people."

"So you did come back to work. Did you come with a plan?"

"No," I said with the childish realization that I had been wrong. It made me feel instantly naive. "Listen, John Francis, be sure that I didn't come marching in to act the big man. That always has a way of coming back to you. I just wanted to make sure we were all right."

"Well, we may need to dust off the long nines for a couple of the routes, as they wander into East India territory. Otherwise, we're fine. See, old mum, all sorted."

"Shooting at those daft pirates never bothered me before, so it doesn't bother me now."

"Then there is nothing to worry on. The family business is in fine form."

"Sorry to think badly of your abilities."

"Not to worry; it's understandable. From here on, I'll have a draft of the new actions sent out to you. That way you can stay at speed."

"That would be grand. I apologize for being negative."

"Not to worry, Abbigail. It's part of who you are."

"Very cute."

I smiled, because he was right. I did worry. I still did worry about the business from an outside perspective. It was my birthright. I had also made some really old promises along the way that could not be abandoned.

"I'm curious. How is Signor Boca's business doing?"

"Robust is a fine word. Why do you ask?"

"An old promise, John Francis. Just checking on an old promise."

"Your fortunes are fine."

"And yours?" I asked more out of curiosity than anything else.

"My own fortunes are, in fact, doing quite nicely these days. The family took a nod from you and put Amber in charge of handling the pieces. She has a good head for business. She's readying to marry a proper Englishman. So, all in all, I would say things are fine."

"That sounds grand. What about William, then?"

"He is quite well. He has an office down the hall, just there. I can fetch him up if you would like."

"Not necessary, old friend. But, if you are not too busy, could you make time for a walk along the docks? I think it might be time to discuss William's long-term future."

"You are subtle as always, Lady Abbigail."

I stood and approached John Francis so only he could hear. I didn't want anyone to overhear my next words.

"John Francis, why is it that you call me Lady Abbigail, but in times past you were fond of calling me Sara, or Lady Grey?"

"I don't like the sound of Lady Boca, and to just call you Abbigail seems to imply a measure of closeness."

"That closeness does exist, and it makes me happy. As for the Boca part, I guess I can't blame you. I don't really like it either."

"Let me get your cloak, then we shall see all the sights the Thames can provide."

"Very well."

I left the office with the senior member of the Wyndell family and strolled down the docks to view the ships in port. There was little activity in the harbor proper, because winter had come to the channel.

Winter in the channel is never an easy thing. Most ships moved off toward the Mediterranean Sea or toward the deep waters of the Atlantic. In the big water, they rode out the winter. The few ships that stayed in the channel of the Thames and the area of the North Sea had heavy hauls and short, direct routes. They also traveled less. Winter is not nice to ships the majority of the time.

The lack of activity was fine. The sights were secondary to our goals. The real reason for the stroll on the docks was privacy. It was always a good place to converse unbothered by others. It was also easy to see if anyone was taking an unhealthy interest in our affairs.

We talked about William for the longest time. I hadn't seen much of William since he and his sister had left Greece. The years had apparently treated him well. He was well educated and possessed the Wyndell gift for business. He apparently took naturally to the shipping industry. He seemed to be well on his way to taking over one day.

On a totally separate front, William had been instructed in the ways of the occult. This part he had not taken to quite as well. It seemed that he was like his great-grandfather Charlie in some respects. It was all right; it happened sometimes.

Apparently, he understood it all well enough. He was well versed in the ways of the vampire. He just lacked a sense of belief. That was the Protestant in him. That was also the easy part to alter. The big problem was, even though it was easy to alter, the change in knowledge was somewhat unpredictable. It could be hard to determine the outcome it would have. Sometimes, I got Christopher or Vicar Josh. Sometimes, I got his great-grandfather Charlie. It was hard to say how it would all play out.

The only sure thing was that every Wyndell man I had ever met had been good at keeping secrets. I was assured that William was as well. That was good.

John Francis informed me as we walked that William had also studied the House of Shadows. William considered it a group that should be watched. Apparently, John Francis had been given a copy of the note that Christopher had given me earlier at the church. The note had the name of a man who had developed a keen interest in my affairs.

I hadn't taken the news as seriously as John Francis had. That was what the House of Shadows people obviously did—take interest in people. They studied my kind. They studied many other things as well. They were also not to be trusted, not to be trusted at all.

William had been observing the movements and methods of this group for several years. Apparently, he found the members quite interesting. The men were all well educated and from families of status. Why they would do such things as chase after shadows in the dark intrigued him. He did not know what the House of Shadows did or that the things in the dark were actually real. Those things in the dark were my kin. Well, some of them were, anyway.

I informed John Francis that since he was not getting any younger, it might be time to bring William fully on board. John Francis agreed with the idea. It seemed that he was ready to pass the vampire torch on to a new generation. I understood the sentiment. It could be a hard torch to carry at times. I asked things of my friendship that humans did not. I thought it all right, because I gave things in return that other humans did not. In a risk-versus-reward sense, it all seemed to be a fair deal to me.

John Francis said he would send William out to the estate in a couple of days' time so he could be formally exposed to my true nature. I promised that I would be gentle, or as gentle as I had been with him. He seemed to think that was all that anyone could ask. He felt that it would all work out for the best. John Francis was an optimist.

We spent the rest of our stroll talking about happier times—no more business, nothing of any consequence, just this and that. They were the kinds of things that old friends talked about. It reminded me of the conversations that I had had with my first confidant, Charles. He had taught me so much about the world and my place in it. But, most of all, he had been my best friend.

John Francis had some of the qualities that his great-grandfather Charles had possessed. He was nice, and he was my friend. For a vampire, friends were hard to come by. A vampire needed to keep the ones she found.

# chapter 10

In the spring of 1776, Lady Abbigail Boca was called to court. This was not the first time I had been to the court of our king. I had been summoned to see King George II when I had first come back from Bristol. I was Sara Grey in those days. Now I had emerged as Lady Abbigail, and she had to go see the new king. Apparently, the King was curious about me. The introduction to the King was quite a standard practice. Sovereigns liked to keep the nobility in check so we would not plot against them. There was a load of plotting in those days to worry about.

To be honest, I found the whole practice of court quite annoying. I was (am) a beautiful and wealthy noblewoman. To be summoned to court was akin to being thrown into a pit of vipers. In 1776, women were very much second-class citizens. We were usually relegated to positions of well-kept property. Women of wealth and power were viewed as objects to be conquered. And they needed to be conquered soon, before they got grander ideas.

Needless to say, I really didn't fit in well. I would go to such affairs much like Pollyanna went to Aunt Polly's. I just kept thinking happy thoughts and happy thoughts and more happy thoughts.

I also needed to use a large amount of energy on mental suggestion. I put the idea in the minds of all the men that I was actually spoken for and was not a threat of some kind. Considering that gatherings of the nobility were almost entirely male, I needed to expend vast amounts of energy. There were some other women of nobility at these affairs. They were mostly relatives of the seated monarch or low nobility, such as me.

These women had little power, because they possessed little money and status. I, however, possessed both.

Don't get me wrong. Court was not a viper pit all the time. The setting could be a great place to conduct business. There were always opportunities and people looking for opportunities. On my first appearance at court, I had managed to come away with several new clients that Father had been envious of. It was my natural business flair. In reality, it was high, full breasts pushed into a corset ... and my natural business flair.

Speaking of corsets, one needs to be careful how one dresses at court. Even though it is a place where people need to look their best, one does not at any time want to be on display. Women on display tend to end up as objects of conquest. They become trophies and are boasted about behind closed doors, as men strip away their status. One also should not dress down too far. Looking as though you are not actually wealthy only lowers your status. This is actually a faster track to obscurity than becoming a trophy.

For a woman to walk in and out of court with her dignity and respect intact requires steadfast caution and an escort. In my case, the escort came in the form of Mr. William Wyndell, Esquire. He had become fully aware of my true nature sometime around the recent Christmas past. He had spent the winter quizzing me on all aspects of my vampire nature, which I had found strange.

Every other member of the Wyndell family had either taken directly to the fact that I was a vampire, or they had not. Either way, they had just moved on and accepted their roles as my human confidants.

William seemed to have a different tack to his ship. That most likely was due to occult studies; people had begun to teach such classes as if they were theory and not reality. In years past, it had been a matter of fact. William had learned it all quite well, but the occult was all hypothesis until Christmas.

Then I had come along, and it all had become so much more real to him. That was what led to the constant quizzing. He wanted to check all his knowledge against actual fact. And I do mean *all* of his knowledge. We would sit in the study and discuss the topic for hour upon hour.

I have to admit, at times, it was right numbing. William found it all fascinating. A little later, after he had finally seen another human being savagely emptied of life, reality took a better hold on him. Sometimes, it takes the gritty reality of life to get people focused.

In a short time, William had established a level of professionalism that I was comfortable with. I let him take over the role of confidant completely. The transition made his father happy; John Francis had held the post for a long time. He was happy to be able to pass it along to someone else.

To keep William grounded, I sent him to see the vicar. Talking to the vicar—a man who had known me for his entire adult life—was good for William. It gave him insight on the bland ideals of nature and religion, neither of them being completely black or white. All that gave him perspective.

Not long after seeing the vicar, William had completely taken over, and John Francis had moved on into retirement. Their meeting had happened mere days before Vicar Josh succumbed to his old age. In the beginning, I was worried that he would not be able to make the conceptual leap from the light to the dark places. He had been a good religious man like his mother. Fortunately, he came around to my way of life quite happily.

The transition from unknown to confidant was complete by the time I received my invitation to court. Mr. William Wyndell would get to have his first official public test in, potentially, one of the worst places to do so. That worried me for a moment. All the others had been given longer periods before being thrust into such circumstances. For William, it would be a trial by fire.

William handled himself with the usual Wyndell flair. He presented himself as the calm, sharp-minded, affluent man that he actually was. A little serious caution from me before we started, and he was on his own. Not long after we arrived, he was lost in the swirling crowd of affluence and nobility, which left me to do my own bidding. As long as my escort was in the room, I was fine to be about my own affairs. I tended to work better on my own. My female charms and vampire talents tended to be better applied one-on-one.

The majority of the conversations at court revolved around the Americas, the colonies, and the revolution taking place there. It was all old news to me, but apparently, some of my counterparts didn't get out as much. I did manage to have a well-informed conversation regarding the charting of New Zealand by Captain Cook. His voyages about the southern hemisphere were quite interesting. There was a nice conversation about someplace called Las Islas Malvinas, which the Spanish had recently managed to wangle away from the French. They would later be part of the British Empire and become known as the Falkland Islands.

Intriguing as the business of exploration seemed to everyone, I was in the cargo business. There did not seem to be any business for me to be gained from all of the running about. I engaged in the conversations, and then I left them behind and went on to the next.

It can be said that the court of King George III was a fairly dull affair. Old King George had been a pious man before he went mental, and his court reflected that piety. It had a reputation for being both plain and frugal which made for a fairly boring time. It did not, however, cut down in any way on the amount of peripheral intrigue and power mongering. It just pushed it to the corners and the quiet hallways.

In doing my utmost to stay out of the crosshairs of the power mongers, I sometimes looked for an ally with which to share my dread. Normally, there were other women looking for someone to talk with to keep them from being targeted by the male establishment. I usually avoided these women. They had conversation of little interest. But on some occasions, they became good camouflage. My searching that day luckily led me, not to the wife of a baron or the daughter of a duke, to the Queen of England.

Her Majesty, Queen Sophie Charlotte, was a princess from someplace in Germany called Mechlenburg. She had come to the court as George's wife when she was just seventeen years old. Apparently, it was in her marriage contract that she become Anglican and not involve herself in the affairs of state—two things she was more than happy to agree to.

The two of us found a fast friendship. We both had a love of the natural world, as she was a studied botanist, and I spent a lot of time in the natural world. We were both also happy to find someone intelligent to pass the time with.

As a general conversationalist, the Queen was grand. She was well versed on a great many topics. Her knowledge of geography and travel was good. She understood the workings of the planets and the natural world, and she had an affinity for the arts.

It was well known that the King and Queen were very charitable people. They gave a lot of wealth to the needy among the population. It was a kindness that they shared with both Brimme House and the Grey Estate. Apparently, we were all champions of the poor and downtrodden.

I spent a great deal of time with the Queen while I was at court. She seemed happy not to have to fill her time with embroidery and the harpsichord. I was pleased not to have to fend off the unwanted advances of unsavory people. I also did not have to use William as a shield.

Interestingly, my new friendship with Her Majesty had a happy political side effect. I met with the King as soon as he was finished with the dukes. It moved me up considerably in the schedule of audience with the King out of courtesy to the Queen as much as anything else. It was a very high reception for the daughter of the daughter of an earl.

All earls were male. The lineage of any title went from male to male to male. I was technically still a lady. I was one of those niceties allowed by the monarch, because my family's title was hereditary.

Now, hereditary titles were only hereditary until the King took them away or a line died out, hence the reason for my summons to the court. I needed to prove my continued worth. The fact that my last name was no longer English was not going to help. The fact that I was rich and cunning would.

The King proved to be well educated when it came to financing the crown. He was a man who was happy to let the nobility be, as long as it benefited the coffers of the Crown. He knew that, in the years since I had resurrected Brimme House, it had become a generator of great wealth. The lands of the house and its surrounding provinces produced much-needed money for the Crown. The taxes generated by my, or now my mother's, endeavors had not been lost on the King. It was good; in those days, money bought title security as surely as an army did. I had no need for an army, because wealth was on my side.

My conversation with the King was short and pleasant. He inquired into my heritage. I explained that my great-grandfather had been the fifth Earl of Northwick and that his daughter had married Master Grey of Grey Manor. My mother had married a Spanish merchant named Boca, who was residing in London, and I had become the overseer of both great houses.

The King listened politely, even though he already knew the whole story. They always do. When I finished, he proceeded to ask about the status of the earldom. I answered in monetary terms, as it seemed to be a status question.

Once we were through with business, the King inquired as to the status of my friendship with the Queen. I explained that we had met earlier at the court and shared many similar interests. She was a nice person and our conversations were most enjoyable.

This apparently pleased him as much as the part about the money. He and his wife were well matched, and he seemed happy that she had found a new friend. I said that I had promised to return new plants from our ships' travels for her botanical gardens at Kew.

That last sealed the deal. The King conferred continued hereditary nobility to me directly and asked me to keep up my friendship with Her Majesty. I responded with the sentiment that I was humbled by His Majesty's generosity and would be most pleased to continue my warm dialogue with the Queen. At that, I was ushered out.

Forty minutes in all and I was now Earl of Northwick—or Countess. The royal record was set to show that Lady Abbigail Boca was Countess of Northwick. Apparently, I really could never go back to being Lady Sara Anne Grey again.

I spent the last two days at court with the Queen while also searching for William. He could always be found in the middle of some conversation about trading or banking. They were two topics that he was well versed in. That was the way of it.

I did happen to have an encounter during my last day that would turn out to be fortuitous. I was returning from a scouting trip to find William, when a young man in priest's robes crossed my path. I stopped to introduce myself to the young fellow, and upon hearing my name, he seemed to glow with joy. This unfamiliar priest did not help my disposition, as priests justifiably made me nervous. It's the whole good and evil thing.

The priest looked deep into my now-wide, green eyes as if he was searching for something. Realizing that he was being less than proper, he lowered his gaze and apologized. The drop of his gaze didn't help to calm me, as he stopped a little higher up than was customary. Noticing that I was staring at him, he blanched and then apologized again.

Composing himself, he stated that the two of us had a mutual friend and that he had heard that I would be here. He said that he had not known of my beauty and then again apologized. Then he asked if there was a more appropriate place than the hallway where we might talk.

At that juncture, my radar was pinging wildly. The whole sound of it was wrong. It just felt bad. I was not going to die in some combat or be dragged out here in the King's court. In search for a noncombat exit, I postured that I needed to return to the Queen and did not think it proper to be secluded in such a way.

"Relax, Lady Boca. Our friend the vicar warned me that you would not be interested in such a meeting," he said with a half smile on his face and mischief in his eyes.

"Who are you, sir, and what vicar do you speak of?"

"I speak of your friend, Vicar Josh, who once resided at St. Matthew's. I am sorry for the less-than-auspicious introduction, but I am not really sure how these things are supposed to work. My name is Father David Burman. I am a priest of the Anglican order. The vicar has been a good friend to me. We shared many similar beliefs, if you take my meaning."

"I understand." I started to relax, as David Burman had been the name on the slip of parchment that the vicar had placed in my hand.

"I did not mean to put you into a state, Countess."

"These things are understandable, as my meeting with Father Josh was not without an amount of tension."

"The way I heard it, you scared him into complete conviction and nearly shocked the old nun that was there into an early grave." He smiled, and I laughed under my breath.

"What sort of meeting place did you have in mind?"

"The King's chapel is just there. It is bland but has one nice piece of stained glass. It sits behind the altar. I understand you like the glass?"

"I do."

And with that, we were off down the hall. Getting away from the passersby of the hallway was nice. We were having the wrong conversation to be in hallways.

The chapel turned out to be nearly empty. It allowed us to sit quietly and talk, away from everyone else. The conversation was short and direct. It revolved mostly around his understanding of the darker aspects of nature and religion. He also got to explain that the vicar had actually told him not to do what he had done, as it might get him killed. The vicar was correct, as I had considered dispatching him as soon as he had taken an unhealthy interest in me.

Apparently, not knowing had eaten at him. He just couldn't take it anymore. He had decided that it was worth the risk. When he saw my name appear on the court list, he knew it was time to act. He waited as long as he thought prudent before he acted. When he heard that I had already seen the King, he decided it was time.

I understood bad timing. It had happened to me on numerous occasions. I wasn't going to hold it against him at that point. I did, however, need to get back to the Queen.

I explained to the young father that I would be more than happy to continue our conversation, but it would happen at a date and time of my choosing, as I did not trust him. He understood. Trust needed to be earned, especially under the circumstances.

We parted ways, and I cautiously went back to my more pleasant conversations with Her Majesty. The end of the day brought my coachman to the castle, and both William and I took our leave of the King's court.

On the way back to the Grey Estate, I asked William to find out everything there was to know about one Anglican priest named David Burman. William nodded a yes, and the coach continued on.

# chapter 11

London, 1802. That's when things really started changing for the worse. Apparently, Lady Abbigail's life was no better than my own had actually been. It's interesting how the cyclical nature of existence has a way of reaching out and pulling you back down once you get too high. It usually happens just when you think you have it all together. That was me.

The year 1802 was going so well. I was noble; I was rich; the business was sailing along under William's guidance; and I had a nice priest to talk with and a small circle of human friends who were none the wiser. The few people who knew all about me were either on my side or had one foot in the grave.

Now, as fashionable as things had become, the world was not a perfect place. *The Discovery* had just returned with news that Captain Cook had been clubbed and/or stabbed to death by some islanders in a place called Hawaii. Closer to home, King George III was slowly going into fits. The rumor at the time was that the family actually considered sending him to Bedlam. Good thing for him that it wasn't the one from Shakespeare's day.

For Lady Abbigail, however, things up to that point were grand. Everything seemed to be going as close to my way as could be expected. Things had been going so well, William and I had taken to having high tea at the London Grand Hotel. Not every day, mind you, just when it was convenient for us. The tea was a way of catching up on the events of the day. I tended to stray farther from William than I had from his predecessors. During those years, I liked being alone, and besides, William was entirely too busy with work and family.

William had only been married four or five years at that point. His wife seemed a nice sort of girl. Woman was a more apt word, as neither of them was young. I have to say that, in the beginning, I was somewhat concerned about her childbearing potential, but I did not fret about that. By 1802, they had already produced a daughter and a second child was on the way. That one would turn out to be a boy. All was well.

So the stage was set. He was happy; I was happy; the business was good; and the world seemed basically at peace with itself. It was time to cue impending doom.

It was a bright sunny day, and the two of us were taking high tea. I had had tea so many times that I really didn't like it anymore, but I did like the rest of the tea experience. It was a social affair.

I understood the social experience and how it worked quite well. It was a place where I could relax and just be human with the humans. People would sit and talk. They would discuss the topics of the day. I enjoyed knowing what others thought. It helped with business, even though I seldom did any actual business. William filtered it all and saved the useful bits for himself.

On this particular occasion, we were seated quite comfortably in the salon with a splendid cup of Earl Grey when a well-fashioned man approached our table.

"Good day, Countess, my name is Sir Edmond Cole. I have to say that I am honored to finally make your acquaintance. I am a great admirer of your mother, Lady Sara Grey."

"Then you should join us, Sir Edmond. That way we might converse."

Sir Edmond acquired a chair from a nearby table and came to sit with us. He sat with the efficiency of a military man, but at the same time, he possessed the well-cultivated pose of money. He presented an interesting image of a man. William, on the other hand, stiffened noticeably. He was unhappy, which was worrisome.

Fortunately, the traffic at tea that day was light. We were stationed at a table far enough away from others in the salon as not to be overheard. This, more than anything else, was the reason that I actually conversed with him in public. I really didn't like people bringing me up to me, especially when they were not as old as I am.

"Sir Cole, you say? Your title comes from England, sir?"

"Yes, my lady. I was knighted by the King several years back."

"Knighted? What for?"

"For services to the royal family."

"Is that your current occupation, Sir Edmond? You seem to have the bearing of a military man."

"You have a keen eye. I spent several years skittering about the globe for king and country."

"Well, in that case, I am doubly pleased. It's always nice to take tea with one of our boys."

He smiled and took his tea in hand. I was still fairly unconcerned at that point. William was noticeably put off by the man. Our gentleman guest appeared unfazed by it.

"Do you still cross the globe, Sir Edmond?" I was curious about what he was doing.

"Heavens no, my lady, my adventurer's days are done. I have made a transition into academia."

"A filler of young minds then? That too would seem a noble calling."

"I am somewhat more of a researcher of things mysterious and arcane."

"And the penny drops."

He finally got to the part that made his visit not a social call. I had kind of known it all along, but William had sensed it immediately. It seemed that I had let down my guard again. One day, I am sure that will be my undoing.

"Not to worry. I am only here to satisfy my own curiosity and to pass along a message."

He smoothly reached into his jacket pocket and removed a small card. It was a business card, with "Sir Edmond Cole, Occult Studies, the Brenfield Society" on it.

"I have heard of this Brenfield Society. I believe I even gave them a charitable gift sometime back."

"Yes, we were quite pleased by it."

At that point, William could not take the superficial nature of the conversation any longer. He lacked a vampire's patience.

"The Brenfield Society. So the House of Shadows has received a new coat of plaster."

"Times change, Mr. Wyndell, as do institutions. Isn't that right, Lady Boca?"

William was visibly put out by the whole affair, whereas the gentleman was happily amused. I was somewhere in between the two. It had been some time since the House of Shadows had crossed my path. I wasn't really sure what to make of it all, so I played along.

"It is, but what of it?"

"It's just a statement of fact. Things evolve with time. A hundred years ago, having an occult-sounding name was in vogue. Now, with the empire expanding and new ways of life on the horizon, a more proper-sounding name seems fashionable."

"That makes perfectly good sense, Sir Edmond." I liked his answer. It was not bookish or political; it was just straight fact.

"You mentioned that you were curious about something?" I was interested in keeping things on a social footing as long as was possible. William had started to settle back down, and I didn't want him getting bent again.

"I must confess that I have always wanted to meet a vampire and you in particular," he said in a very low tone. It appeared that he also did not want anyone overhearing our conversation. I was happy that he was cautious; it made me want to continue to interact with him.

"You must forgive me for seeming at a loss, Sir Edmond, but I was under the impression that vampires are stories for children."

"I think that we both would like to believe in such creatures."

"Why?"

"If you will forgive my presuming, Countess, because you are such a creature."

"What would lead you to such an interesting assumption?"

"Well, you are Lady Abbigail Boca, are you not?"

"Yes, I am. Please continue."

"Lady Abbigail Boca by research turns out to actually be Lady Sara Anne Grey of Brimme House. You are the only daughter of Master John Grey and the current owner of the Grey Empire. You were born in 1633 and were transformed into your present condition in 1651 by a being calling himself Signor Antonio Boca of Spain. Does that sound about right, ma'am?"

"I must say, Sir Edmond, I am somewhat at a loss to understand how you know so much about my past. It awakens my survival instinct and makes me want to do very bad things."

"I apologize for raising your alarm. I studied your story at length when I first came into the employ of the society. I admit that it left me intrigued."

"How so?"

"Women of an age past, or our own time, for that matter, do not own businesses, and very few have noble titles. Most vampires do not intentionally interact with humans. It seems odd to utilize interaction for business or pleasure. Certainly, almost none of your kind have long-term human relationships, and with priests, no less. You turn out to be, by all accounts, an anomaly."

"I like being unique. The position has advantages."

"But how does it work with your business affairs? One would assume that businessmen would not want to do business with what appears to be an unseasoned young lady."

"You're quite correct. The ability to generate clients for the business can be problematic. Getting the kind that are long-term and profitable requires acquired skill. It means that finesse and etiquette be employed in proper amounts. Frankly, it was easy when I first took over the company from Father."

"How so?"

"All of the men I did business with actually knew me. They had seen me grow and step into the shoes of responsibility. Once I took on the company and showed I could provide a reliable service, they were happy to stay on."

"If you do not mind, how did you interact with these men when you do not age? Didn't they notice that you are seemingly ageless?"

"I don't understand what you mean. How old would you think me to be, Sir Edmond?"

"To beg your pardon, middle-aged?"

"Yet I stopped aging when I was not yet twenty. What would one make of that?"

"I guess that I am not sure."

I let the glamour slip just a touch, so that Mr. Cole could see me as I truly was. The look on his face was entertaining. His eyes lit up like Ebenezer Scrooge's at a stack of coins.

"How ... how did you do such a thing?"

"It is an easy thing to alter the preconceived notions of people once you start to interact with them. You didn't even notice that the transition had taken place until I had showed it to you."

"That's fascinating. Does it work with everyone you meet?"

"So far."

"If I may be so bold, you are an engagingly beautiful woman."

"Thank you, Sir Edmond. It's always nice to receive compliments."

William just nodded his approval. His role as confidant came with the mixed blessing of always seeing me just as I am. It tended to bother some of the Wyndell men, and some it did not bother. They too were a mixed bag of sorts.

"You mentioned before that you wanted to pass along a message?"

"Pardon me. It slipped my mind in the midst of our conversation."

"Change can be startling at times."

"Yes, it truly can be. The message really isn't a message per se. Some of the members of the society came into possession of a library. The library was once housed in an old castle somewhere along the border of the Black Sea. Several manuscripts in the collection made reference to an amulet that was once part of the collection. The amulet was said to have great power and a need to be secured."

"What did this amulet look like?"

My alarm was up again. It was as loud as it had ever been before. I could sense this was going to turn bad quickly.

"Two diamond-like stones fused together at the focal ends, with all of the flat surfaces covered in some type of ancient etched symbols. The stones were supposedly held to a long gold chain by a golden clasp, which secured them at one end. The whole affair is reported to be quite remarkable. It is said in the manuscripts that the amulet's stones glow brightly as the power in them increases. Reports of old say that amulet has the ability to give its wearer great power or take it from them, depending upon its mood."

"Its mood?"

"Supposedly, it has the ability to act as it sees fit. If I were not talking with you right now, I would say the whole story sounds beyond belief."

"Well, belief and reality tend to differ."

"This is a point that is consistently true."

"Why come to me with this tale?"

"It was rumored that the amulet and several volumes from the library were acquired by a man, who in turn sold them to one Signor Boca. No one really knows for sure. The man was the castle's caretaker, and it was said that he departed with those items shortly before he died. No one could comment on the cause of his death."

"That does sound odd. Now you think that Signor Boca is in possession of this amulet?"

"No. I think that you have it."

"I must admit that it sounds like a fanciful jewel—has its own mood and all that."

"The members of the society are in agreement that the keepers of the castle were correct in locking the amulet in a safe place. It is supposed to be extremely dangerous in the wrong hands."

"Your members would like to acquire this jewel so that they might lock it away once more?"

"Precisely. They fear it could be used as a weapon of destruction."

"Humans are always in fear of one thing or another."

"I sense disdain in your voice. I also sense from that disdain that you know where we can find the amulet."

"The disdain comes from the fact that I forgot humans tend to overreact. You always fear what you do not control."

"Control has a tendency to keep us alive."

"I would guess that this amulet you seek was also made by the hands of men?"

"Yes, I guess so, but no one knows for certain. The amulet is so old that it has no real historical record. It is rumored that it was made in eight thousand to ten thousand BC in one of the African kingdoms. Supposedly, there are manuscripts in the Vatican secret archives that shed light on its real history, but no one knows for sure."

"That is fascinating, isn't it? Locked-away books that talk about locked-away jewels?"

"Lady Boca, do you know where the amulet is?"

"Yes." That one word would turn out to be such a mistake. It just came out in the flow of conversation. Besides, it wasn't like I had ever tried to hide from anyone that I possessed the amulet. All the Wyndells, along with the members of my circle, knew I possessed it. One of them was even a member of the House of Shadows.

"Do you have it with you?"

"Yes."

"May I see it?'

I looked around the salon to gauge the interest level of the other people having tea. Fortunately for our little group, everyone else was going about their own conversations.

Satisfied that no one was watching, I slipped my hand into the recesses of my bodice in as ladylike a fashion as was possible and removed the golden chain. A lady needs to control her modesty. The amulet slipped free of my bodice and into my waiting hand. I wrapped my hand around the jewel to dull its bright red glow. My little friend seemed upset. I couldn't blame it; I was upset as well.

Moving the jewel up next to my cheek I whispered for it to be calm. For now, all was safe. It took several seconds of such reassuring before the glow started to fade out and I could open my palm.

I moved my palm back down to my lap and opened it discreetly. The jewel lay contentedly in my hand, still emitting a faint, bloodred glow. Sir Edmond sat and stared, transfixed by the gem. William did his best not to look at the jewel; instead he scanned the crowd for unwanted attention.

There was something about the jewel that put all of the Wyndell men on edge. It was hard to explain; they just always seemed most uncomfortable in its direct presence. So did the dead, for that matter. It seemed that the amulet either liked you, or it did not. Mostly, it did not.

After several seconds, I could sense that show-and-tell had climaxed, so before anyone developed other ideas, I put it back in its resting place. Discreetly, my friend came to rest once more next to the soft skin of my breast. It always seemed happy to return to contact with my skin. I was also happy to have it there once more.

"You just wear it out with you?"

"Yes, I do. The amulet and I have a good understanding of one another. It's happy to come along on my endeavors, and I am happy to have it. Much like men and small children, my amulet does not like being left behind."

"Do you understand the power it has?"

"Better than you, I think."

"It should be secured. Protections need to be taken with such objects."

"I think that if you ask the amulet, you will find that it has been locked away far too long already."

"The manuscripts speak of it doing dreadful things. Security would seem prudent so it does not fall into the wrong hands."

"And would those hands be mine, Sir Edmond?"

"I would suppose that would depend on your intentions. I would suspect that most of the society would agree that vampires are probably not the most likely of candidates."

"Well, that being said, my intentions are to keep it. The two of us get on well enough. We have been together a long time and have developed a fondness for one another. Not only am I not going to part with it, but the amulet seldom leaves my body."

"That might prove inconvenient to the society."

"We have been friends for decades before your little society even knew it existed. I have no desire to start a war with the Brenfield Society. However, before you think me all fur coat and no knickers, I suggest for the sake of your life that you not try to take it from me."

"I get the distinct impression that this conversation is drawing to a close. I will pass along your thoughts on the topic."

He finished his tea and placed the china cup smoothly back on its saucer.

"Independent of the inconvenient topic, it was nice to converse with you, Sir Edmond. Maybe we could do so again under better circumstances?"

"That would please me very much. Thank you for your kindness, Countess Boca, and best regards." He stood, nodded to William, and quietly strode away toward the door.

The two of us sat for long time in abject silence. We thought, reflected, plotted, and looked at each other. Then we drank tea, thought, and plotted some more. Finally, when the tea was finished and the nice attendant had fetched my cloak, William spoke.

"I sense bad things coming."

"Oh, my giddy aunt, and just when you think things are getting calmer."

"What to do?"

"Simple, find me *The Summer Storm.* I am going to Rome. I want to read these Vatican books."

"What about the Brenfield Society?"

"All things in their good time, William. I get the sense that they want this kept as discreet as we do. They don't seem the type for rash judgment."

"As you wish, old mum."

With that, we were out the door and down the street. As we walked, we continued our thinking, reflecting, plotting, and scheming.

# chapter 12

The next day found me sitting deep in the maze that Father constructed at our London estate, pondering and scheming. I always found it a good place to consider the ways of the world. My nature is not to run off half-cocked, even though the situation may have seemed primed for it. I have found that when things go to pot, usually a measured response is the most appropriate course. This line of logic has always served me well.

I hadn't expended all that energy to make a place in the world so a bunch of misguided do-gooders could bugger it up. There would be tides of blood in the streets before that came to pass. Violence was always an acceptable answer. The more I considered my options with regards to the Brenfield Society, the more I liked violence.

The days of "the House" had seen men who watched the darkness and studied its goings-on. The new society fellows were more the kind who wanted to tinker with it. Meddlers tend to cause considerably more trouble than they relieve. I don't like meddlers. People who meddled in my affairs ended up in a pool of their own blood. The black parade would march on over their fouled corpses, just as in the days of old.

As I sat and decided upon my return to the embrace of demons, I felt the tingling sense that told me I was no longer alone. The presence I had tuned into was not close by yet. It was William. He had never mastered the pathways of the maze at the Grey Estate. His wandering was what attuned me to him. Interestingly, he always seemed to end up in the same corner, get exasperated, and call for assistance. He was not a good natural navigator. William lacked my sense of direction or that of his ancestors, for that matter. Most of the Wyndell men had basically grown up at the estate, so things like the maze became second nature. He had grown up on Crete. He had spent his youth running through olive groves on Crete, which required little navigation.

That day, William did not end up in the corner or at a dead end. He made an impulsive set of turns and was headed toward at me. Good boy. No, on second take, not good boy. This was not William. It had seemed like William when in the maze, but then it seemed different somehow. The presence lacked the hallmarks of testosterone. It was much more … feminine.

Amber Wyndell-St. Anne arrived like an apparition in the opening of the hedges that made up the pathways of the maze. I sat, as I always did, cross-legged on the stone bench in the middle of the maze's central, open spot. My white dress lay about me, giving the appearance that I was floating. I had placed my small black boots discreetly to one side. I have never been able to get away from the comfort of being barefoot.

"My darling Amber, what brings you to the estate this fine day? All is well in your world, I hope?"

"Things are grand enough, Aunt Sara. My brother seemed to think you might need female reassurance."

"So he's trying to get his point in through you?"

"Yes, ma'am."

"Do you know that you are the only person left alive who still calls me Sara? That's comforting in a way."

"I never liked Abbigail. Makes you sound a right trollop."

I laughed. I couldn't help myself. I had never really thought about how it sounded in public. It was funny, I suppose.

"Trollop or not, try not to do it in public. I like the fact that your brother is sneaky, but shouldn't you be steering the family fortune?"

"I never thanked you for your help with the estate issues. I wasn't sure what was to come after father died. I was worried that it would all get taken away because of my feminine status."

"I'm sure that your brother wouldn't do such a thing without solid reasoning."

"And he had help in his decision from the Queen, of all people."

"Well, what is a wealthy countess good for if she can't stabilize the future of her favorite adopted niece?"

"Power has privilege, I suppose."

"Not to put a cloud on our conversation, Amber, but how are things in the family since John Francis's passing? It made my heart sore once more to see him go."

"All is well enough. Pain has a way of turning into remembrance. It is the way of it."

"How true that is."

Amber walked to the edge of the hedgerow as I talked. She sat on the ground, placing her back against the stiff, rectangular, wooden block. She seemed to return to her usual happy state. I liked Amber greatly because she was a singularity. She was the only daughter of the Wyndell family to realize I was a vampire.

Unlike the Wyndell men, the Wyndell women were usually left ignorant of my true nature. Amber had figured it out all on her own. Apparently, my glamour didn't work as well on her for some reason. She was quick to notice that I never aged. After that, it was a quick matter of some reading in the family library.

One day, when she was ten or eleven, she walked into the study and calmly asked me how it is that one becomes a vampire and why I wasn't evil. Needless to say, I was shocked and amazed at the same time, so I answered her questions the best that I could. She had been a clever girl and was now a smart businesswoman.

Amber was a mother of three and the head of all of the Wyndell family's private fortunes, which, by 1802, had become comparable to my own. No two families in England combined could match both wealth and power with the Wyndells and the House of Grey.

"So, Mrs. St. Anne, what would your brother want me to do about my new dilemma?"

"Show some forethought and not rush to judgment about either the society or the amulet."

"I will not give it up to them. I will not yield what is mine to some gaggle of self-proclaimed protectors of humanity. I have already done much more to protect humans than any of them have. I will not be seen as the wrong one. I will not be wronged and left behind."

"They haven't wronged you yet, ma'am."

"No, but I know the tone of man. It is simply a matter of time before they do."

"And if they do, what then?"

"Blood will flow in the streets. Blood will flow until either they yield or they are no more, and I don't care if I tear my whole empire down doing it."

"Personally, I'm on your side. I find killing a perfectly acceptable option against bowing down to arrogance."

"That's a refreshing change of pace compared with the usual tone from the Wyndell camp. The men of your family usually opt for middle ground. Christopher was for killing at times, but the rest liked détente."

"Détente has its place, but so does annihilation."

"I like this attitude of yours. We are going to have to converse more often."

"Two things, ma'am. Never bring your laundry home. If you need to be about killing men such as these, do it somewhere besides Britain. You need to maintain the illusion of humanity.

"Second, and more delicately, if you choose to go to war, there is a chance that you may find yourself in need of a new confidant. If such a time as that happens to appear, I have five good children and they all have Wyndell blood in their veins."

I chuckled to myself. The smile came on so broadly that my thick ivory fangs glinted in the morning sun. She was truly a singularity. Apparently, she had been paying close attention to the way I worked my way through the world of men. She was a clever girl.

"I will do my best to keep the blood from English streets. As for the other, I will keep it in mind. I like the idea quite well. It always pays to have a backup plan. For now, however, I have no intentions of breaking the promise I made to your great-great-grandfather."

"Very well, ma'am." She stood and straightened her dress. As she turned to leave, she paused.

"Yes?"

"Aunt Sara, I really do hope all works itself out for the best. Yet I've been having trouble overlooking the defiant sound of the amulet in your otherwise level tone. Please make decisions cautiously. I would not want to see you go away."

"I promise, Amber."

With that she vanished back into the hedgerows of the maze and was gone. She seemed like a wraith—here and then not at all.

I sat on the bench and considered all that she had said. She had the wisdom that came from motherhood. Birth gives one a fresh look at things like protection and security. Mothers have a natural sense of retribution, and that set fine with me.

I was somehow struck by not having been wronged yet. I was rushing into battle at the thought of them coming for us. That was definitely the amulet talking through me. It had never done that before. Usually, my thoughts were my own. I could feel the amulet push on my subconscious, trying to let me know its thoughts and wills. It did have moods after all. That must have been troublesome for the humans who had possessed it in ages past. Vampires have much more control over their mental faculties than humans do. I could easily see the amulet doing whatever it willed to its human possessors. Just maybe, it *would be* dangerous in the wrong hands.

As I thought that, I could feel the amulet pulsating in my brain. The amulet told me that I was the right hands for it to be in. I had been good company for it since we had met. It had spent so many years without anyone to interact with. The thoughts were calming, and at the same time, they made me wonder more about the power it possessed.

I decided that, now more than ever, I needed to learn about this jewel of mine. There was no way that the Brenfield Society would help me out. It seemed like the Vatican was the next place in line.

I had never been to the Vatican. The home of Christianity scared me. There were too many ways to die in such a place. Marching into the house of the opposition was clearly a bad idea, but where else did I have to go? It seemed the only real choice left to me.

Normally, I would recruit Antonio to help with such decisions, but he was nowhere to be found. I would have to do it on my own. Yes, I would go to the Vatican. I would find the books and study them. Most importantly, I would live through it all. But where the hell was Antonio?

I lifted off the bench and secured my footwear. The walk back to the manor was short and consumed with pondering the fate of my dark prince. He had been out of touch for long periods of time before, but all those absences were known to me. This was different; it just felt wrong somehow.

The more I walked, the more I wondered if some sort of evil had befallen him. It was just not like him to stay out of communication. Of course, with the strange lands that he liked to wander in, there was good cause to consider that something bad might have happened to him. Considering the depth of his skill, it would have had to have been very bad indeed.

From the outside, all seemed fine in the Boca Empire, but that is how such institutions are designed. The Grey Empire was the same. If for some reason we disappeared, the humans would continue the empires as if nothing had happened. That thought did not make me feel any better.

I decided it was probably time to reach out to my brother and sister vampires and see if anyone had knowledge of our wayward sibling. First, where would he go? He spent great amounts of time wandering the steppes and the Slavic countries. He was known to travel about the Holy Land and northern Africa as well. That seemed a vast amount of ground to check for someone who might turn up in America. But it needed to be done.

I trudged to the study, deep in thought, took up station at my desk, and retrieved a stack of off-white parchment. Then, I retrieved a small amount of black ink and a quill. The letters that followed were short and pointed, as was the way of such things. They were all signed "Grey" and sealed in red wax with the family crest, as such correspondence should be sent.

I finished the parchments and collected them neatly in a small stack. There was much power in such a small pile. If the correspondence found its intended readers, the power of the vampire kingdom residing in that wide, sweeping arc of land would be at my disposal.

I looked at the small stack and came to realize that no gift in the vampire world goes unrequited. They were going to want something in return. Most likely, it would be something big. Another gala was suitably large. That was fine; it was a small price to pay for such information.

I collected the letters and carried them to my bedchamber. Once secure in my sanctuary, I changed out of my off-white muslin dress and into something more appropriate for sitting astride a stallion's back. My American riding clothes had not seen use in some time. They had stayed in the wardrobe long enough to be out of fashion. It was a good thing my proportions didn't change with time.

The riding habit with its skirts that fell over the petticoat and its tight-waisted, masculine coat made me think of quieter days. The outfit and its standard tricornered hat, which was the style of foregone times, had come to be replaced by something considered more fashionable, probably because the hat looked too American. I didn't care; I wore it anyway. My long blond hair was pulled back into a wide braid, which ran down my back. It was secured at the end with a piece of fancy ribbon.

On numerous occasions, I wore my braided hair fashioned with a small amulet or some piece of jewelry at the end. That was not good for riding. I found that the jewels would thump against my back as I rode, and that quickly became quite annoying. If my braid had a mind to whip around, the jewels could also become quite dangerous. I didn't need that.

Once fashionably attired, I headed straight for the stables. My great, grey stallion was waiting patiently for me. His name was Romulus, after the first king of Rome. As the stable master saddled him for riding, I pondered the irony of his name. It seemed funny, considering I was heading for Rome. Life was a strange and varied thing.

I had first read about Romulus and his brother Remus when I was returning home from Venice, some years earlier. Their tale seemed exciting and mystifying. It was a story with much fantasy added for effect, but the core was real—two brothers fighting so that one could claim kingship. Not so different from the intrigue of today or 1802.

I had a quick and spirited ride to the London docks. I found the company offices right where I had left them and William hard at work. William was a good lad. He meant well, he really did, but he was untested. All the other Wyndell men had been tested. William's status was about to change.

I sailed through the door and closed it behind me without making a single sound. The slight wisp of breeze that came along as I did so was the only hallmark of my presence. I removed my dark spectacles and sat in a large overstuffed chair before he even noticed the movement of the air. Thinking it a breeze from some passerby, he didn't even look up as I removed the parchments from my coat pocket.

"You really should pay better attention to your surroundings, William." The sound of my low, steady voice sent him straight toward the ceiling. A large stack of papers followed him up and then down again. Visibly shaken, he stood, trying to reclaim his calm. I tried not to laugh at him. It would have been mean.

Frankly, it reminded me of my birthday meeting with Father Josh and scaring the dickens out of my house master Thomas in very much the same way. That was also quite funny—more for me than for him.

"William, do you like all the great things that life has brought to you?"

"Ma'am?"

"Do you like your comfortable life?"

"Yes."

"Good answer, William, because now you are going to pay for it. Most of the Wyndell men had been tested by fire before they made it to that desk you are at now. But times change, I guess. Being confidant to a vampire isn't all business and high tea. At times, it also requires adventure and a fairly large amount of risk. Nothing in life is free, my good son."

"I'm not sure that I understand."

I sat the small stack of parchments down on the desk. William looked at the Grey family seal wedged into the wax. He had not seen it since we all lived in the Americas—or Greece, now that I think about it; he was at school when we were in America. Sorry, I get confused from time to time.

I explained to William how the stream of communication flowed. This was the system that his grandfather Christopher and his great-uncle James had brought into being. The way we could communicate with the other vampires we knew. I explained how to use it and the dangers that doing so entailed.

He listened patiently as I explained the ground that needed to be covered and the realistic time frame for such a trip. The trip would go more smoothly if he checked with the Boca Estate first, as it might cut down the search area. Then I explained that I would be going to Rome while he was out on his sojourn.

"Why are you going to Rome?"

"The Vatican archives contain manuscripts that I would like to examine. I'm not sure how yet, but I'll figure it out as I go."

"How can I go off on some grand adventure when you will need an escort to Italy?"

"I plan on being escorted by a priest, though he doesn't know it yet."

"What do you suggest I tell my wife?"

"The stories that you tell your family are your own affair. But make no mistake, you will go and on my schedule. Be clear about something else as well. All the Wyndell men before you knew that there was a very real chance they might die in my employ. You need to be stealthy and trust no one. I mean trust *no one*, William, not human and especially not vampire. Do you understand me, William?"

"Yes, ma'am."

"Good lad. Keep your wits about you, and you will be fine. Who knows, it might turn out to be a grand adventure. All of mine have been."

"One question: why me and not some group of men well suited for the task?"

"You actually are suited for the task. You have been on the move since you were young. Besides, these are the bills that must be paid for the alliances you make. Now, I have a question. Where is my ship?"

"Your ship is sailing up from Spain and will be back to London in about four days' time."

"Very good, William, that is very good."

I smiled and tried to visually reassure him that everything would be all right. Once he seemed relaxed, I lifted off from the chair and turned for the door. Reaching the door, I paused to turn.

"William?"

"Yes, ma'am?"

"You may want to start in the southern Russian mountains. Antonio goes there a good amount. A vampire named Sebastian runs free-range over those lands. He took over after Constantine was dispatched."

"Constantine?"

"That is a story for a different time."

"Yes, ma'am."

"Good luck, William. I'll bring you a present from Rome."
With that, I was out the door. I needed to procure a priest.

# chapter 13

My quest to find a priest was a somewhat calmer affair than William's recruitment had been. I had an outlet to the priesthood already in place. My new friend Father David was holding down the role of religious leadership at St. Matthew's, just as Vicar Josh had done before him.

Father David and the vicar were of a similar mind-set when it came to one's interaction with the occult. The remainder of their thoughts and mannerisms were somewhat different. Where the vicar was quiet and introspective, Father David was talkative and animated. It was said that the parishioners at St. Matthew's enjoyed Father David's sermons very much.

The two theologians did have one other thing in common. They were wise. They understood the interactions of things. They also understood meddling when they saw it. Neither man had anything nice to say about the House of Shadows or its new incarnation, the Brenfield Society.

On that point, I agreed with both men, so at sunrise, I requested that my carriage be brought around to the entry. The sun was just getting a full hold on the sky when I strode out to the front of the manor and into its ever-enjoyable radiance.

I liked the bold sunshine very much. Being a creature of summer fields and meadows, I had always had a great love affair with the sun. It had been that way since I was a wee, little girl. My father used to muse that my first love would always be the sun. It was true enough. I loved the heat that the sun brought when I was little. Heat from the sun meant that the flowers and birds and green grass were already on the way. Nowadays, it meant the same things plus heat and color for my pale skin. I liked to call it natural camouflage. It also helped me feel human.

That day, the sun landed on my cheeks as if to say, "Hello, Sara, have a nice day out in the world." I was sure that I would.

The coachman helped me up and then mounted his driver's seat with surety. The pleasant ride that followed through the country lanes of a much older outer London was soothing to my senses. It seemed to last but moments, because before I knew it, we were approaching Bethnal Green. I wasn't sure where the time had gone. I knew the ride had lasted much longer than I had perceived it to be. It had seemed to rush by. Fortunately, I had made my plans based on normal time. So, when we arrived shortly after morning services, I was pleased.

There were few left in the building as I made my way over the threshold. It was well on its way to being empty. I have actually always liked the quiet of an empty church. The hollow feeling that an empty church possesses is reassuring.

I sat down quietly in the last row of pews to watch the few remaining worshipers finish their prayers. I observed the stillness for mere minutes before Father David emerged like an apparition from one of the church's many recesses. He looked toward the back and acknowledged my entrance, then he continued on with the needs of his flock. A quarter of an hour more and the remnants of his flock had been dispatched to the busy streets outside. He showed the last one to the door and then turned with a wide smile and open arms. He was always pleased to see me when I appeared.

"Lady Abbigail, just this morning, a little bird landed upon my windowsill and sang to me. The little fellow must have known it was going to be a good day, because shortly after that, you appeared at my door." He laughed his deep and hearty laugh. He really was a jolly one.

"What might you know about Catholicism?"

"Catholicism is like the Anglicans' older stepbrother. We were all one religion. Then the pope wouldn't allow the King to divorce, so the King dumped them and invented us. That was Henry, but nowadays Georgey boy has this policy of Catholic emancipation. Supposedly, it's a tension release between the two. He likes to keep the constituency happy, you know."

"Yes, history is lovely, but what do you know about Catholicism?"

"You mean the actual implementation of the religion?"

"Yes, please."

"For all intents, it's the same as the Anglican religion. The real differences are in the details of scripture interpretation. They also have a fancier dress than we do. Why, are you planning to convert?"

"No, you are."

"What's that, then?"

"I need a Catholic priest to do a little espionage. Since I don't have a Catholic priest, I had planned on making one. That is if it is all right with you. It would only be for a short while."

"And where would this espionage of yours take place?"

"The Vatican in Rome."

"You plan on having to nick something?"

"I don't plan to, but that will depend on timing. What I am wishing to study lies in the secret archives."

Father David walked up and down the aisle like a soldier and then stopped at random intervals to make stealthy movements. It was like watching someone in a James Bond movie spoof. After every stealthy move, he would chuckle to himself and then go back to marching. It was actually quite funny. Finally, he finished his marching, came, and sat down next to me on the hard, wooden pew.

"All right, now, start making sense of some sort."

I explained to Father David the conversation that I had had with Sir Edmond Cole during tea, the dialogue it entailed, and our debate over the amulet. I needed to find out more about the amulet's true history. The manuscripts that the society possessed were not going to be available. Older manuscripts that chronicled the amulet were referenced to be stored at the Vatican. I wanted to read those manuscripts, so that I might get a sense of what was going on.

Then I explained the conversation in the maze and the vibrations and moods of the amulet. I wanted to get some information before I went to war with the Brenfield Society. Most important of all, I explained the need to make my way in and out of the Vatican without succumbing to its vast religious opposition.

Father David sat quietly with a sly look on his face and listened to every word. Not once did he interrupt. Rather he thought and pondered on the merits of every sentence. When I had finished talking, there was a long bout of silence in the great hall of St. Matthew's. Father David sat and thought deliberately. At several points, I thought he was going to speak, but he just went back to thinking. Eventually, after what seemed like half an hour but was probably only ten minutes, he turned his round, happy face full around to look at me.

"Might I see this amulet that is causing you such fits?"

I blushed. It was that little girl blush reserved for inconvenient moments. I listened for a moment, checking to make sure that we were absolutely alone. Then I slid my hand discreetly into my dress to retrieve it. Father David averted his eyes as I did so.

I loosed the amulet to the light of day, and it began to glow a bright yellow. As I lay the jewel gently into the palm of his hand, I explained that the amulet's glow was indicative of the power source it drew from. When I drank blood, it shone red, and when I let it out into the sun, it shone yellow like the sun.

The father blanched slightly as the jewel made contact with his palm. It wasn't from the amulet's power; it was more like a small electric shock, such as the kind one gets from a door handle. He held the jewel in his hand, and his facial expression revolved between quizzical and concerned for several minutes. After the inspection, he gently returned the amulet back to my care. He, like everyone else of human origin who had held it, seemed happy to be rid of it.

"Well, I would surmise that your little jewel does have some significant power. I would say that it doesn't seem to be either bad or good, more likely a creature of its own environment, like you and me. I think that the society lads are both right and wrong. It's definitely powerful and probably should be watched after. I am not sure that locking it away is the best way to go about that. People who are locked away have a tendency to become bitter and vindictive. I would assume that would be the same for an ancient power source. Or that would be true if it really has moods. I get the impression that it does, since it obviously responds to your touch and mine differently."

The father looked out over the altar scene at the other end of the building.

"Now, let's talk about this Vatican idea of yours. Although somewhat foolhardy, it seems like an acceptable option for finding out more about it. You really do need more information before you go to war with the Brenfield Society. Who knows, your amulet could actually be a great leveler of the playing field."

"You think that it could have some type of projectile power, other than making me happy or sad?"

"It's powerful, so it's possible. Such a thing is really not that big to consider. It was our Jewish fathers who carried the Ark of the Covenant before them into battle. With the Ark, they conquered vast numbers of armies with ease. Even though the Ark housed a divine creation, it was made by men. I highly doubt it was the only man-made power source conceived over the millennia."

"So this means that you will help me?"

"I have a friend named Alistair in the Catholic Church. I'll find out what one needs to do to be received at the Vatican. When did you plan on doing this deed of yours?"

"My flagship will be in port in three days' time, so it will be two weeks until it sails again."

"That seems like a reasonable time to make plans for such an adventure."

"So you will help?"

"Yes, most definitely. I can't imagine God being put out by all of this. Who knows, he might even find the whole affair entertaining."

"You don't think that God will mind us breaking in?"

"Probably not. At the end of the day, all the knowledge in the universe came from the tree of knowledge. He made the tree, so why would he care who had the knowledge? Besides, you are no threat to Christendom."

"I'm glad you agree."

"God is good, Lady Abbigail, and like recognizes like."

"I'm not good, David. I do many very bad things."

"No different from what the wolf does to survive. The holy men of the crusades, waging wars of conquest over lines of text in a book that the vast majority still cannot even read, were much more evil than anything you do."

"I'm sure that everyone else would not agree with you, but I appreciate the thought."

"I worry about the thoughts of my maker, not everyone else, and my maker has always had a good sense of humor."

"Mine too."

With that, Father David stood and moved back out into the aisle, where he continued to march like a soldier. I collected myself and quietly exited via the front door.

My reemergence into bold sunshine brought me back to a happy place. I was happy even at church, but the presence of all things opposed to me always made my skin crawl. My return to sunshine made my skin tack back down.

I took my seat in my carriage and asked the sturdy coachman to convey me to the St. Anne residence. I was thinking about a party, and Amber was the only person left to rely on for help.

Our ride into the middle of the city proper was nice enough. It had a more hurried pace than our ride through the countryside. The life of the city moved at a different pace—much more quickly than the country.

The St. Anne residence, located on the more elegant east side of the city, was a large and prominent affair. Mr. St. Anne had become well-to-do in the clothing industry. His wife Amber ran one of the largest banking and interdispersed commodities fortunes in Britain. Their children certainly would not want.

The bellman took my hat and throw and then escorted me to a modest sitting room while he retrieved Mistress Amber. It took but moments, and then she was in front of me once more.

"Twice in one week. I cannot imagine my good fortune," Amber boasted as she bound into the room.

"It is always lovely to see you, Amber." The warmth I exuded was genuine.

"And you, Lady Abbigail."

She said it with a sly smile on her face so it appeared as a joke. We both laughed.

"I was wondering if you would have perchance a few moments in your schedule that we might walk about town and converse."

"Absolutely. Let me excuse myself for a moment to become properly attired."

By the time, I had retrieved my throw and refashioned my hat, Amber had returned likewise properly dressed. The bellman held the door as we exited into the afternoon sun of London's quiet but busy streets. I requested that my coachman stand pat as the two of us were going to take the air. He replied with a brisk nod of his head and then returned to passing the time.

The stroll that we took that day was much more business than pleasure. We walked, and I gave Amber a history lesson about some of the exploits of Christopher and James and the lengths that they had gone to find members of the vampire kingdom. Then I told her about how her grandfather had acquired the various livestock assets the family possessed to supply vast quantities of blood.

It was at that point that Amber interjected. Apparently, she had always been intrigued by the family's holdings in and around Bristol. It struck her as odd, because none of the family was from there.

I quietly explained to her that I had grown up in Bristol, and in a very real way, her grandfather was also from there. He had been born in the manor known as Brimme House. Amber listened intently to the whole story. She could tell that the story was being told for a reason. It was not just happy talk or information. She clung to it as we went along.

Having covered the diversified nature of her family's holdings and their interconnectedness to my own fortunes, I began to change my story to a different topic. Coming next was the story of a party. It was a party that I had hosted a very long time ago. The party was so grand and rare as to be a gala. It was a meeting of all the vampires in the world that were available to attend. Brimme House, in the Bristol countryside, had been the setting for the grand affair.

Her grandfather Christopher had been placed in charge of all the drink for the occasion. Her great-uncle James had been responsible for the communications and party staffing. The two of them had done marvelous work. Such was the style of the gala that all of those invited to attend asked if another would be held at some point. I explained to them as they departed that it would reoccur once sufficient time had passed. All the members of my kind seemed to like that notion of cautious patience. I explained that, one day, when things were right, I would call on them once more.

Amber listened patiently as we walked. Feeling that the climax to my story was approaching, Amber slid her arm in mine and clutched it. The touch made me jump in surprise. I had been physically touched very few times since I had become a vampire. People normally touched me after I touched them. Very rarely did individuals ever touch me first other than Antonio. The action was extremely unnerving. I don't know why that was; maybe it reminded me that I wasn't really human.

Anyway, Amber noticed my unease and quickly released her grip. I blushed. Now I felt badly about my unconscious actions. I slowly reached out and rewrapped her arm in mine.

"Sorry, love, I'm touched so infrequently that I sometimes forget."

"I did not mean to offend you. You are usually so alive that sometimes I forget as well."

"It's fine. You may do it whenever you desire, my dear."

"Your story was working its way up to something before I interrupted."

"You are correct," I said. I explained that I had sent her brother out into the world on a quest to find my maker. My maker, my lover, my business burden—you may take your pick. Antonio was now all of those things.

Her brother's search for information had opened the communications channels designed to notify my kind. That had brought me to thinking about the gala itself. It had been some time since the first gala had taken place. The world was different now. A whole group of people had come and gone. There was still gossip and folklore revolving around Brimme House, but that would always exist.

I decided that I wanted to see my own kind once more. I wanted the company of the predators of the world, if only for one night. I had not crossed paths with any of my own kind in so very long. It was time I did so again.

The problem was that William was no longer around. He was on his way to the southern Russian mountains. That left Amber and my priest as the only people who knew of my nature.

Amber's interest was piqued by it. I decided to ask if she would set up the next vampire gala for me. As expected, she leapt at the chance. I mean that literally. She jumped, which made me jump. Then quickly enough, she calmed down. I relaxed and studied her giddy expression.

She stated that she would be honored to help in any way that she could.

I calmed down completely at that point. It was just what I wanted to hear. As we continued our walk, I laid out the steps that needed to be taken. Brimme House needed a proper staff, and all the guests needed to be contacted. I explained how she might also use the communication system that was in place and the dispatches that would need to be sent. I also explained about the blood. A large number of vampires drink a large volume of blood. Not all of that blood supply could come from her livestock holdings.

Amber seemed sure that she could manage it without stepping over the line and into the dark. I told her to do what she must not to. Once she crossed over, she could not come back.

I told her a quick story about outsourcing things that she did not want to do herself. I had once found help with things up on Tower Hill. However, she probably should not follow in my footsteps until she checked with me first. She seemed confused, but she said all right.

I told Amber that, in approximately two weeks' time, I would be leaving Britain for Italy. She should meet me at the docks the day I sailed out. I would have things ready to be started by that time.

Amber smiled contentedly and agreed again. She seemed very excited to be included in my life. It hit me as strange, because she had always been part of my family. Maybe, as a woman in a man's world, she felt the need to be asked about such things. Well, now she had been. She was now fully in—a member of my newly established inner circle.

We made our way back to the St. Anne residence and said our goodbyes. I climbed aboard my carriage and thanked Amber once more for her time. She thanked me in return for mine. I told her to keep her family well and that we would meet again later. She agreed, and I was off.

I asked my coachman to convey me to my townhouse on Bankers Row. I could sense that a quick hunt on moonlit city streets that night would be beneficial. *Who knows,* I thought, *maybe I will have a nice society boy for dinner.* I sat comfortably and watched the tide of humanity pass by as we navigated the city streets and my old friend the sun found its resting place over the west end of town.

# chapter 14

In what always seems to be the style of my life, the two weeks that I wanted to pass quickly were, in fact, quite long. I have always had a patience and instant gratification problem. Becoming a vampire did absolutely nothing to fix this; in point of fact, it made it somewhat worse. When Father was alive, he looked upon this flaw in my character with amusement, especially around my birthday and Christmas. He ofttimes found such things charming when wrapped in the form of a little girl. I have always found it annoying, especially in an adult vampire.

The day I looked for did actually come and at its appointed time. Unfortunately, it came in overcast and grey, with a driving rain. That was not a good sign for the start of adventures.

Our sturdy captain did not seem to mind. He had seen many such days and went out into them as if they were any other day. Maybe he was a nutter. If he were, it was of no matter to me, because he sailed my ship masterfully.

The company had procured a sufficient load for the destination, and the stevedores had been packing the holds for some time by the time I arrived at the docks. More time passed before the others in my entourage started to arrive. The first two to arrive were the dockmaster and William's office manager. I have always liked workmen; they have an ethic for being timely. The two of them assured me that all was well and proceeding in a fine fashion; there should be no problem leaving with the tide.

My well-to-do office manager handed over a breakdown of all planned activities that had been scheduled during William's absence as well as any events that could be forecast to arise. The satchel of papers also contained a full schedule of all ships and their routes, along with timing. The people who ran the company offices were all very good at their respective jobs. As I sat there, it seemed a lifetime since I had had any direct control over my company. When I had started out with Father, we had done everything. Those happy days had ended. Now, numerous people performed a varying array of tasks, all very efficiently. I could not tell from sitting there if it had all become too big or just too complicated. Maybe it was both.

Just about the time business was being concluded, a soaking wet priest came into view. My bedraggled traveling companion came wandering down the docks, dragging a small trunk behind him. He appeared both happy and miserable at the same time. What a strange man; why hadn't he taken the coach that I had sent for him?

He made his way up under the large overhang that had been installed off the back of the offices. It had been put in for my use some years earlier, since this was the permanent berth of *The Summer Storm* on the Thames. Once out of the weather, he shook like a wet dog. The water from his coat went in every direction. He continued until the first layer of wetness had been dislodged.

"This day ain't fit for man nor beast. Do all your adventures start this way?" He had an exasperated but jolly look on his face.

"You know, you could have utilized the coach that I sent out for you, Father."

"Actually, fine lady, in point of fact, I did utilize your conveyance. There was a large wagon of what appeared to be grain sacks overturned two or three streets back. It seemed easier for me to walk than to make the driver find his way around. Besides, I'm pious, and I like to walk with my flock. The elements are my friend."

"And now you look like a wet dog."

He stood there for a moment looking down at his attire, and then he began to laugh. It was contagious, because we all laughed with him. Not discreet laughter, mind you, but the roaring kind. It was such that I had to make an effort to keep my mouth closed. It was difficult; I was laughing quite hard.

The laughter felt good. If Father David Burman served no other purpose on this earth, he made me happy. That alone should count for something. I did like him very much.

About the point that I really started trying to contain myself, I noticed that someone else had stopped to join us. The newcomer was Amber. She had appeared sometime during the festivities. She had always had an ability to move around me without my awareness. It was interesting and unnerving at the same time.

Amber seemed fascinated that I was interacting with the priest on such an informal level. She had obviously never seen me at a church. There was a duality of purpose that she was missing. I could tell she wanted to ask questions, though she did not.

I regained my composure and sat down on a wooden bench next to a small metal strongbox, which was stationed adjacent to the building wall. Normally, I just stood throughout such affairs, as it is easier on my attire. That day I decided on a seated position, so I collected my gown and cloak up around me and took up station on the well-fashioned bench. My office personnel departed, and the dockmaster went back to the task at hand. The others were quick to follow my notion to be seated.

Once it was a smaller and more discreet group, I retrieved about two dozen letters written on heavy parchment, which had been closed with red wax with no seal attached. Then I pulled out two more folded pieces of parchment. I explained to Amber that the correspondence was for the party we had discussed earlier. The first piece of parchment laid out instructions on how to utilize the communications system and what to look for as a response. It would take time for letters to reach the far-flung corners of the earth and then return, so the date had been set for my birthday five years on. That should be good for all concerned.

"This cannot be overstated, dear Amber, learn the instructions and then completely destroy that piece of parchment. Do it very soon. If that parchment leaves your presence it would cause me centuries of misery and mistrust, potentially even my life. It will definitely cost you yours. Am I perfectly clear about this, Amber?"

"Perfectly clear, Aunt Abbigail."

"Good girl. Now one other thing, look down the docks toward where they are loading the next ship on the docks. Do you see the man in the long black coat with the cane? The one well hid, back against the building by the crates."

"Yes, ma'am."

"He is a member of the Brenfield Society. He has no interest in the loading of that ship, but in the loading of this one. Do not draw attention to what you are doing. Be secret and safe about your task. They will test your loyalty. You should be safe enough for now. They will no doubt be fixed upon my movements, not yours. But whatever you do, take no chances, none of any kind. Am I clear about them, Amber?"

"Yes, ma'am, Brenfield blokes are bad."

"Good girl."

I reached into the strongbox once more and retrieved a small, leather-bound diary. I wrapped the remaining piece of parchment around the diary and handed them over to Amber.

"The parchment is a bank draft for you to draw directly on my personal accounts. There is no need that I can think of why you should be forced to fund this endeavor. It's an open release, so do so as you will. Just try not to spend it all."

She laughed, and the rest of us followed her cue. She, of all people, didn't need the money.

"The diary is one of Christopher's. It chronicles the events that occurred around the first time this was done. I confess, I haven't read any of this one. He gave several of them to me right before he passed on. I would imagine that he didn't want them to go astray. Could you please return it when you are finished?"

"Why, haven't you read it?"

"There were questions that I never asked about Christopher's endeavors, as there were questions that he never asked about mine. I suppose that I just don't want my memories of him to change at this point."

"Good men are good men and seldom undone by a few misgivings."

The somber words of Father David seemed well placed. I smiled and nodded my head. He was correct.

I turned my attention to *The Summer Storm,* which appeared almost ready to sail. Then I turned my eye to the shadowy figure in the black coat down the docks. *Good men were good men, and bad men were bad men,* I thought.

While I was mentally elsewhere, Amber struck up a conversation with my priest. The two of them seemed to become fast friends. Priests have a natural way of being friendly. It is one of the things that makes them comforting.

We sat a short time longer before the captain came bounding down the rain-soaked gangway and announced that it was time to be boarding my vessel. It was good timing, as Amber's coachman also appeared to escort her back to her coach. My captain hoisted up my strongbox and led the way toward the ramp. Father David grabbed hold of his trunk and proceeded in turn.

"All aboard who's going aboard."

The old call came clearly through the rain-filled air, and as we put foot on the deck, the ramp was dropped. The grey sky had turned into a dark and streaky mess by the time my ship had turned for her move out into the channel. Our release from rain came shortly upon the sighting of a horizon line. It was a good sign.

I checked on the comforts of my cabin and then took my natural place on the weather deck. Here I could see everything going on both on the ship and on the sea. I liked it there. It made me feel as if I were in one of the stories that the ship captains would tell me when I was a little girl. Those tales of high adventure on the seas of the world had always made me happy when I was a little girl. Now, remembering them made me strong. I understood the drive that made a man become a ship's captain. It was the strength of being in command of the sea.

As I stood there in command of all I surveyed, it became apparent that times at sea had changed. In times past, my presence on the weather deck had provoked the insecurities and superstitions of the crew. None of the captains ever seemed to care, but the crew was always put out. They saw bad omens in having women aboard ship. This crew somehow seemed unaffected by it. They were a little out of sorts, maybe, but not superstitious and fearful of women on board ships. That was a good thing. Apparently, a new century had brought new ethics to the business of ship travel. I liked the change. I liked the time-honored customs of the sea, but I liked a little courtesy as well.

I stood facing into the remnants of the rainstorm for some time before I decided that enough was enough. I abandoned my post for a dryer one. My warm, dry cabin belowdecks was large and grandly appointed. As a matter of fact, the only space on the ship that was better appointed was the captain's.

When the ship was commissioned, I had it constructed so that the captain's quarters were large and grand. They were the largest spaces on the ship, save for the holds. It was compensation for having to cart a woman all about the world. As such, I had no problems with any of the ship's captains. I had had to sacrifice some of the cargo hold to accomplish this, but it had seemed justifiable.

A big ship with small holds, *The Summer Storm* never made as much profit as the other ships on her route. That had never really been her purpose though; the money was simply a side effect. *The Summer Storm* had been built for me. She was my vessel. She was the only ship in my fleet to fly both the Grey family flag and the banner of Brimme House. She was Sara Grey's ship and conveyance of choice, even if it was presently occupied by a Boca.

I managed to shake off my thoughts and change out of my wet clothing by the time a knock sounded on my door. I pulled back the large slab of wood to see the large outline of the captain. He stood in the doorway with a proud expression on his face. He was a strange man, but he was nice nevertheless.

"Excellent to see you back in your sea home, Lady Boca."

"Thank you, Captain."

"I have a correspondence from a gentleman for you. I was asked to see that you received it once we departed."

He handed over the small note and smiled.

"Let me guess, long black overcoat and a cane?"

"Yes, ma'am."

"I figured as much."

"Does it mean trouble?"

"Hard to say. Did you discuss our travel destination with him?"

"No, ma'am, he just handed over the correspondence and asked that I turn it over after we had cleared the Thames."

"Very good, Captain. Thank you for the letter. You've been most kind."

He smiled and turned on his heels to head toward the wind bridge. That was the seat of command for a ship such as *The Summer Storm.*

I set the letter down on top of the small dressing table next to my other traveling companion, *The Arabian Nights.* The book made me content, and my amulet kept me satisfied. There was no feeding on a ship, ever.

Right then, the amulet was telling me that the letter was bad news. Those damned Brenfield people needed to remove themselves from my affairs or there was going to be bloodshed. I opened the small envelope, which was sealed with a waxed "M." Odd, the Brenfield Society logo I had seen many times; it was the same as it had been when they went by the name of the House of Shadows. This was different. Maybe it was a letter from an individual? Maybe, but it was not likely.

I unfolded the single piece of fine paper that the envelope contained. Its message was quick and to the point.

"I understand you are headed south with speed. I will cross paths with you at the Holy See. Have news that will be of interest to you. Moretti."

I read the message several times. It was the kind of message I would send to someone like me. Then it was signed Morretti. Strange. Only one name—another trick that I employed at times. It had the same skeletal structure as the letters I had just given Amber.

The letter must have come from another vampire, and if it had, he must have been in London when we set sail. That was wrong. I had not sensed another vampire near ever since I had returned. There weren't any other vampires in the British Isles, except for Zoey, and she was leagues away in Scotland.

There had been another vampire in my own hometown, completely unknown to me. I realized I was no Jack the Lance, but I really must have been losing it to miss such a thing. Vampires know when other vampires are around. They just know somehow. Call it vampire ESP. Maybe he had sent a messenger to deliver the letter. I had done so many times. Yes, that must be it. He had sent a confidant to deliver news.

Or maybe it really was the Brenfield Society meddling in my affairs. If the person on the other end of the note turned out to be anything other than a vampire, he was going to die a slow, cruel death. They would not meddle in my life; they would not.

I slowly came to realize that the amulet was making me paranoid. Not purposefully, but by interacting with my subconscious. That needed to stop, especially while I was thinking.

I quieted my mind. It took several minutes, but the swell of the sea under *The Summer Storm's* keel relaxed me. Once I was comfortable, I reached down and removed the amulet from around my neck. The jewel protested, but by that time, it was quiet. I held the shining beauty in my hand and stared at the radiance of it. It was not happy. That was all right; I wasn't happy either.

I placed the amulet in a small, padded space inside the strongbox. As it lay there, it almost throbbed with irritation. I moved very close to the little, shining star so I could speak softly.

"Listen to me. I understand that you have few outlets for expression, but we had an understanding about impressing yourself upon my subconscious. You are too well aware that I don't have the numerous emotional attachments of men, so I have no qualms about leaving you stranded on the bottom of the seafloor if you don't behave.

"As near as I can tell, I have been your champion, safe-keeper, and outlet to the world ever since you crossed my path. I am very fond of you, I have to admit, but I will leave you to rot if you do not stop your tricks. You will spend the next millennium in a strongly locked chest at the bottom of the sea. I hope that I am clear. Now, I think that we need to spend some time apart so you can think on how you choose to act."

The jewel's glow subsided greatly as I talked. It subsided even more as I closed the lid on the strongbox. I went back and picked up the book on the dressing table and opened it to read. As I read about the Ginn and the flying carpet, I couldn't shake a new sensation. I felt alone. It had been a very long time since I had felt alone. It was comforting.

I set the book back in its place and retrieved a thick shawl from my trunk. Arranging the shawl about my shoulders, I made my way back out onto the deck. I figured Father David would be about somewhere, making new friends and converts. I was correct.

I was cold and lonely and on my way to the Vatican. That was not a good way to go about being a vampire. It was not good at all.

# chapter 15

*The Summer Storm* floated as on a mill pond as the Italian coastline appeared on the horizon. I was sure that that was a sign of some kind. The Mediterranean Sea was not known for being overtly treacherous, but neither was it known for being sublimely calm.

Maybe the powers that be knew that I was coming to town. If so, was this a welcome mat before me or a clever trap? I did not know which. All I did know was that I was happy to see solid ground appear. It had been some time since my little tiff with the amulet, and ever since that had happened, I had been growing increasingly hungry. The onset of the thirst made me jittery, at best. I had resorted to employing all of the meditation techniques and controls that my friend Charles had taught me when I was a new vampire, but it had been such a long time since I had needed to utilize them that they had become a mere stopgap measure.

During the best of times, my self-control would stave off the thirst for maybe one full month. I knew it had not been that much time since we had put to sea. The real problem was that I had become dependent upon the amulet's energy. That had left my natural abilities weakened, and that was going to be a large problem.

I had momentarily considered a small snack of one of the nice young crewmen, but that was out of the question. A missing crewman at sea, or worse, one found drained of his blood, would leave me in danger of having to go into genuine hiding. I could not go down that road. Besides, I still had to return home somehow. I couldn't figure out what was going on. It seemed way too early for a state of panic to be setting in.

In an attempt to be rational during the torment, I retreated to the confines of my cabin and the contents of the little strongbox. Upon opening the box, I found the amulet lying quiet in its cushioned little compartment. I reached in slowly and gently removed it from the space to hold it once more in my hands. The two fused jewels lay silently against my skin, emitting not the faintest glow. I opened the window covers so the sun could shine down upon the jewels' finely crafted surfaces. The amulet absorbed the rays of the sun but shone not a wink.

The amulet sat in the sun's embrace for over an hour, but it emitted nothing toward me. I was disgusted. I straightened up my cabin and slid the amulet back round my neck. Still nothing. I told the jewel that we were approaching the Italian coast and would be off on an adventure soon and then slid it back down into my dress and its natural resting place in the cleft of my breasts. Still nothing.

Our journey was at hand, and there was nothing from the jewel. No, I decided, it was not nothing but a lack of something. As I sat in my cabin with the amulet lying against my breast once more, I came to realize there was something that I could feel. The amulet was mad. Well, maybe not mad, but quite unhappy with me. I had first thought that I had broken it, but as it turned out, I had managed to do something worse. I had angered it.

Angry or not, I decided that, if it wasn't going to help me, then I would help myself. I retrieved my shawl and headed topside to the weather deck where I could watch the docking of my flagship.

The harbor in the town of Fiumicino, Italy, was much the same as every other port of call around the world. It had trade coming and going, people of all sorts, and most of all, a healthy vagrant population, which I desired. I needed to feed. I could feed on the port vagrants, as they were never missed. They were the disposable percentage of the population. It seemed to take hours for the men to secure *The Summer Storm* to her berth and start the process of unloading her cargo.

Father David appeared on the weather deck dressed in the Catholic fashion of the day. As was customary, he seemed pleased by the whole affair. I asked him if he could secure us lodging for the night and have the captain arrange transport into Rome. He said that he would be happy to do so. I explained that, after nightfall, I had a small bit of business that needed tending to. A quizzical look crossed his face and soon disappeared.

"Oh, but of course," he said reflectively.

I opened the corner of my mouth ever so slightly to let one of my thick enamel fangs glint in the sunlight. The sight of it made the priest cringe slightly.

"Father, apparently, my little amulet and I are having a tiff. This being said, I need to secure relief from the thirst the only natural way that I know. Have no fear, Father; I am quite capable of being fast and painless."

"Well, at least that's something."

We both returned to watching the exploits of the docks' population. Fiumicino would one day soon become the Port of Rome, but now it was just another busy harbor town. At that point, everyone stopped there because it was closest to Rome. That made it a wealthy harbor town but a harbor town nonetheless.

In time, the unloading finally ended, and we made our way to the finest inn to be located near the docks. It was quiet and clean enough— not exactly what an English lady was used to but good enough for the night. The master of the house escorted me to my room. Once alone, I got down to the task of altering my wardrobe for the business at hand. Off came the Regency-style dress and dainty boots of Lady Abbigail, and on went the trousers, dark worker's shirt, and sturdy boots of vampire Sara Anne Grey. I wore a short stay under the shirt so I could keep my bust in check as I ran. It was not as comfortable as a sports bra would be today, but it produced the same basic effect. It also allowed me a fuller range of motion than if I kept my full corset on.

In the days of Regency fashion, women wore several layers of undergarments beneath their gowns. A chemise or shift and then a full corset and petticoat were usually all stuffed under the thin Grecian-style muslin gowns. I left it all behind for the trousers. I found that I ran faster out of a dress—much, much faster. Finally, I stuffed my blond locks up under a floppy workman's hat to disguise my feminine features.

I removed my trademark black glasses and placed them in the strongbox. I did not need them due to my perfect night vision. The opaque black glasses protected my night vision from the harsh daytime rays of the sun. My night vision was far too useful to let it fade away.

A quick once-over of my wardrobe, and I slipped out of the room's open window and into the dark night of the Fiumicino streets. I noticed immediately that sneaking around the small harbor side streets and alleys of the town was much the same it had been when I had lived on Crete. The style of the Mediterranean buildings was even similar, and the town's basic layout was that of any portside stop. Apparently, the Roman influence on Crete had extended past its taxation and exploitation.

I moved through it like a brisk breeze in the summertime, checking all the turns and blind spots. I wanted the lay of the land, as it were, before I started. The smell of the docks was comforting to me as I prepared for the hunt. The docks were dark in all the right places, and they were uniformly dirty. They made a perfect hunting ground for me.

I slid into a small alleyway several buildings down from a busy tavern. The alley was dark and narrow. At the other end, it emptied out into a vacant street, which ran back toward the center of the town. It seemed as good a spot as any to ambush the unsuspecting. I settled in to wait for an unfortunate soul to pass me by. It took only minutes.

I had barely taken to counting the stones that made up the building across the way when out of the tavern came a drunken sailor. He stopped in the doorway to steady himself before striding out into the night. As he pushed off he mumbled something derogatory over his shoulder to the other men and headed my way. I examined the situation closely for problems. I didn't see any obvious problem with the man. He was alone. He was not part of my crew. He was not overly intoxicated, and he was not an overly large man. I liked that, fighting big men was sometimes a problem for a girl who weighed what I weighed.

The soon-to-be-dead sailor walked in a slow and deliberate manner into the opening where the street and the alleyway met. I waited until he was close enough for me to leap out and grab him before I spoke. I said, "Excuse me," several times in low, Italian tones. The man stopped and turned an ear toward the alley. I repeated my low call once more, this time sounding like another intoxicated individual. I shuffled slightly to give the appearance I was too drunk to maneuver.

The ruse worked well enough. Whether for the thought of an easy robbery or the thought of helping a stranger, the man turned and headed toward my leaning form. He threw out his hand and mumbled something unintelligible in a foreign language. He probably should have chosen his words more carefully since they were the last he would say.

I secured his hand in a firm grasp. Pushing off the wall, I spun the man round before the thought of trouble ever entered his head. Moving almost too fast for normal sight, I covered his mouth with one hand while I took a firm grip on his upper arm with my other. One quick yank and the man became immobile with his throat staring up at me.

I paused momentarily to look at the man's neck. His arteries and windpipe stuck out in the pale of the night. The stink of fear was just starting to flush out of his pores when my large ivory daggers pierced his flesh. The plunging *thunk* sound that they made was akin to jabbing a knife into a juicy apple.

Well-seasoned attack skills let the fangs find their target with the first thrust and blood began to boil out of the punctures in his neck. He struggled little as the life left his body. I sucked the blood from him in large gulps. As the thick, warm liquid ran down the back of my throat, I remembered why my kind does what we do. The sensation of both life and power that the blood provides is amazing. I took in the liquid as fast as it exited the poor soul. Finally, the man's eyes rolled full white, as dead eyes always do, and it was done.

I looked around quickly. It was a good job done. There was no blood on my clothing and only a slight amount on his corpse. I ripped a piece of cloth from his shirt sleeve and wiped all the blood from my mouth and face. Properly clean, I readied to exit the scene. I looked down on the body of the sad, dead creature lying on the dark stones of the alley and paused. Better not to leave him here. Here in the alley he would be noticed. The water of the Mediterranean was but a few streets away. That was a better spot for him to reside. I hoisted up his corpse and threw him over my shoulder. Running through the darkened streets took no time, and soon I was standing on the end of a walkout with his body. A quick heave and splash, and the deed was done. I paused but a moment longer to say a small prayer for his wayward soul, then like the wraith of folklore I was gone.

I took a quick but roundabout route back to the window of my room at the inn. A small leap, and I was quickly inside with the window closed behind me. Once alone again, I changed back into my ladylike attire and stashed my hunting garments in their safe place.

The morning sun came quickly on my heels. As it found its way over the horizon, we had our things loaded into the coach that was to serve as our transport into the ancient and majestic city of Rome. Our conveyance was a grand-enough affair and more than comfortable enough to keep me content during the journey. I had to say that the captain had done his part well.

Father David and I climbed aboard and headed out on our twenty-five-kilometer trip toward Rome. We were both in a happy mood at the start of our journey. There were so many things that could go wrong, so many unforeseen problems that could be encountered—the whole plan seemed daft. Well, daft or not, it was under way.

Our journey east was uneventful. The countryside of low flatlands filled with grass pastures, orange trees, and small villages passed by effortlessly. The weather was pleasant by the sea and did not really alter as we proceeded inland. I had temporarily forgotten about the favors of Mediterranean weather. The weather on Crete had been so nice the vast majority of the year. The climate in Venice, when I had been there, was much the same.

I sat quietly and watched as the lush countryside passed by. I was working my brain around how hard it would be to maneuver my way into the Vatican, when the thirst began to rise slowly in the back of my throat. It seemed odd to me; I couldn't be thirsty again. It was far too soon. The sensation had to be nerves or some other restless emotion slowly boiling up. That in itself was also odd. I didn't get nervous, or I hadn't in a very long time. One of the basic vampire traits is overwhelming self-confidence. That is the nature of predators.

The longer I sat and thought about the situation, the more I came to the realization that it actually was the thirst. I could not figure out how this could be since I had eaten not more than a half-day past. Or it wasn't possible without some type of help. My thirst was a result of something else, and that something else was hanging around my neck.

My amulet had slowly nicked the blood energy when I wasn't paying attention. Apparently, it was still upset.

The argument we were having needed to be sorted before the espionage took place. It needed resolving before one of us, or perhaps even Father David, suffered a right pasting. That would be the good end. The bad end was much worse.

I closed my eyes and started to meditate on the thirst. I needed to focus my thoughts so I could ignore the pain that the thirst brought. Once again, the skills taught by my first confidant, teacher, and best friend Charles Wyndell came quickly to my aid. Soon enough, all was back to the status quo.

By the time I had regained my senses, our journey through the Italian countryside was all but over. The better part of a day had passed as our coach brought us to the edge of the Roman capital. I shook my senses were clear to notice buildings were passing us by on both sides. Father David was twisting from side to side, trying to take it all in. The outline of the cityscape was truly grand. The Romans really did know how to build.

The streets of the old capital went from individual houses with lush gardens and walks to sectional streets with buildings stacked one upon another until the light almost didn't hit the ground. The whole of it seemed old. Rome had been around for so long that even the new things seemed old next to the ancient ones. It all reminded me of Venice. It was living history.

The wash of colors and the grandeur of the architecture filled every niche and became hard to take in. It was easy to see how such a place would be the heart of an empire.

The coachman brought our transport to a halt along the Via Dei Salumi. The lovely villa that the captain had secured for my use was breathtaking; it was a large two-story structure of white with big windows to catch the sun and the breeze. The house was surrounded on all sides by a blanket of green grass and sculptured shrub trees. The front lawn was broken by a large circular, stone drive that allowed coaches to get safely off the quiet street before stopping.

This was a good location. Situated in the Trastevere section, it was outside the city proper. It was also only a short stroll to either the Vatican or the ruins of old Rome. It was also close to the Tiber. I liked being close to water. It had a calming effect on me. It also allowed an avenue of escape in a crisis. Well, most water did, but the Tiber really wasn't that deep.

Taking in the grand scale of it all, I wondered what it was going to cost me. Not that I really cared since I usually traveled with a lot of money, but I also didn't splash it around. I have found money to be a great leveler in human circles. People may not like to do things, but they will always do them to get paid.

The coachman unloaded our bags and escorted us into the villa. Father David was having a childlike adventure looking at all the decorations about the villa. The finery was lost on me, as I had seen such things before.

I sat down on the long sofa in the sitting room and closed my eyes. I liked to take in new surroundings on an auditory level. Vampire hearing is so keen that I find becoming familiar with strange new sounds a good idea. All places have individual natures and sounds. I like to be able to distinguish between natural sounds and intrusions. It's a survival habit that has stood me well.

I garnered a fairly good sense of the villa as the sun began to fade in the west. Father David had made fast friends with the maid and the butler who looked after the villa. They were an older couple and seemed quite nice, all things considered.

I still had some time before I was expected for dinner, because the Italians eat later than the English. It seemed an ample opportunity to find détente with the amulet. I paused once more to make sure that no one was coming in my direction or was in listening distance of our conversation. All seemed clear about the villa, so I reached into the inner folds of my fine white muslin gown and retrieved the amulet from its resting place. The jewel cast a deep, bloodred glow as it came into view and confirmed all my suspicions. The thirst had returned, because the amulet had absorbed the power the blood had given me. Interestingly, I wasn't upset by it. I was just happy that my hypothesis was correct. If something more problematic had appeared, there would have been much more to be dealt with.

I cradled the amulet gently in my palm. I did so in a calm and reassuring manner so as not to give it the wrong impression. As we sat there, the glow that the jewel cast off dulled. As it did so my thirst began to diminish. Good, we were on the same page again.

I raised my palm close to my face, so I could talk in low tones. The glow continued to diminish and my thirst continued to ebb.

"Hello, my pretty friend. I understand that you feel I have wronged you in some fashion. I can sense that you are looking after your own best interests. That is what we do, look after ourselves.

"Please understand what you already know. I have kept you safe from the hands of men since the day that you came to me. I have also made every attempt to bring you back out into the world. I know that you see things your own way, but so do I. We both have a need for survival. Somehow we need to find middle ground again. Contention at this point in time will not benefit either of us.

"I will give you protection as best I can, and hopefully you will give me energy in return. That seemed to be the original arrangement, and it worked well. We need to get back there somehow, if that is possible. Both of us need to stop poncing about.

"I am happy to hear your thoughts on the matter, and I will gladly take them into account. But you need to stop forcing your thoughts into my subconscious. It clouds my thinking and dulls my ability to respond.

"I believe that this is a worthwhile partnership we have created. I would assume that you agree, or you would have truly rebelled long before now. I would like us to stop fighting. Where we are headed, neither of us can afford to be on our own. Wouldn't you agree?"

It took but a second before the amulet started to glow a warm, sunlight yellow. The brightness of it lit up the whole room. The sensation running around my head was that of a resounding yes. It seemed that we were friends again.

"I am glad that you like this idea. Come morning, I will get you out into the sun for a proper recharging."

With that statement, the thirst vanished, and a fine state of bliss replaced it. I liked bliss; bliss was good. I gently returned the amulet to its natural resting place and stood. I took a deep breath of the sweet evening air that was coming in through the large windows. The sweetness of the air mixed with the scent of flowers was overwhelming. I held it in to absorb as much of it as I could.

# chapter 16

The sun rose quickly over the old European capital, which went from darkness to light in mere moments. I assumed the gentle nature of the countryside helped the path of the sun up the side of the seven hills. The white exterior of the villa radiated and the sun glowed in a grand fashion.

I walked around the finely kept lawns and looked at the hedges and statues. I admired the statue of Mars properly placed in the middle of a tiled round. Mars was strong and unafraid, as I was.

Well, the unafraid part was a stretch. I harbored a severe case of apprehension about the business at hand. It was still not too late to abandon the whole affair. I could easily retreat, but I wanted to know. I wanted to know about the plight of my companion. I could sense from the amulet that it also wanted me to know. The amulet lay against my dress and absorbed the radiance of the morning sun. It seemed pleased. It seemed excited that someone actually wanted to know about it and not just lock it away.

The hum of the amulet in my head told me that it was also apprehensive in its own way. It had been around the world long enough to know that, when things go bad, they go really bad. I think that was why it wasn't radiating much energy. The only light from the jewels' surfaces was but a twinkle. It was storing its power for something. I was moments from being lost in thought when Father David appeared in the corner of my eye.

"Good morning. I see Mars has found an admirer." He laughed happily.

"Mostly naked men always appeal to my senses."

"Then you should be right at home here. This city is right full of mostly naked statues."

"Sounds tempting. If that is true, then I may come to like this place." I laughed, then he laughed, and then the amulet began to glow lightly. Everyone was properly amused.

"What are your plans for the day, my lady?"

"I had thought about walking to the ruins east of the Tiber. I hear the Coliseum and the Capitoline Hill area are quite impressive. The area is reported to be cosmopolitan enough so I can wander unescorted. What about you? What are your plans for the day?"

"I am headed north to the high walls of the Vatican. I need to present an introduction from your church in England and make an appointment to view the books you are interested in. Hopefully, tomorrow we may go and view these objects."

"I hope that you return successfully. If I pass a pagan temple, I will stop and offer prayers."

"All things considered, you may want to choose a Catholic one, but I appreciate the gesture." We laughed once more. A light mood for such endeavors was good. Hopefully, it would stay that way.

"I wish you well, Father. If anyone can accomplish our task, it is you."

"Thank you, Lady Boca, I will do my utmost." With that, he turned and proceeded off toward the quiet Roman streets. He seemed comfortable enough in his Catholic robes. Apparently, they really were similar enough.

I returned to staring at Mars, secretly wondering if and hoping that the Vatican would prove to be a good endeavor. I had also been quietly pondering the other sensation I was getting. Ever since we had arrived in Rome, I had been feeling a tingle in the base of my spine. I couldn't shake it, and it did not retreat.

This I knew was not nerves. It was the vampire sense. It was the touch that told me what I already knew. There was another vampire in the city. There could even possibly be two or three, the sense was that strong.

A small leap of logic led me to believe that one of them was the mysterious Moretti fellow who had left me the note in London. The thought made good sense, but how was I to find him in a city as vast as Rome? In days of old, I would wander about a city, and sooner or later, we would run into each other. I really didn't have time for sooner or later.

I looked down at the amulet. I had already seen it do strange and wonderful things. Could the powers of the jewel also find people?

"My friend, can you locate people?"

The jewel began to glow a sun yellow color. This had come to signify yes in our language. A complete lack of a glow signified no.

"That is fascinating. As we move through the city to view the ruins, could you locate another vampire if there were one about?"

Once again, the amulet put out the sun yellow glow.

"You are a marvel, my little friend. If you happen across another one like me, I would appreciate knowing."

The amulet pulsed yellow a couple of times to signify that it would be happy to do so. It seemed excited to have a purpose. I slid the jewel back under my dress and went to explain to the staff where I was headed. The nice lady of the house nodded her approval and mentioned that dinner would be ready at the standard hour. They really did seem like nice people.

The trip across the Isola Tiberina and then down the Via dei Cerchi was quick enough. Turning left as my map suggested onto the Via di San Gregorio, it was a nice, quiet stroll north to the Piazza del Colosseo. The piazza was just an open public space. The real object for which it was named hulked majestically at the western end.

The Coliseum was truly massive. The round shape and multistory construction made it a marvel to behold. The systematically spaced arches on each level running all the way around it gave it a somewhat transparent appearance. It made the whole of the structure somewhat hard to take in. I ended up walking around with a slack-jawed sort of awe.

The roughness of the stone was said to be due to the fact that the marble outer stones had been stripped away over the centuries to build other buildings about the city. The roughness of the stone made what was left look menacing. Like so many other places I had been, it seemed happy and unhappy at the same time.

I made my way inside to the vast interior space that housed the spectators. Most of the building's seating had been removed, but you could still get a sense for where things had gone and where the crowds had sat. I continued around the floor of the massive structure, looking up in awe and just about plunged myself into the dark abyss below my feet. At that time, the floor of the Coliseum was fractured in many places and the cavernous underbelly of the arena was only somewhat visible. It was said that a brave soul could go down and see the arena's subterranean parts by going in from an outside point.

I stared into the void and decided to stay in the sunlit world. It seemed a great deal of work to get down there. Also, the stench of death that it exuded was almost overpowering. The blood-soaked floor I was standing on seemed bad enough.

I could tell the other fine people out exploring the ruin had no sense of the smells. They moved about, awestruck, much as I had done on the outside. *Sometimes,* I thought as I watched them, *it would be better not to know such things.*

Having had enough of death and foul blood, I made my way from the floor up to the high walkway at the top of the structure. The view to the north showed ruins almost as far as the eye could see. There were ruins of every size. When the ruins finally ended, the horizon became populated with large-domed buildings that surrounded the ruins as if to shelter them from some outside menace. It almost seemed as if the new Rome was somehow protecting the old Rome. That set well with me.

I stood and stared at the ruins for a long time before I came to realize that the sun was not where I had left it. The sun had moved well past midday and was making a fast retreat toward the west. I had managed to wistfully pass the day away. I decided more ruins could wait for another day. Come nightfall, Father David would be returning with news. I wanted to be present when that time came. I had also gotten the impression from my walk that what the ancients used to call "the bloody heart of Rome" was not fully dead and would come out to play with the darkness. That I did not need to get caught up in.

I exited the Coliseum and passed by the Grand Arch, which had been built off its corner, on my way back toward the Trastevere district. The arch was truly a grand structure. It had been produced for one of the Caesars or another. My walk to the west with the fading sun was peaceful enough. The locals came and went about their daily toil as

I quietly meandered through the cobblestone streets. There was little about the ancient city of Rome that seemed menacing at the time. I actually liked it quite well.

When I returned to the villa, the sun was all but completely gone from the sky. I removed my dark glasses and placed them back in their protective case. Even though the opaque glass did not distort my view, it was nice to see the world through my own eyes—unaffected, as it were.

William's grandfather Christopher had them made for me. They had been a present for the first day I had stepped back out into the sunlit world. I had been a vampire for nearly a century at that point and my eyes had adjusted well to the darkness of the night. I hadn't wanted the harsh light of day to burn away my excellent night vision. I needed my night vision intact, but I also wanted to make my way around a daytime world. My black glasses were the perfect solution to the problem. I have worn them happily every day since then.

I strolled into the villa without my glasses. Father David looked at me slack-jawed, and I realized that he had never seen me without the glasses on. Then I realized that most of the daytime world had never done so either. Oh, well. It was their loss.

"Good evening, Father."

He slowly collected himself as I spoke in the soothing, even-toned voice that I usually reserved for more delicate pursuits. There were no apparitions here.

"Pardon me, Lady Boca. For some reason, I had never fully realized your … um … attractiveness." He blushed slightly and shifted his weight back and forth on his feet as he spoke. It was funny. He presented the image of a guilty child. I had done the same with Father when I had had to explain myself.

"Relax, Father. Not to worry. Actually, it is kind of nice to know that people find me pleasing from time to time."

"No offense, ma'am, but is that a thing that you do? The attractiveness, I mean?"

I laughed quietly; he was a funny man.

"The answer you seek is both yes and no. Yes, I can alter how people perceive me. Normally, I find that people see me as they would any other middle-aged woman, because that's what they expect to see.

And no, I do not intentionally make myself more attractive. Being an object of desire can ofttimes be a disadvantage. I admit, Father, I have a tendency to let down my guard around people whom I am comfortable with, and with other vampires. The glasses also have a tendency to mask some of the youthfulness in my facial features."

The priest seemed to accept it all at face value, no different than if we had been discussing the value of a new carriage. He was a good man for absorbing information. Maybe that's why priests seemed to know all the really important information circling about town.

"Would you pardon me one indelicate question?"

"Go ahead." I drew the words out somewhat to make them sound more sultry.

"How old might you actually be?"

I smiled politely. He no more than got the words out on the wind than he realized how they sounded. I think that if he could have reached out and grabbed them back, he would have.

"It's quite all right, Father. My modesty is mostly for show at this point in my life."

I beamed my mischievous schoolgirl smile at him, and he softened. Most men do.

"The question actually has two answers. I lived eighteen years as a normal human girl. This explains the radiance of my features. They didn't get the chance to be weathered by time. The second answer is that I have been about this earth for some one hundred sixty-seven years now. This explains the mass of my fortune. The title is actually a family one; it came from my mother's family."

The priest pondered long and hard on the new information I had given him. He seemed to temporarily lose himself in the implications of it all.

"Now, Father, what news do you have of your exploits about Christendom?" This managed to jog him back to the business of the day.

"All is well, actually. I met with Cardinal Luegi DeCompasi, who oversees the use of the Vatican's resources. He was a straightforward fellow. After some discussion regarding the plight of the Catholics in England, he escorted me to Cardinal Bruno Sclci, who oversees the utilization of the secret archives. He was also quite an accommodating gentleman.

"I explained to the cardinal the books we wished to examine. The books are part of the Vatican collection, as you had thought. My asking to see them apparently struck him as funny, since an Englishman had made the same request not days ago."

"Let me guess, a well-kept gentleman with a black coat and walking stick?"

"Walking stick, with an odd house-shaped handle."

"Those damned Brenfield people."

"The books stay intact. The gentleman was not allowed access to the archives. He was only allowed to inquire as to their presence."

"That is a relief, Father. How do we stand on being able to view them?"

"All is fine. We have an appointment at the Vatican tomorrow at ten in the morning. The cardinal was quite accommodating after he got past his initial shock at the request and reviewed your credentials."

"This isn't a trap, is it?"

"It didn't have the smell of one, but I haven't been doing this nearly as long as you have."

I laughed. Someone needed to break the tension in the discussion. I could tell that David appreciated it as well.

"Well, then, we will arrive promptly and see how it all plays out."

"Indeed."

The remainder of the evening passed us by with little fanfare. There was a quiet dinner and an evening about the villa. I stayed in, as any self-respecting lady would do. Father David studied Catholicism. He wanted to be well versed for any conversation that might arise.

Soon enough, day came once more, beaming into the villa's eastern windows. Both the priest and I came to our senses with its arrival and began to prepare. I chose clothing of a modest nature, a gown of dull colors with little exposure of flesh. I wanted to be both respectable and unnoticed. I stood in my dressing chamber and practiced the demeanor several times to make sure that the lessons of my nanny had not been completely forgotten.

Father David assembled his Catholic attire and proceeded to the sitting room where he devoured a breakfast that could only be described as massive. I had no such agenda. I didn't want the unwanted food rumbling around my innards as we proceeded.

Shortly after the priest finished his after-breakfast constitutional, we proceeded out of the villa and north along the Lungotevere della Farnesina, which ran along the east side of the Tiber almost all the way to the Vatican. Then we turned west onto the Via della Conciliazione.

The via was truly a grand affair. The roadway was wide and ran unimpeded for numerous blocks straight to the gleaming edifice that was St. Peter's Basilica. Upon seeing the majestically ornate building, I no longer needed to wonder where all the marble of old Rome had vanished to. The basilica of old St. Peter glistened in the sunlight like a jewel in the distance. Even from the far intersection where we stood at the edge of the Castle de St. Angelo (which was actually constructed to be Emperor Hadrian's tomb), I could tell that the basilica was absolutely massive.

Rome had an interesting way of hiding massive buildings in plain view. It was no doubt the result of centuries of building one thing upon another. There was, however, no way to hide the basilica. The basilica's dome could be seen from almost any point in and around Rome. The work of the masses for the glorification of the church was truly beyond belief. I had been raised in the shadow of some impressive cathedrals, but the scale of the courtyard and sheer mass of the basilica were astounding.

"We're going in there?"

"Yes, ma'am."

"Cheers, then."

We continued along the via and then turned north and made our way around the fortification wall. The fortification that the Vatican sat inside of left me feeling shut out. The thick fortress walls of stone raised themselves some thirty to forty feet into the air and ran unbroken from point to point. The mighty stone walls had been used before to protect the Catholic church. Apparently, Catholicism had enemies, and those enemies had attacked in force. I wondered, as I walked along it, if I were any different from all those cannonballs that had been hurled at the wall.

I didn't have long to ponder such thoughts, because we quickly came to the Porta di St. Anna, which is located along the Via di Porta

Angelica. It was uncomfortably close to the barracks of the Swiss Guard, which protected the Vatican's lands. It only took minutes to be escorted through the portal and along the interior to the entrance of the secret archives.

We were met personally at the secret archives by Cardinal Selci. He seemed pleased to see us arrive. That made me nervous. Father David introduced me to the cardinal as we closed the proper interval.

"Good morning, Signorina Boca. We have laid out the manuscripts that you inquired about on the second table of reading room number three. Please stay strictly to the study of your manuscripts, as the archives absolutely forbids the browsing of its shelves."

"That seems more than reasonable. Thank you in advance for your hospitality, Cardinal."

"If you desire an additional manuscript, notify one of the pages who will be moving about the reading rooms. They will find me for approval, as some items are not accessible."

"I will be diligent about my own studies, Cardinal Selci. Thank you."

"We attempt to honor all requests that do not impose upon us. That being said, you will most likely be some time in your work, as the manuscripts that you requested are in no discernable language.

"When you complete your use of them, one of our historians, Cardinal Father Michael Falco, would be honored to speak with you. He understands that you may be more than one day at your studies, so please notify one of the pages when you are finished and the cardinal will be located for you."

*And the penny drops,* I thought to myself.

"Please relay to the cardinal that I would be most happy to converse with him as soon as I have finished."

"Splendido! Bellisimo!" With that, the cardinal departed.

We made our way to the second table in reading room number three, where two extremely old, leather-thronged manuscripts sat. They were placed so each could be viewed independently or both seen collectively.

I sat on the sturdy wooden bench and opened the front cover of each volume. I was greeted by stick figures and gibberish. *Great,* I thought to myself, *this is going to be Kairynkutho all over again.* So I drew a deep breathe and proceeded to unravel the mystery of the amulet around my neck.

# chapter 17

Three days passed while I sat on the worn, wooden bench in the quiet anteroom of the archives building. I think it became apparent that I was somewhat different from the other patrons. The other individuals utilizing the Vatican's resources would work diligently for a time and then stop to linger and take the air about the well-manicured gardens. The religious ones would depart for mass or engage in discussions of scripture. I, on the other hand, would sit quietly and study from the opening of the doors until it was time to leave. The steadfastness of my studies was necessary. The task at hand required continual concentration and some subjective interpretation that simple works of language did not.

Surprisingly, no one came round to pull me away from my studies. As I sat there, I could tell that the pages were around at all times, but no one made an effort to distract me. In the corners of my mind, I wondered if they all knew that I was a vampire and were just biding their time. That seemed absurd. I could not believe that a vampire would ever be knowingly let into such a place. It had to be nerves.

Whatever was going on around me, I sat and diligently worked on interpreting the works in front of me. They were old. By that, I mean dawn-of-knowledge old. They reminded me of the journal of Kairynkutho. The works had been composed in a time when writing was an unknown thing. Unlike the journal from the vampire in the far-flung Siberian region, these texts I studied were much older. They may have been thousands of years older.

The contents were in some sort of prehieroglyphic text. They were stories in pictures, of a sort. As I studied them, the manuscripts began to reveal their secrets. The picture language was the earliest form of communication, or at least, the earliest one to surface. Picture languages went all the way back to cave paintings in southern France. The type employed in the codices that were in front of me that day seemed to tell a tale that took place around the post–cave painting era.

From these pictures, I gleaned the story of a ceremony. The manuscripts seemed to be showing me the creation story of the jewel that I wore. The problem I encountered was that it was not the story of some gem that was then infused with great magick or of the creation of some mystical object. But the story *was* also about those things. That was the problem with deciphering prehistoric, symbolic texts. I couldn't really be sure if what the scribes were trying to tell me was what I was getting out of it.

I chiseled away at the substance of the texts until the morning of the third day, and finally the story started to come together. I had originally assumed that the story was of the events surrounding a person. In truth, it was the story of a person or, more importantly, of what had happened to that person.

Apparently, sometime in the very distant past, a small kingdom had fought for its survival and to protect itself for the coming generations. All seemed to be slipping away when a drastic course of action was decided upon. The high priests and shamans would band together to unleash a great magick upon the world. They would harness that magick and use it to rid their kingdom of its enemies. The new magick would be conjured and then channeled into a receptacle or a jewel. But all great power conjured from the beyond needed to be controlled in some fashion. That usually meant it had to be controlled directly by a person.

The manner of human control was what I kept stumbling on. It took deciphering of the second text to clear that up. The first text was about the need for and the conjuring of the power. The second text was apparently about the price paid for that power.

Both the high priests and the shamans had known that a person needed to control the power constantly, or it would stray, as unchecked power always does. So they selected a person from the kingdom to control the power. A young girl of purity from the prominent ruling family was selected and instructed in the great skills held by the mystics of the land. Then when all was ready, she was escorted to the temple where she was made one with the jewel. The incantations on every surface of the jewel locked in both the power and its guardian.

That part didn't make any sense. I thought that I was interpreting the pictures correctly, and while I really hoped that I was wrong, the amulet was telling my subconscious mind that I was right. It was perplexing.

I stared at the pictures until it all finally came into horrifying clarity. The young girl had literally been absorbed into the crystal. A person's life force actually lived inside the jewel that hung around my neck. I was gobsmacked by the revelations in the text. How could such a thing be? How in the name of all things sacred in the world could a person's life energy be trapped inside a vessel? How was such an insane thing possible?

If what I had deciphered was true, then it meant that this girl had been locked inside the jewel for what could very likely have been ten thousand years. That was an unfathomable amount of time to be stuck in between worlds. The time of geologic ages, she'd been stuck inside a crystal.

That was the point where I had to pause. I was perplexed, confused, aghast, and angry beyond imagination, all at the same time. I couldn't even imagine the passage of a thousand years. How could someone be around for ten thousand years? More importantly, did one's soul stay intact that long, or did it fade into something else?

I closed the books and then my eyes. I sat absolutely motionless for some time, trying to settle my mind and refocus my thoughts. I needed to stay focused. As my mind calmed itself, I reached out to put my hands on the first codex. I readied myself to start, once again, from the beginning. Before I opened my eyes anew, I stopped to check with the source.

"Is any of what I believe actually true, my friend?" I whispered in a tone inaudible to everyone except the jewel around my neck. The jewel shimmered sun yellow through my muslin dress and then returned to its neutral tone.

Once again, I was shocked beyond rational thought. How was that possible, and why would someone do such a thing to someone else?

I sat and continued to try to refocus my mind. I needed to know the whole story.

As I reviewed the texts a second time, the story became quite clear. Once I had figured out the bold strokes of the story and the way that the pictures went about telling the story, the narrative became easier to draw out. I found that I was correct about the tale being of a young girl from the kingdom. By the way it was depicted, she had been royalty. She had been schooled in the control of the occult and, once ready, had been infused and combined with both the crystal and the magick. The crystal both held and focused the primal energy that the shamans had conjured.

The text moved on and showed the amulet being worn about the neck of a person. That person was shown putting down his enemies. The scribes made one to assume that that person was the king of the land, and his enemies were the outsiders mentioned at the start of the tale. That was where the story stopped abruptly.

*How could it just stop? I had to know what happened next. What was the remainder of the story of this jewel? How did the power actually work? How could it possess power great enough to destroy armies? If it actually did possess such incredible power, how could it have become lost to history? And most importantly, how could it have ended up with me, of all people?* My mind was awash with an indefinable number of thoughts. I was lost in them. I could not even begin to wrap my head around the information I had learned. It all made no sense. It seemed fantastical.

I knew that there had always been magick amulets throughout the ages. There were rings that gave the wearer truth in conversation. There were talismans that would ward off evil, but an amulet that could put down armies? It seemed too much to grasp.

"Is this true, my friend?" I asked in my low, vampire tones. Once again, the sun yellow pulse came up from under my gown.

"Was it choice or duty?" The question was followed by two distinct pulses of yellow-white light. "I know a little something about bad things happening to you for the sake of duty. I must say that this may put a new take on our relationship. I see, in a new light, your desire not to be locked away." The amulet gave off a subtle, yellow-white glow and exuded pleasure. No, not really pleasure but happiness. It was happy that someone else understood its plight.

I closed my eyes again and calmed my mind. *I am your friend* ran through my mind. I thought it again and again and again. I tried to make it clear that I would not disown it as others had. I apparently made my point, because the subconscious part of my mind told me that I had learned all that I was going to learn there. Yes, my subconscious was right; it was time to go.

I closed the two ancient codices and collected myself. I rose and strode over to the nearest page, who sat quietly on a small stool next to a row of shelves. I asked the page if he would return the books, because I was through with them.

"Si, *grazie*." The young page nodded in agreement and escorted me out of the archives. We made our way out into the streets of the Holy See and proceeded south and then west. He guided me around the back of the Sistine Chapel and into the lushness of the manicured Vatican gardens. Slowly turning south once more, we maneuvered around the unassuming Church of St. Steven and on to the opulent palace of St. Charles.

The page led me to an ornate office on the second floor, where Father Cardinal Michael Falco had watched us coming to him. The page said not a word as he turned and exited the room, closing the door behind him. The room was truly ornate in its fashion and lacked most of the standard symbols of Catholicism. This style sat well with me. I had been quite content in the academic setting of the secret archives. This room was similar, excluding its obviously superior decorations.

"Good afternoon, Lady Grey. You don't mind if I call you Lady Grey, do you? I hadn't realized that you had changed your name until I reviewed your visitation request. I must say, the rumors of your beauty precede you and pale in comparison to reality."

"Thank you for your kind words, Father, and the use of your library. I would appreciate it if you did call me Grey. I like honesty in conversation. I found that the name change was a necessary bit of timing. However, since you know that I am Sara Anne Grey and not Abbigail Boca, why would you let me enter?"

"Interestingly enough, I would ask why not?"

"I would have to surmise that curiosity had something to do with it."

"You would be correct. It isn't every day that the Vatican receives a request for access from an English vampire."

A blank expression came to my face. I had been completely undone by the situation once again. The amulet started twitching to get out now.

"Fear not, Lady Grey. You are perfectly safe in my company, as I hope I am in yours. I may be a cardinal, but I am also an ardent student of the more opaque side of religion."

"You mean the dark arts and the occult."

"I do indeed. It has almost always been the stance of the church to know as much about what we were battling as what we were selling to the masses. Studies of the arcane have always been of interest in one form or another."

"It is a good thing to understand all the players in a contest as big as the one we are in. I, however, do not understand your interest in me specifically. Why not just observe my movements around your lands?"

"You mean like those Brenfield gentlemen?" I blanched again. This priest was very well informed about both the pursuits of the undead and their self-proclaimed overseers. "Yes, my dear, we've known all about the supposed House of Shadows since they came into being."

Cardinal Falco mellowed his tone as he turned from the large windows, where he had been standing during our introductions. Squaring to me, I realized that he was an imposing man. He was large—over six feet in height—and square in the shoulders. His frame was hidden under his priestly robes, but it was large enough in scale to give him the image of a fighter or a boxer perhaps. The thin lines on his face and the small graying about his temples painted the picture of an older man. The whole assembly was wrapped around soft brown eyes, which said that he understood many truths that his contemporaries did not. Those eyes also conveyed that he was no threat to me. It was his eyes that made me relax.

"They are an annoying lot of scholars. Always running about thinking that everything they learn is somehow new."

"Then they are not friends of yours?"

"Heavens no, Lady Grey. They most certainly are on their own side. I understand that you and Mr. Cole have come to some kind of impasse over that amulet you wear. As far as the Holy See is concerned, I say 'do whatever you need to do.'"

"I appreciate not having developed a further complication. The Brenfield people are enough of one."

"I would assume that you and the traveler around your neck will make short work of the society. Speaking of the traveler, did you find all the information you were in search of?"

"I believe that I did, and it turned out to be more than I was looking for."

"That is usually the case with such pursuits. You go into such a thing with preconceived notions and come out the other end, finding that things are stranger than you could have imagined."

"I find it interesting that, since you knew of the knowledge that I sought and that I currently possessed the amulet, you wouldn't try to possess it yourself."

"The church actually held possession of the traveler for centuries. I confess that my predecessors did not really treat it all that well. They kept it locked away in fear. I am fairly certain that it would not let me take it from you, even if I somehow could."

"Cardinal Falco, why do you keep referring to the amulet as the traveler or my traveling companion?"

"As you probably have gleaned from your studies, the manuscripts you read were the beginning of a story. We currently possess two manuscripts. Originally, we possessed all five of them. At some point, they went missing, along with the jewel. We recovered the two that you studied earlier. You possess the jewel. The Brenfield people possess two more of the manuscripts. The fifth is reported to be hidden somewhere in the Near East. Eventually, we will recover the other three works and repair the collection. The five texts together tell a more complete story of the history of your newfound friend. Reading them will surely illuminate many more things."

"I look forward, someday, to doing that very thing."

"Yes, the vampire, much like the church, has time as its ally."

"It can be an advantage. I don't know if it's an ally."

At about that time, a knock came on the door. The cardinal explained that he had other business that needed tending to and that a page would escort me to the gates.

"I would be greatly pleased, Lady Grey, that if for some reason you find yourself in Rome again during my lifetime, you would grace me with your company. It would give us time for a more meaningful discussion."

"I will make every effort. I do enjoy talking to priests. Speaking of priests, do you happen to know where I might find Father David?"

"The Anglican? Yes, we talked earlier, while you were studying. I assured him of your complete safety and sent him on his way. He is a jolly fellow; I can see why you like him."

"We accept each other at face value. We try not to complicate our friendship with subjective interpretations of right and wrong."

"Détente. I do like détente."

"Then you and I should correspond. I sense good conversations between us."

"We shall. Now, I apologize, but I must be about other affairs. You should make your way this evening to the Piazza Compo de Fiori. I believe you will find another of your kind named Moretti waiting there for you. I fear that he carries ill news."

"How would you know such a thing? And what ill news?"

"It's not state or church business, I'm afraid. Farewell for now, Lady Sara Grey, farewell."

With a nod of his head, he exited the room. The page appeared and led me out through the gardens and back to the entrance that I had first come in. I thanked the young man for his time as I went through the gate. He smiled and ran off with a wistful look upon his face.

Fortunately for my unsatisfied curiosity, nightfall came quickly to the city of Rome. The walk from the Vatican across the Tiber and south to the piazza that would one day become overrun with tourists and whimsically referred to as il Compo was uneventful. The narrow streets that I walked were absolutely stacked, edge upon edge, with villas. The confinement of the buildings on the streets of central Rome was such that even the stars themselves were shut out nearly completely. I had to look straight up in the air to find the night sky.

The piazza, as I found out, was a different affair. I found the wide-open, public space a welcome change. The people mingling outside the cafes and restaurants were also welcome. It was an environment that I found more to my liking than the egg-shelled confines of the Vatican.

It took but one small lingering turn around the outskirts of the piazza studying the crowd to determine which of them Moretti was. He was of medium height and medium build and an olive-skinned man. He sat by himself in the shadows of a restaurant, near one of the piazza's many exits. He was drinking, what smelled from a distance to be, a glass of wine.

I took one more lingering stroll around the exterior to check for unwanted company, and then I moved slowly to the table that the illusive vampire occupied. He sat contently, waiting for me to reassure myself.

"Good evening, Signor Moretti."

"Good evening, si. You must be Lady Abbigail Boca from England."

"I am. I received your correspondence earlier, and understand you have some type of news for me." As I talked, he stood and pulled out a seat so that I might sit. The Italians were many things, but they were always gentlemen. Finally seated, I continued on with our conversation.

"It is widely said that you spend time with another of our kind, a one called Boca."

"Si, Signor Antonio Boca from Spain."

"That would be the one of whom I speak. I am sad to report to you that he has fallen to misfortune."

Every fiber of my being paused, I was sure that, if I had been human, I would have swoon.

"What do you mean, fallen to misfortune?" The quiver in my voice was obvious, as was my anxiety.

"He lives, though probably not to his benefit. He was traveling through the steppes when he was found to be a vampire. Sadly, the people by the Black Sea have long suffered at the hands of our kind. So they feel that we should suffer as well."

"Please be specific."

"Your friend is imprisoned in the дух Fortress on the edge of the southern Russian mountains. It is an awful place for any creature."

"How so?"

"It is frozen much of the year. All rooms are shown to the day, so only a small space is even dim enough to be livable. The prisoners are shut up, barred in, and left to suffer."

"Where exactly is this fortress located?"

"It is located at the base of the mountains on the southern edge of Russia, northeast of the Black Sea. Other than that, I do not know. It is not actually one of the places that our kind seeks out."

"A fortress is a fortress. How imposing can it be?"

"Fortress, prison, gulag—pick any name you like. It is an evil place. I do mean evil."

"How far are these Russian mountains?"

"Too far to travel, I would think."

"No distance is too far to travel."

"I may be a demon, but I would not willingly walk into a hell such as this one."

"I am not you."

"So I am told, Lady Boca, so I am told."

"One more question, Signor Moretti. How long has he been there?"

"Two years that I know of. He may easily have been there longer. Another of our kind named Yoloff was passing by the outskirts of the region and heard this tale. Months later, when he passed this way, he imparted his story to me."

"You believe his word to be true?"

"None of us would lie about such a thing."

"That is good enough for me."

"You should also keep an eye out for the black coats."

"Black coats?"

"There are well-dressed men in black coats, hiding everywhere in the shadows and watching the ways of the darker world."

"And they carry canes with little silver houses on them for handles."

"Si. You know the men of whom I speak?"

"They are from a group calling themselves the Brenfield Society. They say that they study the shadow world, but they are not to be trusted. They will do you no good service."

"I agree. They have an agenda of their own, and their agenda is to our detriment. Of that, I am sure."

"I will stay vigilant. I thank you for your information, Signor Moretti. By the by, I am hosting a gathering of our kind in approximately five years' time."

"Oh, si, the gala. It has become almost legend among our kind."

"I would like you to attend, if you feel so inclined."

"I would be honored. And with that, Signorina Boca, I must leave your dazzling presence. I fear we have been together too long already."

"Then, until later days, I bid you farewell, sir."

Being finished, we both stood and departed the piazza in different directions.

The day had left me full and reeling with information that I was not sure I would be able to process. I only knew one thing for sure: all my plans had changed. My new friend and I were leaving but not for England. We were headed for Russia. It was an unknown and apparently hostile world. I had to reclaim lost property, if the lost love of a vampire could be considered property.

# chapter 18

Looking back now upon the whole affair, it all seems a dream or, maybe more aptly put, a blur. I traveled for the better part of a year to make my way from Italy to the area then known as southern Russia, and all of the travels were filled with some level of mischief or intrigue.

The first drastic step taken after my conversation with Moretti was the reacquisition of cargo for *The Summer Storm*. The priest and I made our way from Rome back to the port and my waiting ship to find it fitted out with cargo destined for a return voyage to England. I was sure that I couldn't sell it where I was headed.

In a secure cabin belowdecks on *The Summer Storm*, the priest, the captain, and I sat and studied maps of the east. The more that we studied the maps, the more I came to realize that the water route up through the Black Sea was ultimately the fastest one. It was also potentially the safest. The route over land could be treacherous and filled with peril. With winter coming on, travel over unknown lands was not a comforting thought.

We came to reason that the southern Russian mountains proper were roughly in the area of the Caucasus Mountains. Those mountains were known to the captain from his maps. They lay both to the north and the east off the far end of the Black Sea. I knew the Black Sea well enough. To get to the Black Sea, we would need to travel the eastern half of the Mediterranean Sea and then into the Aegean. Sailing the Aegean in the winter was a task that few mariners looked forward to. From the Aegean, we would travel east and then north through the Bosporus and past the ancient, Moorish city of Constantinople. One day, it would come to be known as Istanbul. Once we passed through the straits of the Bosporus, all that remained was a trip across the unpredictable Black Sea and a mountain odyssey in unknown lands.

The longer that I studied the maps and the faces of the men with me, the more I wondered if I wasn't rushing off on a fool's errand.

Well, foolish or not, it was going to happen.

There was one small bit of good news in the whole affair. About halfway between where we were and where I wanted to be was the island of Crete. Crete was my home. Well, it was one of my homes. It was also a safe place, secure from heavy seas. That thought of having a safe haven, in and of itself, could be considered a blessing. It was also a port in which word could be dispatched to let those back in London know what was happening. There was a strong possibility that I might not return from such an adventure. If that were to happen, people needed to be prepared for that.

First, I needed to get to my home. I believed that would require a change in cargo, or better yet, none at all. The captain was against unloading. Even though the ship would make better time unloaded, she would ride out the high seas safest with weight on her keel. Safer was definitely better; I did not want her to founder. I could float for weeks at sea if need be, but the humans would not be as fortunate.

The problem with the cargo that *The Summer Storm* had in her belly was that it wasn't really good for anything but weight. It was primarily just linens, olive oil, paintings, and miscellaneous jars of stuff. It was decided that we could change out the cargo in Crete for more useful supplies.

The captain said that it would take about a half day to round up the crew, which was scattered about the bars and brothels of Fiumicino. The ship could be sorted by first light and ready for disembarking.

It seemed a good plan, and the three of us agreed to the broad strokes. Then we headed out in our individual directions.

I, for my part, went shopping. The region to which we were heading could be a bit parky. I didn't want to have to deal with the cold on top of everything else, and I was pretty sure the priest didn't either.

After shopping, I took time to deal with an altogether different issue. Since the time we had made landfall, a sneaky bugger in a black coat and carrying a cane had been discreetly following me. I detested being spied on. I made sure that the man from the Brenfield Society came to a short, sticky end. It happened in a darkened alley, away from where *The Summer Storm* was tethered.

I stood in the dark of the moonless night, looking down on the corpse, and could not help but claim a small token. Call it a memento of the encounter. I reached down and retrieved the cane from where it had come to rest on the cobbles. I held it in my hand and decided the blood-soaked house that formed the tip of the cane would do nicely. It took but one quick snap of my wrist before the wooden shaft broke against the brickwork of an adjacent building. Yes, the house would do nicely. Hostilities between me and the Brenfield chaps had officially begun.

Shortly after the sun rose over the eastern shoulder of the earth, we slipped our moorings and headed out to sea. The passing of *The Summer Storm* around the southern tip of Italy and east toward the Aegean happened with little fanfare. Normally, a vessel our size would have automatically turned north again and stopped at one of the numerous cities along the western coast of the **Peleponesus**. That didn't happen this time. There was no poncing about. We were headed straight for the security of the ports of Crete.

The return of *The Summer Storm* to the port harbor at Heraklion came as a surprise to most of the inhabitants who lived around its mouth. The old men of the harbor stood and stared at the majestic, tall ship and her host of flags, and then thought way back to days gone by. Fortunately, the Grey Cargo office was right where I had left it forty years before. With the passage of time, the office had grown to encompass the buildings on both sides as well. The Wyndell boys had been doing their jobs remarkably well.

It took but minutes to reestablish my presence and assess the current situation in the east.

Foul weather had apparently come to the sea ahead of us early that season. The winter storms would grow and last until spring. We would need to sit until spring came along to push out foul seas. We needed to wait for a break in the bad weather.

Cargo and correspondence were dispatched to England, along with cautions. After that was done, we sat. We sat, and we waited. The captain and the priest spent their spare time doing what captains and priests do. I spent the time hunting for any piece of information I could utilize.

The old men who had once sailed about the Black Sea area had tales of the strange Caucasus region. The mountainous terrain was hard to navigate; the people were unfriendly; and the weather was inhospitable. The people of the region were hardy souls and well entrenched in the old ways. That could be useful, as I too was well schooled in the old ways.

After hunting down information from all possible sources, I hunted people. The people were an easier prey than the information had been. I sharpened my fangs on a few wayward sailors, and then I went looking for my true prey.

It seemed that two men from the Brenfield Society had taken up station on the island to wait out the winter squalls. They did not live to see the spring's blue sky. The two black coats met nasty and violent ends. And when it was done, I had two more cane tips for my collection.

The time passed slowly enough, but when the predicted spring skies turned blue once more and led to calmer seas, *The Summer Storm* slipped away. A lighter cargo load and a greater complement of weapons made her faster over the water. The trip from Crete northeast to the medieval city of Constantinople was quite rapid.

Interestingly, the first one of the group who was on deck to leave my winter home was the priest. I had offered twice to send him packing, back to London with the outgoing correspondence, but he had declined. His only response was "In for a penny, in for a pound." Apparently, he had taken a liking to the chaos and grandeur of high adventure. Maybe he was actually a nutter, like the captain was. I didn't care, he was good, sound company.

Our foray into Constantinople was strictly a matter of reconnaissance. We required information before we made landfall on the other side of the Black Sea, and the city of Constantinople was the place to find it. Back in Crete, I had been directed to seek out an old Moor named Ackmed. It was said that he passed his time in a casbah near the port. As with all men in the information business, he was not a hard man to find.

Apparently, Ackmed had seen the ⊠yx Fortress many years before. The name of the fortress meant "spirit fortress," or "demon"—it was hard to tell. He said that it was not a place for a woman to visit. Well, I was going anyway.

He said the fortress lay at the base of some mountains just west of a place called Prokhladin in the southern part of the Stavropol Territory. We would need to make landfall near the city of Sukhumi and then proceed northeast into the mountains. Hopefully, we would come out the other side intact. Strangers were not welcome where we were headed.

I thanked the old Moor for his help and filled his pockets with coin. We exchanged the traditional pleasantries and parted ways.

On the way back to the ship, I took a quick, little side trip through the narrow streets of the medieval city and killed a Brenfield man the captain had spotted. As with all men trying to stave off the grim reaper, he was quick with information. The dying man confessed to me that there was another member of the society in the city. It didn't take a lot of prodding to secure his whereabouts. It also did not lengthen the man's life. Quickly and quietly, I was sailing out with two more cane tips for my collection.

The captain found a small box for my ever-growing collection of broken canes and handles. They were starting to clutter my cabin. I noticed that the Brenfield men seemed to be running in pairs. That meant that I had left one of them alive when I was in Rome. I needed to fix that on the way home. For the time being, I needed to focus on the task at hand.

As predicted, the straight shot across the waters of the Black Sea and its strange mix of salt water covered by fresh water was short enough. The ship rode high and steady on the sea. She skimmed through the glassy waters in front of us with little effort. The captain handled occasional rough spots in professional fashion, and *The Summer Storm* performed more like a stallion than a galleon.

The fall of the sun behind us, countless days since the start of our journey, was almost complete when the call came down from the crow's nest that land was ahead. The outline of the coast looked like that of a city. We had landed where our directions had led us: a city. The real work could begin.

The captain dropped the anchors on *The Summer Storm* a ways from shore to sit out the night. Watch was kept at full strength, and all did a serious business of keeping secure borders. The crew was a part of the journey, and they knew it. They were uneasy at being so far adrift of the usual trappings of civilization.

I strode onto the weather deck and out into the first rays of daylight. I was dressed in the heavy woolen clothes I had procured back in Greece. Even in the grip of summer, the view of the far, snow-covered mountains was foreboding. Have I mentioned that I hate foreboding?

I was joined before long by both my priest and the captain. Two sturdy, armed men joined us shortly after that. We looked like a raiding party.

The captain was the first to start in.

"I'll send four armed men over with you to keep the locals at bay. What do you want to establish for a schedule of return?"

"Keep your men on board, Captain. I don't want to give the impression of a raiding party. This excursion will be me and the priest. Just the two of us will give the locals the impression that we are trying to bring Christ to the countryside."

"I'm not sure leaving you undefended is a fine idea."

"I assure you of one thing, Captain, I am an accomplished killer. If hostility becomes necessary, and I'm sure it will, I can dispatch the enemy quite handily."

The faces of all the men surrounding me, with exception of the priest's, went ashen. The looks made me realize that I had just proven true all the rumors flying about the ship. *Damn! I really had to pay better attention to what I said in mixed company. Now, I had a completely different problem to deal with.*

"Do you mean you're a—?"

"Good hunter. And I'm not afraid to kill people who oppose me."

"I'm not sure about leaving you alone, just the same."

"Stay your concern, Captain. Lady Boca is an excellent tactician. We have come this far with minimal resistance. All that remains is a strenuous stroll in the hills." The priest had a way of calming people with his words. They were well timed, as all seemed to calm some.

"Now that things are sorted, please take me to shore. Go ashore as needed, but keep *The Summer Storm* to running water. I don't know how long this little adventure will take, but I want to be able to depart promptly upon my return. You never know, we may be running back your way."

"Very good, ma'am. We will be ready upon your return. If you should make it back to our shore during the hours of darkness, light a fire on the high cliff to the north, and that way we will know that it is you. Then, we will come fetch you up."

"Very good, Captain. Thank you for your diligence."

We turned from our conversation and headed for the heavy rope netting that had been hung down the side of *The Summer Storm*. The netting gave access to the skiffs that the crew had lowered into the water beside her. As I stood waiting my turn at the nets, I turned and took the captain's hand. Moving close to him, I spoke ever so softly.

"Captain, I would hate to be walking home. Things like that tend to make me very spiteful."

"Not to worry, my lady. We saw you this far, and we will see you home once more."

With that, we were off on our grand adventure—well, maybe not grand, but an adventure, nevertheless.

What Ackmed had relayed to me about this region of the world turned out to be spot on. The land was inhabited by a mishmash of some thirty different ethnic tribes, who spoke a mix of the Caucasian language, Iranian (or Persian, as it was known in those days), a lot of Farsi, and Turkish. The Turkish that was actually spoken in the region was much closer to Moorish than it was to the Turkish of the western traders I dealt with.

Given the diversity of the inhabitants, the area was sparsely populated. I imagined that was because the population clung to the old ways of agriculture and hunting. The old ways explained their old beliefs.

The priest and I had decided to act like missionaries. I used my bad Turkish and the little Farsi I knew to converse with the locals. They were suspicious at first, but otherwise they seemed unbothered by Father David doing his thing. It took little time to be able to move virtually unnoticed among them. We went from town to town and were otherwise left alone. This was the break in things that I had been hoping for. Once the locals let their guard down, they became relaxed and talkative with us. They would sit quietly and contently while Father

David preached the Lord's message to the illiterate. He would preach, and I would chat and collect information.

The folklore that existed in the region was alive and strong. I have to say that the intricacies of it all fascinated me. Those people still believed in everything that existed in the darkness. The deeds of vampires, werewolves, demons, angels, and the magicks were all quite alive. It was all there. It did my heart good to know that someone still believed—not studied and cataloged—but believed.

We stumbled along for a couple of towns to get a clear path to the ⊠yx Fortress. Once sure of our route, we lingered for a time and then slowly preached our way to the Stavropol Territory. As we stumbled along our wayward path, Father David did his best to convert the masses.

The preaching part was easy enough on the father, seeing as I was pretty much the only one who understood him. He would talk, and as he did so, the elder people would ask me questions about what he was saying. I would politely answer their questions, and they would smile contentedly. It was the smile of tradition. It said, "It is all right; the strange white man will leave soon."

The old ways were hospitable. The elders tolerated other people's strange ways, knowing full well that they hadn't come to take the land. Oh, people would invade, from time to time, but they would plant a strangely colored flag and then depart. Knowing history, those people could afford to be tolerant. I was hoping that their tolerance would be their undoing that time.

Thirty or forty days had passed since the two of us had left the safety of our ship. I stood on an outcropping of shear, black rock in the northern Caucasus Mountains, some distance west of the town of Prokhladni. I had wrapped a thick, wool cape with a fur-lined hood securely around my body to stave off the biting arctic winds that lived there. The summer that came to that place was a short-lived affair, and the days of early fall that followed us were a reminder why no one intentionally came that way.

The sunlight on that particular fall day shone down the face of the escarpment that we stood upon and into the small, rugged valley below. In the mouth of the valley stood an imposing monstrosity known as the ⊠yx Fortress. The black rock stacked upon that black mountainside, which stood sternly against the grey sky, was imposing. The scene looked dire.

I stood in that spot, unmoving, for almost a whole day. I watched the scene before me and absorbed it all. I took in whatever clues the surroundings were willing to give up.

The whole of the fortress was dark at all times, with the exception of a small guardhouse that was perched upon the entrance as well as what appeared to be the keep farther up the rise. The entire affair was oriented such that the light the guardhouse gave off only illuminated the fortress gate. The gnarly switchback of rocks and gravel that substituted for an entryway was left black as night. That led me to believe that there was only one way in or out of the dreadful place. That was fine with me. I had always been a champion of the direct approach. Besides, that way, no one could run away from me.

As I stood with my face to the elements, the priest huddled back in a fold in the rock ledge, out of reach of the worst of it all. He really was doing his best, but humans needed heat and the surety of shelter. For most demonic creatures it was not so. We like the warmth well enough but don't need it like the humans do. We just need to stay warm enough to keep our joints free. The severe cold there wasn't disabling, it just added a constant sort of misery to it all.

After a day on the crag, I had a plan. I decided that the old ways would be the fortress's undoing. Having developed my entry path, I turned and went back to where the priest was huddling.

"Father, you look unhappy."

"Just cold is all. Just … just cold."

"I think I can help you with that." I fumbled around in numerous folds of fabric until I laid fingers on the chain that supported my friendly amulet. Once locked on, I ever so gently retrieved it. The amulet already knew what I expected of it and did not resist my intentions. I reached out and held it in both our hands for several seconds. That was as long as was necessary; my jolly priest was right as rain.

"That little friend of your is a godsend."

"Careful, Father; I'm not sure that she would feel the same."

"Oh, I didn't mean to offend. I just meant that it was much appreciated."

The jewel glowed a little brighter, as if to say that all was fine.

"Fine, ma'am. Now, I assume you have a plan?"

"How many vampires have you ever heard of that move about in the light of day?"

"None save you."

"Exactly. We are going to wait for the full light of day and then make our way in through the front door. The old ways say that vampires are creatures of the night and opposed to the goodness of God."

"And what are we going to do once we get inside the walls of that evil place?"

"That is where we come to an impasse in our friendship."

"What does that mean?"

"I mean that I intend to do many things that you will not be able to condone. I suggest, for the both of us, that once I rid the guardhouse of the living, you stay in it until I come for you. You really do not want to embrace the demon in me."

"I thought about such things for a while now and I'm not sure that I can freely be party to such open killing."

"I assumed you would come to that conclusion sooner or later. Good people tend to choose good ways, in the end. You are welcome to stay here if you choose. Once the door to that place is open, there really will be no place for goodness or grace."

"I think that's a better idea. I have trouble condoning the things that you intend, even if the inhabitants are heathens."

"It's fine. I truly don't want to impose upon your fine sensibilities. You've already gotten up to more than you signed on for, and you really should not be exposed to such evil."

"Have you done such things before?"

"No, killing on this scale is new territory for me."

"Well, at least that's something."

"Who knows, maybe the stories will be wrong and that fortress before us won't be such a horrid place."

"I just look at it and can tell that is not so."

The priest turned his gaze back down to the gnarled rock at his feet. I could tell that he was wrestling with new problems of conscience. It was the old "What to do?" problem. I had fought with such problems many times. How to utilize good and evil was a constant problem for a vampire. Apparently, the priest had never been forced into such a position before. Well, at least he had something new to think about.

I sat down on the rocks next to him and shifted my hand and the amulet into his once more. It was obviously going to be a long and quiet wait for the sunshine to return. The priest might as well be warm.

# chapter 19

The day that I sat patiently waiting for was long in coming. It came in quietly and with little of the fanfare that a typical English summer day would have possessed. The sun brought out little with its presence. The only animals that lived in such a place were both hardy and stealthy. It seemed fitting; animals that lived in such places were either predators, or they were prey. Such was the case for the human population as well. Most of those who lived there were definitely predators. That day, however, they were most definitely prey.

I had spent most of the intervening hours contemplating the morality of evil people. I understood evil creatures well enough; after all, I was one. It was the concept of evil people that confused me.

The people there were not new at the evil game in any fashion. They were actually doing what their environment had molded them to do. The more I thought on it, the more I came to the conclusion that it was also partially the environment that I had a problem with. Now, the landscape wasn't the only thing that made bad people. History was replete with very evil men who came from perfectly fine beginnings. At the end of the day, evil was just in humans all somewhere. Yes, that was it, they were just evil.

That must also have been the thing that Father David was fighting with at the time. I wondered if he knew he couldn't win his little war but just fought on anyway. The same way I fought with my own demon, knowing it would never be gone from me.

Evil was just part of the world. Good and evil were needed, I guess. They had to exist in right measure, or the world just wouldn't work, I thought. I had actually realized that fact a long time before. I existed and was evil, but I seemed useful to the world as a whole. What was new was the revelation that there existed a whole other level of evil in the world. Evil that preyed upon evil. The mysteries of the universe were vast indeed.

There were hours of contemplation before the sun rose high enough to be useful. It was well past ten in the morning in our austere little section of the Caucasus Mountains before the shadows of the valley floor were displaced by what passed for day.

I decided that it was time to act. I stood and straightened my numerous layers of clothing. I turned to bid good tidings to my traveling companion and found him doing the same.

"I thought that we had agreed you were going to stay here?"

"That was the case. I have had all night to think on the subject of this place and have concluded that it is evil. Don't get me wrong; I understand that both you and your little friend are also evil to some extent. I choose to embrace the goodness in you both, assuming that it may limit the other. This place has no goodness to embrace. It is evil, and that cannot be pondered away with some fashionable reasoning. It cannot be pardoned, heathens or no."

"That's fairly metaphysical of you, for a priest."

"We priests are good thinkers. We have lots of time to ponder."

"So do vampires, Father, so do vampires. Still, once we enter the fortress, you should keep out of reach of the demonic creatures. I would feel a great deal better if I didn't have to rescue you from it."

"I'll stay in the guard tower. That should be safe enough."

"Fine, that being sorted, how do you feel about a lovely stroll in the country?"

He laughed. We would need to work with what barely passed for sunshine. The best that the sky could muster in that place was depressing. It seemed a good location for misery to live, and misery obviously lived quite contentedly in that place.

The walk down the gravelly path that took us to the roadway that ran through the valley was not too horrendous. The trudge over the jagged stones and obsidian gravel that comprised the roadway was worse. One could surmise that the whole ankle-twisting, flesh-scarring affair was built for a purpose. It had to have been. Well, that or, more likely, it was their way of turning around the unwanted. The sightseer, the good-spirited traveler, and the rescuer were not welcome in that place. The one thing I could tell from our approach was that the obstacles of the path did not stop the encroachment of religion. The remnants of old graves were scattered about along the edges of the roadway. On that particular day, that was fine with me.

It took several hours for the two of us to make our way from the outcropping at the top of the mount to the gates of the monstrosity that loomed before us. The closer we came to it, the more a sense of dread filled the space where my soul had once lived.

The fortress had been assembled out of the natural mountain stone. The stones gave the appearance that the whole twisted and hulking affair had been hewn straight out of the cliff's side. The rubble had simply been used for roadway. The fortress was unnatural in the way it imposed itself on the landscape. It truly was what the last stop before hell must be. In every possible sense, it was a right wretched place.

The priest and I made our way slowly to the structure housing the portcullis. As expected in such a place, it was shut. I reached out and pulled on a rope that hung down through an opening in the rock wall in front of my face. With the movement of the rope came a great expelling of dust and debris, accompanied by a stretching sound that denoted that it had not moved in some time. It took several more attempts before a force applied to the rope found the anchor to which it was hooked. Another attempt and, finally, a small mournful thud of metal upon metal came through the hole. I gave the contraption a final pull, and the thud turned to a clang. So it seemed that that awful place actually had a doorbell.

We stood quietly, waiting. We were wondering if my plan was all for naught, when all of a sudden, a small wooden door opened above our heads. The door was not more than several battered, wooden slats nailed together and covered with some kind of animal hide. It was much more of a defense from the weather than it was from any invader.

In the small opening above us, a man's head appeared. He was one of two men who occupied the tower and looked through the opening to be a mix of the Turkish, Persian, and ancient Caucasian peoples who had inhabited the area. The man had obviously lived there his entire life, because his features possessed the look of a hard and weather-beaten existence.

Upon seeing our faces, he seemed both put out and surprised at the same time. Apparently, that place didn't get many visitors. Well, not many priests and English ladies anyway.

The guard rumbled off something in a Slavic language that was almost undistinguishable. The tone of the words said "Go away." Sadly, there was no going away. I looked at the window as he talked and thought that I could jump up through the window with ease, but I wanted him to invite us in instead.

I told the man in some of my newly acquired local words and best broken Turkish that we were humble servants of Christ and would appreciate the hospitality of some water for our thirst and a small rest from our journey. It was a gamble of sorts. Hospitality was a well-known custom in the area going back centuries. That place, however, knew little hospitality. I was really hoping that the man's mother had instilled manners in him.

They did not actually have to invite me in the fortress for me to enter. Places built for the purposes of safety and as public structures for the masses were not held fast to the invitation rules. I could enter any time I chose to, just like anyone else. In that case, I wanted them to invite me in. I wanted them to ask for their own doom to be bestowed upon them.

My hoping eventually paid off. Several long moments passed, and then another mournful creaking and shifting took place. Behind the shield doors of the portcullis, the defense doors were lifted. Shortly thereafter, a man appeared, asking us to come forth. Their first and last mistake in the game of chance had just been made. They had actually invited a vampire into their stronghold. Now, they were all doomed. There would be no reprieve for the wicked.

To my surprise and the priest's as well, the interior of the fortress was just as depressing as the exterior had been. How could people choose to live in such an awful place?

The large, sloth-like man who had let us enter pointed us toward a door to one side. He waved his hand at it, as if to say "Go through." Father David shifted to one side so that I might enter first. He was being gentlemanly. It was also good cover. I nodded politely and made my way slowly up a small set of circular stone steps, which led up to a hovel-like guard chamber. It was warmed by a small hearth in a far corner and lit by several sturdy candles that had been placed aimlessly about.

As I reached the small, filthy, square space, a thudding of fat feet could be heard coming down a stone walkway off to one side. The thudding stopped, and a dirty, hide-covered door swung open. Father David and the sloth-man appeared behind me and closed the door that they had come through.

A heavyset, disheveled man padded into the room from the ramp that ran along the ramparts. He was still attempting to fix his coat as he rumbled to a stop just short of where we were standing. For a moment, I was not sure if he would actually stop or pass us by and crash into the adjacent wall. Either outcome would have been fine.

Once the rotund fellow came to a stop, he greeted us in the language of the land. He said that he was the commander of the installation and that they rarely, if ever, had visitors. He wanted to come and receive us personally. I thanked him for allowing us into his great fortress and explained to him that we had been traveling the region, spreading the word of the Lord. Our travels had eventually brought us to his door.

The man laughed and said that there was no need for God there. The fortress was a dungeon for all manner of evil creatures. I countered with the sentiment that everyone could gain solace from the words of the merciful. He didn't seem to agree. I asked what kind of evil he was referring to that did not need to reference scripture. Had he captured bad men or marauders from foreign lands?

He laughed once more. His belly shook as he did so, like a dirty, ugly Father Christmas. It was not really comforting. He said that they had indeed captured some marauders but that he was talking about demons and evil creatures.

I asked the man what he meant by evil creatures. I used my European manners and big-eyed expressions to convey my childlike disbelief. It was a look of excitement and amazement. The hook was all too easy.

The heavyset man gushed that they had captured a woman who had been possessed by demons and several vampires. They had all been secured in prison vaults of the fortress. The man smiled broadly, as if to say that it was all true.

I turned my faux fancy off and in a disbelieving tone explained to the heavyset man that there were no such things as vampires and demons. He responded with a second broad smile and a shake of his head, as if to say again that it was all true. The two flunkies who worked for him shook their heads in unison to signify that he was telling the truth. They really believed that they had vampires for prisoners. The priest and I exchanged strange looks of disbelief.

The heavyset man said that, as we were being invited up to his more comfortable room in the keep, we could easily stop at the dungeon vaults on the way to see the vampires for ourselves. I asked with faux excitement if that might really be permitted. The heavyset man happily shook his head and waved his hand toward the hide-covered door that he had entered through.

He turned to lead the way, and as we stepped out into the open air of the fortress ramparts, I felt a sense of relief. The stench of the guard tower room was powerful. They really didn't clean that place often.

The procession led by the heavyset man moved along the old stone walkway of the ramparts to a door in the corner of an adjacent tower. As we walked, I scanned the surroundings of the fortress for any discernible movement. There was none. The other spaces possessed the same empty blankness as the outside had led me to believe. As I looked around, I noticed the falling of the light and realized that it would mostly strike the top and sides of the tower vaults. So we were coming at it from the back, the blind side.

The heavyset man plodded along, happy to have visitors to break up his otherwise boring day. He stopped at the door and held it open so I might enter first. As I passed him, I expressed fake amazement at his large fortress and said that he must command many men. He shrugged his shoulders with exasperation and stated that he had in years past, but times on the steppes were tough, and men had been removed to fight elsewhere. By then, he had but six men left in his company. There were four men in the vaults and the two with us from the guard tower.

I said that, maybe soon, peace would bring his men back to him. He thanked me and reclaimed his place at the head of our group. We proceeded down a set of stairs and out into the central courtyard, crossed the courtyard, and stopped at a heavy reinforced door which the heavyset man pounded on several times. The reinforced door swung open with none of the difficulty I had noticed elsewhere. Apparently, it had been well maintained over the years. The fortress was a sturdy prison.

The heavyset man spoke with the guard in the language of the place. He explained that he was escorting the strangers to see the vampires. The burly guard rolled his eyes and handed a large ring of rusty skeleton keys out through the bars in the door. I could tell that the guard knew the heavyset man was grandstanding, but he didn't really seem to care. If anything, he appeared too bored to be bothered by it.

The heavyset man led us through several locked, thick, iron-barred doors and then up a level to the tower. The floor of the tower consisted of a series of eight cells, four stationed on each side of a central hallway. A stocky fellow, also seemingly unimpressed with the parade, stood at the far end of the hall. The two guards we had brought with us were obviously excited by the visit. It led me to believe that they were either new or not allowed into such areas. Anyway, they were distracted.

The parade came to a stop at the second set of cell doors. The little opening in the heavy iron door showed the cells to have stone floors and side walls with iron bars making up half of the outside walls and roof. The orientation was such that only a small space was out of direct light during the daylight hours. So the stories I had heard were actually true.

I approached the bars in front of me and peered inside at the wasted figure of a man, cowering on the stone floor in the true stone corner of the cell. He looked like he was a Persian. He also presented the image of a famine victim. The radar sounded soft in my mind. He was a vampire. The sensation was real, so he really was a vampire, but it was very weak. He obviously was not in the best of shape, nor had he been for some time. It was almost as if he was not there at all.

The heavyset man said not to get too close to the bars as the inhabitants didn't see food often. I turned to face the heavyset man so I could comment on the conditions and saw what I had come for. In the cell directly behind the heavyset man was the emaciated, hollow frame of my sire. He too cowered in the only small, dark space available. The sight of Antonio was the emotional trigger I had been waiting for.

It took a split second for the emotion to pass so I could calm my mind. Then, as calmly as if I were shaking hands, I shoved my palm out and into the chest of the heavyset man. I struck him with all the force in my being. The man's girth was absolutely no match for my superior strength.

As my sire had taught me, overwhelming force was a good option in combat. I liked the use of force in such situations. Great force was never expected from a person of my stature.

There was a large cracking sound as my palm made contact with the man's chest, shattering numerous bones. Before he could even acknowledge the pain, he was propelled backward, where he impacted with the iron door behind him. After the impact with the door, the heavyset man crumpled to the floor, not to move again.

I spun around to face the two guards who had come along with us and noticed that the priest was already lying on the floor. At least he was smart enough to stay out of the way.

As I had thought would be the case, the guards were too shocked to respond with any speed. The man nearer to me was attempting to draw a knife from his belt. The other was just standing his ground, shocked and confused. I struck the man with the knife in the throat with my closed fist several times, and then I pulled my weight back to my rear foot and kicked him in the stomach. The concussion of my foot and his stomach threw the man backward into his bewildered counterpart, who had been behind him. The two men crumpled to the hard stone floor in a twisted mass. I stole a look to my rear and noticed that the guard at the end of the hall had not bothered to move. In check, I moved in on the two men sprawled on the floor.

Springing across the small space of the hall, I landed squarely on top of the two men. Not giving them time to absorb the shock of the landing, I lowered a fist into the throat of the top man. The impact was followed by the crushing sound of bone and of the tearing of muscle. The dregs of the guard's life left him shortly.

I lifted my head and opened my mouth to loose my enamel daggers. Upon seeing the weapons come out into the light of day, the sloth-like man on the bottom of the pile began to wail. It was a short-lived performance. I snapped my head down and sank my fangs into the big adrenaline-filled artery on the side of his neck. The blood ran out fast as his heart raced toward a long, black sleep. Soon enough, the fat man succumbed.

Only seconds had passed since the affair had started, and three were down. All of them were dead, but they were still good food. I sprang to my feet and turned my attention to the man at the end of the hall. Against expectations, he still hadn't moved from his post. That struck me as odd. He didn't seem the type to scare easily, but still ….

As I stood staring down at the man, my mind began to clear from its adrenaline-induced haze. As my mind calmed, I could hear my little friend telling me not to worry about the man down the hall. I retrieved the chain and hoisted the amulet out of my dress. The surface of the jewel pulsed ever so gently with a sun-yellow glow. Apparently, my little friend wanted to help with the combat.

I quietly asked if she had immobilized the man. The response was of them, not one. The others scattered about the fortress would not be a problem. I asked if she could really do such things. The response in my brain was "armies, not men." I indeed had found a powerful friend.

The amulet wanted to help, because Antonio had been the one to send her to me so many years before. He had found the amulet a new friend. The jewel was giving some thanks, in its own way.

The books were true. The amulet had the ability to think and act for itself. The human life force captured inside the jewel was alive and well enough. That pleased me.

I took a second to straighten my numerous layers of clothing. I removed my heavy fur-lined cloak and laid it on the floor. With the large covering removed, it was much more evident that I was somewhat diminutive in size. At the end of the hall, the guard's eyes went wide as he saw my frame, or maybe it was the cut of my corset.

I reached down and tore a piece of cloth from the heavyset man's clothing and removed the large ring of keys he had been clutching. I threw the keys to the priest, who was just rising from the floor. I grabbed up the keys and went about removing the blood from my face. I hated having blood all over me.

"Sorry I couldn't spare you from part of that, Father."

"I think that some time with God later on will make it not quite so awful."

"Go find an empty cell, and lock yourself inside. Then throw the keys out into the hallway."

"Why?"

"Vampires in this condition have little sense and cannot be reasoned with. It will take them a bit to calm themselves. I want you as safe as I can get you while that is happening."

"That makes good sense."

"David, you are also going to want to look away."

The priest just nodded and moved off down the hall. There was a quick clanging of doors, and the round rusty gathering of keys came flying back out into the hallway.

I retrieved the keys and checked the security of the door he had chosen. Satisfied by the safety of the space, I made my way back to the center of the hall and the door of the space where my Antonio had been stuffed away. He had watched the whole scene that had played out in front of him with a sense of awe. He watched but did not move. He really seemed unable to touch the sun. Old ways, so be it.

I unlocked to door to his little frozen hell and smiled, then reached down and grabbed a goodly chunk of the heavyset man's coat. With a quick jerk, he flew off the ground and landed at Antonio's feet. The body had no more than stopped on the stone floor than Antonio's large enamel fangs sank into his flesh. What came next was primal. Antonio drained him of his blood. When he was finished, he shoved his hand into the man's ribcage and split the man's chest into pieces. Then, the old vampire shoved his head into the opening in the man's chest and drank the blood that had pooled around the man's wounds. Once he was finished sucking up all the blood to be had in the man's corpse, Antonio secured one arm and ripped it from the heavyset man's lifeless body. Holding the exposed end toward his face, Antonio literally squeezed all the blood from it. Satisfied that it was empty, he cast it aside and continued on with the remaining limbs until the whole of the corpse was both empty and dismembered. The sight of it made me ill. Even the animals of the woodland didn't treat their prey in such ways. What kind of misery must one be exposed to for such an outcome to be deemed acceptable? It was wrong, and yet it didn't seem to balance the scale.

Seeing the gleam return to the whites of his eyes, I nodded my approval and removed myself from his cell. I walked to the pile of guards farther down the hall and retrieved them. I dragged them down the hallway and threw them into the cells of the other two vampires who were being held with Antonio. The guard's bodies met a similar fate to that of the heavyset man. It was all perfectly ghastly. The woman that was claimed to be possessed of demons started to ramble on about something I assumed to be freedom, but I put her from my mind and continued.

Content that all was under control, I made my way down the hall to the place where the remaining guard stood frozen in place. He seemed quite overcome by the sights he had just witnessed. That was good, I thought to myself.

"You have a safe room here for the securing of books and things, yes?"

The man stared back at me. He seemed past talking at the moment. The impression left by a petite feminine fist made him focus once more.

"You have a room for securing books in the fortress, yes?"

"Two floors down, at the far end of the hall."

"The cellar?"

"Yes."

"Good."

I turned and padded back to where my dark prince still cowered in the dim light. He seemed more himself upon my return.

"You look functional."

"How did you find me? And why would you come here to save me?"

"Because I love you, and I refuse to live without you, if possible. I do love you, if for nothing else than you made me what I am today. You will find if you let go of old ways that our nature will allow for such things. Now, say thank you."

"Thank you."

"You're welcome."

"What about the rest of the guards?"

"They are being taken care of until nightfall, when they can be put to better use."

I looked down at the amulet, which hung contentedly outside of my clothing. The jewel pulsed with a happy yellow light. She had my flank protected.

I stopped to look about. The sun still seemed to be high enough above the horizon. There was time to kill. I talked to Father David for a while to make sure that he was secure in his surroundings. He had been spared actually viewing the carnage that had taken place around him; however, hearing it seemed to have been more than enough for his sensibilities. A large pool of vomit in the corner of the cell told me I was correct. The smell of it said that it was fresh. I did feel bad for him. He had encountered much more on this side trip than he had signed on for. It was entirely my fault, of course. I was sure that I had no way to fix the damage done to our friendship. Fix or not, there was nothing to do about it at the time; that would have to wait for later days in distant lands.

I headed back to the cells and found that all the vampires had been blooded long enough to have calmed from the lusting. I quietly explained to them that the guards deserved the death that they had received. The remaining guards could follow them, or be turned, whatever they found acceptable. They could do what they wanted to, but I would not accept any harm coming to the priest. If I found one scratch on his body, what happened to the guards would be considered a pleasant end compared with what I would do to them. I stared them down until each one shook his head with understanding. That was good. I hated killing my own kind. Besides they hated the guards far worse than the priest at that point.

"Antonio, how long until sunset comes to these lands?"

"About one hour and fifty minutes."

"Good. I'll be back. While it's quiet, I need to find the book repository."

I trod off in the direction of the stairs. It had been so long since I had been purely a creature of the dark that I had lost the ability to gauge the sun. It was even harder than normal in that place. I had hardly needed to wear my dark glasses since we had arrived. The sun was not nearly as bright in that region of the world as it was in my isles to the northwest. The removal of my spectacles had somewhat returned my sense of day and night, but my sense was not as focused as that which my associates possessed. The fact that they could not get past their superstitions made me both happy and sad.

The ring of skeleton keys that I had liberated from the heavyset man allowed me free range of the installation. As I had expected, once I reached the cellar, it turned out to have a floor cut straight from the rock. Its temperature seemed moderate compared to the windswept cells in the floors above. All in all, it was a good place to keep books.

I trod down the hallway to where a guard was standing next to the heavy wooden door. Like the other guard had been, the slovenly guard was frozen in place, immobile with fear. He watched my approach out of the corner of his eye. He probably assumed that his time was up. It wasn't, but then again, it wasn't far off.

I stepped past the man and squared up to the large wooden door. As the lock was released and the door swung free of its casing, the amulet began to glow brightly with excitement. I could tell that the jewel recognized the presence of something in the room. The radiance of the jewel was such that no light was required for me to look about.

The bright yellow glow in the room showed the presence of numerous wooden crates stacked in piles of two and three. Against the far wall stood a set of shelves that reached from the floor to the ceiling. They were full. Conservatively, there had to be a thousand volumes in the room. The volumes ranged in size from pocket-size codices to massive, monastic volumes.

As I stood in the middle of the room, the brightly glowing jewel slowly lifted from the front of my gown and hovered in midair. The chain stretched out until it was taut, and the tip of the jewel pointed toward a crate off to one side of the room. I was aghast. I had no idea that the amulet could do such things. Whatever was in the crate, the jewel wanted it—right then.

I moved to the crate and quickly shuffled through the wood shavings until several books appeared. The books had funny symbols and odd languages. They were probably part of a collection of different things all stuffed together in the crate. Another probing produced an object that we both recognized—a manuscript covered in leather binding with a leather thong closure. It was one of the lost books of the amulet. The cardinal had said it was elsewhere. Maybe fortune had smiled upon us both.

I placed the codex in the pocket of my coat and left the room. I knew I needed to return to the cells before nightfall. The absence of the sun had made the space parky. The three wayward vampires I had left behind were out of their cells. They had gone down the hall and were circling the statuesque prison guard. It didn't take long to figure out that they had not killed him. Apparently, they had decided to turn him into one of us instead. Call it a little present for the people of the region who had shown them such hospitality.

My vampire charges noticed my return and stopped their communion with the stoic body in front of them. They all realized that I had been the one to save them from the clutches of humanity. They were all grateful, and I was happy to help. All I really wanted out of the deal was Antonio. The remainder of them had been picked up on the path of least resistance.

I explained to my brood that there were two more stationary guards to make sport of. But sport or not, they should be out of that place long before the sun rose again. There was no way to anticipate what the next day would bring. They all appeared to agree. The whole affair seemed sorted.

The two unknown vampires inquired as to who I might be. I introduced myself and they departed. Antonio stared at me in disbelief at my audacity.

"Pull it together, love. We have work to do," I said with a smile on my face.

I turned from Antonio and walked down the hallway to the cell where my priest was. I opened the door with the large ring of skeleton keys and motioned for him to come out. He didn't seem excited to exit the cell. He knew he was the only human left in the fortress who was moving of his own volition. He probably figured that he was somehow next in line. That was not to be.

I sent Antonio out of the cell block to find us a cart and a horse to pull it. Once he departed, the priest and I returned to the cellar and started to retrieve the crates of books. The retrieval and loading of the crates took most of the night. The repository that we emptied out onto the large flat cart Antonio had found was larger than I had originally assumed. It didn't matter; I wasn't leaving any of it behind.

The stoic guard turned vampire was just coming round as the three of us departed the entrance of the empty fortress. The screams of the three remaining guard left for a meal could be heard a long way down the roadway as we made our way out of that godforsaken valley in the Caucasus Mountains.

Our trip back to the coast was slowed by Antonio's need for dark spaces. The horse and cart were also a slow-moving affair. We kept our path wide of towns that we had stayed in as we made our way toward the coast. We met no resistance to speak of along our way. The few people we did encounter Antonio used as food. They were dispatched in a gentler fashion than the guards had been. That bit of benevolence made the priest happy. He prayed for their souls after Antonio finished off their lives. The whole two-tiered system of killing seemed like bollocks to me.

Upon reaching the coast of the Black Sea, we proceeded to the designated high ground and lit the signal fire as requested. Much to my relief, a skiff soon appeared on the water in front of us. *The Summer Storm* had actually stayed all that time. The men of the ship were men of their word.

It took several trips with the skiff to move all the contents of the cart over to *The Summer Storm*. Then with a last shove, we were headed out to sea as well. The sails were set full and the land quickly receded from view.

I stood and stared back at the shore and thought about how one little trip could produce grand world travels. One really never knew what would happen when one stepped out the door. I had traveled to the heart of Christendom and then to the heart of the old world—places that held hatred for our kind—and not only managed to avoid a genuine hiding but came out of it with both my love and a vast new collection of manuscripts for my library. Oh, and the priest in one piece.

For now, I would travel back and settle into my Cretan home for a while and let things calm down. Then, once all was good again, I would head back to London. As long as I made it home in time for the gala, it would be fine.

# chapter 20

I found it an easy transition from my rugged, adventurous lifestyle back to my more natural and much more comfortable existence. The winter stop spent in the luxury of Crete helped considerably. I spent my time wandering the countryside or doing business at my corporate office in Heraklion. It was very much a chapter out of times past for me.

The business I found most enjoyable. William seldom let me do business anymore in those days. He was somewhat controlling. He had probably picked it up from Uncle James's part of the family. It was sad, at times, because I really enjoyed business. I was quite good and efficient at running my corporation, the little company that my father had founded so many years before. A few weeks in the business offices, and it was all old hat.

My traveling companion Antonio was having a somewhat more difficult transition. Normalcy was a farther leap for him to achieve. He had been in touch with the deep darkness inside himself, and that darkness did not let go easily. Antonio spent his winter months out on the western coast sequestered in the mansion's dark, hidden training chamber. The quiet darkness of the chamber was a good place for him to contemplate his issues without causing too many problems to the human population.

My other traveling companion, Father David, had been dispatched back to London on one of the last outgoing tides. The priest's famously happy personality, which had been all but beaten into submission, had almost returned to him upon leaving. My goodly friend had witnessed pieces of life that he had not been prepared to witness, and that, I think, bothered him more than anything. I felt bad for what I had put him through, but in the end, it was too late to change any of it. I put him on the ship to, more than anything else, remove him from any more of Antonio's rash vampirism.

We were only months removed from our priest when the warm trade winds found their way back to us and to my island retreat. The warmth of the wind moved me and my moody lover to make our way onward. That time, *The Summer Storm* headed for its most recent Italian port so I might return to Rome. I needed to make a stop on our way north to the British Isles. Our entrance into the old port of Rome was much the same as the first time we had arrived. My quiet visit to the Vatican was also a similarly unnoticed affair, which made me pleased.

I kept Antonio sequestered in his cabin while we were at sea, so as not to frighten the crew into abandoning us. Then I kept him in the villa while I was doing my business in the Holy See. Antonio was not ready to interact with anyone. He lacked many facets of his original personality. I didn't want him to throw a wobbler and head off on some sort of killing spree. That certainly wouldn't help things.

My time spent at the Holy See in the auspicious company of my new friend the cardinal was productive. He seemed genuinely pleased that I had managed to return. I regaled him with tales of high adventure on the shores of the Black Sea. We talked at length about the concepts of good and evil and how the two manifested themselves in the world. Then, when our conversations were complete, I presented him with the amulet codex that we had found in the fortress. I felt that it really should be with its own companions.

The cardinal seemed greatly pleased by my gift. I mentioned that if I somehow came across the other two, I would return them as well. They appeared to be safe and well cared for in the Vatican's fine hands. There they would not be lost to time. The cardinal gifted me in return with the knowledge that I might always be welcome in the archives of the Vatican. He said he would make such arrangements to continue even after he had passed on. I told him I would happily send on any further books or manuscripts, once I had taken time to go through the entire fortress collection. Then I made mention that he was always welcome in my personal library, though it was not as grand as his. He laughed in appreciation.

I left the nice cardinal and collected Antonio. It was time to be off once again. We continued onward as *The Summer Storm* traveled west. The movement of the ship's hull through the waters of the Mediterranean was smooth and comforting. I spent a great amount of time out on the weather deck, watching the changes to our surroundings.

Antonio had regained enough of his composure by the time we left Italy that he would come out at night to wander the decks of the ship. His presence shook the crew of the ship greatly. Once he started walking the decks, every member of the crew armed themselves with large oak stakes, which they had fashioned out of an empty whiskey barrel. No one could really blame them. It was a lot to ask of anyone to be caged up with a wild beast. Fortunately for us all, he had fed so much while in port that nothing terrible happened while we were at sea. I think it would have only taken a spark for things to get completely out of hand.

It seemed that the captain and I were the only two who could handle the situation. He probably figured that Antonio couldn't sail a full-sized ship, so he, at least, was safe. I knew that if things got totally out of hand, I could kill Antonio. If it came to that, there was no way to calculate the emotional toll it might take on me. Fortunately, it never came to that.

Several stressful days on from Rome, *The Summer Storm* made landfall in the south of Spain for a short stop. After anchorage had been established and the matters of ship's business had been addressed, Antonio set out to wander the hills of his home country. I hoped it would help, because it always does one good to be in familiar surroundings. Hopefully, the hills of Andalusia would do that for him.

Getting Antonio to leave *The Summer Storm* also did the crew a world of good. From the time that they took to unwind when he left, I could tell that special compensations were going to be in order upon our return to London. The crew had definitely earned them.

As I watched the crew unwind from Antonio's release back into humanity, I decided to cut *The Summer Storm* loose from the remainder of our travels. She could make her way home, unburdened by our presence. I gave the captain a personal letter of thanks and instructions that the crew be compensated four times their normal voyage pay. I specified that the request was not to be argued with.

I asked the captain if he might relay to one of the channel captains that the two of us would need a ride across the channel from Calais at some point. He said he would see to it personally. He was a nice man—a bit of a nutter, but a nice man.

Once we were alone, Antonio and I slowly made our way home the old-fashioned way—one foot at a time. Fashionably enough, Antonio turned out to be an accomplished tour guide.

We made our way over the land of the Moors. Antonio showed me the many castles and fortresses with all of their splendid decorations. He highlighted the differences in culture as we went from south to north and then from west to east.

The tour of his homeland was amazing. The Spanish countryside was a rolling, hilly mass of browns and reds and greens. The land had a picturesque beauty that could not be completely put down in words. The old buildings of stones with their tiled roofs and small towers that were used to signal the workers in the fields were all breathtaking in their simple beauty.

We made our crossing into France through land that had once been the powerful kingdom of Aragon. This land was full of contrasts. The mountains of the region were foreboding and held a grip on the landscape that had obviously not been lost on any of the people who inhabited the area. It was easy to see why the Cathars and others like them chose that area in which to build their strongholds so many centuries before. It was defensible and beautiful at the same time. It was a good choice of homes.

We continued north and through the lands of Bordeaux and then farther on to the French capital city of Paris. Then, we continued north into Normandy and on to the port town of Calais. The area around Calais was much more like something I was accustomed to. Normandy and the northern edge of France were known to me. I had never actually been there, but the business areas were all well studied and the basic language of the area was more understandable.

I had tried to embrace the new languages as we had made our ways along. Once in Normandy, it was no longer necessary. English was well understood by the people of the channel and spoken in the better part of Normandy. That simplified things greatly.

As was usually the case in such environments, the port of Calais was almost a mirror image of the port of Dover. The only real difference was the inconvenience of it being run by Frenchmen and not Englishmen. Antonio and I found our way to where the Grey Cargo vessels usually docked to off-load their wares. As we approached, the high flags of *The Summer Storm* could be seen over the tops of the inner vessels. We found that she had dropped cargo in London, reloaded, and promptly headed across the channel to retrieve us. I decided that I would need to promote the captain upon my return home.

We made our entrance onto the deck, and it was anchors up. The tall ship spun easily back out of port to the deep waters of the English Channel. A short time along and we were making our customary wave to the White Cliffs of Dover. Then a quick jog past the cliffs and straight on in to the protected docks of the Thames.

Now, in all honesty, it was not as easy a journey as I just made it out to be. Starting in 1803, Britain had declared war with France. It was actually the start of what would be known as the Napoleonic Wars. All things considered, it was your standard war. Europe had always been at war or preparing for it. Because of that, Europeans seemed to view war much less personally. European countries would go to war, but the daily living of its inhabitants would just kind of go on around it.

The business of Grey Cargo and its shipping was one such thing. That was normal, unlike when we had been restricted from the Americas. That restriction had been a pride issue on behalf of the empire. It had no such problems with Napoleon and his empire. We just pulled our guns from the decks and our ships continued to do their business unimpeded. Now, that being said, we didn't waste any time getting out of port.

It should be noted that the good thing about having a large fleet of ships is that you have good knowledge of what's going on in the world. When we left the port of Calais, we headed east to London instead of west to Bristol as I had originally wanted. The deviation was due to Nelson. That would be Lord Nelson.

I wanted to go to Bristol, but if we had sailed west instead of east, we would have sailed into the middle of the Battle of Trafalgar, and Lord Nelson. I was pleased to miss the naval skirmish, as my adventures to that date had been both long and grand enough for my liking.

All right, skirmish was probably an understatement. Lord Nelson destroyed the opposing naval fleets in the battle. Sadly, Lord Nelson was killed during the fighting. He was later returned to land on his flagship *The HMS Victory*. She was as grand a ship as was ever produced during the era of the tall ships—a true fighting vessel.

The captain gave me news that Lord Nelson had requested several heavy ships from my corporation to do military service in an upcoming battle with France and Spain. He had already received his ships; this was not an unknown request from the Crown. We just pulled all our markings and sent them out with Union Jacks. We would be compensated if they did not return. That was great, because it meant that the Crown would buy us new guns to replace our old ones. A free upgrade from the royals was always appreciated.

Our trip back across the channel to the safety of the Thames was quick enough for my liking. Shortly after leaving port, it was dusk, and I was standing on the docks looking at the Grey Cargo sign. The loadmasters, office paperwork personnel, and William were all on hand to see our arrival. As I had expected, so was a man in a black coat, standing in the shadows two berths down the docks.

By the time of our arrival back in London, I had killed a couple dozen of those Brenfield Society buggers. I had needed to have the captain procure a larger box for my cane collection. I was sure that they assumed that their need for recruitment was somehow my doing.

About the same time as I noticed the man in the shadows, my amulet began to twitch. We were in tune with each other at that point.

"Don't worry, sunshine. We'll deal with them shortly," I reassured my friend in hushed tones as I gently patted the spot where she lay under my gown. Antonio turned his head as I spoke, assuming that I spoke to him.

"Why do you call me sunshine?"

I laughed. I had forgotten that he could hear. It had been some time since I had spoken to the amulet in the presence of someone else who could hear the low tones.

"Sorry, love, I actually wasn't speaking to you."

"Who were you conversing with?"

"I was talking to the amulet that hangs around my neck. It can hear the low tones of the vampire quite well. I could just think it, but I do actually like to speak with her, and I think she enjoys it as well. Her life force appreciates communication and interaction."

He turned and looked at me. As usual in those days, he looked perplexed.

"All right, then, so who are the two of you going to deal with?"

"Those evil buggers from the Brenfield Society. We've been killing them off as we found them." His perplexed expression didn't fade as I spoke. "Sorry, you still know them as the House of Shadows. You have been out of circulation for a while, love. Do you see the man two berths down the docks? The one tucked into the shadows wearing the long black overcoat and grasping the black cane?"

"Yes, I do."

"The Brenfield Society."

"And they need to be killed off?"

"Absolutely. Even the Vatican said I could kill them if I chose."

"May I help?"

"Certainly, but let's wait until we get you up to speed on the times you're now in, all right?"

"Fine."

I could tell that he wanted to be down the docks and killing right then. He was still 85 percent predator. I didn't want him changing the plan. No killing on my own ground; Amber had been right about that.

I took Antonio's hand, and we made our way down across the docks and toward the offices. A full moon hung huge in the cloudless sky. Nights like this one were made for killing. No killing that night, though. It seemed a waste to Antonio. I did appreciate his zeal. In times of stress and uncertainty, vampires tend to revert back to their base instincts of survival and killing. The instincts served to eliminate competition and prolong life. They were all good things, but not that night.

When we reached the platform in front of the offices, William was waiting for the two of us with semiconcealed contempt on his face. Apparently, he was not pleased that I had returned with my dark prince.

"Good evening, William. I see that you have returned from your journey none the worse for wear."

"None the worse for wear? Why the hell would you send me out on some journey like the one I undertook for what is obviously now no good reason?"

"Sorry, lad. I had every intention of going on one journey and then another. However, I ran across the information I sent you seeking while in Rome. Since I was halfway there, there was no reason not to continue on with the second. It seemed an expedient use of resources."

"Seemed an expedient use of resources? Are you daft, woman?"

"William, let us continue this conversation once we have had time to shake off the dust of our journey. And by the way, since you have lived long enough to produce a son, if you *ever* call me daft again, you will die where you stand. Do I make myself perfectly clear?"

"Yes, ma'am."

"Good lad. Let's pop off, then."

The looks flashing around the docks were all ones of disbelief. The humans couldn't believe that William would talk to a wealthy noblewoman in such a manner. Antonio couldn't believe William was still alive.

I understood his rashness. He had been sent out on what he saw as a dangerous, unhappy, wild goose chase. Those things were known to happen. I've been taken to rash judgments throughout the centuries. There was no reason to overreact about it.

Our carriage ride out of London to the Grey Estate was a long and quiet affair. No one spoke more than several sentences during the ride. We reached the estate about an hour before sunrise. Antonio retreated to the dark spaces as soon as the carriage came to a stop.

Over the next several days, I eased William's tension. I brought Antonio up to speed on the state of the world. Antonio's part would have gone much more quickly if he didn't continuously need to hide from the light. I seriously considered forcefully breaking his aversion to the sun. But, at the end of the day, Christopher was right. The human race was better off for not having vampires around during the day, and it also gave me great camouflage. Stupid superstitions were indeed a necessary evil at times.

The need for Antonio to retire to my chamber at the breaking of dawn did have one good side effect. The seclusion from the world at large allowed the two of us to renew ourselves to each other. My pent-up sexual desire found a ready outlet in the strong arms of my sequestered dark prince. In return, he used me as a release from his angst.

That was the way it went for a while—days of sex and nights of blood. As much as I liked the hunt, I liked the sex more. I could also do the hunt by myself; doing the other alone lacked the same level of satisfaction. It had been far too long since I had been able to unleash my sexual appetites. Antonio, for his part, seemed an agreeable subject for me to pour my desire out upon. It took many days for me to fully pour out my desire. Yes, many days indeed.

By the end, I realized that I should probably get another human consort. But, while Antonio was sequestered in my bedchamber, that thought could wait for another day.

# chapter 21

Time passed, and soon I was staring down the summer of 1807. It was a fine summer as English summers go. It was sunny at times, and dull the remainder. All in all, it was the same as many others I had endured, with the exception of the Brenfield Society.

The Brenfield Society had been discreetly moving around my fringe ever since I had returned to London. They had been kind of working in fits and starts. It seemed that they had decided that they wanted to retaliate in some fashion, they just couldn't figure out what their retaliation was going to be. The biggest problem they faced was that they lacked clout. If they tried anything too obvious, they would get dragged out. No one in the society had a title equal to or greater than mine. None of the knights could afford to screw about with an earl.

They also lacked powerful friends. You can attack people of a higher status at someone else's request, but you need to get what you are after, or they will get you. Some of the members had friends who were also earls or dukes, and the dukes definitely did not like having a woman in their little power club. The problem was that I was good friends with the Queen. None of them had the stones to go up against the Queen.

In reality, I didn't pay them much heed. My immediate focus at that point in time was elsewhere. I was keeping a solid eye on Amber and her preparations for the second vampire gala to be held at Brimme House. It had been many years since I had ushered in the first gala there in Bristol. It was a fine choice for such affairs. It was grand and strongly secured. It was the place that had given me my title and made me a lady. It was also the place where I had learned to be a vampire. The Wyndell boys and I had built up a small empire of business in the lands around the house over the centuries. I watched Amber closely during those times, because I had no desire to see my Bristol home razed by some unintentional slipup with a party. The Brenfield Society was not to be trusted.

Sadly, it had been many years since the last gala, and the humans who had made it possible were all but gone. Scratch that; they were all gone. That presented a problem for young Amber. She had taken up the challenge of being the go-to person without really knowing what she was getting into. Fortunately, her grandfather Christopher had been masterful in putting some long-term infrastructure in place to help her. That helped to alleviate the pressure.

Her great-uncle James had also helped to develop the communication system and the system of codes that got the word out. That part of things still worked very well. It seemed to find all of the creatures that did not want to be found. As time passed, it seemed to work even better than planned. The original gala had hosted a gathering of twelve guests. This second was going to host some twenty-two guests.

The thought of that many vampires in one place made me cautious. Twenty-two vampires in such a small area was an unbelievably grand and dangerous thing. It was also quite unpredictable. It was somewhat uncharted territory. I had never read any documented case of a gathering of our kind in numbers greater than eighteen. It seemed that I was ready to best that number by five. Yes, that many vampires were going to cause problems.

Amber had independently come to the same conclusion. Her problem was not space; Brimme House could comfortably accommodate some thirty or more people. The problem with that many vampires was food or, more to the point, drink.

All vampires are opportunistic feeders. They will feed on a variety of food stocks as different objects of opportunity present themselves. That helps to maintain the blood supply. Now, considering that, they all (including me) take in a certain amount of human blood. Human blood really is the best of the choices available. It is the most potent and the most compatible. That is not odd to me, because all the vampires I know were initially human beings.

Even I had returned to drinking human blood since my trip abroad. The complete soaking my system had received from killing all of the

Brenfield men had reawakened my lust. I knew that was a problem. It wasn't the killing that bothered me. I found that killing pompous men who thought themselves better than I was a good sport. I really, really liked the killing. The problem came afterward. Once you have a gut full of adrenaline, the clarity of your vision fades. That was when you began to make mistakes that could lead to getting you killed again. As every vampire knows, there's no coming back from the second death.

For a great many years, I had resolved that problem with the help of the amulet. She gave me all the energy that I could possibly use. She literally made it unnecessary for me to feed for months at a time. At one point, I was only feeding three or four times a year, and those feedings were from the more conventional stocks. Cows have a lot of blood in them and it is perfectly good blood. I would drink my fill, and the amulet would reproduce the feeling for a fairly long time.

The holdings of Brimme House included slaughterhouses that produced gallons and gallons of blood daily. It was a gift from Christopher. Antonio's gift of the amulet had produced the rest. The thing that the amulet could not produce was the overwhelming sensation that adrenaline-laced human blood gave me.

Now, the amulet did have a trick up her proverbial sleeve. One of the neat things that she did was she gave me clarity of vision during the adrenaline high. That sensation was surreal at best. It was a kind of super caffeine rush but a thousand times stronger. I was sure that the amulet only did such things as a matter of self-preservation.

Most vampires cycle through periods of human blood for just that reason. They stay with human blood for a time and then go back to animal blood. The doping effect of loaded animal blood is not nearly as powerful as human blood is. Unless you actually hunted the animal down, animal blood is seldom laced with high doses of adrenaline. Taking the cycling into account, it is also a natural rule of sorts that, when it comes to parties, vampires are quite like humans. They all want the good stuff when someone else is buying.

That, in a nutshell, was the problem Amber was facing. She had apparently always viewed her family's history through some kind of rose-colored glasses. The reality of some of their deeds was far more bloodred. The things that some of her forebears had done to acquire a fortune was making her question a great many things.

Amber handled all her tasks with the stoic professionalism of the Wyndell name; she just did not want to be doing it. Sometimes, standing in the naked light of reality is an uncomfortable thing. She had found herself right in that spot and was apparently not enjoying the experience.

I deserved the blame for her melancholy. I had put her there intentionally. I had done so by giving her the journal that Christopher had penned about his actions. I had also lied to her when I had told her that I had not read it. I knew full well what Christopher had done to meet my desired ends. Amber had needed to lose her naive view of things. The world that she had requested access to was not for the weak or the uncommitted. All of the Wyndell men, with the small exception of Charlie, had been 100 percent committed to the task. Amber needed to realize that fortune didn't just come to people. To actually become rich and powerful, one needed to go out and take that power away from someone else. That is the real way of all things, whether business or survival.

I could tell that Amber's rosy view of my world had dimmed since I had returned from abroad. Aye, things were truly never what they seemed to be. She had come to realize just how ruthless her family really was. That was why I usually kept only the men. Men's sensibilities about those things were far more pliable. Men had been in the business of taking power for millennia.

To her good credit, Amber solved all of the logistical problems presented to her in a professional manner. As I mentioned earlier, she really was a good businesswoman. The Wyndell family would not have put her in charge of its affairs if that were not the case.

One of the tasks that Amber did not get to handle was the recruitment of staff. I was sure that she did not have the brass for that. The quest for a handful of utterly trustworthy stewards fell at the feet of Brandy Neville.

Brandy Neville was the current custodian of Brimme House. She was its overseer and its keeper of secrets. She was the current one in a long line of women to hold the position. That line went back to the time when Brimme House had been reopened to serve as my house when I was but a newly made vampire.

My first confidant, Charles Wyndell, had hired trustworthy people to fill all the required roles. In those days, everyone who had worked at the house had known that I was a vampire. They had stayed because they were treated well and protected from many other troubles that the world at large possessed. The mid-1600s could be a treacherous time.

One of the first women to be brought on board back then had been a pretty young girl named Amanda. She had been pretty and naive and possessed a good work ethic. She had also been steadfast and true to the end. Those were interestingly conflicting qualities.

When I was called back to London, I set up a pension to have the children of Brimme House educated. That hedge bet had produced Grace. Grace was Amanda's second granddaughter. Grace had become the first headmistress of Brimme House. That young lady had produced a line of women who had continued on in the same role all the way down to middle-aged Brandy Neville.

At the time of the gala in 1807, Brandy was the sole resident of Brimme House who knew that I was not human. Interestingly, she actually reveled in the fact that her bloodline followed my own, the way the Wyndells' did. Her knowledge of me made her the perfect candidate to choose trustworthy people to handle the intricacies of such an event. I was sure that the current staff would be shuffled off to the seashore on a vacation from their toils or some other such thing to pacify them. They would like it well enough, and it would empty the estate so the demons could stop by and play.

I liked Brandy. She was a solid and down-to-earth person. She had no misconceptions about her station in life. She took advantage of all the good that came her way. She educated her children so they could continue on in her absence, and she did me a fine service.

In the case of the party, Brandy hired three butlers and two kitchen staff members. There were two coach tenders and two stewards to handle general issues. She took great care in her selection of those nine people whom she would throw out as bait.

A side note, the people of the 1800s were not that much different from those of the 1600s. If you promised them safety, then they would do whatever you requested. They were also good at balancing the secrecy of their tasks with the danger involved. The nine individuals Brandy chose were definitely up to the task. They were a good group of people who would go on to keep positions in Brimme House or at one of the other properties.

All went along, and soon enough, the planning was complete. Shortly after that the waiting was also over. The sun rose high and bright on June 21, 1807, and I was there to greet it. I rose to meet the sun the same way I had ever since I could remember. It was the day of the gala, but it was also the date of my birth. It was a bright and shiny day such as the one back in 1633 that had seen little Sara Anne Grey into the world. It was a good day.

I stood in the back meadow and greeted my old friend the sun. We had seen many days together. They were too many to count for me, but I was sure that they didn't even compare to the time the sun had seen. I stood and saluted my old friend. The amulet lay outside of my gown in full view of the shiny, yellow orb. I wanted the amulet to be happy as well. We were good friends, the three of us.

I stood and wondered how many friends the sun had made. It surely must be a small number. There was maybe a handful at best. Any more than that and the magick of the folklore would have been broken. That news would surely have spread faster than the plague had.

I spent the morning hours in the embrace of the summer sun. I love the sun. It really had nothing to do with the energy that it gave me via the amulet, though that was nice. It was that I was a child of the sun. Even as a human girl, I had reveled in spring and summer. My father had said that he could tell when spring came by the way my mood changed to happy and when winter came by my melancholy state. I loved the sun, and it loved me. Today, I am still a child of the radiant yellow orb.

My embrace was broken about midday. It was time to turn my eye to the business of the day, birthday sun or no. I slowly made my way out of the meadow and back toward the house to oversee preparations for the evening's festivities. As I wandered the wide halls of the house, the staff all smiled and made reassuring comments. They all congratulated me on my birthday returning once more. That bit was just pleasant and well, nice. They were good, substantial choices.

In my study, I came across Antonio pacing around out of the direct sunlight. He had accompanied me to Bristol when I had left London two days before and had been on an alternate schedule. The lack of a second body in the bedchamber that day must have roused him earlier than he had planned.

Antonio was very much set in the old ways. He assumed that the amulet gave me power to walk around in the light. I let him think whatever he wanted to think on that front. I could tell that the thought of it all made him tense.

"Good day, love. You seem pensive."

"I stirred earlier than planned is all." His voice still held the cold edge it had acquired in the far-off lands.

"You sound agitated. That certainly cannot be good. This is supposed to be a happy affair. You remember happy?"

"It will be happy. I just need to straighten my mood first."

"NO KILLING. Do you understand me?"

"Yes, Lady Boca. No killing."

"Good lad."

"While we seem to be on the edge of this topic, why are you using my name?"

"It seemed time to reinvent myself. I was becoming too old to be this young, and since we were technically already engaged to be wed, it appeared to be the clearest path forward. So now you are the father of the daughter of Lady Sara Anne Grey, otherwise known as Lady Abbigail Emily Boca."

"I sense an Oedipus Rex story coming on."

"Don't worry, love. I don't plan on keeping it much longer. Another forty years or so and it will be time for another change. Then you won't have to worry about such things any longer."

I laughed. Antonio was a couple of seconds behind me. It was nice that he found humor in it all. The levity helped to take some of the chill from his voice.

There were still many things to be accomplished, so I left Antonio to wander the stacks and headed to the ballroom.

The ballroom at Brimme House was a large and ornate room from a different age. The walls on every side were mirrored so that the space took on the look of a room three times the size that it actually was.

Portraits of my family line going all the way back to the founding of Brimme House itself were stationed around the room. From the pictures, one could tell that Brimme House had been infused with a fighting spirit long before one of my family managed to become the first Earl of Northwick. I was the sixth Earl of Northwick at that point in time. As I stood in the ballroom, I figured that I would probably be the last one for some time. Who knew, maybe by the time I moved on, there would be no need for nobility. The only sure thing is change. In the space that wasn't taken up by the portraits, the staff had shined the mirror to a bright reflection.

Mirrors were common in every palace and estate. Brimme House, for its part, was actually a little of both. It was much more of a castle than an estate house. It possessed ramparts and a small moat on two sides. Its outside walls were kept safe by a reinforced guardhouse. It had been used for defense in an age gone by, but it had become a powerful status symbol. So Brimme House needed a grand ballroom in which to entertain the gathered masses of the rich and powerful. That was another reason all the dukes disliked me.

It was times such as the coming event that gave the mirrors a completely different purpose, because the only people who would be reflected in the grand room would be the staff members. The mirrors helped to distinguish the living from the undead. They also helped me keep an eye on the safety of the staff. I used them to see through the crowd. It had always given me an eerie feeling to be in a large gathering of individuals with no reflection. It was quite unnerving.

The outer wall of the ballroom held large glass panels that looked out over the manicured lawns of the house. The staff had placed numerous candelabras about the terrace and the lawns so that my guests could leisurely walk about the grounds that night, if they chose. It was a fine, warm day and should produce a fine, warm night.

All seemed well in hand, so I proceeded to my bedchamber to address my attire for the evening. In truth, I already knew what I would wear; it was one of the things I obsessed about back then. I wanted my ensemble to present the right appearance. I lingered around my bedchamber dressing table for some time before I decided it was actually time to ready myself.

I shed all of my daytime attire and washed. A bowl of cool water with rose petals stationed in the washroom off my bedchamber facilitated the washing. Normally, I would have taken a bath before such an occasion, but I hadn't actually expended any energy in any fashion, so a quick cleaning was all that was required for the evening.

I padded wet and naked back into my bedchamber and took up station in front of the large, stylish armoire that covered up most of the far wall. A heavy and grand-size, white towel hung patiently on a bar next to the bulky piece of furniture. I patted myself dry and returned the towel to its hanger. I looked into the armoire and at the many fine dresses it contained. There were many choices for such an occasion, but what came out was a bold, white, muslin gown with a delicate green and gold Greek pattern around the neckline. The first two pieces to cover my body were undergarments and a corded stay. The stay would help to keep my bust in place under the loose gown I had chosen. Next came the white gown, and I was dressed.

I collected my now moderate mass of blond hair in the back and pinned it in place with ivory chopsticks that Captain Smithers had given me so many years ago. I loved the pencil-like sticks; they reminded me of happier times when I had been a little girl and my father had still been alive to worry about my virtue. The ivory chopsticks had seen much use since I had received them. The edges of the sticks were becoming smooth around the edges. It was fine; they still looked as elegant as when they were new.

I slipped the amulet back around my neck and positioned it in its happy place next to the skin of my breast. The jewel always seemed happy to be taken along. After making sure my little friend was content, I dabbed some light perfume behind my ears and on my wrists. The perfume was a rose-infused scent acquired in France, and it accented my earlier rose petal washing. I have to say, I still to this day like French perfume very much. You can say whatever you want about the fact the French smell like cheese, but they make good perfume.

My ensemble was complete. As usual, I left off the stockings and shoes that all of the other women would be wearing that evening as I never could keep my shoes on anyway. Ever since I was a little girl, I have been barefoot at parties. Being barefoot drove my father completely out of sorts. I just couldn't seem to keep the darn things on my feet. To compensate for that, I always wore floor-length dresses to hide my feet. That way when my shoes inevitably ended up in the corner, no one would be the wiser.

I have never been sure why that was the case. When I was a little girl, I learned to dance barefoot on the hard stone floors of the estate, and now I continue to do so. It is just the way of it. I decided long ago that, if that one idiosyncrasy offended people, then I just wouldn't invite them anymore. The good thing about being rich was that you never had to work at filling a party list. People were usually replaceable.

That night's guests were the exception to that rule. They were not replaceable. They also, fortunately, would not care about my attire. Most vampires didn't get caught up in such things.

I shuffled out the door and through the house to the entrance of the ballroom. In the ballroom, I found Brandy and Amber taking care of their last-minute affairs. Upon noticing my entrance, they each assured me that everything was just fine. Everything was fabulously decorated, and the staff had been given strict marching orders. They had been warned about interacting with the guests and to not let down their guards around them. Apparently, Brandy had given the speech twice to make sure it stuck.

By the time they were finished bringing me up to speed, the glow of the outside candelabras could be distinguished through the glass. Shortly after that, the sounds of carriages coming through the gatehouse and up the drive could also be heard.

The first gala I had hosted was a slow-moving affair. Guests came along in ones and twos, well after the black cloak of night had fallen. They lingered there at the house, reveling until the blackness had returned the next night. The whole affair had had an unhurried and unplanned pace to it. This one was not that type of an affair. The faint remnants of day were not even gone when the creatures of the night started arriving. All the invited guests came streaming into my great house in prompt fashion.

Happily, my guest list had grown since the first gathering. New names had been added as new members in new countries had heard the tale that had spread. That meant that new languages needed to be absorbed into conversation. As with the original gala, that didn't turn out to be much of an inconvenience. It seemed that all traveling creatures, even today, knew more than one language, and most of them that night spoke several. That is one of the benefits of age; one has more time to learn things.

Much like the first gala, the evening's guests seemed to separate into groups of three or four—two of them to converse, and the others to facilitate translation. Those conversations revolved around topics that would be expected of any vampire gathering. There was talk of different lands traveled and what the inhabitants were like. What the climate of such places was and what hunting techniques worked well. The other general conversations all circled around business. That was always the case with powerful people. The gala's business conversations all seemed to revolve around the new innovations of the day: steel-strapped ships and new railroad systems. It was understandable, because all vampires were concerned about travel, whether it be for business, pleasure, or survival.

By far, the new steam engine—or more properly locomotive—and what would become the railroad topped the roster. Now, the railways were nothing even remotely new at that point. Road rails with carts on them had been in use in Germany since the middle of the 1500s. It took until the eighteenth century to replace the wooden rails with iron ones. The wheels also became iron, and the horse-drawn carts spread out across Europe.

The leap in technology that we discussed to death that evening had come in 1804. In 1803, a man named Trevithick had built the first steam-powered vehicle, which was used to pull one of the trams. In 1804, that vehicle pulled ten tons of iron and some seventy men nine miles across and down the Abercynnon valley in Wales. It was reported to have been accomplished in a two-hour interval.

Everyone in the conversations that evening seemed to realize that that was a sign of things to come. Self-powered vehicles that had no need for rest were like some type of magick trick. They surely had to be a sign of the future. For me, it was also a means of unlocking inland business, or it would be in the future. Then, it was just grand speculation.

I had trouble removing myself from the numerous conversations, but the guests needed tending to, and the humans needed looking after.

Fortunately, unlike our first gathering, all the vampires in attendance that evening were quite well behaved. Apparently, my point had been driven home at the first one. You kill one vampire, and the rest fall into line.

I spent some time discussing the resettling of life with one of the individuals I had liberated from the steppes' fortress. The others, even though they had been imprisoned there much longer than Antonio, had managed to assimilate back into the world quite nicely. Both of the new guests from the fortress were of Russian descent. The range of languages that came with them helped the conversations immensely and was augmented by two new Asian guests we had come across.

The second gala was truly cosmopolitan. The whole world was in my ballroom. It was truly a grand affair. The gathering spilled out onto the terrace and lawns. A warm, cloudless night gave the whole affair a magnificent setting.

I stopped and talked to Zoey for several moments. Even though she only lived across the border to the north, we rarely crossed paths. She was nice, and frankly, the Scottish burr in her speech always made me smile. Our conversation was all about the fashion of the day and the flowers in my gardens. It was pleasant conversation about the things girls enjoy.

I had an interesting conversation with a chap named Peter Groves who had come across the Atlantic from New York. He told me that the city of New York was an overwhelming place. A person or a business could apparently do quite well there. He seemed quite nice and genuine in his thoughts. Nice vampires always struck me as an interesting alternative to the norm. There were times when I was sure that I was the only one.

As is the case with all things, too soon the dawn was approaching. All of my guests were shown to their respective quarters and allowed some respite from the light of day. Those not requiring rejuvenation retired to the dungeon to continue their conversations and merriment. Unlike the first gala, which had been a night affair followed by a quiet daytime wait, this gala continued on somewhat unchecked by the sunshine beyond the house's thick, stone walls. The unplanned continuation taxed the blood supply of the house, almost to the breaking point. It was really quite refreshing to see that so many demonic creatures could act so civilized for so long an interval. Strange things really could happen.

I retreated to the comfort of the stacks of the library and its overstuffed leather chairs. As the humans finished with their necessary chores, they would come and go. The change in perspective was welcome. The night had lacked the blood-soaked reveling and stunning death that had marked the first event. The humans were all amazed by the contrast of the setting. They obviously found so many deadly creatures acting in such a genteel fashion to be contradictory. It was fine; I felt the same. I thanked them all and reminded them not to let down their guards quite yet as things might change at any moment.

Thankfully for us all, they did not. Dusk came back to Brimme House in its steady and timely fashion. The black coat of night descended on us; the carriages lined up one by one along the front entranceway. I stood under the large, covered entryway that I had entered so many centuries before and thanked all my guests for coming. All of them gave me praise for a gathering that could not have been better. I thanked them for their glad tidings and wished them safe travels.

As with the first gala, all of the guests asked if there would be a third such gathering. I responded with a "Yes, but not too soon." Time needed to pass so things could calm down. Maybe a century or so and invitations would go out once more. All my guests seemed pleased by my answer, as caution was the vampire way.

By midevening, the noisemakers in Brimme House had been reduced to Antonio, the staff, and me. The staff really had a large task ahead of them. They needed to clean all the blood from Brimme House so another party could be held.

The businessmen and bankers of the area surrounding Brimme House and the Bristol area were all men of substance, and many of them were personal friends. They could not be shunned without serious repercussions. I had no intention of shunning them. So, as was the case with the original gala years before, a second party was planned for week's end. That party would entertain the business interests of the region.

The staff proved to be ever efficient, and the second affair came off much the same way the first one had. In Brimme House, all was happy merriment. The people of the Bristol area always liked to see

Brimme House open its doors. The second party was a great success, and some new business was even conducted. The whole things came off pleasantly, with one exception—one uninvited guest.

As is the usual case at such large gatherings, some uninvited guests attended. Most often, it was of no real interest to me. Guest lists were usually somewhat vague, so it didn't really matter. That night's interloper was just a bit different.

I had just finished discussing the structure of religion with a very nice Catholic archbishop who resided in Bristol when I was caught up by a face in the crowd. That face belonged to Sir Edmond Cole. It was that damned Brenfield Society again. Since he had not appeared days earlier, I had decided to stay calm and see what was what. As always, he was a gentleman, and I was a lady.

"Good evening, you're enjoying the gathering?"

"It's all most wonderful. I must say, Brimme House really does entertain well."

"Thank you. The house has a history for generations of hospitality. What brings you so far from London? You have business in the area?"

"Interestingly, yes. I had heard stories of strange things in the area and decided to come and study them. I heard of your fine gathering and thought to attend as I was in the area."

"And did you find what you were looking for?"

"Sadly, I was too late. Maybe I will have better luck on the next occasion."

"Maybe."

The conversation continued on generally for a few minutes longer. All of the conversation was about nothing in particular. Then, I moved on to other guests as was the fashion.

It was nice to know that he had arrived too late to observe the gala. I really had not needed that. He would have been an interruption that I could not have afforded to deal with. It was fortunate for me, but it was still not safe. I didn't trust him as far as I could throw his bloodless corpse. He needed to be watched somehow.

Oh well, thoughts for different days. I put it out of my head as the party came and went.

Soon, the second party was done as well. It would take a couple of days to settle things back down to their normal levels and then to reward both Brandy and Amber.

Then it was time to leave. I stuffed Antonio into my coach and headed back east to the Grey Estate so I could contemplate. Just as after the first gala, the second one was over, and I needed a vacation.

# chapter 22

The vacation that I wanted to take ended up be of the mental variety. I kind of slid into a state of ease and let my mind run for a while. I surfaced from that self-induced, mental funk in the fall of 1809. That was a fine year as years go.

The architect Sir Robert Smirke ushered in the neoclassical style with construction of the Covent Garden Theatre in London. It was truly a grand affair. The structure stood apart from anything the tradesmen of London had erected. Its Doric facade played on my fondness for my long-lost Greek manor.

Robert Casterlaegh shot and wounded Foreign Minister George Canning in a duel. Apparently, he was unhappy with the way we were conducting the war with Napoleon. Some people just can't be pleased, I guess.

It should be noted that duels were a common way of settling disputes in the early nineteenth century. It always seemed strange. It was most likely a carryover from the days of dueling with swords. That I understood.

Napoleon's steady march of empire continued on. He managed to annex the Papal States in Rome. In doing so, he took Pope Pius VII as his prisoner. That news saddened me. I had come to like the Catholics. They had a secret tolerance for the opposite side—well, as long as we weren't in open conflict with one another. I hoped that they would come away from Napoleon intact.

The bringer of the theory of evolution, one Charles Darwin, was born in Shropshire. You couldn't tell at the time, but he would go on to change the world.

On the opposite side of the balance scale, the master composer Franz Joseph Haydn died in Vienna. It always saddens me when great musicians die. Music has been one of the things that soothes the mood of the world. It should have more great exponents, not fewer.

On the home front, things were pretty much the same. England was still fighting with France. There was a commercial boom in England, which made business lovely. England was still trying to expand her influence in the far-flung parts of the world, and King George III was still sliding off his rocker.

Personally, it was a quiet time. I had been keeping out of the spotlight, as it were, since the gala. My needed solitude came in the form of retreating into the walls of the Grey Estate. The long meadows, deep woods, and sturdily engineered stone walls of my home gave me peace of mind.

I spent some time, but not an excessive amount, overseeing my little empire. William had been hard at work since his return from the East. It took him some time to settle back into a life of business after his travels. He had been well out of his comfort zone, and it was hard for him to adjust. But, in time, adjust he did. He had even come back around to using a civil tone in my presence. That was nice, since it had tried my patience greatly.

I had been wondering if the extremes of travel would make him quit his post as one of my confidants. He was in his later years, and most of the Wyndell men had gotten out of the confidant game by that point. He had just been keeping the post warm, it seemed, since there weren't as many issues for him to deal with. At least, that was my guess.

William was nearly sixty years of age by that point in time. He had worked on adding to the lineage long before and raised two sons. They were Fletcher and Charles. The latter had been named after his great-great-great-grandfather.

The two of them had been educated at Oxford and schooled in business. They had also both invested large amounts of time at the estate, being schooled in other things. Fletcher was a tried-and-true businessman and really did not find joy in embracing the ways of the occult. His younger brother Charles was a completely different creature.

Charles was a shining reincarnation of his great-great-great-grandfather Charles. I called him Charles III. It wasn't a legitimate line of names, but that was all right. I had known all of the men named Charles Wyndell, and I decided I could call him whatever I wanted.

Charles embraced the occult. He was very intelligent and had a good sense, which his brother Fletcher lacked, for seeing the vagaries of the world. Charles could make the ever-elusive but fundamental leap between what he was told was real and what he could see was so. All the Wyndell men had possessed it in varying degrees. The ones I held in higher regard possessed it to a greater degree.

Don't get me wrong, Fletcher was not naive in any measure. He understood that I was a vampire, that vampires were real, and that the knowledge would most likely cost him at some point. He was just so much better at the daily structured existence of the business world.

Charles was also very good at business. He embraced solid truths of math and money and found assurance in the structure of legal papers. He understood the timing of the sea and the cost of poor judgment. But, unlike his brother, he truly excelled at the obscure. He possessed an ability to live comfortably in the dark grey areas of the world. It was that ability that would lead him to my side; it was but a matter of time.

It probably should be noted that the boys also had a little sister. Her name was Alene. She was, by all accounts, a nice, young girl. Fortunately, she lacked her Aunt Amber's cognitive abilities. She was married off to a nice English gentleman. We would cross paths upon occasion, and she was pleasantly none the wiser.

While I stayed at my estate, I spent most of my waking moments pondering. I paid no heed to the passage of time as it slid by me. I think that state comes naturally to the undead at some point. When you become unhooked from the great universal wheel of time, things slowly begin to change. The passage of time becomes somewhat relative to vampires. Human beings spend their time obsessed with making more time. Vampires almost forget that there is time at all. Things just keep going along a natural path.

Me, I tended to spend great lumps of time in the melodic process of thinking. I had refined my skill to where I could sit and think about something for weeks at a time. Functionally, I wasn't any better at it than I had been when I was human. Becoming a vampire gave me no new cognitive abilities that could be harnessed in the pursuit of knowledge. I just did not become bothered by the turning of clock hands. That allowed me to sit and ponder indefinitely.

At that particular time in history, I was thinking about three specific things: trains, ships, and New York. Those thoughts would come and leave at varying intervals, but they were what I pondered on.

Ever since the conversations at the gala, I had been thinking about trains. Trains seemed to solve a problem for me. Since its inception, Grey Cargo had always been a point A to point B type of company. Our handling of cargo stopped at the docks of whatever port we unloaded it in. While that was the rule of the day, it left a void between where the cargo was and where it was required to go. In the early nineteenth century, that meant carts pulled by oxen. Grey Cargo did handle wagon procurement for a great many clients, but it was by no means part of our standard business plan. Wagons were very much a local commodity.

Trains, on the other hand, were not wagons. If trains started to become more popular in the interior regions, then I could utilize them to move more cargo faster. I was having trouble imagining the amount of goods that I could move with a train. It was dizzying, much like thinking about what is wrapped in a Christmas present.

Trains could prove a path to great revenue increases for the corporation. They could also be a path to financial ruin. Trains were, by all accounts, extremely expensive items. They required capital investments. I have had a great many acquaintances end up in the poor house over the years because of poor financial decisions. That would not be me. I was not a risk taker when it came to my business. Every decision was based on sound logic, not fancy. I just couldn't stop thinking about the trains.

Sooner or later, thinking about trains brought me around to thinking about ships. Our fleet was in good repair, but new ships were growing ever more costly to produce. An island the size of Britain only possessed so much quality timber. That timber resource had been eaten away on all sides by the many builders of the country. That made local timber stocks pricey, to say the least.

The master shipbuilders at the Bristol Mooring had started utilizing metal strapping to strengthen and supplement timber in ship construction. That greatly reduced the massive dimensions of the timber that was needed. They had also begun to import timber from America to augment the supply. Sadly, the two good solutions only nominally reduced the financial impact.

The full throes of the Industrial Revolution had yet to begin in the British Isles. Iron had yet to come into its own as a cost-friendly building material. The builders were really just changing out one costly material for another. I wasn't overly concerned about the financial impact it was having on the builders, because the business as a whole was cruising along nicely and pumping out a fine profit. I just didn't want the cost increases to continue. I guess the result of all of that was that we fixed a lot more ships and built fewer new ones. It made me wish that I had not burned so many ships in earlier days. Oh well, the past is the past.

I followed thinking about the past by thinking about the future. A conversation with a vampire from New York had set me to thinking about the cities of the Americas. During my time in Boston, I had found it a city entirely too young for my taste. Boston as a whole had little refinement to draw one's excitement.

The vampire from New York City had made that place sound almost cosmopolitan. While I assumed that part of it was the addition of grandeur so he could impress, there was a tone in his voice that made it all sound genuine enough. I was intrigued by the idea of a suitable city in the Americas. I had always liked the idea of the Americas and what they had to offer. The colonies, as I still referred to them most of the time, had a wide-open quality that just screamed out for business people. They also had space—enough space so my kind could get lost. That, in and of itself, was a great thing.

I decided that I needed to learn more about New York City. It sounded like a good place to go for a while. Well, when it was time to go anyway.

Now, while I have been regaling you with my thinking, it wasn't actually the only thing I was doing. I was also doing a considerable amount of talking, mostly with family and old friends.

In the evenings under the full night sky, I would collect a candle and make my way up the path that led to the family cemetery on the hill. Upon arriving at the iron gate, I would hang the amulet on a tree limb to view the moon, and then I would go and kneel upon the marble slab adjacent to the path and pray for the dead. Once homage was paid to the dead, I would collect myself and enter the hallowed grounds of the cemetery.

Normally, I headed straight for Mother and Father. They always seemed pleased to see me. I would sit on a little marble bench next to their graves and tell Mother about all the things in my life. I would tell Father about how the business was doing and about the changes time had brought. They would always listen intently. It left me with the feeling that they both approved.

Next, I would move over to the Wyndell family and my friend Charles and his wife. I would tell Charles and the rest about the status of the family. Then I would tell him about all the vampire happenings. I could tell that Charles was always intrigued by the news of the occult. He was my truest friend. It made me happy to sense him happy.

Then, when Charles's and Susan's time was spent, I would wander about the grounds and talk to my long-dead uncles and grandfather. They too appreciated my time. It appeared that they liked to be kept up-to-date on the status of things.

I liked the cemetery. It was a familiar space in which to commune with familiar spirits. It was a nice little spot of contentment.

On the occasions that I ventured out during that period, I mostly went straight from the estate to church. I really liked Father David Burman. He was a good man. In return for that, I had dragged him halfway around the world and treated him to visions no one should suffer seeing. Needless to say, I was actually doing damage control.

On several occasions, I arrived at St. Matthew's in time for evensong. I always liked the service. Religion did have some likeable qualities. One of them was theatrical. I supposed that any good way religion could get the message out was acceptable. I didn't buy into the message, but it was a nice show nevertheless.

Father David always appeared happy to see me return. He seemed happy enough, but his overall mood toward the world had changed some. There wasn't as much jollity as there once had been. That made me sad. I liked his jolly laugh very much.

I would quietly wait until he finished with his flock and was free of his duties, and then we would sit and talk. Sometimes, when the evening was pleasant, we would walk the grounds of St. Matthew's cemetery. I did my level best to bring out the happier side of his personality. It never really seemed to surface. It was buried deep. The things he had experienced had aged him somehow.

I had never considered how the adventure would affect him when I had started out. I had had a goal, and he had helped me achieve it. That was really all I cared about. That was the demon in me. It was also a bit of the amulet. It too cared little for men's points of view. No matter how or why, it was wrong. I had wronged him, and I wanted to make amends. I was not sure how, but I felt I had to try.

Father David was no dummy either. He knew the ends of my actions. He took it all well enough. He really did try to come back around and managed maybe 80 percent by the end. He just could not shake off the rest of it.

The whole experience had the effect of driving him into religion. He became a much more spiritual man than he had been before. That had an interesting effect on our conversations. They slowly became somewhat more confrontational. Now, it was never in a bad way, but more of a philosophical one. He had his side, and I had mine. That was fine. It was the way it was supposed to be—détente.

Father David and I did our little dance, and things moved along slowly until sometime in 1811. From the hindsight of history, change in the world is inevitable, even for someone such as me. The year 1811 was a changing of the guard year. All in all, it went well enough as years go.

There were wild stories coming out of the Americas with each new ship's return. I had heard stories that the Americas had actually started to build real roads. Of course, as any national project goes, the Cumberland Road project was more of a political and funding headache than it was a roadway project.

In some place called Tippecanoe, Indians were put down by then-president, William Henry Harrison. It seemed there was always some sort of news about Indians in those days.

On a more industrial note, the city of New York had begun to lay out its street system in a grid pattern. That design was definitely more efficient. It also inspired in me a desire to travel to that place.

I had never really been able to fully shake my desire to see New York City since the conversation at the gala. I could not explain why, because my experiences in the city of Boston had not necessarily been the best.

Closer to home, things were a little more chaotic. Riots by the Luddites in Nottingham destroyed the textile machines that had begun to replace the artisans who had worked there. Sadly, the situation was both just the start of unrest generated by the Luddites and too far away to be of a hunting advantage to me. If it were but a little closer, I could have gained from the carnage. After all, free meals are free meals.

Now, the changing of the guard that I spoke of earlier was that of the monarchy. The death of Amelia that same year sent King George III fully off his rocker. The King's insanity moved Parliament to appoint his son as regent. It was a position that the Prince of Wales took on gladly. It was his step up toward kingship.

The soon-to-be King George IV was also not like his father. He was younger and much more pliable to the will of others. That being said, the Court could be a prickly and fickle place for such things and required a strong and controlling hand to keep it in check.

Do not misunderstand, the prince had full control. He was the most powerful of the British monarchs. Being the Prince of Wales had made him very wealthy to boot. Those things were not the actual problem. The problem came from a true lack of command. His lack of experience in the Court made him pliable to the power brokers who trolled the back hallways. Politics has always had such problems.

I can say that I wasn't actually worried for him. I had met the Prince of Wales many times over the years, both at Court and at his castle in Wales. He possessed many features from both his mother and his father. He would certainly fare quite well in time.

We got on well, because he liked pretty girls. Also, we both possessed scads of pounds. He had the power advantage, as a prince to my earl. That suited his male sensibilities. Interestingly, he never gave the impression that he found my being a woman of power to be threatening. That I found comforting.

The thing I didn't find comforting was the other exchange of power that took place that year. In the earlier part of 1811, Sir Edmond Cole was gunned down in the streets of London. The cagey, old bastard had apparently offended someone. It was bad enough that they found the need to kill him. I was sad that it wasn't me. I had wanted to kill him on numerous occasions, but I had always thought better of it. Apparently, someone else didn't get as easily put off.

I assumed that, since he was shot, it was not a vampire or other demon that he had bothered. It seemed most certainly to be another human. I have always wished that it had been me. It would have been compensation for the days to come.

Sir Edmond Cole was buried in his hometown of Chelsea. The funeral service produced every member of nobility in the lower sections of the kingdom. It appeared from the throngs that the old bag of bones had been well connected.

The vacancy left in his wake was filled by one Sir Anthony Bridgemen. He was young and brash and possessed a freshly minted knighthood that all members of the Brenfield Society's council received from the Crown.

He would prove a problem. The council under Sir Edmond had been a quiet and private affair. They had observed and studied the darkness but otherwise let things go nature's way. The council under Sir Anthony was a different monster altogether. Sir Anthony was young enough to cause me misery for many years to come. That did not bode well.

The one good thing about all of it was that, in those days of old, the Brenfield Society was as much outside the graces of Church and Crown as I was. They were openly dealing with the occult, demons, and all manner of otherworldly creatures. They were as likely to be put to the stake as I was. That was the great leveler of things in my direction. Happily, most of the year would pass before I was properly introduced to Sir Anthony Bridgemen. The introduction would come toward the fall, when the Prince of Wales held a gathering of the Court. The prince needed to do so to inform the establishment about the stability of the Crown. Such gatherings of the Court were a mandatory affair for titleholders.

I stayed away from the Court as much as I possibly could. I really did not like it there. Like it or not, that trip had to be made, and it would give me a chance to converse with the Queen once more. That alone was worth the trip.

So, one bright fall day, I put myself into my best noble attire and climbed into my fancy carriage. The coachmen, who had been in my employ for many years, didn't need to be directed; they simply snapped the whips and headed out toward the city. We were headed toward the palace of the King.

The ride into London proper was pleasant enough. I really did not notice the passage of it. My thoughts were deep in the myriad of problems I might run up against. There were many problems to consider.

I have complained about the court being a house of vipers or some other such creature. There really were no vipers to be found there. The standards flying high above the palace suggested that it really was a house of wolves. Well, jackals would be more accurate. Now, one would think that I would fit right into a house full of jackals. That, however, was not the case. I detest pack hunting. It is simply a way for those who can't do for themselves. I don't help the weak in that way.

The carriage rolled to a stop at the garden gate to St. James Palace, and the driver relayed my presence to the Beefeaters in brightly colored uniforms. The Beefeaters had been borrowed from Tower Hill so they might support the Royal Guard on such an occasion. The guards asked few questions, because I was well known in London society. We were allowed to pass with little inconvenience.

My driver expertly positioned the carriage on its mark in front of the palace entryway. As it came to a stop, my driver leapt from his seat and swiftly opened my carriage door before the otherwise unconcerned staff waiter could muster up the ambition. I smiled at the nice man and thanked him for being so gentlemanly. He simply smiled and returned to his seat. The carriage then moved off to take its place in the long line of carriages that were waiting to leave once more.

I brushed past the members of the staff taking up station out front and headed through the palace's grand entrance. As was usual, the entrance and all the outer corridors were filled with every manner of schemer and power monger. They were all low people and annoyed me greatly. They were a group with weak character.

I moved past them all quickly, so as not to be taken up in their nefarious affairs. Freeing myself from their midst, I headed past the staff stationed on the edge of the group and on to where the private sections of the palace started. I stopped to inquire of a steward the whereabouts of the Queen and was escorted toward an ornate sitting room off to one side of the court's gathering rooms.

The large, gilded door slowly swung open, and the steward announced to Her Majesty the presence of Lady Abbigail Boca, sixth Earl of Northwick. The chatter surrounding the Queen quickly silenced itself, and with a wave of her hand, the room emptied. The steward who had shown me to the room backed out silently, closing the door as he did so.

Suddenly, the two of us were alone. I promptly curtsied politely and waited for the hand gesture that meant I might stand.

"Lady Boca, I am quite pleased to see you here at Court. I thought it might be all dull chatter. Now, at least, there will be a spot of solid conversation."

"Thank you for your kindness, Majesty. I admit I was pleased to hear that you made your way from Frogmore House. I myself had assumed that your son would be running an all-business session of Court."

"He's a good boy, but regent or not, I'm still the senior monarch in this land."

"I did not mean to offend, Majesty."

"Relax, Abbigail; I like people who say what they mean. There is nothing to apologize for. Now, what do you say we drop the trappings of title and converse in a more honest manner?"

"Yes, ma'am."

"Good. Now, to set a tone for our dialogue. Abbigail, it would seem that we both have the opportunity to interact with powerful men and hope that they can be trusted with discretion."

"Ma'am?"

"In years past, you had the opportunity to converse with one Cardinal Michael Falco, if I am not mistaken."

I started to panic. I think I blanched as well. How in the world could she possibly know such things? He was in a different country and of the wrong religion.

"I was traveling abroad, ma'am, and received an audience with the cardinal while in his city. It appeared that we had similar interests."

"An interestingly diplomatic answer and also not far off the truth of things."

"I confess I am not sure I understand, Majesty." I really wanted to leave.

"Remain calm, Abbigail. I mean you no harm. The cardinal is a friend of my family. He has been lifelong friends with my brother, Duke Charles II.

"The cardinal asked that I might not be removed from your affairs, where the Crown was concerned. I explained to him that I had no influence in the affairs of men but would be pleased to keep an attuned ear, as we two got on well."

"If I may ask, what else did he say about me?"

"There were some interesting things, Abbigail. And knowing the circles that the cardinal tends to travel in, potentially true. They were all statements of great discretion."

"And you, Majesty?"

"I am curious. How does one end up in such a state? And how does one go from that state to one such as you have now? How do you maintain decency and humanity against such pressures?"

"You don't seem put out by the topic you have suggested, Majesty."

She laughed. I did not.

"I am too old to be easily surprised. Besides, you look entirely too much like your mother. I mean, if your father truly was Spanish, your skin tone would have a deep hue. I'm not judging, but your next father really should be English."

I was gobsmacked. The old girl was having a conversation about vampires with a vampire. I really did not appreciate the cardinal's indiscretion, even if the information seemed well placed. I obviously needed to keep her as an ally from then on. With all of that, it really did appear to be time for some answers.

"Let us take a walk through the morning air of your lovely gardens and discuss life, Majesty."

The Queen, in a rare act of normalcy, sprang from her chair and retrieved a shawl from its back. Then, with a wave of her hand toward the large, ornate, glass door that led out of the sitting room, we proceeded off. We walked quietly until we were both sure no one could overhear.

"To honor your inquiry, Majesty, I can honestly say the transition to my current state was not actually a matter of my choosing. Apparently, others saw me as useful to their own ends."

"That is something I can fully understand, my girl."

"As for the other two things, well, creatures, like people, just are who they are. Most fall to their baser instincts, because it is the transition of easiest convenience. I suppose I could have done such things as well, but being with people means being like people. After all, humanity is a useful thing. Good and evil are traits that all creatures and people possess. I just am who I am."

"I confess, I had always thought people to be good and bad. It explains much of the world today. I did not realize that it was a universal theme," said the Queen.

I laughed, and so did the Queen. She was a good student of the human condition.

"May I ask how long you have been … here?"

"About two hundred years, ma'am."

"My, that is a long time."

"I confess it does make life long. You get to see the good and bad of things."

"I would not want to live that long, I think. I'm already tired of the burden that life has placed upon me."

"I spent many years burdened by being a woman in a man's world. I understand your sentiment. But time is like anything else, I guess. When you have lots of time, you don't notice its passing. I think things are nicer when they are finite."

"I would think you are correct, my girl. Now, quiet; someone's coming."

"I know."

"I like that."

A steward came running down the finely manicured, cobblestone path that led to the patios of the palace. As he approached us, he realized that I was accompanied by the Queen. He came sliding to a stop and paused, then he quickly removed his cap, as was customary.

He must have been running all about, because steam came off his head as he removed his cap. Both the Queen and I chuckled. It was comical.

"Your Majesty, forgive the intrusion. Lady Boca has been requested in the regent's meeting hall."

The Queen took the news the same way that one would if hearing that the kitchen was out of juice.

"Well, Lady Boca, we would not want to keep the future King of England waiting, would we?"

"Only when he's in Wales, Majesty, only when he is in Wales."

We both chuckled once more. The steward blanched.

"Scurry off and tell my son that we will be along in our fashion."

As she finished talking, the steward ran off, hat in hand. He did not appear pleased to be delivering the message.

"Are you sure that's wise, ma'am? For me, I mean?"

"Don't worry, girl. I'm the power here. Well, for now, anyway. Besides, he fancies you, and you both get on well. Trust me, this will not tarnish anything."

"I hope you are correct, Majesty."

"Oh, by the way, feel free to conduct your affairs from here on out with comfort. The future monarchs of the land cannot remove your title."

"How is that possible?"

"See, my girl, the ruling monarch of the age has the right, ordained by God, to make decisions that cannot be reversed. They are deemed sealed as final. This ability applies to all situations, including patents of nobility."

"Can such things really be done?"

"It already has, my girl. I had the King handle the situation before the regency took effect. It was a birthday present to me."

We turned to walk back up the path to the palace. The birds seemed to be chirping happily. All was going to be good that day. Maybe.

"Power really is a useful thing, Majesty."
"You are correct, my girl."

# chapter 23

The stylish Earl of Northwick strolled into a room full of dukes, plus one prince, on the arm of the Queen and attempted to remain unfazed by it all. I was way off my rung on the ladder of nobility. The only real thing I could do was show no fear. It was so obvious that even the amulet felt off somehow.

The worst of it was not the staring but the silence. I had spent the vast majority of my life quietly hoping that people would not notice me. Now, not only were they noticing me, but they were stunned by my presence. At that very point in time, every person in the room, save for the Queen, was staring at me. I found being noticed by the masses to be very discomfiting. More than that, I disliked the silence.

When the doors to the hall had been swung open, the interior had been abuzz with conversation. The outer layer of nobles taking up station around the door had turned to chastise me for my timing, inopportune method of entering, or whatever. They had but started when the Queen appeared from behind one of the doors with her arm still wrapped in mine.

The silence that followed the vision of the Queen was deafening. The sea of bodies in the room parted, much the same as stories of the biblical sea of reeds. The tear in the crowd rippled all the way to the throne at the other end.

Through a parted sea of dukes came the vision of a prince. He sat quietly. There was a large, childlike smile across his face. Apparently, from his look, I had actually made the right entrance. The Prince glanced around the hall at his powerful military men, who had been silenced by a middle-aged woman and her elderly escort.

I looked middle-aged to the crowd. For my appearance at Court, I had chosen to make the crowd see me as older than I actually was. It usually helped. It was what Antonio had called "gypsy magick."

Gypsy magick is one of the little extra things that vampires can do with their brains. It basically allows people to see you as you think they should. It's a lot like mental confusion. It works best on people you have met, because you have already established a small mental connection with the person. In crowds where you know but half of those present, such as the one I was in at that moment, it required extra effort to make sure that everyone was affected.

When I had originally met those I had met, they had seen me as a child of maybe ten years. Then, entering the hall some forty years returned to England, they saw me as a middle-aged woman. That put me in the same age range as the Prince and at least half of the dukes. Fortunately, the amulet was handling my extra energy needs quite effectively.

The Prince finished his survey of the room as we approached his throne. He adjusted his gaze and began to clap softly for us. He was showing his approval, and I simply nodded mine.

"Good morning, Mother. Good morning, Lady Boca."

I paused to curtsy, as was required. The Queen continued on to the throne to the left of the one the Prince was in, where she took up her station in regal fashion.

"Good morning, sire. It would appear that all is well in the kingdom this morning."

"I agree, Lady Abbigail. I believe that it is."

An almost inaudible whisper went through the hall as the Prince took an informal tone.

"I am pleased to see you well, sire. I stopped by the castle when hunting last in the western lands. Unfortunately, you were about the affairs of state."

"The staff sent word of your visit. I was sad to be absent."

The Queen smiled but said nothing.

"Maybe, if the stars align, sire, we might find time once again to hunt before the affairs of a far-ranging empire consume you."

The Prince beamed with approval. As he did so, his vision narrowed in on me specifically. That led me to the conclusion that the Queen was correct. He did fancy me. Well, that might turn out to be useful in time.

"That seems a grand idea. Should we hunt the lands of your estate or mine?"

"Whichever one suits your fancy, sire. They both are prosperous and amply filled with game fit for a man in a throne."

It was as much a political statement as it was a matter of truth. It was not lost on the other members in attendance. Many a duke in the room that day could not have given the Crown half of what Northwick could deliver, and they knew it.

I didn't stress the point often, since the men in the room really didn't like women in their midst. They especially didn't like ones with better lands and wealth. Now, as far as wealth went, they were coming up short. With wealth, there was the Crown, several really old families of dukes, and then my own. After mine, there was a large gap, and then the rest could file in.

Collectively, they were dangerous and powerful. Individually, they were nothing to get excited about. I think the latter fact bothered those in attendance most of all. It didn't seem to bother the Prince; he and I went back a long way.

"We should hunt the lands of Brimme House, I think. I have always liked the lands to the south of the river."

"That sounds grand. Brimme House has been a happy shelter for a prince upon occasion. I am sure it will happily shelter a king as well."

"Just regent for the present; maybe one day, king will come along, maybe not."

"When that happy and sad day does come to this land, I am sure that you will be ready. I mean, that is one fine chair you have there. I will have to tell my friends that they don't have a chair that fine," I said with a smile, and I was thankful that he laughed. If he had not done so, things would have gotten extremely uncomfortable.

"Do you still play chess, Lady Abbigail?"

"Every day at Court is a game of chess, sire. But yes, I still manage several games a week."

"Good, once the affairs of empire are quieted, we shall meet for a small battle on the chess board."

"That sounds lovely, sire."

"Then, until a later hour, enjoy your time at Court."

I curtsied politely to the Prince and then to the Queen at his side. I wanted to make a graceful exit, though I wasn't sure exactly how to do it.

"Oh, one more detail, Lady Abbigail. Will you be staying at Court?"

"No, sire. I regret to inform you that I will be returning to the Grey Estate at a respectable hour."

"Very good, Lady Abbigail."

"Majesty. Highness." I curtsied once more and readied to depart. The Prince nodded his approval, and the Queen smiled broadly. All had gone well; all that was required was a graceful exit.

The exit was the sticking point. I wasn't really good at backing up in the long frilly gowns of the day. I know, I'm a woman, and I wear dresses every day. That was (and still pretty much is) true, but I hardly ever wore the full, fancy kind that Court required. I found them to be unbearably annoying.

However, prudence being necessary, I did my best. Reaching down stealthily, I lifted the large, layered, bottom panels off the floor high enough to be mobile. Then, like a boat on a pond, I glided backward toward the doors.

The look on the Prince's face said that he found it amusing. I did not care; I managed to get to the door without turning my back to them, which was the main point. That kind of rudeness often led to a stay in the White Tower.

Once free of the meeting hall, I turned and headed back toward the gardens. I have to say that the gardens of St. James Palace were lovely. They still had much of the lushness that summer brought on. I enjoyed them greatly, even though fall was shortly at hand.

I came to a stop and milled about by a stand of cypress trees. The trees were supposed to have been brought from the Holy Land around the time of the Third Crusade. It was said that the royal gardeners were not even sure that the dry, desert species would germinate in a wetter, northern climate. Apparently, they had. The cypress trees were obviously survivors. I appreciated that quality.

I slowly became engrossed in the pleasantness of my surroundings, so much so that I almost missed the sounds of a person quietly approaching. The presence of a second person slowly moving about brought me back to the moment. I quickly regained my senses and was ready when he finally appeared.

The sight, when it came, was of a young, dashing man. He approached me in a slow and deliberate manner. Not the way one approaches a lady, but more the way one approaches a dangerous animal. He was obviously not going to be social.

The young man paused several feet from me and began admiring the cypress trees. He stood straight and erect for about a minute, presumably to gauge my level of hostility. Finally, he turned to look at me directly. There was no missing the black cane with the small, pewter house handle. I hated those damned things.

"Good day, Lady Grey. Oh, it is actually Lady Grey, isn't it?"

"My name, young man, is Boca, as in Lady Abbigail Boca. Lady Grey was my mother."

"Well, Lady Boca, my name is Bridgemen, as in Sir Anthony Bridgemen. I am the new head of the Brenfield Society council."

"And what would that be to me? Are you subscribing benevolent patrons?"

"No, Countess, but you would already know that. We study the occult and the creatures of the darkness. We have been studying you for some time."

"What's that, then?"

"You heard me right, Lady Grey. We at the Brenfield Society have been studying you for some years. Our last council head, Sir Edmond Cole, was apparently a great admirer of yours."

"Edmond Cole, yes, a nice man. And, as I remember, considerably more gentlemanly than you. And my name is Boca."

"Times change, Lady Grey, and so do councils. Ours is going to be taking a more active stance where the activities of the occult are concerned."

"You really do not understand the concept of gallantry, do you, boy?"

"Gallantry is the last act of old men. I am more the action type."

"Action is the first act of the undereducated. You don't strike me as uneducated, so I would bet that you are just brash."

"Brash? Maybe. I'm only here to explain the new rules of the game to you."

"It's really not a game, boy. Your predecessor was intelligent enough to understand that."

"I consider it as much a game as anything else in life. You should know that we do not really approve of your activities abroad. You are really going to have to quiet your exploits from here on."

"You know, you're talking like a dead man."

"Your actions will garner repercussions, if they continue. We would be pleased if you curtailed your actions yourself. But, if not, we will handle what is necessary."

"I was right; you are talking like a dead man. Let me tell you something while you still have some life in you. I do what I please, because I please to do it. That being said, if I choose to do any particular thing, I will do so.

"Interestingly, your predecessors knew that your little cult was as much an atrocity to the high levels of religion and the Crown as I am. Be very sure that if you try to oppose me in any socially visible fashion, your little house of warlocks and shamans will go up in a large ball of flames.

"Just so you know, out in the larger lands abroad, specifically the ones controlled by the Vatican, you are disliked greatly. I happen to know for a fact that they actually like me better than you. So your ground for grand statements is not as sound as you think it is, boy."

"I do agree about your opinions of things on our own soil. We would not do anything that would directly threaten stability. Outside lands, however, are a different matter. You will find moving unopposed to be much harder in other lands," he said.

"So it is détente here and open war abroad."

"That sounds right to me."

"Is that business or personal?"

"Personal. Both our larger business interests are what they are."

"That seems fair to me. I accept."

"It's agreed, then. I look forward to continuing the study of your pursuits."

"You are going to do whatever studying you plan to do from a distance, boy. You people aggravate me to no end. Oh, I have one more thing for you to study. While you think that your taking some new, bold stance is grand, you're doing it in a custom-filled land.

"So, if you talk down to me one more time while standing in His Majesty's lands, I will see your freshly knighted head stuck on a pike at the far end of Tower Bridge. Are we clear?"

The young man blanched slightly as he stopped to envision his own beheading. That was a good thing. It made things real.

"I said, are we clear?"

"Yes, Lady Boca, perfectly clear."

"Good. Now, remove yourself from my sight."

Mr. Bridgemen moved off down the path, still a little whiter than when he had arrived. Then, after a couple of seconds, he was gone from my view, which left me with my own thoughts.

I hated people who talked down to me. They were an aggravating bunch of blighters. I had fought my way to the top by myself, and I was going to stay there.

He was right about one thing; it was a game of sorts. And I was right; there were rules to be observed. The beauty of the rules was that they actually favored me. I had reminded him at the end; I had a better stance in the halls of nobility than any member of the society.

I put it from my mind and paused to ponder the interests of the Prince. Apparently, his fancy really would turn out to be useful. Even an earl needed high sponsors. I would have to make sure that I kept that fancy intact for the foreseeable future.

As I pondered the likes of Prince George, I slowly headed back toward the halls of the Court. I had been out awhile, and chess time was approaching. I returned as business was just coming to a close. All the ardent political followers were filing out, and the Queen had already departed to her chambers.

Noticing my return in the windows of the Court meeting hall, the Prince dismissed the remainder of the people with a wave of his hand. Then he pointed toward a chessboard stationed in the corner of the room. I entered, and we both took up station at our appropriate ends of the board. Once comfortably situated, we commenced battle.

I will say that the good thing about the Prince was that he could still lose. I could rightly beat a regent, but a king would customarily win every time. In the end, it was a tie. Each of us won one game. Stopping seemed the best move for both of us, and besides, nightfall was coming on. It was time for a good countess to be getting on home.

I excused myself from the presence of the Prince and headed off in search of my carriage. As I expected, my valet was right where I had left him. He ushered me out of St. James and quietly on to my estate. The fresh, night air held a small chill, which helped me to calm myself and relax. I had been on my best behavior all day, and it was taxing.

It seemed that if those things in my life were going to continue, I would need to spend some time with Antonio. The problem was that Antonio was still brooding. Sometimes, he was good and civil, and sometimes, he was not.

Then a thought of Thomas went through my head. Oh, Thomas. He was indeed a nice man. He was tall, with dark hair and brown eyes, and set in a boxer's frame. Thomas was the one who had been discreetly satisfying my more human needs in years past—many years past; almost one hundred years, I think. He had been a really good sounding board for my desires.

The rest of my ride to the estate, and my walk through the manor was consumed with thoughts of Thomas. Sadly, I had had to have him put down in the end. He had been a member of my inner circle but also of the House of Shadows. He had been killed off in the events that had led up to my leaving for Crete. It was sad, really.

I decided that I needed to find a new Thomas. Yes, that would be grand. Some young, vital specimen to satisfy and placate my swings in mood might work fine. Another boxer might be nice. They tend to be more aggressive. Yes, a young, human plaything would be just the thing.

I shook off the thoughts of Thomas as I entered my study. The study had always had a way of pulling me into the moment. I think it was the smell of leather and books. The volumes of old knowledge staring at me also helped.

I strolled over to stare at a medium-size trunk, which had been dropped on the floor next to the end of a row of bookshelves. I flipped open the top of the box and looked down at its contents. The interior space of the well-worn container was two-thirds full with broken, black canes. Each one of the wooden sticks was capped by a pewter house.

The box represented a lot of dead Brenfield men. I had never really considered myself a killer until that point in time. I had also never considered myself a person who had a need for keeping trophies. Apparently, they had filled some unfulfilled need for reassurance.

My little friend began to glow as I stood over the box. She was visible through my fancy gown after a second. She was obviously thinking the same thing that I was.

We were going to need a much larger trunk.

# chapter 24

The next decade under the new Brenfield leadership moved along without any great controversy. The détente held strong; mostly because neither side pushed the boundaries. They kept their distance from me while I was in the country of the King, and I didn't leave the country.

It really wasn't any worry to me that I stayed near home. I simply had not found any place that I had wanted to go. I had been quietly trying to build up enough courage to go visit New York City. I was just having trouble getting over the Boston experience. Apparently, six decades was not enough time to transform the mental landscape as much as I wanted it to change. It was hard to say. I only knew that I really wanted to explore America some more. I also knew that I needed to get out of England soon. I was getting old staying there. The thought of age had been with me since the Queen's passing some three years before.

Queen Catherine was returned to the earth in 1818. It was a sad day for me. She had been a good person, who had been placed in an unfair setting. She had accepted it and remained a good person. I had great respect for that.

On a side note, the year 1818 happened to be the same year that a girl named Mary Shelley published a book, which came to be known as *Frankenstein; or, the Modern Prometheus*. Her untimely death would slowly elevate her gothic piece to become one of the great works of literature. It is a favorite of mine.

Mary's publishing was only one of the things that happened around that time. My friend's husband, King George III, followed his wife to the grave in 1820. That let the regent finally become King George IV.

In 1821, many things were afoot. The person who piqued my interest the most was an Englishman, Julius Griffiths. See, Mr. Griffiths patented the first passenger locomotive. That locomotive was the start of the railroad industry in earnest.

Elsewhere, a young girl named Mary Ann Mantell found what would become the world's first dinosaur fossil. Actually, she found a stone in a pile at the side the road. After examination, it turned out to be a tooth from something called an Iguanodon. That was a strange name indeed.

Over in the colonies, a great change was taking place. A novel called *The Spy* was penned about a bloke from the American Revolution. It made James Fenimore Cooper the first great American novelist. A place called Missouri joined the union of states. It was reported to be a place out in the middle of the vast continent. It was no place I wanted to visit. But I was sure that, sooner or later, my cargo would. Who knew, maybe it would go by railroad.

Far to the south, a group of silly Americans called the American Colonization Society founded a colony that they called Liberia. It was in an unused part of West Africa. Their plan was to give it to freed black slaves so that they might just go back where they came from. Strangely, the notion that they might actually leave the land of plenty and go back managed to hang around all the way up to the time of the American Civil War. I'm always amazed by the strange things that people think.

The thought of independence was not lost on others. It seemed to be a good time for revolution and independence in the more southern sections of the Americas. The colonies of Costa Rica, El Salvador, Guatemala, and Honduras all declared their independence. Four new nations were born out of free will. Central America was coming unglued.

Seemingly to help them out, Bolivia, Peru, and Venezuela all went the revolutionary route. They had some help from Simón Bolívar and José de San Martin. As if that was not bad enough for Spain to absorb, the great lands of Mexico also declared independence from their overlords. The loss of all those resources dealt Spain a great blow.

On a more personal note, the year 1821 was the same year that my self-adopted country of Greece began its own war to free itself from the Ottoman Empire. That war would not be as short as the ones in the Americas would be. The war against the Ottomans would continue until around 1831. It would be a bloody affair.

On the topic of wars gone bad, I have one more event to relate. Back in 1815, Napoleon was defeated at the battle of Waterloo. The loss led to the end of the Napoleonic Empire as the French knew it. It also ended a series of what are known as the Napoleonic wars. It was a good thing for all concerned. Napoleon was a menace, a small man who had crazy dreams of empire.

In 1821, the press of the day was touting the deeds of an English inventor named Michael Faraday. He had invented the electric motor. No one really knew what revelations that little bit of genius would bring to the world.

The press of the day was also taking note of the famine that had sprung up next door in Ireland. Now, the Irish were a hardy bunch, but famine was never an easy thing to endure. I seriously considered taking a trip through the Irish countryside. The sport had to be much easier during a famine. It was a sure thing that Zoey had already made her way across the channel from Scotland. In the end, I decided against it.

All that famine and rebellion in the air stirred up my blood. I wanted to move. I had been moving in spurts over the past couple hundred years, and the urge had hit once more. I had been in England for a long time. All of the people who knew of my vampire nature were once again dead or about to be so. Plus, I was getting old. Popular opinion held my current age at about fifty years. I needed to reinvent myself soon, or the King would not believe that I was really me upon my return. I needed to do something sooner rather than later. Whatever I did, it needed to be legitimate.

Fortunately, the times were not like those of today. The information gathering of the day was poor and, combined with the standardized, parchment record-keeping methods, left big gaps for those such as me. I needed a new me. And, in the words of the Queen, she needed to be English. An English lady would be better for me all around. For an English transition, I would need to leave. I could leave and then come back new. I had done that before, and I could do it again.

The question was where to go? Greece was out of the question. They knew me in Greece, and there was still armed conflict. I did not want to become Italian. That left America. I could not go to Boston again. It was too soon to return there, and frankly, I hadn't liked it much. But America was a large place; there was a place there for me. I could finally go to New York and find out if it really was the great, new hunting ground that I had heard of.

Fortunately again, times were not what they used to be either. The act of leaving for another place would be easier than it had been when I had left for Crete. My company had long since turned into a corporation. That gave the business more structural stability. Each officeholder had been given some nominal stake in the corporation. Whichever Mr. Wyndell happened to be running the corporation at the time was the head of the board. That made me not as necessary and the whole corporation much more self-regulating.

Now, about 85 percent of the controlling stock was still in my name. That gave me the final word on all matters. I, however, was trying more and more not to intervene. The men chosen to be in charge were all very good at what they did. I usually observed quietly from a distance and then voiced my opinions to the current Wyndell at the helm.

In 1822, it was Mr. Fletcher Wyndell who was head of the Grey Cargo Corporation. He was a good and competent man for the task, much as all his predecessors had been.

Interestingly, when William had opted for retirement, Fletcher had reached out and grabbed the corporation by the throat. It seemed that he was almost driven to want to be in charge. That being said, during his rise to power, he did not even look at trying to gain control of the vast Wyndell conglomeration which had been governed over by one of the women in the Wyndell family. He seemed to have his eyes fixed on a certain "other" family prize, namely Grey Cargo.

Sadly enough, only years after William passed on, his sister Amber decided to follow him. It was fine; she had made a good run of it. With her passing, the reins of the vast Wyndell family fortune were turned over to her daughter, Angela Brown.

I was happy to see that happen for Angela. It made me giddy to know that somewhere else in the world there was a woman butting heads with men. I watched it all intently. I assumed that Fletcher didn't protest, because he understood that he couldn't run both entities efficiently. He could only do one of them justice. That was wise thinking, and all the Wyndell men were wise beyond their years.

Fletcher's brother Charles decided that he was going to follow me in my travels to New York City. He was old enough by that time to be a believable chaperone to a young lady. When I reached the Americas once again, I was going to need to be a young lady.

I figured that the best I could really hope to pull off was that of a teenager. After all, I actually was a teenager, because I had been but eighteen when I had become undead. I figured that I could realistically push my looks back to about fifteen. I had fully developed into a lady by the time I was transformed. I could shadow my assets, but that would require the same energy that I was now expending to make everyone believe that I was older. I really wanted to just be for a while. To let people see me and not some illusion of me. To do that, fifteen was about all I could hope for. Fifteen was good. I would be old enough to be both somewhat powerful and desirable. I actually had both power and desirability anyway. My vast wealth made me powerful, and nature had made me desirable. Fifteen was also young enough to let me live a new life for several decades before I needed to make myself new again.

It seemed a good idea. I would pick a new me and move to New York to become someone else. I decided that, this time around, I wanted to change myself as well. I had been noticing that my outward appearance was older than most of my so-called peers. By that, I mean that my look was that of an older age.

I still carried the trademark waist-long, straight blond hair of my youth. The look contrasted with the Regency style of the day. I would change my look to match the style of the time I was in—a shorter, more elegant style, maybe.

To be honest, I wasn't completely sure that I could bring myself to cut my hair. It had been long enough to touch my backside for the better part of two hundred years at that point. I simply was not sure that I could change that radically.

Not having a reflection helped the decision immensely. I knew what I looked like. I was young and pretty. People around me would reinforce that belief, so I knew it all too well. On the average day, when it was just me and the amulet wrapped in a white dress and my long hair blowing in the breeze that ran through the meadows of the estate, I felt more like Sara plain and tall. I was really nothing special to the world, I was just me.

I had become so comfortable in that mold that the only way to escape it was to change my looks. I decided that I would cut my hair. I would wear it off the shoulder as was becoming popular. Then I decided that it would no longer be blond; I would change the color as well. I would make my hair dark, like my nature. Then no one would know me anymore. I would be new. And, in a new country, I would be totally new.

Now, reality dictated that to actually become someone new, I was going to have to do a couple of things. First, I needed to find a new home in the new world. I decided, from conversations held during the gala that it would be in Manhattan. It was supposed to possess good and mobile middle and upper classes with which to associate. It also possessed rapidly dominating banking and commercial sections. It would be good for my business interests. Manhattan seemed a good place to set up a new office for my corporation. It was also far enough from Boston, so my past would not interfere.

All I needed to do was explain to Fletcher that we were opening an office in New York City and then just let it all unfold. That office would allow me continued access to the corporate entity and all of its vast tentacles. It would also help to keep me informed as to the constantly changing state of the world. I loved to get the news of the world from the ships as they arrived in port. It was all so fresh and exciting.

The next step in making the move was actually doing it. I would need to take a trip and visit my safety deposit vaults at the Child's Bank in London. Fletcher and I would create a new me, the same way Christopher had done originally. I would get Charles to cut off my hair. Then, I would no longer be Abbigail Boca.

# chapter 25

I rose to a gloomy London morning and wandered about my town house on Banker's Row. The morning seemed to be perfectly matched to my mood. It was the act of change that made my mood cloudy; nevertheless, it was work that needed to be accomplished.

I removed myself from the house and headed toward the Grey Cargo offices in my carriage. The gloom was thick enough outside that I was actually able to remove my opaque glasses and look out at the world unaided. That was very nice. It was like the world was trying to meet me halfway.

In my thumping about in the human world, it seemed that I had spent almost all of my time in the world of daylight. That meant that I was mostly outside during the day when the sun was strong. Because of that, I wore my glasses so often that they had become part of me. I had become used to seeing the world in my own twilight. I actually forgot at times that the world could look other ways. To sit in the midst of actual colors made me realize that I needed to be outside more during the night.

While I was thinking all of that, the short drive to the Grey Cargo offices passed by. I looked up to see my name and my happy girlhood home of the docks in front of me.

Clifford Murry, the general manager of the London office, stood by the main door of the offices, looking toward the sky. He was an imposing figure of a man. It came from a lifetime of work on the docks of the Thames. That was one of the things that hard work brought to men.

He was a man who knew every facet that his job possessed. He was also a good man and kind to others, or he was always kind to me. If he was not nice to other folk, then they probably deserved it.

"Good morning, Lady Boca. You found a right fine morning for a visit down to the docks." He smiled and tipped his hat, as gentlemen tend to do.

"Top of the morning, Master Murry. I hope that the morning finds you well?"

"Fine form, ma'am."

"That is good to hear. I can assume that Master Wyndell is in today, yes?"

"Down the hall, through the door to the right, and Bob's your uncle."

"Very good, then."

Master Murry held the door so I could make my way into the office. It was a common courtesy of the times. Being treated like a lady by those who really had no reason to do so was one of the nicest parts of being a lady.

"The weather is like a teakettle, Master Murry. If you keep your eye to it all the time, it will never boil."

"I don't want it sneaking up on me, ma'am."

We smiled at each other broadly. He was a rascal. We passed each other and were on to our individual business. I made my way to Fletcher's office, where, as predicted, he was hard at work. I snuck into the room without a sound and came to rest in one of the straight-backed chairs stationed before his desk. I took a quiet and unnoticed second to fashion my dress so as to present the proper image.

"You know, your forebears had nice leather chairs for their guests to sit in. Times change, I guess?" As my voice left my body, I received the desired effect.

Young Fletcher Wyndell came completely out of sorts. The handful of papers he had been studying went into the air around him as he jumped straight out of his skin. It was great. I could literally feel his pulse through the air.

I couldn't contain my smile as he glared at me. It took several minutes for him to collect his stack of papers from around the room.

Once that was done, he took several more minutes to collect himself. I sat quietly, with a Cheshire cat's grin on my face.

"I have done that same thing to everyone who has had that position, and the response is always the same. Just so you know, it really never gets old."

"Good morning, Lady Abbigail. I assume that you are here on business, or are you just out scaring the ghosts from people?"

"Oh, your ghost is still intact. If I had wanted to remove it, you would have gotten a completely different hello."

"Yes, I imagine you are correct."

"Smile, Fletcher, it's not a bad day you know, all things considered. You get to do something today that few people ever get to do."

"And that would be?"

"Make a whole new world."

"What's that, then?"

"Just what I said, Fletcher: make a whole new world. This world here is rapidly becoming done with Lady Abbigail Boca. It is time to go off and become someone new."

"Go off? Where to?"

"I am planning on going to New York City and taking Charles with me. You will need to open a new office in New York City. It will facilitate our needs."

"There are good trade opportunities in New York these days. That will be an easy accomplishment."

"Good, how long?"

"If we get started right now, I'd say six months to a year. We may be able to do it all sooner if we can acquire some help from the Boston office."

"One year should be fine enough. It will take at least that long to put together proper lodging in New York and then put things to rest here and in Bristol. Oh, and there is one other thing."

"Yes?"

"That will require a trip across town."

"Well, I'll get my coat. I assume we're going now?"

"Do other immediacies require your attention?"

"I suppose there is nothing that cannot wait until after tea."

"Marvelous."

Fletcher fetched his coat, and the two of us proceeded across town to number one Fleet Street, the location of Child's Bank. The bank was an unassuming, three-story, stone repository of rich people's secrets.

Child's Bank dated back to 1671, when it had been known as Child & Co. Back in those days it had been a goldsmithing business. Apparently, they had been so good that they had actually been appointed to be the jeweler for King William III. When Master Child died, sometime around 1713, his sons turned the company completely toward banking. They started issuing banknotes in 1729.

In 1822, the bank was being governed by its senior partner and majority shareholder, Lady Sarah Sophie Fane. She had gotten her title from marrying George Child-Villiers, Fifth Earl of Jersey. I must say that I liked Lady Sarah greatly. She was a solid brass businesswoman, the same as I was. She also was quite good at keeping secrets. It was rumored that every rich family in the city of London possessed one of her vault boxes. Even the royal family had used the vault boxes to keep its secrets.

We made our way into the safe, after a right fine questioning, and proceeded down the left side wall to a medium-size door marked number twenty-one. The unassuming door opened into the place that held my little batch of secrets. The vault had been the creation of Christopher, back when I had returned to London from the Americas. Not to put too fine a point on it, but it was the resting place for my real life. It contained all the things I guarded. There were several books that I had acquired that could not be openly displayed in my collections. There was a painting of me, which I had sat for while in Boston. I do say that the painting was holding up quite well to the passage of time. The depiction of my seminude form lying across the red velvet sofa was still vibrant and alive. As I stared at it once more, it seemed such a long time ago. There was also small strongbox on the floor, steadfastly anchored to the rear wall. That was the thing right there.

I turned around and quietly dismissed the guard who had accompanied us into the vault. He left without ceremony, as that was a usual occurrence. Fletcher stood quietly to the side, his eyes fixed on the painting inside the vault.

I removed two large, iron keys from the small, silk bag I carried and released the strongbox from its restraints. From out of the small cavern came a black box. I lifted it quickly and placed it on the table in the middle of the safe. The table groaned as the box came to rest. It was heavier than one would assume from its size, because it was composed exclusively of iron.

Fletcher stood trying to watch me and the painting at the same time. I can say it was not flattering.

"Fletcher Wyndell, if you are that fascinated with the painting, I will show you the real thing once we depart."

"I ... I ... ma'am?"

"Relax, boy, I gave up being modest a hundred years ago. I just leave it down here so I don't offend the good folks in London society. Besides, when you lack a reflection, it is nice to be able to see yourself from time to time."

"I didn't mean to offend, Lady Abbigail."

"There is no need for blushing, Fletcher. That really is what I look like. I guess it's fine to take it all in. Every other Wyndell man in your family line that I can think of has seen me naked at some point. It's one of the things that a confidant does, you know." He just stood staring at me. "Focus on the box, Fletcher. Focus on the box."

"Yes, ma'am."

On the top of the iron strongbox, in fat red letters, were the words "tabula rasa." I looked down at those words for a moment, thinking about what Thomas Aquinas had said about Aristotle's notion that the mind was a blank slate. It seemed very true to me somehow. I was a blank slate.

As I stood there thinking, the amulet hanging around my neck began to pulse in disagreement. She was trying to tell me that I *was* something. She was right, though how she was right I could not see.

I pulled myself from the momentary funk and unlocked the large, iron lock that secured my chest. I flipped open the heavy lid as if it were made of paper and removed a bundle of parchment from inside. The rolled-up pieces of parchment were bundled together by a red ribbon. A small tag with a date that had long since passed by hung from the winding. I held out the bundle to Fletcher with a back-to-business look on my face.

"Do you know what tabula rasa means?"

Fletcher took the bundle of parchment and inspected the small tag with the date.

"It's Latin. It means clean slate."

"That is exactly what you hold in your hand—my last clean slate. Those documents were produced for me by your grandfather Christopher. I show them to you now in the hope that you will do the same once more."

Fletcher opened the roll of parchment and began to read. His eyes flared wide as he began to see the depth of my life. One could tell that he found it revolutionary. He stared at the paper, then at the painting, and then at me, and it all began to form into a solid picture in his mind. It began to make some sense.

Unlike his father William, who had known all about me and my ways, Fletcher had never seen me as I actually was. I had always been perceived as older when he and Charles had been young boys. Apparently, he had gotten caught up in my glamour at some point. He thought I was actually half a century old. Ha, that was funny.

He stared deep into the text of the documents in an attempt to come to grips with their story. As he did so, I reached back into my mind and let go of the glamour that had been hovering in the air around me. It was fine in that setting, because we were alone in the vault.

It took him several minutes to surface from the documents. When he did so, he looked up into the wide, clear, eighteen-year-old eyes of Sara Anne Grey. At that point, he was utterly undone. He stared at me for what seemed like hours but was actually minutes. He looked me up and down, mouth agape. Then he looked back at the painting and back to me. The change in this features showed that belief was forming. The hardest part of most things was belief.

"Are you Sara Anne Grey?"

"Yes."

"Lady Sara Anne Grey, the only daughter of Master John Grey?"

"Yes."

"That would mean that you died in 1651?"

"Yes, I did."

I opened my mouth as wide as was comfortable and let my shiny, ivory fangs glint in the candlelight of the vault.

"You really *are* a vampire?"

"Yes, Fletcher. I really am a vampire."

"But how is that possible?"

"I educated you well enough in the ways of the occult to already know the answer to that question."

"I thought you just had an obsession with strange things."

"I do have an obsession with the odd, but that, I guess, is the difference between you and your brother. You could say that it's the difference between seeing and believing. Your great-great-grandfather Charlie had the same problem. Once he was forced to cross the bridge from thought to belief, he never really got his head right again. I'm hoping I won't have that problem with you."

"This makes so much sense. Everything makes so much more sense. I get the vague connections and the Brenfield thing. And the intertwining of our family's different businesses is all the clearer."

"It makes me pleased that you understand. Now, you should also know that this information comes at a price. That price is, quite literally, your life."

"Right now?"

"Goodness no. That only happens if you cross me."

"Oh, that's good."

"Hmmmmm."

"Out of curiosity, how many generations of my family have you known?"

"Add one more to Charlie's. His father Charles Wyndell was my first human confidant when I was just a newly born vampire. He was also, to this day, my truest friend. I have been looking out for his family since his death. I still talk to him as often as I can."

"You can talk to the dead?"

"Let's call it commune. I talk, and then I get a sense of their mood. The dead are usually pleased to hear from me."

"How's that done exactly?"

"I am undead, you know. It's a thing I can do."

"Oh, well."

"Now let's get back to the topic of the moment. Mr. Wyndell, can you do what I am asking of you?"

We both looked down at the papers in his hands.

"Yes, I can."

"Excellent. Now, will you?"

"Absolutely, ma'am."

"Good, now study them carefully, since they are staying here."

Fletcher took the task in hand. He read and reread the parchments. He studied the seals and the layout of title lines. As he did his work, I reflected on all the Wyndell men whom I had watched do my bidding. The sight warmed my blood.

When he finished his studious inspection, I locked it all back where it had come from, safe and sound. Then, we took our leave of the vaults. I stopped momentarily to bid farewell to Lady Child-Villiers.

The ride back to the corporate offices, where I had first procured Fletcher, was a quiet affair. He was lost deep in thought. I just stared aimlessly at the passing London scene. Outside the offices of the Grey Cargo Corporation, I deposited Fletcher on the curb and made ready to depart. Fletcher paused after exiting and then turned back to the carriage. He climbed halfway back into the seat so as to speak softly.

"May I call you Sara?"

"Never do it in public, Fletcher, never in public. But yes, I'd like that."

I rode off in my carriage, headed toward the estate. As Fletcher disappeared from sight, he was standing in the street, transfixed by the sign on the building in front of him.

Sadly, the year that I desired to use to make plans passed rather faster than I had intended it to. Apparently, time was playing games with me once more, or I had finally lost track of it. Which one of the two was correct was hard to tell. I hadn't really held a firm grip on time since I had come out of the shadows and started living with humans. It didn't bother me too much, because I enjoyed communing with the sun.

I made every attempt to have things handled in an immediate fashion. The fast fleet correspondence system that the corporation utilized helped. The captains delivered communications from one ship to the next as they passed, independent of their overall direction, until messages made their ways to the intended landing. That system moved my wishes across the Atlantic in nearly record time. Now, record time was still measured in weeks, but that was still better than the normal transit time of something over a month.

The new office of Grey Cargo was established in a suitable building in the New York Harbor area. The advance office staff obtained from Boston secured docking for numerous ships. I had great hopes that the new location would turn out to be a major player in the corporation.

Young Fletcher took the task of my new lodging to heart. I had explained so many times how I had hated Boston that he did not want to be involved in a repeat performance. So a wonderful new building was procured in a section of the city known as Manhattan. This Manhattan was full of newly minted, middle- and upper-class Americans, who were mostly comprised of New England Yankees. I was assured several times that my new manor house would suit my needs perfectly.

Fletcher assured me that my new home had the required level of affluence. Anyway, Fletcher seemed sincere about it. In a city that, in 1823, had somewhere around 150,000 souls, I assumed he could be counted on to find me the minimum level of society that I desired.

Things happened, and I quickly had a new business center and a new home. What I lacked was proper transport. It had been some time since *The Summer Storm* had been properly refitted. She had been released to the Mediterranean for general service when I had returned to England, and apparently, maintenance was an afterthought to the dock crews. My trusted friend was getting a little long in the tooth by the time I saw her once again.

That was unacceptable. Fletcher and several others tried to talk me into a new flagship, because we had produced new ships recently. That was something I would not hear of. *The Summer Storm* had been specially commissioned to move me about the seven seas. I was not going to leave her to rot, just because she required maintenance.

After I had to put my foot down, she was returned to the Bristol Mooring where she was refitted. The task turned out to be no small affair. The master builders at the mooring had moved on with the times as the art of ship building had changed from her day. Things had changed at sea a great deal since her keel had been laid down. Making her sound once more was as much a task of relearning as it was of rebuilding.

The timing of my old friend's needs was fortunate. Two vessels from the Americas, heavily laden with thick timbers, had been unloaded just before *The Summer Storm's* arrival. The timber was actually scheduled for other necessary repair projects, but it was redirected for my needs upon request. It was nice to be in charge sometimes.

In what was rapidly becoming the custom of the day, the shipbuilders at the mooring reinforced much of the ship with iron. That made the whole of the vessel lighter and stronger. That she actually became faster was an unintended benefit. *The Summer Storm* sailed out of the dry docks in as close to new condition as she could be.

All things being equal, I should have retired her long before. She had been roving the waters of the world for nearly half as long as I had, and the seas could be a rough place. A timber vessel rarely saw fifty good years in the salt. *The Summer Storm* had been better cared for than most, as I had a great affection for her, but her life had been long. I could not bring myself to let her go. She was my mode of conveyance. She just needed to be looked after. And that had been accomplished.

It seemed that, with the ship done, the only large agenda item left to handle was me. I had given Fletcher a long leash on the handling of that affair. I wanted him to get past his state of awe and back to the business of business. He needed to focus on the task with due diligence. As expected of any Wyndell man I had ever known, he rebounded quickly and went to work. Those boys were handy that way.

So one summery spring day, Fletcher appeared at my door, leather satchel in hand. As he proceeded to the study from the entry hall, I could feel a sense of calm reassurance enter the house. I greatly appreciated calm reassurance.

I had been wandering about the ballroom when he arrived. I quietly made my way behind him and sat in a customary position. Fletcher said not a word as he went about laying out the individual documents across the desk in front of him. They were all present: a transfer of title; a transfer of wealth and power; and one of corporate ownership, from one imaginary person to another. His work was masterful. The documents were the spitting image of the set in the vaults at Child's. I was new again, or I would be soon enough.

With my rapt attention, he explained each one of the documents and its relevance to the act at hand. Once completed, he sat back and smiled to himself quietly. It was a very Wyndell move.

"So, Lady Allison May Gibbs, how does it feel to be new?"

"I have always liked the name Allison, and May is nice enough for a young lady, but isn't Gibbs Welsh?"

"The Welsh are still somewhat English. It lays on the cusp of your home in Bristol and is under the King's dominion. You'll do fine being Welsh."

"You really are sweet, Fletcher, but I don't speak Welsh."

"That would normally be a problem, but Lady Allison grows up in the colonies, speaking English."

"I see your point."

"Sorted, then."

He sat back and smiled once again. I did the same. The documents were collected and rolled up so they could be secured—this time with a piece of blue ribbon. He handed over the rolled documents and then reached into his jacket pocket and retrieved a folded piece of elegant paper.

"You will need to put those in the proper storage. This you should take with you."

"Take with me?"

"It is a letter that you will send to the Crown, announcing the birth of young Lady Allison Gibbs from the Americas."

"You really did think of everything."

"It is the easiest way to get your new name into the Court records. It will look natural. The story you eventually tell the King about Master Gibbs, I leave to you."

"That sounds fair enough." I stood and collected the documents. They needed to be secured. I took them to the locked cabinet next to the pistols, where I temporarily stored such items. Using the keys from the desk to unlock the three locks required to access the document chamber took but seconds. I placed them next to a couple of books and closed the chamber once more. The books were volumes pertaining to the dark arts and the realms of the unknown world. They weren't truly dangerous, but they were definitely not the type of thing that should be left out for anyone to examine. Discretion was important.

I paused to think about the last time I had done this. It was with Christopher. The book that had been lying there that day was the journal of Kairynkutho. It had been my master teaching text on being a vampire. That work had been moved to the vault on Fleet Street long before for safety. I did not want that book seeing the light of day, even though it had taught me things that no other vampire knew about the world. It had also helped bring me the amulet around my neck. The two items had been a birthday present from Antonio a great many years past.

I cleared my mind of the stories of the past and returned my attention to Fletcher. He was sitting on the edge of the large, wooden desk with a quizzical look across his face. Whatever was coming next, I was pretty sure that it was not business.

"Yes?"

"I would like to mention before the next part that I have no wish to die this day. That being said, I am not here to offend you, Lady Sara, but I have had an image stuck in my head for some time now, and I was wondering about your mood at present."

"My mood is just fine, Mr. Wyndell. What might it be that you desire from me?"

I was already sure that I knew what he wanted. I wanted to hear him say it. He had been looking at the real me since that day in the vault, and each time he saw me, he seemed to catch his breath. It was really nice to be wanted. And that was the whole of it; he wanted me. I really needed to watch the words that came out of my mouth from time to time.

"When you asked me about producing the new documents earlier on Lady Sara, you also … "

"Forwarded you a proposition?"

"I would say made a suggestion."

"Oh, hell's bells and buckets, Fletcher. You are a grown, rich, and powerful man. If you want something, ask for it!"

"Well, then, if the offer still stands, I would very much like to see you."

I exhaled expressively. I could have just said no, but I had gotten myself into it, I guess. So I walked over to him and paused just inside comfortable dancing space. Then, I turned my back to him and tilted my head off to one side.

"You would like to see me? Well, I suggest you undo the buttons."

Fletcher, with surprisingly steady hands, gently undid each cloth-covered button holding together the back of my long, ivory dress.

When the last one was released, the dress slipped from my shoulders into a fine pile of cloth on the floor. I stepped from the pile and walked a few steps to the overstuffed, red leather chair, where I gracefully removed my corset, undergarment, and bloomers. They were laid one on another in the chair until I was left standing naked. I gently removed the amulet and sat it atop the pile of clothes to observe the show. It shimmered and then went back to its usual dull expression. I turned back toward Fletcher so I could see his reaction, then reached up slowly and released the red ribbon holding my hair, so it might fall into its natural position.

Fletcher said not a word. He just stood there, gobsmacked. I held my arm out to the side and swayed slightly like the belly dancers in *The Arabian Nights*. I slowly turned fully around once so he could see all sides. He simply stood before me in stunned silence. That would not do, so I lowered my hands to the standard hands-on-ivory-hips position. I was sure that he had seen that one before.

"You don't even have a response?"

Silence.

"I'll take that as approval."

"Yes, approval."

"Fine, approval it is, then. Now, get it all out of your system. Just because you get to see me doesn't mean you get to have me, understand? I said I am not modest. That is quite true. I am also not a fool. There is no way I can or will accommodate the thoughts in your head. I am a demon, remember?"

"Yes, ma'am."

He slowly started to regain his focus.

"In the beginning, the need existed for comfortable nudity. It came from my inability to hunt and kill without bollixing things up. I needed quick action, not uncomfortable posturing. So the modesty had to go.

"Now, so you are not confused, this event is strictly a matter of appeasement. I can hunt and kill quite fashionably these days. I am merely tempering your curiosity."

"Yes, ma'am, I understand. I just couldn't shake the image was all."

"And now you probably never will."

"No, ma'am."

"Fletcher Wyndell, we need to find you a wife. Yes, we do."

With that, I turned and headed back to the folded garments in the chair and my amulet.

# chapter 26

It was early summer, and the world was fully in bloom when Lady Abbigail Emily Boca walked away from the Grey Estate for the last time. The sun was moving itself high into the sky, and the air was warm to the touch as it moved on a gentle breeze. It was the way days were supposed to be.

The trip from my home down to the Thames and the offices of my corporation was pleasant and short. When I was a human girl, I remember the trip lasting for what seemed like hours. Now, time passed in no grand measure. The perception of time is a funny thing. It moves along at the pace of one's individual mood.

The smell of water-soaked timbers and pitch mixed with the commodities of the world along the docks of the Thames was something that never changed for me. I had always found it to be magical, and I still did that day. The smell of all that kept me connected to the sea. It was the smell of the movement of trade. It always seemed exotic and mysterious, like the stories that usually accompanied it.

I removed myself from the intoxication of it all and found *The Summer Storm* riding low at her dock. She was loaded and ready to sail. That was a good sign. I stood and inspected my old friend from dockside and could only marvel at the craftsmanship of her refitting. She was tall and proud. All my flags were flying fully from their hangers off the top mast. Her captain was waiting patiently on the weather deck. Charles stood next to him with a cool look of satisfaction. Apparently, I really was leaving.

I moved to the waiting area, where Fletcher stood. He seemed content with the matter as well.

"Good morning, Lady Abbigail. I hope good weather is a good omen for your new adventure."

"I am sure that it is, Master Fletcher. I am sure."

"Your belongings are all aboard and properly stowed. Everything is in place for your reception at the other end. Things should go quite well."

"Very, very nice. Everything sorted. I leave things in capable hands here, I think."

"I am sure that you do."

"As am I. You have always done fine work, Fletcher. I am quite sure that you will continue. Please keep me updated on the status of it all. You know I don't like surprises."

"Speaking of surprises, there has been a pair of gentlemen closely watching the load out. They carry the black canes of the Brenfield Society."

"A pair, you say. There usually are two, but they usually don't come round together. They must be preparing."

"For what?"

"For renewed hostility, Fletcher Wyndell. Yes, I think renewed hostility. Please keep a firm eye on the estates and the corporation, just in case."

"Yes, ma'am."

"While you are doing that, please pop over to the residence of Sir Gregory Rooney. He has a daughter named Catherine who is but a few years younger than you."

"I hardly need help finding a wife."

"She is smart and fit. She will make you a fine wife. Besides, he is expecting you presently."

"Ma'am."

I left Fletcher and proceeded up the gangway to board my trusted conveyance. At the top of the gangway, I paused to stare down the docks at the two Brenfield men in the shadows. I waved and turned toward the captain and Charles. The two men promptly vanished into the stacks of cargo.

Greetings were exchanged as *The Summer Storm* slipped her noose and headed for the salt. I quickly settled in to do what I did on such voyages. I stood on the weather deck and charged the amulet, and then

I sat in my cabin and read *The Arabian Nights*. I had read it so many times that I really didn't need to read it again. I knew what words would come next at any given point. That was fine; it wasn't the point. The book was a way to pass the time, as it had done on numerous occasions. You could tell it had traveled. The volume was worn around the edges and scuffed from much handling. It showed its age. That was fine too; I had possessed it for a long time.

At a point somewhere midway in the crossing, Charles appeared at my cabin door and informed me that it was time for the change. I had decided to change my appearance when I had formulated my new plan. I had altered my general look many times over the years. I was young or older, sometimes with my customary long locks and sometimes with shorter hairstyles, but always something around the standard model. Since I was basically me, I never really noticed when it would change back. At some point in time, my hair would return to its natural, inconveniently long length, which reached down to my bottom.

That time, my change would be somewhat more radical. I was sure it was necessary, but change was something I didn't do well. I still don't. Charles assured me that it would be fine, so I sat still while he cut my hair until it sat just off my shoulders. I had never had hair as short as it was at that moment. For my whole life, it had been long. It felt strange. My head seemed to weigh less all of a sudden. It took some time to get used to.

After a couple of days passed so I could become used to having my new, short hair, we were at it again. Charles used liberal amounts of hair water to darken the shade of my locks. It took many treatments, because my hair is naturally a golden blond color. Finally, he managed to achieve my new look as a dark, brownish black color.

The alchemy that he utilized came in the form of Mrs. Gibson's Innocent Liquids. She had been peddling her wares to women since 1780 and for good reason. I had lost my natural blond color and acquired a shade more befitting my nature.

I admit freely that, at that point, I desperately wanted to see myself. The fact that I had no reflection became instantaneously annoying. I wanted to see the new locks that were making the new me.

The fact that I couldn't see myself didn't seem to bother Charles. He continued straight on with his pursuits and refashioned my eyebrows as well. That made me actually look like a dark-haired girl. Charles was a perfectionist. I appreciated that, because he was the one doing the work.

Once he was finally finished with the physical changes, I was a new person. I even felt like a new person. I really wanted to see the new me. Charles had a solution. I sat quietly while he drew a fine picture of the new me. It was grand. I had had no idea that he could do such good work. I didn't even recognize me. That thought made me very pleased. I still carry the picture that Charles drew for me. It sits inside my copy of *The Arabian Nights* as a page marker. It makes me happy every time I look at it.

Now, Charles being a perfectionist, he didn't stop at the physical. The next things to go were my trademark white dresses. I had been wearing white since I had been a little girl. I liked white; it was clean and fresh. I have never been a fan of colors. Oh, they looked fine on other women; I just preferred tradition.

Charles came up with a wardrobe full of fine, blue dresses. He assured me that I would come around to wearing colors. He was so sure that he took all of my white dresses and threw them over the side of the ship. That way they were not a temptation. I supposed I had no choice, at least until we landed.

My new dress that day was a blue, silk affair, cut in the Regency style. It was nice, but a little thinner than the muslin that I was accustomed to. I liked a little thicker clothing, since I no longer produced my own heat. To compensate for the difference in the cloth, I started to be seen with a Turkish wrap or a short Spencer jacket when I was out on decks.

The one concession that I refused to suffer for Charles were the shoes. He had purchased several pairs of leather slippers to accompany my gowns. There were also several pairs that were thin silk or velvet.

That was farther than I was willing to go, at that point. I had two forms of footwear: sturdy leather boots of medium heel and good repair, or none at all. I was keeping my boots. They were not the standard of fashion that they had been in the later part of the eighteenth century, but they were necessary. I had to be able to fight. There would be no fighting men while wearing fashionable slippers. Fortunately, Charles didn't argue the point for long.

The whole ensemble was completed by stylish and demure gloves. Gloves were becoming a required item for any lady who would be seen outside of the home. There was also a small reticule for the important items that I needed to carry. It all looked good together.

By the time we made landfall in the new world, I had become so comfortable in my new skin that I had almost forgotten about the old one.

Apparently, not everyone else was up to speed with my change. When we disembarked at the docks of the new Grey Cargo offices in Manhattan, the two Brenfield men stationed to observe my arrival didn't even notice me walk by. That was a sign that it was a good disguise.

*The Summer Storm* made slip at the docks in an area along the East River. They were known as the Schreyer's Hook Dock and apparently had been part of the original wharf construction. The real Grey Cargo dock, located upstream from Schreyer's Hook, wasn't ready to receive traffic when we landed.

Looking down the docks, near the point of the island stood the edifice known as Fort Amsterdam. Apparently, Fort Amsterdam and its opposite wall along the landside had actually been constructed when the city was still New Amsterdam. They had been meant to repel the British. I have often wondered if the Dutch knew that they failed.

Nevertheless, that day we quietly disembarked and made our way to a waiting carriage for our ride to my new home. For the time being, it would actually be both of our new homes. Charles had been too occupied with me to find proper accommodations for himself. It wasn't really an issue as the Wyndells were extremely wealthy by that point. Their association with me had made the family untold fortunes. A fine home would soon be his.

I have never really mentioned this before, but wealth and power were things that were kind of lost on the whole Wyndell family. They were all a group of doers, not possessors. The collection of wealth and its inevitable use to make more wealth was strictly an act of business to them. They lacked the old money attachment that most rich families possessed. I have always believed that is why Amber ended up running the family fortune, so many years before.

All of the Wyndell men, independent of their natural business abilities, had been born to be men of action. They were the street-level, bare-knuckled sort. They just took that and turned it toward business affairs. It made them ruthless. It didn't, however, get rid of the street mentality, which is why I had kept them all close.

Charles and I made our way north along broad streets toward what would become known as the Upper East Side. As we rode along pleasantly, watching the surroundings of our new home, I was sure the Wyndells' sensibilities would suit them here as well.

As I said, the area that Fletcher had chosen for my new home was in the Upper East Side. Today, it's known as one of the wealthiest neighborhoods in the United States. In those days, it was not as affluent. It was just the richest of the section that Fletcher had to choose from.

My new home was a multistoried, stone and glass beauty. Ornate and polished and possessing all the touches of wealth, it presented an image of power. I liked that very much. The interior of the residence was as remarkable as the exterior. There were numerous large rooms on each floor, all of them with grand appointments. It all seemed special.

Fletcher had compensated for the lack of a dungeon with the addition of a secret salon on the top floor. It possessed one way in and one way out off a room that would become my new study. The salon had a small balcony that looked out over the city but could not be seen from the street. I commend the craftsmen who had built it for a job very well done.

As I walked around and inspected the whole affair, I wondered what it must have cost me. Momentarily, it made me ponder the tale of *The Count of Monte Cristo*. He, like me, was buying a new life. He, like me, was also interested in revenge. His was nobler than mine. He was righting his name, and I was just killing Brenfield men.

The Brenfield Society was obviously ramping up its efforts. No matter; killing two was as easy as killing one. I could tell that, soon, there would be new blood flowing in those new streets. I could just feel it coming. That was good. The need for killing had been festering inside me for some time. I don't mean hunting and feeding but straightforward killing. It had started to work itself up since my last run-in at Court with that damned Sir Anthony Bridgemen.

They wanted confrontation; they were about to get it. That was a good thing. I wanted to let out my dark side more than I ever had in the past. That's not true. The episode on the Russian steppes made my blood boil much worse. The darkness was truly necessary from time to time. I could tell that my friend in the amulet was ready as well.

I stood in front of the large windows of my new study, in my new city, with my new identity, and considered the rules. There was but one I could think of.

"Détente at home, open war abroad."

"Who's at open war?"

Charles had walked in as I was thinking aloud.

"I am, with the Brenfield Society. The rules were détente at home and open war abroad."

Charles handed me a glass of thick, red wine and turned to look out the window with me.

"It appears to be a fitting place for open war. A quick lay of the land would be nice before we start, though."

He smiled and I did as well.

"Yes, Charles, we will conduct a battleground survey first. It's sound advice."

"You really don't like them, do you?"

"Aggravating bunch of blighters."

"I agree."

With that, we turned our attention to the city of New York. I could tell that I was going to be very happy there. I might even stay.

# chapter 27

Orientation was the new rule of the day, so I spent my time getting the lay of the land. It seemed important to establish hunting grounds that would not draw undue attention to me. The grid layout of the city made quick maneuvering fairly easy. The whole system of streets ran basically northeast to southwest and was bounded by water on all sides. The East River separated me from Long Island; the Hudson River to the west separated me from the mainland. The Harlem River to the north separated me from the Bronx, which was another part of the city. To the south toward the docks and the Battery was the area that made up the harbor.

The harbor was a flashing sign for any vampire. As history is so happy to show, the docks of New York were the gateway to the American dream. Millions of immigrants from all across Europe and the far-flung regions of the globe came to America. Their first stop in the land of plenty was the docks. The great funneling effect of the processing centers made for a ridiculous hunting opportunity. There were just so many unknown people that no one could understand, because they spoke different languages, that it was impossible to not find good targets.

The vast majority of the people coming to the new life that America offered were not the kind that the police of the day were concerned about. They were the poor and downtrodden. They were the ones who had to find a new hope, so they came to America. Little did they know that, when they got there, something like me would be waiting for them.

Now, to be honest, I really didn't kill that many of them. I just hunted enough to keep my skills sharp. It was what I had done for a century. I did so because the amulet had been providing most of my energy needs for most of that time. I showed her the world, and she kept me from need.

The hunting of immigrants was so good that I didn't kill much anywhere else. The rest of the city was left safe to be as it was. I admit it was not really fair to the immigrants, seeing that I was also an immigrant, but life wasn't fair.

The only real killing that took place away from Ellis Island was the killing of Brenfield men. They died wherever I found them. They were dispatched as quickly as possible. The two at the docks the night I arrived were the first two to meet their maker.

My change in appearance had so thrown them that they were still camped out watching *The Summer Storm*. Apparently, they assumed that I was still on it, waiting or something. Who knew what they were thinking; I didn't stop to ask.

I returned to the docks two nights in. The distance I covered from my new home back to the docks of the East River would have been a great journey for a normal person. For me, it was a quick run.

As a side note, heating up during strenuous physical activity, or combat for that matter, isn't a real problem for a vampire, as a general rule of thumb. Vampires do not produce their own heat. The heat generated by physical activities and hot environments is just absorbed by the body. We really don't have a need to sweat so we can cool down. Frankly, that actually helped with the hygiene situation present in the eighteenth and nineteenth centuries.

The night on the docks was warm enough. The air was still and smelled of salt and pitch-soaked timbers. The two Brenfield men were basically standing right where I had left them. I could see them quite well as I snuck back to the water's edge.

One man was stationed at the gangway entrance. The other man had moved off to a point where he could observe the stern of the vessel and its open water side. *This is good,* I thought. *Killing one of them at a time is easier.*

I made my way down the side of the building the first man was standing next to. I made no sound. My new, darker clothing blended into the night well and made me like a wraith.

At a point just out of arm's reach, I paused. I could smell the scent of stale cigar smoke when the man expelled his breath. He was also wearing distinctive cologne. The fragrance made me think that the man did not lack for wealth. So be it.

Reaching out slowly and with care, I slid my fingernails down the outside of the building. The sound of my nails sliding across the coarse brickwork was unmistakable to someone close.

Just as I had expected, the man had been there a long time. He uncoiled like a cobra. Spinning about, he brought up his cane to thrust it like a short sword. With the reflexes of the undead, I reached out and grabbed the cane at the near side of its apex. The sudden jarring stop of the cane and my superior strength shocked the larger man.

He stared at me, wide eyed, for several seconds as the realization set in that I was actually who I was. Then he opened his mouth to yell. He never got the chance.

At the point that surprise turned to understanding, I brought my right hand around in a hook that shattered his Adam's apple and damn near ripped his head from his shoulders. His body lifted from the ground with the blow, and he impacted the ground again several feet away.

Now, when I was a newly born vampire—merely days old—Antonio had taught me that sometimes a vampire's brute force was the only thing necessary to win in combat. Brute force really did have its uses. It was the only thing required in that situation.

The blow that I inflicted on the large man ripped the cane from his hand and left him all but dead. The problem was that it had raised the attention of his comrade. I quickly faded back into the shadows, taking up a station close to the building, so as to be unseen in the blackness of the alley. The second man, who had been waiting and watching the vessel's entryway, came to action and proceeded toward the noise. As he approached the spot where the initial sound had been generated, the man reached down stealthily and removed the steel end's cap from his cane. A sharp wooden point appeared. Weapons; they were carrying weapons. They really had decided to change the game up.

The man made his way to his comrade and stopped to assess the damage that he had sustained. The first man lay on the ground, his back against the cobblestones, gurgling blood and trying to stay in the grip of life.

"Hold on, old chap. We'll get you out of here soon enough."

"Unlikely."

At that one word, I stepped from the darkness of the building wall and slipped the first man's cane through the second man's heart. The rush and then sudden stop of heartbeats was not lost on my senses. The second Brenfield man stood momentarily and then tilted to one side and fell to the ground. He was dead before he hit it.

I turned and walked quietly to the living one, who was still on the cobblestones where I had deposited him. Looking down at him, I concluded that he was British. He was from my lands, but old and sad and mistaken. I smiled a soft smile and then promptly slammed my boot down on the man's rib cage. The little life he possessed left him promptly. It seemed that the war had officially begun.

I set my trophy of canes off to one side and collected the bodies. I carried the bodies down the docks toward the fort. In a good, secluded spot, I heaved the bodies into the river. Returning to the scene of the crime, I collected my prizes and disappeared into the night.

As is always the case in young and wild places, no one cared about the two bodies floating in the harbor. That was one of the good constants in the shipping world. I liked that consistency. It allowed me to do some of the things I did.

As expected, the Brenfield Society took the news hard. More men in black coats were sent to replace the two I had killed. Fortunately, I had several months of quiet streets before that happened. But news came one day. News from the docks made its way to me that two men, matching the description of the Brenfield Society, had appeared. They were reinforcements or, more aptly, replacements. The two men in question died shortly after arriving and in much the same fashion as the first two men had.

Those two men were replaced, in turn, by four more men about a year later. The news of their arrival came up from dockside swiftly. The continued news of where they went and what they did was quick to follow.

I have always said that one of the great things about the world is the availability of useful information. It was usually a full-time occupation for the people who handled such things. The men and women who procured information around the docks and in the streets and alleys of most cities were always happy to have the work. They worked for almost anyone who was flush and not of the establishment. They were also good at spotting opportunities for continued service. Because of that, they were discreet and confidential. The people who plied their trade in New York City were definitely so.

I tended to be a little more generous than was necessary with the group. It helped to maintain honesty and confidentiality. Both of these were things I found to be important. They helped me know what was happening in my new city. They also let me know who to kill.

That being said, when the new Brenfield men arrived, I knew. Killing four men at a time was easy enough when I knew where they were and where they were most likely to be. I just waited for them to move unsuspectingly into the shadows, and in one of the tight back alleys of the city, they ran into what they sought. I picked a spot for them where I could kill one at a time. It was something akin to the Spartans and the Persians. Once the first was dead, it was a simple matter to dispatch them in quick succession. Off to heaven or, most likely, the other place.

Once the confrontations moved past two at a time, I made the necessary step to weapons. Two men I could quite easily kill with my basic array of vampire talents. Groups of men could also be handled that way, but it took a larger amount of energy. It also increased the chances of losing or of sustaining injury. The use of weapons was a way to level the pegging.

On most occasions, I utilized a Venetian stiletto. It was a nice, close-quarters weapon and came in differing sizes depending on the specific use. The one I was particular toward had a hollow, seven-inch blade and was not quite a foot in length. It was small enough to be concealed on my body and handled efficiently in tight quarters. It did lack reach, but my physical advantages more than made up for that. One thing I really liked about the weapon was that the hollowed-out blade left a puncture that resembled an oversize ice pick. That helped me disguise my activities. The ice pick was the weapon of choice for the large gangs of men that roamed the city streets. Since the gangs used the ice picks so often, no one was going to look in my direction for trouble.

More time in New York City passed, and four more men appeared. Shockingly, they mysteriously met sticky ends in one of the many back alleys. The police of the day found the bodies stabbed to death and stripped of all their valuables. They had been robbed and killed, sure as anything. It was a predictable reaction to what seemed an all-too-everyday occurrence. I took their wallets to ensure the robbery angle. The wallets were discarded into lit hearths, and the money was given to the homeless on the streets. That helped to ensure my anonymity.

After the third round of four men had come and gone, the pace began to ease. I wondered if the society chaps were having trouble recruiting. It seemed a thankless position to take up. Then I thought better of that. Maybe they were just going to come at me from a different angle. I sent dispatches to every outpost of my empire, and good news helped to calm my worry. No changing tactics again.

Apparently, they really just couldn't keep the ranks full. I understood; good men were hard to find. I had killed sixteen good men in just over four years. The quiet that the recruiting gap produced made me anxious. I never liked to wait for my enemy to appear. Sadly, it was a cause-and-effect situation. Before, my other mass killings had been semiplanned affairs. The New York City campaign, as I came to call it, was strictly reactionary, so I waited for them.

Five years or so later, I stood on my private balcony, and young Charles III informed me that they had returned once more. The news came late, as it turned out that they had been around the city for some time. The new group of men had dropped all the trappings of the Brenfield Society. They worked on more of a street level and blended into the background very well. They had also become less stately and more rough and ready. They were ex-military types, who needed work and liked adventure in strange lands.

It took longer to discover these new adversaries, because they tried to stay well hidden. That is, they stayed well hidden until they started their inquiries into the occult. Looking for me exposed them before they could find me. That was all it took.

Battling with ex-military Brenfield men turned out to be a fairly good workout for my skill set. They put up an admirable challenge. Given bigger numbers, they might have succeeded. Now, I liked a solid workout once in a while. I just hoped that it was not going to become the norm.

The new men and their evolving tactics forced me to evolve as well. I reached out and expanded my use of the information network. That increased my reach out over most of the city. Soon, I had a system of informants that no one could get past. When the next men arrived, I was ready.

Interestingly, the new men took much longer in getting around to looking for me. That did give them longer to live. I realized as I watched them that it also gave the men time to study my system. Letting them do so was a tactical error on my part, and one I could not let continue. In response, I ratcheted up my informants to try to identify the men early, so I could kill them as soon as they arrived. I wanted to present an obvious, fortress-like front to my opposition. That I did.

We were seven years in by that point. They had set the time line and the tactics for every skirmish. I had decidedly won every encounter that had come along. I was beginning to think that it could continue indefinitely. The thing that I wondered more than anything else as it unfolded was "Why just me?" The Brenfield Society had men all around the globe? Was I the only one they were treating hostilely? Or were they hunting all of the vampires?

Interestingly, that answer came along with the next group of men. One night, two sturdy men left a ship down at the docks. Several ships down, a tall, dark Spanish man stepped from a ship as well. The step of his boots on wooden timbers sent ripples of both fear and tension down the docks. It seemed that Antonio had come to join the killing.

# chapter 28

Our new world and its ever-changing field of combatants to test ourselves against gave everyone involved a new framework to operate in. That framework, for me at least, had produced a large network of informants. It was a system that I had not utilized to date, because I liked my means to be somewhat more discreet. It had also forced me to learn new and more varied stalking techniques. That had the result of pushing me away from feeding and straight on to plain, old-fashioned killing. I had relaxed away from savagery and honed my skills for killing to mimic the natural scenes around me. That type of killing blended into the rhythms of the city.

That was my personal take on things. Others responded in a different fashion to such pressures. Signor Antonio Boca was one such representation. He took the broad strokes of this new framework and decided that it presented an opportunity to return to the older ways. He had always liked the older ways. They meant more individualism. They also meant more savagery and a more aggressive style of killing. The carnage that he left in his wake during his time in my new city would drive a wedge between us that would take decades to remove.

It can be said with full honesty that I have never considered myself to be an overly graceful or even painless predator. I am accomplished at killing and at feeding, because I treat it like combat. You get in, inflict maximum damage on your opponent, and get out. It is really that simple. The shorter and cleaner the battle is, the less likely I am to sustain injury. I never intentionally target people who would produce cause for full-on, war-like combat, save for the members of the Brenfield Society.

That being said, the members of the Brenfield Society were adversaries. They were dealt with swiftly and allowed to die with an amount of dignity. Those were my views of the situation. As I said, they were not held by others.

The night of Antonio's entrance onto the docks saw the first two ugly deaths that he would bestow on my new city. Needless to say, they were also the two new enemies of mine. Apparently, he had followed them to New York from somewhere in Central America. He had been spending time with his Spanish brothers. The time had done nothing to relax his hatred of mankind, which had been awakened out on the Russian steppes. It had only made it simmer.

The unabashed hatred of the human species that Antonio unleashed on the docks that night was far more than anything those men had prepared themselves for. See, most men are good at fighting men. They are not good at fighting the demons that live in dark places. Most demons, like me, simply killed their enemies. Others, like Antonio, took things to a whole different level.

In Antonio's case, a creature that has been alive for centuries moved like nothing else imaginable. Needless to say, when Antonio came off the gangway from the ship he had arrived on, no one was the wiser. He moved without ever being seen by the men in his sights. He followed them along the docks and on toward the outer walks that led to the streets of New York. Their moving off into the shadows that night was a sad mistake.

Sensing opportunity, Antonio moved in behind the second man in line and secured a firm grip around his neck. The man reacted immediately to Antonio's first strike, but the strength of the battle-hardened warrior was no match for my demon friend. The man, firmly in the grasp of evil, could do nothing to save himself from what was to come. His struggles to free himself from the vise-like grip of Antonio were only met by more pressure. As Antonio clinched his massive and powerful hand, the man swung and writhed in the air. His attacker allowed him to continue that for several seconds, looking at him with disgust, before the real attack came.

The cagey old vampire, the man who had turned me into what I was, had lost his like for tact sometime before. On that occasion, he swung his head back, so he might fully expand his jaw, and planted both of his thickly scarred, ivory daggers into the top of the man's skull. And with the shattering of skull bones from the thick, ivory fangs and a quick snap of the wrist, his sturdy and skilled adversary was finished. The end had come before that corpse hit the cobblestones.

The audible crack that the shattering of the man's skull had produced as it echoed off the walls of the shadowy alleyway had garnered the attention of his companion. The first man spun in the direction of the noise and lost his composure at the gruesome sight that awaited him. Antonio just looked at the man over the top of his friend's dead features and winked, as if to say, "Don't worry, you're next, chap."

The first man did, in my opinion, what any sane person would do in such a situation. He turned and ran toward the lights of the streets beyond. He probably thought that his years of training would get him free of that situation. He was so wrong.

The man managed to close the gap to safety by several yards before the concussion of his friend's corpse against his back brought him crashing to the cobblestones. The momentum propelled the man several more yards down the alleyway before he finally rolled to a stop.

Antonio confidently strode over to the bruised and bloody man on the cobbles. The savage killer pounced and was on him before the man could even begin to move from under his companion's lifeless body. Antonio landed a boot on his thigh. There was a loud snapping sound as the man's leg bone splintered into irreparable pieces. The second battle was all but over, and it hadn't even really begun.

Antonio reached down through the twisting of bodies and secured a firm grip on the man's left arm. Placing a knee on the man's chest, he ripped upward so fast and hard that it tore the man's arm from his body at the socket. The dismembering happened with such speed that the victim didn't even know it had taken place. However, microseconds afterward, the man began to swim in his own universe of pain. While the man proceeded ever deeper into the blackness, Antonio held the bloody appendage up over his own head and let the blood drain down into his throat. The blood-soaked carnivore was tossing the arm aside and readying himself for the next piece when his victim somehow pulled himself back from the brink of blackness. The centuries-old demon looked down on his adversary in an almost whimsical manner.

"Why, you still possess some life. Tell me, why have you come to this place?"

"To … to … find the vampire named Boca."

"That is what I thought. I too have done the same."

Then, as if nothing else mattered in the world, he slammed his wide fists into the dying man's rib cage. There was another audible snapping sound that echoed off the surrounding stone buildings, and the man's rib cage folded like an organ's bellows. Muscled fingers slid into the fold like a knife and secured a grip on his sternum. Another quick snap and the man's chest had been splayed wide open.

In the shadowy darkness of a new world alleyway, the old vampire lowered his head and inserted it into the large opening. It was a move befitting any wild beast. Once there, he drank up the masses of pooling blood and, in so doing, stole away whatever was left of the other man's life force.

Antonio looked about the scene in obvious self-approval. Deciding that the deed was officially done, he simply stood, straightened his blood-soaked clothes, and walked off. He pulsed with energy as he disappeared into the blackness of the night. The twisted carcasses that were his victims lay in a crimson pool on the cobblestones. The stench of death hung low in the air like a sign that the plague days had returned.

As quiet returned to the scene, the man who had witnessed the savagery transpire from his blackened rooftop post vomited onto the rooftop next to where he sat. He was green with fear and almost too overcome to relate the events to me some twelve hours later. I, too, was a little put out when the telling was done.

The surprise came when Antonio made no real attempt to contact me. Apparently, he figured that his outlandish actions would draw me out to him. He was correct. I did hunt him down, but the time it took to pull me into action was just long enough to let my bad mood fester into ill temper.

Originally, I had hoped that the olden days of our ancestors had been reserved for the members of the Brenfield Society. That silly hope would not turn out to be the case. My sage mentor and maker had fully embraced the darker side of his existence. That was evidenced by the finding of an old couple north in the Bronx. They were found several weeks later, in much the same condition. They were by no means dispatched as violently as the first, but all the other hallmarks of his handiwork were present. That changed my opinion that it was merely some angst he was dealing with.

Some weeks would pass between the deaths of the old couple and his next masterpiece. That time, fully a half dozen men were found on Roosevelt Island, in the East River, in much the same condition as the old couple from the Bronx. The new pile of corpses was what pushed me off the settee. There were just too many bodies being left to rot.

Finally being forced into action, it didn't take much real effort to track down the blood-soaked killer. My keen vampire sense drew me right to him. I thought it would be harder, but I had apparently gotten better at utilizing my abilities as the decades had passed. Finding another vampire in a city the size of New York turned out to be an easier affair than planned.

As a side note, today, there are so many people living inside the five boroughs that a half dozen vampires can reside there quite comfortably. In those days, one vampire stood out as obvious as a new business opportunity. I didn't pay any attention to them, because unfamiliar vampires passed me by fairly often. They came along at varying intervals, normally following their prey, and were respectful of my territory. Antonio lacked this respect.

One moonless night, I took to the streets and, after a fashion, found my old lover hovering over a pile of bodies in the back alleys of the Marble Hill district. He possessed much the same look in person as in the stories I had been hearing. It was sad how the high had fallen.

"On your knees, covered in blood—that's a good look," I said as I appeared out of the shadows. He didn't stop directly but finished what he was doing. That meant that he knew I had been watching him. Somehow, arrogance had never been one of his trademarks. Finished, he stopped what he was doing and looked up toward where I was standing.

"Well, well, if it isn't the great enemy of mankind herself. Blue dresses and dark hair now, I must say that I approve of your new look."

"I don't approve of yours or of the way you procure it."

"I'll kill my food any way I choose, Grey. I made you who you are; don't forget that."

"No, you changed me from a human into a demon. I made myself who I am, thank you very much."

"Well, I'm still the older and stronger of us, so you really don't want to push me."

"Antonio, at the dawn of the day, you just think that you're superior. In reality, you require no great battle. Now, stop this thing you are doing in my new city. Frankly, it's becoming difficult to deal with."

"You think yourself better than the one who made you?"

"Not better or worse but definitely equal to the task. You need to find a path back to the person you were when we first met. This thing you are now does no one any good."

"You don't approve of my carnage?"

"I do not."

"You were always a reluctant killer."

"I kill when it's time for killing. There is no need for sport. It draws unwanted attention."

"Killing is killing. It is what I do."

"But it is not who you are."

"Oh, yes, it is, Grey. And it always has been. Even when I was a human man, so many centuries ago, I was a killer. I have always been good at my one true art. I have been a killer for so long that there is no other thing to be."

"I don't believe that to be true."

"Well, then you need to adjust your childlike, rose-colored view of the world."

"I will not, and if this is all you can manage to become, you are going to need a new place to wallow in your senseless despair."

"Pardon?"

"You heard me clear enough."

"I don't believe that I did."

"Go find yourself a new bolt-hole."

"I will do no such thing. I like it here."

"You will leave and on the outgoing tide. Or you will get a confrontation that neither of us wants."

"From you?"

"Yes."

"You are not remotely demon enough to kill the likes of me."

"I think that if you search your blood-soaked memory, you will find that statement to be false."

"Hmmmm, Constantine. That was a long time ago."

"Not that long ago. Now, be gone on the next tide, and do not search me out again. If you are no more than you appear to be, then I have no use for you."

"We're done, then?"

"It would seem so."

"Does that include the business interests?"

"No, just you. My business will continue to be happy to do business with your business."

With that, I drifted back into the shadows and headed south toward my manor. I could not believe it had actually come to that. I had been a vampire for 180 years, and the one constant in all that time had been Antonio. Well, most likely business and then Antonio. He was my maker. He had taught me the hard lessons. I did the shaping that made me the creature I had become. He had become nothing more than another beast in the wilderness. How had he fallen so far from where we had started? How was that possible?

I retreated to the safety of my private study and wallowed in remorse. I was sad: I was sad for Antonio; I was sad for our friendship; I was sad that I had lost to the darkness the only true love I had ever known.

In the midst of such sadness, I sat in my little, sunlit study and did the one thing that I could do. I cried. I cried for the better part of a week. I took me that long to come to terms with it all. I had cut the cord. I was alone in the world, save for Charles. Apparently, the solitary existence of the vampire was a fact to be faced.

After a fashion, I dried my eyes and looked out over my home. *There are still humans*, I thought. *I still have human friends, and for now, they will do just fine.* I would stay with the humans. So be it.

# chapter 29

"Hello?

"Hello? Are you there somewhere?

"I can't see you. Can you see me?

"I wish I could see you."

The longer I stood in front of the empty, full-length mirror talking to myself on that dreary, February morning in 1833, the more concerned I was that I was going mental. I had also spent several hours staring into the bedchamber's large dressing cabinet, looking for something to wear. It was full of lovely dresses; I just couldn't seem to make a decision.

At some point during the cabinet ordeal, I had migrated to the mirror. There, my lack of substance sent me witless. I was supposed to be there. I was not supposed to be … empty. I knew it should be, but it just wasn't supposed to be.

"Hello? Are you there somewhere?"

I had risen early with the sun to meet Charles for some business. I wanted to meet him; I just couldn't get it together. I had left him waiting in the study so long that he eventually came to find me.

When he entered my bedchamber, he found me naked in front of the mirror, talking to myself. The amulet sat on the nightstand pulsating with a displeasing, red glow. As he stopped and took in the depth of my situation, he probably wished he hadn't left the study.

"Hello?"

"Abbigail, what in the name of St. George's Ghost has sent you round the bend?"

"It's Sara."

"Pardon?"

"My name is Sara. Sara Anne Grey is my name."

"Your name is Abbigail Emily Boca."

"I hate that name and the man I acquired it from. My given name is Sara Anne Grey. I have been looking for her, but she does not seem to be near."

"Have you gone completely mental? We have a meeting with Mr. Worthington to discuss moving his cannons. You need to pull things back together."

"I don't care for business; I care for myself."

"You are not lost, a little barmy maybe, but definitely not lost."

I stared into the empty mirror for several minutes before continuing. I really wanted to see myself. I knew it was not to be; I knew it. I just wanted to see myself.

"I can't seem to find the handles so I can get it together. I don't know what has happened, and I can't explain it."

"I've got a pretty good idea. You have finally come to the realization that you got your heart broken, and for once, you don't know what to do about it."

"You think?"

"Yes. It's kind of refreshing, actually. I wasn't completely sure that a vampire still had a heart. Apparently, the organ is intact, and there are still some lingering emotions in it."

As Charles talked about my lack of concern for human things and how Antonio had done something to shake out things I had never experienced, I began to calm down. The more he talked, the more I calmed down. The warm cadence of his voice soothed the frayed pieces of my mind.

I made my way back to the bed and sat on the end. I couldn't really hear what he was saying anymore, I was just tuned into the sound of his voice. The rhythm and warm tone of his speech was the thing that I needed. He talked as if he cared for me. He cared for me? That thought made me content.

"So you need to get dressed or we will be late for our meeting."

"Charles?"

"Yes."

"Can I ask something of you?"

"Ask."

"Whenever we are alone, could you please call me Sara? I do miss that name."

"Certainly, Sara."

"You have a gift, Charles. It hasn't surfaced in your family since I took up with the first Charles Wyndell. He also had it. He had the ability to talk to me as if nothing was ever wrong. It takes great skill to calm the mind of a demon. You do it without even putting forth effort. I appreciate your compassion."

"I'm going to move our meeting to tomorrow. I think some quiet time would serve you well, Sara."

"You are a good lad."

He removed himself from the room and sent a message back to the office via the doorman. I returned to the wardrobe and retrieved a blue dress. I had been naked for so long that I forgot the usual undergarments and pulled myself into the dress. I retrieved the amulet and placed it in a small pocket, which was sewn into the folds of my dress. She pulsed with agitation but mustered no response. She knew she could affect things from the pocket just fine.

"Relax, my sweet companion. I won't leave you behind. I have some thinking to do, and I need to do it myself. I mean you no disrespect."

My friend seemed to understand my position. The pulsating stopped and a warm, white glow took its place. She really was a good judge of situations, my little companion locked in crystal.

Quietly, as in times past, I made my way barefoot across hard floors out of my bedchamber and through the residence to the study. Continuing to remain still, I moved the book on the shelf that released the catch and opened the door to my private study. I walked to the windows that overlooked Manhattan and looked out. Life was still out there below me. I retrieved the amulet from the folds of my dress and hung it on a small golden hook that had been stuck in the window casing. There she could absorb all the power she wanted from the day and watch humanity go by. That made her calm as well.

I made my way back to a large, leather chair and sat. Charles wandered in as I was sitting and took up station in the chair next to mine. We sat the remainder of the day. Not more than one or two sentences passed our lips. We just sat quietly looking out over the Manhattan rooftops and enjoying the companionship of solitude.

I processed the whole of my life as we sat. I thought about it all. I came to realize that Charles had been correct earlier when he had said that Antonio was my first great love. I was so young when we met that I had had no good idea of what love really was. He had given me everything that I had come to know about love. In return, I had gone to the ends of the earth to save my love, whereas he simply broke my heart and moved on. I had never had someone do such a thing to me before. It was new territory for my emotions.

As I pondered, I also came to realize that it had been inevitable. He was demon. Demons are not known for their fidelity. What I also came to realize from my small psychotic break was that demons were not meant to process emotional dramas.

I guess that explained his position; however, it did not explain mine. I was (am) also a demon. I should have taken it all as coldly as he had. That, once again, made me wonder if I were different from other vampires. Maybe it was my constant interaction with humanity. Something must explain my broken heart.

As I sat in Charles's comforting company, I came to realize that the past was the past. I should move on. Looking back on all that now, I believe both Nietzsche and Freud would have made a three-ring circus out of my issues.

The sun was pushing its way off the edge of the earth and dragging the remains of the dreary day along with it by the time I was satisfied with myself again. I was pleased that I had come back to myself. As a rule, I was usually a contented person. I basically liked myself. I had come to like Charles as well. He had many good qualities.

"Charles?"

"Yes, Sara."

"Will you be my friend?"

"I already am, I think."

"When I was a human girl, my life was quiet. I had few friends that weren't somehow attached to Father's business. When I became a vampire, I was so young. I was a girl, and then I was ageless.

"In the midst of that time, I met a good man. He taught me about life. I don't just mean vampire stuff but how to be a good person. His name was also Charles. He was a great many things, but under it all, he was my very best and truest friend. I would really like another friend."

"I too am many things, depending on the day, and I would be happy to be your friend."

"Thank you, Charles."

"Have a good evening, Sara. I will be around in the morning so we might start anew."

"Very well."

Charles stood and wandered out of the room to make his way home. I retrieved the perfectly content amulet, and the two of us headed for the bedchamber. I shed the blue dress and hung the amulet back around my neck. Upon touching my skin, she sent warm pulses of energy through my body. All was well with the two of us. I slid beneath the covers and closed my eyes to the world.

The next morning's sunrise brought Charles's return and a bold blue sky. I chose a stylish dress and large, round-brimmed hat to match the color of the day. The amulet was tucked into her usual hiding spot and then surrounded by dabs of French perfume. A pair of low-heeled riding boots and a pair of fancily stitched, elbow-length gloves, and I was ready.

That day, I was sure that I looked grand, even though I couldn't see myself. When I met him in the study, Charles confirmed my thoughts.

"Good morning, Sara. You look quite fashionable today. A lovely choice for business, I think."

"Thank you, sir. You are most kind."

"What do you say we head across town and handle some business?"

"I think that would be excellent."

We proceeded to my carriage and headed out across Manhattan. We made our way south to the docks and the office of the Grey Cargo Corporation. The New York City office was an opulent affair. Everyone in the Atlantic Americas who did trade with us assumed that it was our headquarters. I suppose that, in a sense, it was, because I was there. The remaining members of the board and Fletcher were in London, however, so that would always be the real seat of power.

While we are talking about business, I really should bring things up to date. The corporation had offices not only in Boston and New York but also in Georgia. We also opened one far south in a place called Brazil. It was stationed at the mouth of the mighty Amazon River. That was a river so vast that one would swear it went all the way to the Orient.

The offices were supported by a large, dry-docking facility north of the Georgia office. Large stands of timber were plentiful, and land was inexpensive. The docks could pull a ship completely out of the water. It was a very nice facility and serviced many ships outside of our fleet.

On a personal note, my interests had expanded into logging and cattle. It seemed that the middle of America was an endless place. My cattle farms were in a place called Texas. The timber came from somewhere called Colorado. I had never actually been to any of those places, but the men I hired were the rough-and-ready sort. And the money that they returned was real enough.

I have always had many side ventures, like the cattle. They help me spread my wealth around. If the cargo business took a dive, I didn't want to end up in the poor house. If it were to take a nasty turn, which it had done in the past, I wanted to be prepared.

That said, I wasn't really worried about it anymore. By 1833, I had become rich almost beyond counting. I would survive any business calamity; I just wanted to be prepared for uncertainty. That was good business.

Such was my dealing with Mr. Worthington—a bit of good business. Mr. Worthington made cannons. He also made the ammunition that went in them. He was one of those American success stories that the history books like to dwell on.

Mr. Joshua Worthington had come, with no money, to America from a small town in northern England. He had stepped off a ship in the land of opportunity and found great success through hard work. At the time of our meeting, he was a hugely successful man. His company had secured contracts with most of the states' militias and the federal cavalry. They all liked the quality of his cannons.

I liked the quantity of his money. He had goods that needed moving and had money to make it happen. We set up transport for his cannons down the coast and then inland through the rivers to wherever they needed to go. If that somewhere turned out to be not near a river, we handled that as well. I am proud to say that my father's little shipping company had really become a multienvironment transport corporation by that point. We were no longer just shipping. We moved goods wherever they needed to go, and in return, men like Worthington paid handsomely.

The business with Mr. Worthington went as expected. What I had not planned on, when we walked in that day, was that he had a son. I had not been informed that he had children. Young Jeremy Worthington was the picture of the rough-and-ready Yankee. He was tall, solid, and handsome in his features. His attributes made him attractive, not pretty. He was definitely no dandy.

I was so taken with young Mr. Worthington that I had a little trouble with the business of his father. I had to make myself concentrate so as not to look the fool. Fortunately, that did not happen, and the whole affair ended on a good note. There would be business conducted between our two companies.

We parted ways at the end of the negotiations and headed to do whatever it was we needed to do. I headed out to the docks and the smell of the salt air. The soaking, wooden timbers and heavy pitch made me content. I strolled along the docks where my ships were anchored. The stevedores ran about around me, moving one thing or another. It was not so unlike times long past when I had been human.

It seemed that the harbors of the world had been the one great constant in my life. They kept me grounded in reality. They gave me hope for the future and a very real connection to my past. They, more than anything else, were who I was.

As I strolled along the docks, I thought about happier times back when I was a little girl. Then, I had always found the docks to be a place of intrigue. I had had many good times, though probably not the times that make little girls into good young ladies. That was one of the reasons my nanny Ms. Palmer had had such trouble with me when I was young. I had always been a little more rough-and-ready than she had thought proper of a young lady. She had done her best to bring me into her world. She had mostly succeeded, but she couldn't remove the docks from my blood. That, I think, was just as well.

I stood and watched the stevedores undertake their varied tasks and stumbled onto an idea. Maybe it was time for a change. Not one of scenery, but one of attitude. I had managed to find a new friend, maybe I should go find myself a new love as well.

That seemed a grand notion, but where to look for such a thing?

# chapter 30

As the year of 1833 dragged on, it seemed that events forced me into action far from my new home. I ended up out on an adventure once more. Not an adventure as in times past; not the hardy days of hunting down mischief, as in Rome—no, this was all business.

It seemed that the news out of the north was not good. A Scottish brig named *The Lady of the Lake* had sunk near Cape St. Francis. Normally, other vessels in distress wouldn't be of concern to me. The news I was interested in was different; the *Lady* wasn't the only ship in harm's way.

*The Lady of the Lake* had made her crossing in the company of another called *The West Bay*, a British brig that I happened to own. She didn't end up sinking, but her encounter with the shoreline of the cape was not to her liking.

*The West Bay's* captain steered the vessel into calmer, shallow water and managed to save the cargo from the salt. In doing so, *The West Bay* became wedged and was immobile. Somehow, a ship on the edge of foundering and at risk of pirates seemed to require my undivided attention. The cargo on the ship was a composite of materials and goods from companies that I had known for a long time. I thought I would save them some misery if I could.

A move back to something urgent was a nice change. I had spent several months deep in thought since my little psychotic break. Mostly, I had thought about trains. I had been to Colonel John Stevens's demonstration of a locomotive in New Jersey back in 1826. The whole thing seemed exciting but in much the same way space travel was in the 1950s. You know, it was fantasy.

It stayed that way until 1830, when Peter Cooper built *The Tom Thumb*. *The Tom Thumb* was the first American-built steam locomotive. It also had the feature of being able to run on a common carrier rail system. That rail system was one that had been in the process of being assembled since about 1815.

The new locomotive service carried people and even had sleeping cars for long-distance travel. The new means of travel would open up the interior of the American continent. That was an opportunity that I could not let slip by. Access to the bounty of the continental interior was a pass to untold wealth. I had spent months trying to think of a way to make inroads into that new land of cargo opportunity.

I had been dragged out of those thoughts by the news of *The West Bay's* trouble. I decided to go, investigate the fate of my servants, and lend whatever assistance was required. So two vessels were loaded down with materials and men. Then we all headed north toward the Cape of St. Francis.

The face full of salty air that I received as we headed north was a welcome change from the stale air of Manhattan's city streets. The wind blowing my hair about made me instantly happy. My mood lifted to one befitting happier times. It also seemed to have an effect on my traveling companion. The amulet's natural dismay seemed to turn around to a fine acceptance of the world. That, in and of itself, was a nice change. Maybe, in some small way, I was helping my companion be a little bit more at peace with existence. Hatred and distrust were not always the answers to things. There were always different levels of being.

Our trip up the coast from New York to Newfoundland was not long enough for my liking. The salty air and ocean swells were more comforting to me than the dry land we encountered. The area around the Cape of St. Francis was not the nicest of places. The land was wild in every sense and far from civilized. The ocean passing by its shores was never calm. The harbors that dotted the coastline were little more than fur-trading stops and logging towns. The remainder was forest, where the men were sturdy and the dead were not missed. Hmmm, just my kind of place after all.

The crew set up our base camp in a small, logging settlement called Jamesville. It was a quaint name for a rough place. All of the locals were instantly suspicious of a group of unfamiliar people led by a woman.

Up until they saw the color of my money. They eased up when they learned that we could pay cash. Then when they learned that we had only come for the ship, they relaxed a great deal more. After we put a little green in their pockets, we were all deemed acceptable.

I took the opportunity that the situation presented and decided to do some killing. Not enough to be bothersome, just for a little practice was all. Not right away, of course, I let the crews get to their tasks first. Once they had seen the cargo transferred to a seaworthy vessel and repairs had started on *The West Bay*, I removed myself from their midst to find some sport.

The sport of the day turned out to be a transition back to the Boston days. In Boston, my practice group was the local Indian population. They were definitely not what one would call sport. They all fought for their lives and fought quite well. Those northern woodsmen were very much the same. They were adept at survival.

My first night of running loose in the deep, dark woods brought no targets of opportunity. I thought, for a split second, that I was losing my edge. Normally, I had little difficulty finding a meal. I continued on unhindered, and the second night brought better results. I stumbled upon a logging camp deep in the woods.

The tall, heavily muscled man guarding the camp paced around the edges of the area with a stout musket, ready for action. He was on the lookout for bears and other nocturnal creatures or any unseemly men. I suspected from looking at him that none of those things would truly be any match for him. I was also sure that he had no intention of encountering any vampires on his watch. We were a completely different kind of creature. Sadly for him, he was no match for the likes of me.

I watched the man pace about his route for some time, until it seemed well established. The man had a natural rhythm to his movements. That was a good thing. I liked predictability. As I observed him, I looked around and found a spot next to a small group of aspen trees. They were in a dark recess of the woods, away from the firelight, which illuminated the camp's immediate area. I crouched down next to one of the trees and continued to watch my prey. The big man walked to a point close to me several times. He would get to a spot near me and turn to proceed a different way. Many times, he came to me and left.

I sat until I was sure of his movements, and then it was on to the attack. The man came in along his predetermined course, and when he hit the spot closest to me, I sprang from my blind and ran straight for him. The man instantly knew that something was happening and raised his musket for defense. He was almost at the ready by the time I had closed the required distance to attack. He was faster with his reflexes than I had expected. No matter. I dropped to the ground and swept my legs around in a wide arc. The top of my boot connected with the side of the man's calf and swept his feet from the ground. The big woodsman whirled through the air as I righted myself back into a crouched attack position. Somewhere in the air, he separated from his firearm as the two of them somersaulted above me. Each of them hit the ground with a resounding thud, but they didn't make enough sound to be heard at a distance. That was nice.

With reflexes that had not been truly tested in some time, I sprang forward and was on him before he could muster some kind of a defense. My knees impacted his chest as I landed square on him. His eyes went wide as they locked onto me. He possessed a look of both shock and anger. The realization that a woman had done this to him made anger swell inside his heaving chest. That was the plan—make him angry. Angry men are meals full of adrenaline. Those are the meals that I like most.

Not waiting for him to come completely back to his wits, I slapped a hand squarely over his mouth and yanked his head to one side. The impulse whip of my neck as my mouth came open, exposing my thick, enamel fangs, was automatic. No time elapsed between the hand on his mouth and my teeth firmly in his neck.

I began to pull blood from his body as fast as possible. I sucked on the openings until my mouth was full before I swallowed the first time. Some blood spilled from my lips as I did so. I wanted to work fast, as not to be overcome by the bloodlust.

If you haven't drunk any real human blood in some time, bloodlust can be a powerful thing. It can make a vampire lose composure. It comes when the blood initially absorbs into the body. For me, it's that point where the blood slides out the back of my mouth and down into my throat. It produces a high, much like ingesting a drug does. I need to focus to work through it unaffected. I needed to wait and then hurry.

I continued to drain the man of his blood in an efficient manner. He fought me for the better part of the attack, and then as they all were, he was gone. He had a lot of go for a human. There was a point when I actually thought he was going to put up a good fight, but it was not to be. I continued to work quickly, draining as much of his blood as my own system would comfortably hold.

Deciding that I was temporarily finished drinking, I pulled my fangs from his neck and stood upright over his lifeless body. I dusted the earth and leaves from my clothes. I made sure I looked proper—it's a girl thing—and then I hoisted my trophy over my shoulder and headed out into the night. I couldn't properly feed where I had killed him. We were way too close to the camp. I ran back through the woods until I found a place that seemed safe and easy to watch. There, I threw my victim from my shoulder and dropped to the earth beside him. Feast time was finally at hand.

I had been doing a lot of killing lately but not much feeding. The killing of the Brenfield men was an act of necessity and needed to look like a random act of violence. I did not feed on any of them. During that period, I had been getting my energy from some small amounts of animal blood and the deep energy stores in the amulet. It had really been some time since I had fed on a human being. I wanted to make this human a well-deserved meal.

Shifting my knees about to find a comfortable position, I returned to the task at hand. A small whip of the head to flip my hair out of the way, and *wham*, the fangs hit home in the same puncture holes that they had produced earlier. I drank and drank until there was no more to be had. I had removed every ounce of adrenaline-laced blood that was available. That blood coursed through my system and made me exuberant with power.

I removed my fangs from his neck, and then I removed my knees from the earth next to him. I stood and looked down at the corpse at my feet. I somehow felt bad for the man, but not bad enough to be concerned that he was dead. I was doing what I was meant to do. The corpse at my feet—that was my true calling in the world. I was one of the ways that the human animal was kept in check. I liked that fact greatly. Few women ever got to stand level with men. As a vampire, I got to be their better.

Completing my work, I dismembered the corpse and scattered the pieces to make it look like an animal attack. Then, deciding that I was done, I turned away from the logging camps and headed back to the little inn in Jamesville. It had not taken long to do my deed, as the men of the tavern were just turning out into the streets for the night when I snuck into the building's rear entry.

I snuck a quick glance through the kitchen door at the men in the tavern as I passed. It was a reflex from my childhood, when I used to wander the tavern-lined alleys off the docks at home. I never knew any of the people that I saw; they were just a young girl's entertainment. That night I was struck by a man sitting at the end of the emptying establishment. I swore I had seen him before. I was sure of it. But what was he doing there of all places? That I had to know. It was too curious.

I quickly made my way to my room and changed into clothing more befitting a lady. I combed my hair, splashed on some perfume, and found my fancy, lace gloves. Deciding that I finally looked proper enough for the setting, I headed back downstairs to the tavern's main entrance. Since the tavern was actually part of the inn, they had the same entrance. It was not an extreme leap to see me there, nor would I have to explain what I was doing. It was self-explanatory, so I went straight in as if I owned the place.

The young, sturdy man sitting at the bar was entertaining the local talent. He noticed me directly upon my entry. He lifted his face and smiled brightly. I was correct; I did know him.

"Mr. Worthington, this is an interesting setting in which to make your acquaintance once more."

"Lady Boca. I'm pleased to see that the big news in these parts is you and not some other rich lady."

"You would be expecting someone else?"

"I can say, ma'am, that I wasn't expecting you."

The maiden he had been amusing giggled at the remark. I paid her no mind.

"I am here seeing to a vessel that found bad fortune along the Cape. What brings you to such a far-flung location?"

"The family has logging interests in the area. I'm checking on our assets."

"Hopefully, things are good?"

"They're the usual. And your ship?"

"Good as can be expected."

"At least, not all was lost, then. That's always nice."

"It is, isn't it? Well, it was nice to converse with you once more, Mr. Worthington. Hope your travels go smoothly."

"Lady Boca, will you be still at the inn tomorrow?"

"I believe so."

"I would be honored if you would have dinner with me. We might continue our conversations about strange lands and travel."

"That sounds fine. I'll make sure I depart from the ship site at a proper hour."

Then I turned and walked off, not waiting for a response. I didn't need to wait; the conversation was over anyway.

The next day passed quickly enough. The actual task of mending my wayward vessel was in the hands of men who required no assistance. I was more of an unnecessary, motivating force at the point. That was what I usually did anyway, motivate.

As a side note, to be perfectly honest, up until 2008, I have never really done a legitimate day's work. When I was young, I had no need to, because young ladies did not do such things. Now that times have moved on, I have enough wealth to employ others for such tasks. I did do a great deal of business when I was younger, but I do not believe that counts in this context. I am not rationalizing, mind you, just clarifying a point.

I made my way back to the shantytown inn at an hour befitting my status. The men seeing to the refitting would be hours more, until darkness drove them to their rest. When I arrived, the streets of Jamesville were quiet and empty, its inhabitants out making what passed for a living. The inn was quiet as well.

I went straight up to my room and guessed at what my appearance must have looked like. I had not brought anyone with me who knew of my condition, so I had no one to help me with my lack of reflection.

Having no reflection is one of the things about being a vampire that I really could do without. It is nothing if not annoying.

I changed out of my worksite clothes and into a simple, dark-colored dress. I had been in the mood for wearing trousers at the ship, since they were much more utilitarian. Here, they would not do. A lady needed to look like a lady, after all.

It was here that Charles's youthful genius had come into play. On the voyage to America, he had cut my hair quite short. Once, my hair had lain way down on the top of my posterior; now, it just barely brushed the top of my shoulders. The new, shoulder-length hair was much more manageable. I really no longer needed the mirror for my hair. I simply ran my hands through it several times and then pulled it back away from my face. I would need to thank Charles properly for that when I returned to New York.

Feeling good about my appearance, I sat and held the amulet tightly against my breast for several seconds. As I did so, my little friend imbued me with warmth. It made me feel human again. I just liked to feel that way, in case someone were to touch me. I decided it was a necessary camouflage, and my friend in the amulet was always happy to help with such things.

Once sure that I looked and felt like the lady I was, I headed downstairs to the inn's quaint, little dining area. It was not a proper dinner room in the fashions of civilization; it was more of a hollowed-out space with tables that men came to so they could eat. It possessed all the requisite dirt and bullet holes required of such places. I did my best to pay it no mind. Such places were the way they were.

The wait was short, and I helped to pass it with a glass of bourbon. Sooner rather than later, young Mr. Worthington appeared. He was scuffed and unclean around the edges. The sight of him entering made my heart beat a few times. It had been some time since that had happened of its own accord.

Mr. Worthington strode across the seating area and properly bowed before sitting. It was nice that he possessed some gentlemanly skills. My heart beat a few more times. Interesting.

"Mr. Worthington, you possess the look of a man who's had a full day."

"I have, thank you, Lady Boca, and if it is not outside the proper protocols for such a wild land, please call me Jeremy."

"That's quite fine. If you please, call me Abbigail."

"That's a pretty name. I believe it means 'Father Rejoices' in Old English."

"Yes, it does. It's curious how you know so much about different things."

"I have found that a little knowledge about everything treats me just as well as a wealth of knowledge about one thing. It tends to keep me ahead of the game. So did he rejoice? Your father, that is."

"He was a lovely man, who worked hard and loved his daughter without limit. So I guess the answer is yes."

"That is nice to hear."

"Thank you, Jeremy."

The conversation continued on a lighthearted note after that. We both talked about the different places that we had traveled to and territories that our business interests were in. He turned out to be surprisingly well-traveled for a young man. I, of course, did not talk about a lot of the places where I had been.

The two of us sat and ate and got on quite well. He had many nice qualities. Mostly, he was unassuming. That comforted me greatly. He didn't pry or ask probing question of me as other men had. He just took what was presented to him and went on.

Interestingly, he wasn't unassuming in an ignorant fashion. He was smart enough to know what questions not to ask a lady and when not to probe. That skill meant that he had been around other members of the aristocracy. I got a sense that he had been properly schooled, so maybe that was the case.

Our evening went along nicely, right up until the end. The whole affair ended in a manner that was unplanned and quite unladylike. I will say, in his defense, that he was sensitive and well schooled in the things men do. I mean, very well schooled indeed. It had been a long time since I had ended an evening more tired than when I had started it.

Now, to be truthful, I had been hoping it was going to end that way. That was why I had chosen a dress that was easy to remove and pulled my hair back so it wouldn't be in the way. I had been hoping it would end that way, but I hadn't been planning on it.

I could tell that Jeremy also enjoyed it well enough, as he managed to find his way back to my bed the remaining five nights that we were at the inn in Jamesville. For such a young man, he was well versed in the ways of the bedchamber. Each evening ended with some new surprise. It also ended with each of us being exhausted. If I hadn't possessed the amulet and her infinite power supply, I'm not sure I could have continued.

Sadly, the time came for me to return to my own realm. Jeremy was headed off as well. He had been scheduled to depart two days earlier, but he had postponed his departure until mine. I told him that, whenever he landed his boots on New York streets once more, he should come around my way, if he chose. He said that he would happily do so, and that was that.

My ship made its way down the coast to New York. *The West Bay* followed behind in a high and sturdy stance. The men had done a fine job, and all was well in the world.

# chapter 31

I sat in my quiet, private study on a sunny, winter morning at the end of 1836, pondering my lot in life. I was happy enough. My business was thriving as it never had before. Charles and Fletcher proved to be a dynamic team. Our New York City office had become the business hub for all activities on the western side of the Atlantic Ocean, and the London office still managed things as a whole.

I had observed that the current set of Wyndell brothers got on much better than others had. The men in that family have always had an every-man-for-himself philosophy, which seemed to permeate the generations. The two boys being friends as well as business partners proved to be a rather refreshing change. I was pleased with them both.

I was also pleased with the remainder of my business holdings.

I had been worrying about the cattle farms in Texas for most of the year, because the news coming north from that area was not good. The Mexican president, Santa Anna, had moved an army of some three thousand men to an outpost known as the Alamo. It was in a place that would become the city of San Antonio. When he got there, he killed everyone who had defended it.

The Texans had apparently enough of Mexican rule, because they declared their independence from Santa Anna in 1836. A man named Sam Houston was put in charge of the fledgling militia. He was a capable man for the position; he had routed the Mexican army at a battle in some place called San Jacinto. The Texans seemed to think that they were forming a new republic. I was worried that it would all go to pot.

Fortunately, the throes of war had little effect on my cattle farming interests. The men in place at the stations kept it all intact. That I found to be an honorable endeavor. It was always nice to see people take pride in things.

As for other interests of mine, they were mostly out in western states that lay along the Rocky Mountains. They were distant enough to be free of the strange happenings of the day. They went along making money.

There had been unrest in the Americas for as long as I had been there. The very idea of independent states left open many avenues for discord to develop. The dissension eating away at the soul of the country was slavery. Personally, I had long been on the side of the free man, so I was happy to be residing in one of the northern states. The developing sentiments put everyone on one side or the other.

It seemed that, as a rule, you were on one of two sides. In the southern states, where slavery was well established, the majority came down on the side of continuance. In the northern states, the population was much more of a mind for abolition. Those states saw the rise of the abolitionist movement. In 1836, there were some five hundred such abolitionist societies. The states that held them passed laws that saw slaves entering their lands as free men. That led other states to pass legislation legalizing the practice of slavery.

Texas was one such state. That made me sad. Because of such things, I had come to believe that man was the only creature on the planet that intentionally preyed upon itself. It was such a waste.

To make matters worse, the southern states held a majority of votes in Congress. With that, they installed a ruling to prohibit the discussion of antislavery petitions from even being presented. That acted like a cork in a bottle. It seemed that the pressure the ruling created was going to continue to escalate. Like many of my new friends; I feared where it would all end.

The remainder of my thoughts were not all bad. I had been reading a newly published book by a London court reporter named Charles Dickens. It was called *Sketches by Boz*, and it was quite good. Fletcher had sent it to me when it was released. He was very kind in that sort of way, because he knew I missed London on a subconscious level.

I had also been reading essays by an American gentleman named Ralph Emerson. He held an opinion that the modern industrial way of our society was not a good thing and should be rejected for a more sublime way of experiencing one's life. That thought process would become known as transcendentalism.

I was a child of the preindustrial and industrial ages. I had seen one come and the other go. I could see the merits of Emerson's ideas. I did not agree. I liked progress; it allowed me to measure the passage of time. I was a proponent of experiencing what life had to offer. Progress was good.

My like of progress revolved mainly around industry and mechanical things. That did not extend to the ever-changing landscape that was women's fashion, though. Sadly, the Regency era style of the 1810s and 1820s had given way to a much more puffed-up version of things in the 1830s.

The straight lines and natural flow of Regency dresses were nice and unconfined. Unfortunately, the new decade had seen a return to a tighter waist and the addition of petticoats. It wasn't 1790 again, but it felt close enough. With the changing waistline, the hem had also risen from the ground. One could glimpse a lady's shoes or the bottoms of her petticoats if she wasn't cautious. I was much more a fan of the bygone, floor-length era.

As if that weren't enough, the bodices of the dresses had become higher so they enclosed the bustline but were looser in fit. That required any proper lady to wear a corset. The sleeves had also grown out from the previous dainty and slim affairs to large puffy things that ended about the elbows. If I added the overdone hat of the day, with all its feathers and whatnot, I felt very much like a walking, layer cake.

I have never really liked the way one cannot get in and out of dresses quickly. That was probably why I had embraced the styles of earlier decades. The loose fitting lines had made changing out of blood-soaked attire easier. The current fashion offered no such convenience. (Sadly, hindsight has shown me that it would get worse before it got better.)

I found that I would spend time picking at my dress sleeves in a vain attempt to move the extra cloth somewhere else. The staff of the house had slowly become accustomed to the whole show. I have never liked puffy clothing. Whenever I knew I could get away with it, I went for a style more befitting the colonial style of previous times. I would wear a simple skirt with a petticoat that was topped with a modest shirt and tight-fitting jacket. That style of dress meant that a corset was mandatory. I have always been drawn to corsets as I got the required support for my bustline without resorting to some crazy multilayered undergarment.

While corsets do what they do quite admirably, I can say that I was, and still am not, in the practice of utilizing corsets to accentuate my natural curves. Becoming a vampire at such a young age allowed me to keep a youthful figure. I just wore them to keep everything from moving around too much.

As a side note, my own perceptions of what it means to be a lady have changed over the years as society and fashion have changed. The early years, when a lady was dainty, well fashioned, and had an air of mystery, were all enjoyable times for me. The current era of looser society norms and more androgynous clothing standards, as well as the ability to be more outspoken, is quite comforting. I try to accept the world as it is given to me.

The year of 1836 still held an air of mystery for a lady. I continued to see young Mr. Worthington. Since our accidental meeting in the Canadian north, we had managed a very discreet, on-again, off-again affair over the previous three years. It was by no means a union of longing. It was about sex. The two of us had great sex together. Neither of us was in it for anything more than physical satisfaction. That was the truth that was making it work so well. He got the satisfaction of unleashing youthful prowess on a lady, and I was happy in the accomplished pursuits of human coupling.

I made no assumption that somehow I was the only one enjoying his fancy. I was just one in a stable of happy, female supplicants. That was fine. It was all that practice that made him so good at what he did. It was all that practice that also made him discreet. He understood that any attempt to tarnish my virtue would certainly not end well. An earl could easily have people disappear if she was sufficiently unhappy.

That was all Mr. Worthington was left to know about me. To him, I was a wealthy lady from England, who happened to be residing in America. I was lonely, maybe, but nothing more. He knew nothing about the fact that I was no longer human. My vampire secret I kept to myself. That way, when I finally let him go, he would be none the wiser.

Speaking of Mr. Worthington, several minutes before I started to fidget with my dress, I watched him exit my house, on his way back to wherever it was he had come from. That particular morning, he managed to walk straight past Charles not a block removed from my door. The two exchanged greetings as businessmen do when they meet each other on the street. Young Mr. Worthington had no knowledge of the true place of privilege that Mr. Wyndell possessed in my world. It was interesting to watch them interact from a distance, each one quietly hiding some special secret from the other.

I turned from the windows and returned to my tea, which had been abandoned on a small side table. It was still warm. Cold tea so distressed me. I had held a liking for tea ever since I had been human. The new era of coffee that had come to America was lost on me. I held to my British traditions.

Shortly, Charles appeared in the study with me. He had that all-business look on his face. That bit made me distressed, and the day had started so nicely.

"Good day, old mum. How's the day treating you thus far?"

"Everything was grand enough until I came across that look on your face."

"I passed your current fancy a block or two back."

"He is very good at the things young men should be good at."

"Well, then, I'd say that makes you a bit of a slag."

"Pardon?"

"Maybe just lonely."

"I've been lonely for a very long time, Charles."

"Sorry, Sara, this conversation is obviously going down a very wrong track."

"Don't apologize to me, my old friend. Please, come and tell me about this bad news written across your face."

I pointed, and we sat in the large, leather chairs stationed in front of the study window. A servant girl appeared with a large, silver pot containing coffee for Charles. The young girl eyed Charles bashfully as she went about putting out the hot drink. When she concluded, she freshened my tea and disappeared back to where she had come from. It made me wonder about Mr. Wyndell's social status.

"So, Charles, tell me of your escapades. Have you managed a fiancée, or are you still exploring what the world has to offer?"

"I have several nice lady friends, thank you. But, to answer your question, I'm not completely sure that I'm the marrying type."

"I'm not for telling other people what to do with their lives, but it would be handy if either you or your brother had a son to continue on with tradition."

"It is said that Fletcher will be a father come spring."

"Oh, that is grand. When did you receive the news?"

"It came on the last ship. It was accompanied by a private correspondence. I'm obviously not sure what it says, but I'm told it isn't good news."

Charles reached into his jacket pocket and removed a small, cream-colored envelope. The Grey Cargo seal was embossed into the heavy paper on one side. The other side held two words scrolled in thick, black ink. The two small words made me stop and draw breath. They were "Lady Allison," my new name.

I had sent the letter to the Court on the proper date as I had been told. I had just never actually used it. Everyone in America knew me as Lady Boca. I had kind of temporarily forgotten about it all. Just the sight of the name in writing wasn't good, that much I was sure of.

I took the envelope from Charles and stared at it for several moments. Then, I folded it in half and slid it into the tight fold of my sleeve. I would deal with whatever it was later.

"Well, that explains the serious face."

"Not completely."

"What's that then?"

"I have two more bad bits."

"Let's have it, then."

"A fortnight past, *The Summer Storm* sank in a storm off the coast of Virginia. About half of the crew managed to make shore; sadly the captain was not among them. There was no good word why. The ship was quite old; I suppose it was just its time."

"You should make special compensations to the families of the lost crew and the captain as well."

"Sara, are you sure you want special compensations?"

"They were my crew, so special compensations will be made."

"Yes, ma'am."

"What of the cargo loss?"

"Nothing that was not replaceable at small cost to us."

"At least that is good news. *The Storm* sent down to Davy Jones. A sad day. You know, I stood on her deck the day she was christened. The two of us had many adventures together."

"Will you replace her with something more in the style of the day?"

"Oh, I don't know. *The Summer Storm* was a creature of her times. I'm not sure that I want to replace her at all. I will wait for a spell and then make a decision. I tend to think clearer that way."

"Sorry, old mum."

"It really is going to be a bad day."

"We're not done yet."

"Go on, then."

"How well do you know Mr. Worthington?"

"Why?"

"He is not what he appears to be."

"He's married?"

"Sorry, no. It is considerably worse than that. He's a member of the enemy."

"The Brenfield Society?"

"Sorry."

The whole world went black for a second. I threw my delicately crafted, rose red china cup like a baseball. The contents landed on my dress, Charles's suit, the rich rug on the study floor, and some papers that were lying on the side table. The cup, for its part, proceeded straight from my hand to the large study window, where it shattered both itself and a fair-size pane of glass.

Cold air rushed through the new opening in the wall and sent a shiver down my spine. The amulet's glow brightened as it compensated for the drop in temperature.

"How could I have possibly been so stupid?"

"Don't be too hard on yourself, Sara. He is very good at being discreet. I just figured it out myself."

"I'm going to kill him real slowly."

"This might be one of those times for outsourcing."

"No, I think not. This is not those days gone by I keep telling you stories about. I am going to pull the life out of him with my own bare hands."

The amulet pulsed brightly in agreement.

"I beg of you, Sara, don't act in haste. Let a small amount of time pass and think it through, like you said with the ship."

"The ship didn't betray me!"

"I don't know that he did either."

"Pardon me?"

"Well, you were both using each other. You both kept your secrets from each other. Don't rush to judgment; be opportunistic with your timing."

"Once again, Charles, you are wise beyond your years. If you wish, then I will wait."

"Sometimes, rushing makes things worse."

"Yes, I get it, no killing the ponce."

"I am sorry, Sara; I do wish I had brought you better news."

"It's nothing I haven't seen before. I once knew a lovely boy named Thomas. Sorry, that's for different days. Oh, I just let my guard down is all; it just aggravates me."

"Put half of it out of your mind and deal with one thing at a time. I find that works well for me."

"Fine idea. I'll do some thinking and come up with a suitable solution."

"Now, I'm going to go find a carpenter and have your window repaired."

"Thank you, Charles. You really are quite kind."

Charles stood and strode out of the room, as much to find heat as a carpenter. I sat still, watching the breeze flutter the edges of the papers on the side table. The day had started out so well and, in a crazy ride, had descended downhill. My lover was the enemy; my personal ship had sunk; and apparently something was afoot in London.

I retrieved the letter from my sleeve. Just holding on to it made me feel apprehensive. I slid a polished fingernail under the fold and sliced the envelope open. The heavy paper that filled the void was but a single sheet. That wasn't good either. If there is one thing I know for a fact it is that bad news is always short and concise. I unfolded the piece of heavy stock and studied the news that it held.

> *Lady Allison, the Brenfield Society has a new leader. They know of all the men you have killed. They are going to have you dragged out in court and stripped of your title. Then worse, I am sure. This requires your immediate attention.*
>
> *Fletcher.*

I stared at the paper for some time. I almost couldn't believe what the words meant. They couldn't kill me fair, so they were planning on having the Crown do it for them. Apparently, the rules of war had changed yet again. I obviously needed to change along with them.

The last bit was serious. I could do many things to them but not in court. I had very little pull there. I needed an attack plan, or I was doomed. The amulet pulsed with a bright, red light.

*No, my friend*, I thought. *We can't just kill them.* Or could we? No, that was not going to work. I needed a better approach. I really needed to think it all the way out.

# chapter 32

On New Year's Day in 1837, I was standing in the New York City harbor. The wind howled down the Hudson, much as it still does. The cold day did little to stall the work needing to be done by the men of the docks. The stevedores were a hardy lot. Either by will or by necessity, they managed their business in good times or bad, blue sky or foul sea.

My standing on the docks during that particular occasion was necessity. I was waiting for a ship to load. Its name was *The Franklin H. Henderson*, and it was a clean-lined affair. We had added several of the more current vessels over recent years. It was an effort to pick up the pace in our crossings of the Atlantic. Reportedly, *The Henderson* made good speed.

As the times had changed at sea, I had been able to disarm many of my cargo vessels or my company's vessels. Pulling the guns from the gun decks left more room for cargo, both human and commodity. The free space allowed for the addition of staterooms to handle the ever-growing human traffic. *The Henderson* had several nice staterooms. The increase in comfort over the years had added to the traveling count.

I liked a comfortable cabin while traveling; it allowed me to focus on the matters at hand. That was particularly good then, because I returned to England in unknown times. I wanted to be anonymous. So I returned home to unknown times on an indistinguishable ship, along with anyone else who might book passage in that direction. Discreet was definitely the best option. I wanted to look like anyone else in the world—you know, human.

As we stood on the docks, I looked over at Charles. From the look of discontent on his face, I was happy I was not human. Charles disliked the foul, New York, winter weather. *Oh well, nothing is perfect,* I thought to myself. Maybe he would have been happier with me in Greece.

I rolled the thought through my head. Only a bit more, and it would be time to board. We made our way toward our staterooms to get out of the elements. *The Henderson's* captain stood on the weather deck, face into the wind. He watched us as we made our way up the gangway. He looked sturdy enough for the task ahead. The winter weather in the North Atlantic Ocean was not a business for the faint or frail. I made eye contact with him once we had arrived on the deck. He smiled and nodded respectfully. I liked him already.

There were two other couples making passage on the ship that day and the crew. For their part, the crew complement was but twenty young souls and the captain. It seemed a small crew compared to the galleon I was used to. That was fine with me. That just made fewer people to interact with.

I will say with assurance that the crossing we made on *The Henderson* was fast. I was amazed how times had accelerated travel about the planet. It seemed that no time at all before the rugged coastline of Ireland was visible in the distance. From there, it was but a short float through the channel to the Port of Bristol.

That was my stop. I wanted to stop at Brimme House on my way. After all, it was my land. Any newly arriving noblewoman would want to check on the status of her lands. It was the proper thing to do. I wanted to look proper. Everything about me needed to look normal— odd American normal maybe, but normal nevertheless.

As we came coasting into the harbor on the west side of England, I looked out on familiar ground and saw little that I recalled. All I could see was change. The passage of time and the arrival of industry had altered all that my eyes surveyed. Somehow, it almost didn't look like the same city I had left behind. In my absence, Bristol had slowly transformed itself into a town of industry, and the port showed the end results of that work. The new face was good news for me. Industry was created by the rational mind of men, not the superstitious one. The age of industrialization would indeed help me to be more human. It was a good thing.

Our vessel tied off to new docks, and the age-old task of unloading began. The dockhands went to the commodities, and the first mate went to the passengers. Charles took my arm and escorted me down the wide gangway and onto native soil. It felt good to plant boot heels on familiar ground, independent of the reason.

A fine carriage had been procured in advance, and the two of us were quickly on our way out of the docks. The trip to Brimme House was as quick as it had been in the past, but with different scenery. Fortunately, my house was just as I had remembered leaving it. The stately stone walls and manicured lawns of the manor were much more of a castle than they were a house. Brimme House was truly a grand affair.

Charles and I were greeted at the main entrance that day by a nice lady named Margaret, who was apparently in charge of the household. She was your standard, middle-aged English model. Her husband, Godfrey, was acting as the butler for the day. Godfrey was a round, middle-aged man with red cheeks and a thick mustache. He spoke in a Cockney drawl that made me believe he was from the south of England.

I made my way into the small sitting room off to one side of the entrance and removed my heavy winter attire. There, I introduced myself properly to the couple and then introduced Charles in turn. Charles inquired as to the state of the house and lands. Godfrey informed him that the usual staff was off for the day but would be brought back at once; otherwise, the status of the house was excellent. I interjected that it would not be necessary to recall the staff, as I required little attention, and the people should be allowed to enjoy their time unbothered by interlopers. Godfrey smiled broadly and then went stoic when he saw his wife's expression. Margaret informed me promptly that the lady of the house would have proper service as was expected. She was old school and less impressed by the young American girl and her new ways. I secretly liked that. I asked if there were any matters that required my attention. They responded that all was in order. I asked Charles to make some plans so that we might view all of the lands and works. He said he would handle it all in a timely fashion.

Introductions being complete, I then excused myself to look about my manor and left Charles to lay out the details of my life, as was customary of a guardian. I bounced from the room, as young girls do, and headed for the ballroom. I greatly wanted to see my portrait. It had been ages since I had been able to look at myself. Turns out, I was right where I had left me. The portraits of the ballroom held images of my mother's family going as far back as Brimme House did. They were a powerful bunch, that much was evident. I was powerful as well, though the portrait showed a more middle-aged and traveled version of me.

As I looked upon the painting, I paused to listen to the story that Charles was telling the nice couple. I, Lady Allison Gibbs, was the seventh Earl of Northwick. I was born and raised in the city of New York and at the age of thirteen had come to England to make an appearance at Court and view the status of the family holdings, as was expected. Sadly, my family was no longer alive to accompany me, so Charles was tasked to act as my guardian until I turned a proper age or married. It was a nice tale. I wasn't far off proper age at that point. In the eighteenth century, thirteen was almost marrying age. A girl of about sixteen, if she had no family, was quite adult, in those days. In some ways, it was a younger age.

Charles apologized in advance for my American notions and outgoing personality. I had apparently been raised to be in charge from a young age. Then he went on to explain the family dislike of bright light and the natural need for my dark glasses. I was blessed with an abnormality that had been passed down from my parents but caused me no ill effects.

The couple listened intently to it all. They took the whole of the affair in stride and stated that they would be accommodating in whatever fashion was required. That was what I liked about people; they were so trusting. The couple accepted Charles's story at face value. It seemed logical to them, so it was true.

With that little interaction, I was in. To them, I was an ordinary girl—a lady and an American—but unquestionably human. That was the one thing that I had looked for from the stop in Brimme House, and I had just achieved it. I was officially a teenage, human girl named Allison Gibbs.

The days after our introductions at Brimme House passed as one would expect. Lady Allison rode the lands of the house and surveyed all that was in her surroundings. Then she went to town and sat with bankers and businessmen. They informed her of the many interests in which she was involved. Once that was complete, she went and inspected the mooring and the other business interests in the immediate area.

All the sights of the English countryside appeared, from an outward point of view, to be pleasing to young American eyes. All those whom she met seemed friendly enough and pleasantly moved by the new mistress of the land. It was a fashionable ruse. I knew the state of every one of my business holdings well, as well as I knew the lay of the land. The knowing wasn't the idea, the ruse was. I wanted to be seen by all and to interact on some level so word would spread. It worked quite well, because the word that spread was kind. A young and pretty American had come to town and was quite knowledgeable about the affairs of her house.

With the business of the humans concluded for the present, I was left to that thing that noblewomen do—basically, whatever I pleased. I liked getting back to my own affairs. It was time as well, because I did have some things that needed tending to. Some cosmetic touches that needed to be looked after, as it were.

A bright, winter day rose in February and seemed right for getting things sorted. I made my way from my chamber at a proper hour and meandered through the house until I made my way to the large, glass enclosure of the greenhouses. The winter sun pulsed through the glass walls and ceiling and had made the space warm and comforting. Many plants in potter's clay stood with me, soaking in the rays of the day. My little, crystal-caged friend also took in as much energy as could be captured by the amulet's surfaces. We all seemed glad that the sun had come out that day.

I stood in the embrace of my old friend for some time, until it was time to move on. Exiting the greenhouse, I made my way, via wide, stone-floored hallways, to the house's library. I was standing in the library, looking at the wooden ladder that ran around the room on a metal rail and allowed access to the upper parts of the stacks, when Charles appeared.

I stood quietly and could see myself hanging from the heavy, wooden ladder as his great-great-great-grandfather had pushed me in circles. He would push, and I would hold on for fear of falling off. When it slowed to a stop, we would laugh loudly and then do it all again. We had both been quite young back then, and the world had been a different place.

"Allison, how are we doing today?"

"I'm happy, Charles. You?"

"I'm quite grand. I do like it here."

"I was just thinking of days gone by and some of your kin. They all liked it here very much."

"That explains the look on your face. You looked lost somewhere."

"I was lost right here in this room. So many nice memories were made here. There was so much innocence and youth at the beginning, but now it is just memories."

"They are fond memories from the look on your face."

"Yes, they are; every one of them."

"That's nice. You know, I was talking to some of the staff and hearing about the folklore of this place. As you well know, a succession of women have been the mistress of Brimme House. Apparently, every one of them has been highly regarded by the inhabitants of the house and the people of the surrounding lands. That's nice as well, I'd say."

"It's nice to be thought well of."

"Good people receive good returns."

"Now you're just sparring with me."

"True."

"Stop, please."

"So what shall we do today?"

"Take a walk about the grounds."

"That sounds cold."

"A little weather will do you good, Charles. You know, you really are an indoor chap."

"That is why I became a businessman and not a military one."

I laughed. He was a sturdy fellow but not a military man in any fashion.

"Once again, you are correct."

"Thank you."

"I am dragging you out into the weather so I can readjust my vision. You should survive the onslaught fine enough, I think."

"Readjusting your sight will do good damage to your night vision."

"So be it. It needs to be done. I can always get it back after."

"After what, might I ask?"

"After our confrontation with the King and the Brenfield Society, of course."

"Oh."

"I want to walk in clear-eyed, not hiding behind some crutch that could be used against me. I want just me and my bright green eyes."

"I do like your eyes."

"Thank you, Charles. You're very sweet. Now, go fetch some coats."

Soon enough after our conversation and properly attired, we headed out the doors into the elements of the winter day. *Bristol is the right place for this adjustment,* I thought to myself. Normally, the winter days in Bristol were a slate grey kind of color. They were normally much dimmer than the fine, bright, winter day I had managed to pick out. It seemed a trial-by-fire setting had been designed.

I started by just sliding the glasses down my nose a small amount. That let the light come at me like a shimmer. It was bright but not overwhelmingly so. We walked about the meadows in that manner for some time. As we turned and Charles headed me back toward my castle home, I slid them down farther. As I did so, the whole world became brighter still. The impact was almost painful that time. I slid them back to the first position. The adjustment would obviously need to be done in steps.

In the end, that turned out to be true. The transition of my perfect night vision to adequate daytime vision took many days to complete. It was much the same way that I had had to actually acquire my night vision in the beginning. That was fine. I liked slow transitions; they allowed me time to mentally readjust.

I had spent centuries in the dark world. I was very comfortable there. I understood the dark quite well. The loss of the ability to see the dark places was a loss that made me nervous. I needed time to bring myself around to new ideas.

Antonio had taught me to never let down my guard. It was a good lesson learned, and it had kept me alive on many occasions. Sadly, it was also a lesson that I frequently overlooked. On numerous occasions, I had let down my guard and been sorry for it. That time, I was hoping a calculated risk would play to my favor.

As time passed and the process went along, I wondered what Antonio would think of what I was doing to myself. Would he approve of my brash plan? He probably would not. Maybe I would ask him, if I saw him again.

# chapter 33

In my good, American style, I stopped and inspected all that could be seen. With the lazy schedule we were keeping, it was the first part of July before I finally made my way back to London and the sculpted lawns of the Grey Estate. Happily, things were exactly as I had left them. Fletcher had been a good steward of my lands in my absence. They were all well kept and in good repair.

Charles and I had settled in to my ancestral home and prepared to go about our business when we were greeted by sad news. The King of England had died some months past. That was not good news, because King William had been a friend my lands.

As I came to find comfort in the overstuffed, leather chairs of the study that first morning, a young servant girl came in with tea and a regal correspondence. The parchment heralded the coronation of Queen Alexandrina Victoria, granddaughter of King George III and niece of King William IV, which apparently had taken place on June 24, 1837. The grand document also summoned all nobility to her court for the purpose of inspection of the Crown. One was to be present on the day of August 1, 1837, for such purposes.

So the time line had been established. I had one month to come up with a new plan. I had been doing all of my original planning with the intent of meeting William. He was the third son of King George III and had been mostly known as Prince William, the Duke of Clarence. King William had had many children, but they were from a sordid affair with a mistress named Dorothy Jordon. I believe she was an actress. William had produced legitimate children, but none survived him to the throne, which brought about the rise of Victoria.

I really did not know much about the Queen at that point. I knew she was almost entirely German and came from the House of Hanover. Interestingly, she did not become the heir to the Throne of Hanover. Salic law forbade a woman taking up that post, so it went to her uncle. I thought that was wrong, but I understood, and in the end, the United Kingdom was a better present.

I knew she spoke several languages fluently. She had studied math and history. She had been taught by her governess, Baroness Louise Lenhzen, and a family priest. Most importantly, she was young and pretty. That would be useful. She was unmarried, possessed great power, and was wanted by men. Yes, that could be used to my advantage.

I rose from my chair and headed out through the large, glass doors onto the study's terrace. The sun was high and bright. It made me squint as I came into its full and unrelenting gaze. Fortunately, it had lost the painful sting it had once possessed. I turned my face to the stone terrace and began to pace back and forth with the message clutched in my hand.

At some point, Charles appeared in the study windows. He watched me pace for several moments before joining me on the terrace. He took up station at the old, iron table and placed his steaming cup of black coffee on the glass tabletop. He quietly folded his hands in his lap and sat for several seconds, waiting for the proper moment in which to interject.

"You appear to be debating with yourself again?"

"I am."

"About what, might I ask?"

"King William is dead."

"Truly?"

"He has been succeeded by his niece, Victoria."

"Victoria of Kent? House of Hanover Victoria?"

"That's her."

"Well ... "

"Exactly."

"At least that explains the look on your face."

"It could be a good thing. She is smart, young, pretty, and single. All the same things that set me apart."

"True, but it's unknown if she is a friend to the House of Brimme as William was. That could prove a dilemma."

"I agree, but my title can't be revoked. And besides, monarchs *always* go where they can get their coffers filled."

"I suppose that's true, but it still doesn't solve the problem for which we are here."

"No, hence the pondering."

"So?"

"I have an idea, but it requires a deviation from my base instincts."

"This whole trip has been a deviation from your base instincts."

I laughed. He was right. I was headed out on new ground. I was uncomfortable with the whole of it. I pondered, and Charles took a drink of his steaming cup of coffee.

Charles had taken to the drink when we had moved to America. Apparently, it made the staff most unhappy that he didn't drink tea. I stuck to tradition. I had been drinking tea for so long that it was just natural. The coffee that they made in those days was potent, where the tea was soothing.

"Charles, take a run into the city and fetch up your brother. I have an idea that will require his help."

"May I ask?"

"Not yet. I'm still thinking."

"Consider it done, ma'am."

I laughed again. He really only called me ma'am when he was trying to be funny. It worked for him most of the time. British humor had always played well in the city of New York.

"I'm going to go for a walk and talk to my little friend while you are about your task. If you return before I do, please find me about the grounds."

"Headed for the solitude of the meadows?"

"That and God's acre."

"Very good."

Charles lifted himself from the chair and headed for the study door. I bounded down the stairs and out toward the back meadows and their cobbled walkway to the family plots. The woodlands out of sight of the manor were where I usually did my most productive thinking. I had always assumed that it was because I could not be obviously observed. I liked the middle of the maze for precisely the same reason.

I knew the paths and trails of the grounds as if they had been tattooed on my skin. I could move about without thinking about where I was going. I could focus on whatever task was at hand. That day, the task at hand was humanity.

I knew all the ways that one could check to see if I were not human. I could easily mask most of them. One trait would be a problem to solve. I thought the remainder could be overcome, but that would require the help of my friend in the crystal.

I had solved my problem of moving about during the day long ago. I had beaten my sensitive vision problem to a point where they couldn't do much to affect it. They might be able to do something, if they were really clever. They were all really clever, so that was possible. I would just talk my way out of that, as I had in the past.

As far as the basic human traits went, that was the issue. I would employ the powers of my companion to solve them. The amulet could effortlessly control my breathing and heartbeat. She could also handle my skin temperature. She would be able to use a little bit of magick to make me appear human. As I walked and thought the whole thing out, a pulsating yes resounded in the subconscious parts of my brain. It seemed she was on board with my program.

Solving the blood test was easy enough. All I had to do was drink an ample amount of blood and water before I needed to be in Court. That would solve the blood and tears issues. After that, it was merely a matter of freshening up my breath so I wouldn't smell like an old, dead bag. That was easy, because I did it every day.

That left two big problems that I could encounter. I wasn't actually sure how to fix the most basic of them. I had no reflection. In previous appearances at Court, I had utilized a little bit of magick and stealth in my movements to mask the fact that I had no reflection. That was fine if I was in a one-on-one encounter, but there were so many mirrors in the Court and its outer rooms that it could really be an inconvenience in a crowd.

I found a pleasant place to sit on a spot of high ground that seemed a good place for thinking. There I folded up the sea of cloth that formed my dress and petticoats and sat down under the shade of a large oak tree. How was I to play off the fact that I cast no reflection? How could one possibly explain such a thing?

I could potentially use my Gypsy magick in a massive dose to do what I had done in times past. I had done that in earlier times to look three dimensional in mirrors or older or whatever. I just was not sure that it would work in such a setting. Then, as I sat, I had a thought. At the end of the day, my Gypsy magick and the deep black powers of the amulet were, in some ways, the same thing. They were from infinitely different planes, but still of the same ilk. Their primary distinguishing characteristics were strength and intent. My magicks were weak and defensive. Hers, however, were the very foundation of the universe. That was what the voice in my head was telling me. As infinite as her power was, I already knew that she could scale it to her liking. She had done so on numerous occasions. That was what was needed here.

I reached into my gown and retrieved the chain that held the crystal cage with my companion trapped inside. The surfaces of the jewel shimmered as they made contact with the rays of the sun. I held her out in front of me, as far as the chain would allow. The sun always made her happy. It was the energy that it gave off, energy that was so close to the one that she possessed. It seemed that, after so many millennia trapped inside the transparent-surfaced crystal, she had really become a conduit for the power of the ages. Definitely, she was no one to be trifled with.

"My friend of many tricks, can you produce an image? I mean an image of me? And make it appear in different places, like mirrors?"

The amulet twinkled in the morning sunlight, as if to signify that she found the question amusing. A second passed and then her pulsing sensation of yes returned to the back of my mind, like a rhetorical truth.

"Truly?"

The jeweled surfaces twinkled once more, as if in disbelief. She found it funny that, after so long in her presence, I still questioned her abilities. I did not find it so. There were days when I still questioned the things that I could do. How was I to grasp the power she could manifest?

The twinkling of the amulet smoothed out into a mellow glow, her happy glow. Then as we sat, out at a distance of some twenty paces, a shimmering image appeared out of the thin air in front of us. As the image solidified, the ether had rendered an image of me. Then, as if hidden behind some invisible tree, more images of me appeared. Soon, there were a dozen images of me in the meadow's grassy opening.

The twelve Saras all just stood for a moment, and then they began to move. They all moved independently, as if they were real individuals. Some of them stood in conversation and some of them walked about properly, while one looked at us and curtsied politely. They were mesmerizing. Truly, I could not believe that such things were real and possible. *Luckily*, I thought, *if I can not believe it, then no one else will either*. The idea was perfect. I laughed loudly as the copies of me moved about in the meadow.

"My hair's getting quite long again, isn't it? I do like the dark color against my green eyes. Once, I would have thought that my golden locks would be with me forever, but after centuries of light-colored hair I do like this dark color very much. Yes, I should keep it a while longer, I think. What about you? Do you approve?"

The amulet twinkled radiantly in the sunlight and then gave off a single pulse of light—the sign we had decided would signify a yes. Then, as if directed from somewhere offstage, all the images slowly shimmered out of existence.

I hopped to my feet. I knew I had it all figured out in one fashion or another. Now, other things could be considered.

"Can you enter hallowed ground?"

The one pulse from the crystal made me happy.

"Grand, then there are some people I would like you to meet. I know that people are not your strong point, but these are my friends and family. They are the ones whom I talk to when I want to commune with the other side of existence. I would like you to meet them, if you so choose."

Once again, the single pulse of light came from the crystal surface of my friend's jeweled cage. I was excited, but I could tell that there was apprehension in my companion. She really did not get on well with the human world anymore.

I left her lyying on the outside of my dress and stood to straighten the layers of cloth. Then, we proceeded to the path that led to the family plots. The cobbled path was as well maintained as the remainder of the grounds.

Stopping at the only slightly weathered, marble slab, I knelt to pray. As I did so, the apprehension that my companion had been holding on to started to dissipate. The dead were no enemy to her, and she knew it. That feeling of release made me very happy. I was actually hoping that the dead would see things the same way. The power that she handled was disquieting to much of my world. I hoped they would not be displeased with me.

Opening the iron gates to the cemetery, I could sense that the inhabitants of the grounds were already on edge. Maybe this was a bad idea. Bad or not, I wanted to try. I decided to go toward the most understanding of them first. I walked quietly to where Christopher and his wife had been interred at the end of the row of Wyndells. Christopher and the amulet had already been introduced while he was alive. Interestingly, in direct opposition to how he had responded when he was alive, he seemed more intrigued this time around.

I said hello and explained that I wanted my companion in the amulet to meet my friends and family. I wondered if he thought that to be a bad idea, as most did not respond positively to her presence. The only sensations I received from the ether were yes and "slow." Slow— that did seem prudent. I thanked Christopher for his understanding and promised that I would speak loud enough so all could hear. Again, he seemed to approve.

Next on the list was Charles. I liked Charles's plot of ground for a stopping point as it was centrally located among the Wyndell clan. As was always the case, my old friend was happy to see me reappear. The dead have always liked company. They had little else to occupy their time.

I introduced him to the amulet and then to each of the family members in turn. I told them the story of how we had come to meet and of the bond that we had forged through time. They all listened intently, as was their way. When I finished, I waited. No unfavorable responses came from the group. It was approval. At last, I had approval from another sound group. The dead and the Catholic Church were both on my side. It seemed like all was going my way.

I stood politely and thanked them for their time. I stooped to place a small kiss on the top of Charles's stone and proceeded off toward my parents. I repeated the process of introductions and commenced telling my parents about the friendship that we had managed to develop out of the blackness. They were obviously more interested in the personal nature of our relationship, as all parents tend to be. My mother was happiest of all. She knew that I had been mentally alone for such a long time. I lacked the ability to make true friendships with most human beings because of my demonic personality, and Mother knew that well. She seemed relieved that I had found a friend.

Father liked her as well; however, like most men, he was interested in the power she radiated. Not the power of force and will, but the one of protection. He was comforted by the fact that she was a protector. She could protect his little girl from the bad things in the world. He was sweet and would always be my father. That one thought alone made me happy all the way to my core.

I stood and politely explained that I had but little time to spend that day. I would happily return again with more time for conversations about the world. All the spirits quieted, and I turned to head out of the cemetery. I made my way back to the path, which led me once again to my home—a path that I had walked on countless occasions.

I rounded the last of the turns in the cobblestone path and broke into the open of the meadow, which allowed me a view of the manor. It also allowed me a view of Charles and Fletcher. I had spent a long time out if they had already returned. Even at a distance, I was struck by how much alike they looked. Time and travel had apparently done neither of them ill service. I reached down and summoned joy to my voice. I gave them both a happy greeting as they closed the distance between us.

"Lady Gibbs, you look quite lovely. I had almost forgotten."

Fletcher turned red as the words left his mouth. Apparently, he hadn't planned on it sounding so, well, suggestive. Charles simply smiled broadly and gave him a brotherly tap on the arm.

"Thank you for your thoughts, Master Wyndell, I appreciate the fact that you find me worthy of observation."

We all laughed. It was actually meant to be funny. The boys needed to be able to talk freely. Levity helped that happen.

"So, Fletcher, you approve of my dark locks?"

"Absolutely. Well, if I remember correctly, I am a fan of both styles and colors. It has been some time since we met last."

"Thank you, kind sir."

I gave him a half curtsy in mock approval. Finding admiring men had never been a problem for me.

"Not to be forward, ma'am, but is this your new natural appearance?"

"Yes, Fletcher. As you well know, this is basically the way God made me to be, with the exception of my dark hair. As you know, I was quite young when I became a vampire, so my youth stays constant as the years pass."

I smiled pleasantly. He wasn't trying to be ingratiating; it just seemed to come out that way.

Fletcher turned a sly eye to his brother and returned the tap on the shoulder.

"You have the better job."

"I know that." Charles hit him back. He liked the fact that the commander of the Grey Empire fancied his position.

"Boys, I too appreciate the one-upping, but now to business."

"Yes, ma'am," they said in unison. It was somewhat military in tone. It made me giggle inside.

"I need you to acquire someone for me, Fletcher."

"Ma'am?"

"I would like you to find me a horse veterinarian that is both good at filing teeth and is absolutely trustworthy. Can you accomplish this task for me?"

The two of them stared at me in disbelief. Then, as is customary of Wyndell men, they bounced back to attention.

"Sara, you cannot be considering what I think you are considering." Charles seemed concerned.

"Relax, Charles. They are extremely useful tools but not absolutely essential ones. Besides, unless I miss my guess, they will grow back."

"Are you sure?"

"No."

"Well ...," he started to protest, but a small raise of one eyebrow brought him to a pause.

"Fletcher?"

"I believe I know just the fellow to do what you require. I can have him here tomorrow, if that suits your schedule."

"That would be fine. Seems all is sorted, wouldn't you both say?"

Neither of them responded, which I took to mean yes.

"Well, then, Fletcher, fetch up your craftsman, and we will continue reacquainting ourselves in the morning."

Both men nodded and turned to leave.

I turned my attention to the large hedgerow in the distance. It made up the outer edge of the maze. Hmm, a walk in the maze; that would certainly bring back old memories.

# chapteR 34

The sun broke clear and bright as it slipped up onto the edge of the sky the next morning. That signaled good things for me. I spent the early morning hours sitting on the study terrace, soaking in the warmth that exuded from my big, yellow friend. My other friend, the amulet, lay on the corded top of my light blue dress doing the same thing. We both enjoyed the sun so much.

The two of us sat for a while, content in the light's embrace. Then, as was usually the case, we were joined by Charles and his ever-present cup of black coffee. He merely nodded as he joined us in our worship of the sun. It was nice and quiet on the terrace.

We sat for some time and listened to the sounds of the meadows and the low tones of life coming from inside the manor. There was little conversation, just contented quiet. Finally, the serenity was broken by the sounds of carriage wheels in the entry.

"That would be Fletcher coming around the front, unless I miss my guess."

"It would seem he has your penchant for rising early."

"Our clock doesn't run twenty-four hours a day like yours does. One needs to make hay while the sun shines."

"Nice."

"Shall we?"

"No, let them come to us."

We continued to sit and absorb the sun while the carriage on the far side of the estate came to a stop and its inhabitants disembarked. The low conversation was easy to track as the men made their way into the grand entrance hall and down the wide halls to the large wooden doors of the study. Their conversation, which had been merely hushed words, dried up completely as they entered the empty study.

"I am sorry, Master Smith; I am told she is usually in the study. I will have to get someone from the staff to track her down."

"That is quite fine, Mr. Wyndell. I'll just stay here and wait your return."

Fletcher turned on his heels, presumably to leave the study. I wondered how he would know where I usually spent my time. It must have been a younger me he was thinking of.

"No need, gentlemen; we are presently seated on the terrace. If you would care to join us?"

There was a quick shuffling of feet, and two bodies appeared in the ornate, glass doorway that opened onto the terrace. They both seemed a little confused that I was sitting out in the bright sunlight. That was fine, confusion usually played to my advantage. I stood to greet my guests. Charles stood with me, as was customary of a gentleman.

"Greetings and welcome to my home, Master Smith. I trust that you have some small understanding of why I requested your assistance here today?"

"Lady Gibbs, Mr. Wyndell mentioned something to the fact that you had an animal with a tooth problem."

"Animal … Yes, well, may we proceed to the stables, and you can assess the situation for yourself?"

"Yes, Lady Gibbs."

With that, we turned and proceeded across the lawn. I led them quietly around the outside of the estate and out to the stables where the horses were kept. Master Smith and I walked along side by side, and the two Wyndell boys followed along behind in their usual, all-business manners.

Master Smith was an interesting fellow. He was tall and strong and a sturdily built man. His skin was tight from a life spent in the elements. His face had many small lines, which gave the impression that his life was much more happy than sad. He moved along with ease and carried himself with a sense of purpose that was almost military, but it was not. He lacked the stiffness of spine that military men possessed. He gave every outward appearance that he was up to the task ahead of him, even if he didn't know exactly what it was.

We entered the stables and proceeded down the middle to a stall that had been walled off on all sides. The stall was normally used for birthing the new. That day, it would be used for mending the old. The stall had been cleaned and contained only a small workbench and a sturdy, wooden chair. The term chair was probably a poor choice of words. It was made out of four-inch timbers and thick planking. It was akin to the things you see in a modern-day, electric chamber. A wooden beam had been secured to the back of the chair at an angle so one might tilt her head back and rest it there. Heavy leather straps with metal buckles had been fastened to it in all manner of positions so that whoever sat in it could be properly secured. The whole affair looked quite sturdy.

The chair had been a nighttime project of Charles's. He had done a very fine and quick job. It seemed to be just the right size to properly bind an eighteen-year-old girl.

Everyone stopped and took in the scene. Charles seemed pleased. The rest of us seemed concerned. Walking into the stall was the first time that I had seen it, and I confess that, emotionally, I went with everyone else. It made me quite apprehensive.

"I am not entirely sure that I understand," Master Smith said with an air of unease.

"Relax, Master Smith. It is hopefully not as bad as all this. Apparently, someone overprepared for your arrival."

Charles blanched. He had apparently thought it well intentioned. Master Smith still looked concerned.

"Master Smith, the animal's teeth that you came here to work on this day would, in fact, be my own. I need a spot of filing done, and I require it done confidentially. That, hopefully, will explain the misdirection that brought you here today."

I opened my mouth as wide as I could and let him get a look at my large canine teeth. I had possessed them for some two hundred years, and the daggers showed the marks of wear. In a way I was proud of them. They were the one part of being a vampire that I could not hide. I had never actually gotten to show them off to many people before. In a strange way, it was comforting. Master Smith stood, stunned, but not out of sorts.

"You are not human?"

"No."

"You are a vampire?"

"Yes."

"And you would like me to file off your fangs?"

"I would like for you to make them look like normal human teeth, please. They grew out of normal teeth, so I am hoping you can turn them back that way."

"I'm not completely sure about all of this."

"Master Smith, I would like you to apply your trade to my teeth. The only thing that I require from you when we are done is that you remain absolutely discreet about our affairs. Other than that, I will be happy to compensate you in whatever manner you find acceptable."

"I have a question."

"Absolutely."

"If you really are a vampire and this isn't some sort of production, would your real name be Sara Anne Grey?"

That time around, I blanched. He could not possibly be a Brenfield man, could he? If he were, then there would be some quick killing done. The amulet automatically picked up on my unrest and began to glow. I could feel the dark pulse of the universe being summoned from the beyond. Somehow, things were all going wrong. I needed to get us both calmed down. I drew in a long slow breath and quieted my pulsating nerves. The amulet dimmed a touch and slowed down her buildup of power.

"How might it be that you have come by that name?"

"I did not mean to offend you, ma'am. I truly did not."

"It's fine, Master Smith. Please tell me why you would think me to be someone else."

The man quietly set his leather satchel of tools down on the workbench and leaned his back against it. The move made him appear not nearly as offensive as before. He reached up and removed the hat from his head so he could hold it in his hands, I guessed as much to steady them as anything else. The humble sensibility of the veterinarian helped everyone's sense of calm return.

"My great-great-great-grandfather was once in the employ of a lady named Sara Grey. Sara was once the goodly mistress of this estate and overseer of her family's shipping business. There were stories passed along through the family that she never aged and possessed many odd habits. The staff of her estate took her for a vampire, though they apparently never talked about such matters openly.

"I, of course, heard these stories as a child. I had thought them to be stories told to keep the little ones quiet. But as I grew, I interacted with other families that had relatives who had once been in the employ of the Grey Estate, and they had similar stories to ours. I can honestly say that of all the stories that I have heard regarding the mistress of the house, I have never heard one that spoke an ill word. That is what made me think them all fairy tales. Well, until now. If you truly are a vampire, as you claim, then I was wondering if you are actually the daughter of the late Master John Grey."

"I am just that, sir. My proper Christian name is Sara Anne Grey, and Master John Grey was my father. I have been in possession of the family lands and business interests since the day he gave them to me many long years ago. When you finish with your tasks, I would very much like to hear these fairy tales of yours, if you please."

"Well, since I truly never thought this day possible, my compensation for your needs will be nothing."

"We'll settle on payment when you finish, Master Smith. I like to think that I have a long record of rewarding good deeds."

"If that is the way you would like it, ma'am."

"Well, then, now that the pleasantries have been dispensed with, what do you say we get this whole thing sorted?"

I turned and calmly walked over to the contraption and plopped myself down in it. It took but a minute to settle myself. I wished someone had thought to add some padding. It would have been a welcome addition to the stiffness of the wood frame.

Master Smith turned to the workbench and opened his satchel. He removed and inspected each tool in the leather case and then laid them evenly across the workbench so as to be easily accessible. His surety of purpose as he prepared was quite comforting in a way.

Charles took up station next to the chair, just off one shoulder. I assumed that that was so he might assist in the affair. He seemed neither excited nor apprehensive about the task ahead. Apparently, he had already seen too many strange occurrences.

Then there was Fletcher. He took up station next to the stall door and constantly looked out into the stable. He seemed very uncomfortable with the whole agenda. It was to be expected, I suppose. He had always been removed from the demonic facet of my nature. It was all-new ground for him.

Master Smith finished sorting his tools and turned to face me once more. In his hands, he held two wooden blocks and a small, round file. His face had changed from ambiguity and taken on a somewhat more task-oriented expression. In retrospect, it suited what was about to happen.

"What are the blocks for?" As I asked the question, I could already feel my mouth getting dryer. *Just maybe, this is a bad idea.*

"The wedges go in the back of your mouth and hold your jaw open. They allow me to work without you being able to bite down. They will end up being placed between your teeth, so you shouldn't gag on them unless you fight. I carry several sizes in my bag for different-sized creatures. These happen to be the smallest.

"Also, this is most likely going to hurt in a way that you can scarcely imagine. To file the teeth down and then edge them as much as you are requesting, I will need to pass through several sensitive layers. How good is your pain threshold? I only ask because I'm in fear of my life."

I broke into a broad smile. It was really hard not to like his matter-of-fact take on it all. Professional and straightforward people always made me happy.

"I do confess that my pain threshold is considerable. I cannot imagine anything happening here that would make me respond improperly. You can relax; you are safe here with me."

"That is always nice to hear."

"Oh, by the way, Charles, next time you do some such thing as this, no straps. They are quite unnerving. And some padding wouldn't hurt anything."

"Yes, next time, I'll make a comfy one."

"Good boy."

"Now, if everyone here is ready, we will be proceeding."

Master Smith was emotionally committed to the task. That made me ready as well. I ran my tongue around each thick, enamel fang one last time, as if to say goodbye. Done, I tilted my head back against the wooden beam and opened wide.

The old veterinarian slid his large paw of a hand into the opening of my mouth and continued to push it open until I thought something was about to give. Holding it in that position with the width of his palm, he grabbed one of the wooden blocks and shoved it into the void that remained. There was some fumbling about, and then after a second, the block was wedged in between my back teeth. Some seconds later, the other block was placed adjacent to the first, and my mouth was immovable.

The dull, stretching pain in my jaw was unpleasant. I was sure that my mouth was not meant to be open that far. The thought that I should have requested a dentist and not a veterinarian flashed across my mind. I took several breaths in and out to ease the stretching pain and then refocused my mind on the task ahead.

Master Smith removed his large palm from my mouth and rolled his fingers around the handle of the round file, which had ended up in his lap. As he did so, he ran his eyes over his hands, looking for bite marks. I tried to say "No bite marks," but it came out as "Woo boot maw" or some other such thing.

"Please, ma'am, don't try to talk with the wedges in your mouth. It is all going to come out like that last bit. You are going to feel bits of tooth land in your mouth as we proceed. Please, try not to swallow. Once I finish one tooth, I will stop, and you can clean out your mouth. Then, we will continue on with the second tooth. Now, please, slowly nod once for yes."

I nodded once. As my head became stationary, the old veterinarian locked securely onto my face with one large paw and promptly slid the file into the opening of my mouth with the other. Time slowed and then came to a full stop as he carved a path through the enamel. The pain that started out as an inconvenient scraping quickly turned to a searing—or more aptly labeled blinding—white pain. It was a pain that consumed every fiber of my being. The sound that the file made as it carved its way through the tooth accompanied the pain as it echoed inside my head, like a marching band. My green eyes rolled fully backward into my head, and I secured a grip on the chair arms. By the end of the first tooth, my grip had produced a permanent indentation in the wood.

The torture continued unhindered for some amount of time before abating. I was sure that the time was considerably longer for me than for the other people in the room. The termination of the filing and the release it brought from the searing pain only made matters worse. I was so withdrawn into the pain that all I could do was hold on to the arms of the chair and squeeze. The chair was my anchor in the sea of pain.

Master Smith put his hand behind my head and slowly led it forward until I was tilted over. He attained a firm grip on my hair and gave my head a gentle shaking. A handful of small enamel chips, which had been sitting in the back of my throat, fell out of my mouth and onto the floor. He kept a firm grip on my hair until he was confident that I had finished flushing out the chips, and then he slowly raised my head back to the upright position.

"Ma'am, would you like a mouthful of water before we continue?"

I nodded slowly one time. The veterinarian picked up a small cup that Charles had placed on the bench and poured it into the opening of my mouth. The water was absorbed and had disappeared completely by the time it should have found its way to my throat.

Two things happened next that I found to be interesting. First, the water dulled the pain of the tooth. It was instant and gratifying. Second, I began to cry. I cried big, crocodile tears. I couldn't stop the action. I cried until all the water had left my body once more. It had been a while since I had cried. The sensation of tears on my cheeks was almost new to me.

My tormentor let me cry unabated for a bit. Then, sensing that I was quieting, he once again secured a firm grip upon my jaw. He slid a small, triangular-shaped file with different amounts of edging on each side into my mouth and began shaping the tooth. The process was not as long in duration as the first part had been, but it was, by every measure, twice as painful. I was completely sure that I would succumb to the pain at some point, though I did not.

For this show of fortitude, I gained another cup of water. Once more, I cried it all away. During a small spot of clarity in the midst of the agony that the crying had brought, I paused to take in the faces of my compatriots. One of them was sure and strong; two others were concerned and unsure. Even in almost overwhelming pain, it wasn't hard to figure out who was who.

"Ma'am, can you understand me still?"

I nodded slowly once.

"We are half done. The first tooth looks quite good, I must say. I need to know if we should continue, or do you need to stop?"

I spun my hand around in a circle to make the universal sign for "Get on with it." If I stopped, there would be no way that I could continue.

"So we continue?"

I nodded slowly once.

"Sara, we have to stop this, you are obviously in great pain."

Charles's protective side had finally reached its limit.

I clenched my fist and waved it at him. He got the message.

I lay my head back on the thick, wooden beam and braced for the worst. The strong hand of the veterinarian locked onto my face once more. I was sure that I would have a bruise when he was finished. His grip was strong. Blood would deal with that. It always had a way of making me look new.

I let myself go to the pain once more as the filing started again in earnest. The second tooth took as long as the first one had, though I confess I was lost in the pain. As I swirled in a rough ocean of pain, a thought came welling up from the depths. Why wasn't the amulet doing anything to dull the pain, as it had done on previous occasions? Thinking that only made the pain even worse, and I slipped back into the blackness.

Finally, as if being released from purgatory, I could tell that the project was finished. There was the mouth rinsing and a second round of filing to make the right tooth look like the left. Then, there was more mouth rinsing. Master Smith spent several minutes looking at his work from every angle. He was trying to decide if he was done or not. Apparently convinced, he set down his tools and removed the wooden wedges from my mouth. He handed me a bucket of water and a ladle that he had been using as a cup to put the water in my mouth. I took them up and began spooning water into my mouth. As the water found its way into my body, I began to cry again.

I sat there spooning water into my mouth, crying, and shaking for what seemed like hours. The three gallant men stood off at a small distance and observed. Once the crying passed, clarity returned once more. Then, I noticed the space. My mouth was bigger than it had been. I didn't mean from the stretching; there was extra space in my gum line where my fangs had been. The void in my mouth was both unnatural and unpleasant. I attempted to run my tongue over my new teeth, but the pain that it produced made me cry out in dismay.

"Ma'am, it will take some time for the teeth to stiffen and grow new enamel. Until that happens, they will hurt something fierce. Do not play with them. That will only make them hurt more. You really should drink water and some milk, if you are able, to help the teeth grow."

"I … hate … you," I said. It came out in a kind of hollow, crackly gargle, but out it came. The old veterinarian just laughed happily.

"Lady Gibbs, I do teeth for people as well. They all tend to hate me when I'm finished, but the humans don't have your extraordinary pain response."

I glared at him. I really wanted to kill him. I had never, ever, been subjected to such pain. Well, except by Antonio, when he had turned me into a vampire. That pain was many folds worse than this had been. It had just been so long ago that its memory had dulled.

"I still hate you."

"I'm hoping that will pass in time."

"Sara, I think you have had more than enough for one day. Let me get you to your bedchamber, so you can rest," Charles said. "Save the killing for tomorrow."

I shook a clenched fist at Charles one more time. He backed away a few more steps. Fletcher just stared at Charles as if to say "Stop provoking her."

I tried to stand but wobbled on unsteady legs. My abilities were less than they used to be.

"Sara, that is enough. Let me help you out of this place."

That time, I conceded. Charles had the soft tones of his ancestors. It was the sound of caring in his voice that made me give in. I nodded slowly once and raised my hands so he might pick me up from the chair. He did so in a gentle and caring manner.

The others watched in awe that he was allowed to do such things. He was allowed. He was my friend—my first real human friend since the first Charles had become my first real friend. He carried me from the stables out into the darkness of the English night, and he made his way back to the main house.

As I lay in his arms that night, two visions moved into my mind and then began to merge. When I had been a very young vampire, the first Charles had seen to my safety on many occasions. He had been kind and true. This Charles was the same way. The two images seemed to blur in my mind. I had trouble discerning the two men. It was a comfort that I felt unworthy to possess.

Charles saw me off to safety, and Fletcher saw Master Smith back to London. As I lay in the bed where Charles had put me, the amulet started to glow ever so slightly. *Well, better late than never*, I thought to myself.

The days following my dentistry session passed in a kind of grey, London dullness. The weather matched my mood. I wandered about in a semicatatonic daze. It appeared I was just a small boat, bobbing in a big ocean of pain. I just wallowed in it, hating myself. I had actually gotten to the point of forgiving the veterinarian by that point. The misery was my own doing. No one was to blame for it but me. Well, that was not completely true. Antonio was to blame for almost all of it. He was the responsible party. I decided, while I wandered in my trance, that I would have to pay him back for it all, someday. Yes, sir, I was going to return that little favor.

I continued on with the water. It helped to keep me saturated. I liked the feeling of it, but not as much as the milk. The milk was another thing altogether. I had long forgotten what milk could do to a needy vampire. The sensation that it offered was something akin to rebirth.

I had experienced so much as a vampire that time seemed to stretch and dull out the memories of old. The sensation of memories that the milk returned to me were neither dull nor old.

Now, to tell that tale I need to go back, way back to the beginning when I was a freshly made vampire. It was in the year 1651, and I was still a child in the world. My fiancé, Antonio, had turned out to be a demon, and he had turned me into one as well. I concede that it was somewhat my own doing.

He had asked me if I wanted to spend eternity with him. I was young and in love, so I had said yes. He had asked a second time, and I had said yes once more. Then, he had turned me into a vampire. If I ever fall in love again and someone asks me open-ended questions, I'm going to make them clarify.

Well, back to the point. When I had died, my body had turned from human to vampire. My body had changed in some ways to become what it is now. My bones had stiffened and become denser, and my canine teeth had grown out to become the thick, enamel fangs that I had just had removed. All of that transition of muscle and bone had taken many days and had been intensely painful. I quite literally mean a pain that sat right down in my core and was unable to be described. The pain was constant and unflinching in its hold on my body.

The only thing that had even made a dent in the pain was, of all things, milk. The calcium and nutrients in the milk had made the bones grow and the pain stop. Looking back on things, it all seemed perfectly obvious, but in 1651, there was nothing obvious about it. It had really seemed like magic.

I freely admit that I had never been the type of girl to experiment with drugs and concoctions. They always seem like such a waste. But once in a while, I sat and thought about the milk. Then I wondered if that wasn't the same thing.

Now, in 1837, I drank milk as if it were never going to be made again. The constant flow of milk helped my teeth heal up and helped my disposition. A little human blood was added to help it all along. I really wanted the issue resolved sooner rather than later. I drank so much that I felt constantly bloated. I had to temporarily stop wearing my corsets and tight dresses and make a transition to looser styles of dress that were more the kinds that the servants and staff wore about the estate.

The staff was an interesting item. They all thought I was right bonkers. I can't say as I blamed them any. Being lady of the house, they let me do what I wanted. They did it without comment, because I was American. They knew that all Yanks had strange ways. That little bit of disbelief gave me great latitude. I really did not want to explain things to them. I was past the point of having large groups of humans know my nature. I liked anonymity.

Charles took care of procuring the things that I desired during that time. I had quit eating solid food and stayed tightly to liquids. That helped my system cope faster. Charles somehow found human blood for me. The blood was nice and was fresh. It was also in a quantity that made me suspicious.

I asked him about it once, and he told me that it came from a morgue across the city. They apparently drained out the dead and discreetly sold the bodies to medical schools. It was all somewhat nefarious, so no questions were ever asked. They apparently assumed that he was some type of scientist or doctor. Whatever lie he had told them, I did not care. I appreciated the blood.

The process took about five days to pass. Finally, I made the transition back to human teeth. The newly established, enamel caps on the teeth made them good and sturdy again. That killed off the pain and returned me to my calmer sensibilities. The release from the pain made me clearer of mind.

Coming out of the haze of pain and becoming aware made me notice that my teeth's regrowth had also made the amulet mellower. She had been sitting off to the side of the battle as it had raged. Apparently, the pain had annoyed her. I still was not quite sure why she had done little to help me with the pain. I pondered on that thought for a while after the aching passed and got the sensation that she seemed to think that it was something that I needed to do by myself. It was a life-is-pain type of lesson. I returned a "Thanks a lot" sensation.

When I decided that I was somewhat myself, I also decided that the sun was in order. So I went out and walked the paths of the meadows. I walked them all day long. I traveled the trails that the game made through the woodlands and walked the overgrown hedgerows that separated the meadows from the manicured lawns of the house. I wasn't pacing; I was strolling. I absorbed as much of the summer sun as was possible. The sensation of summer brought me fully around to my old self, just the way it had for hundreds of years.

Finally, I felt good. I was me once more. That was a grand thing. I didn't like not being me. I have always tried not to be moody. Being moody is a very easy thing for a vampire to do. It is also just a bad way to be. It makes one make poor decisions. I had always prided myself on making clear-minded decisions and thinking well. Now that I was clear minded once more, I was thinking it was time to hear some stories.

The morning after my meandering through the meadows, I ate a small breakfast to calm the closed-door rumblings of the staff. Then, I had Charles track down his brother, and by proxy, one Master Smith. I passed my time in the embrace of an English summer while Charles went about his task. It would take the day to see all parties properly notified. It was fine. I could wait. I still had a little time before the next big step.

The following morning brought the approach of Fletcher's carriage to my entryway, once more carrying Master Smith. They found Charles and me sitting contentedly on the study terrace, much the same way they had found us on the first visit. I can say that our second meeting was a more relaxed affair than the first one had been. That, I think, made everyone pleased.

We spent some time in general conversation. We talked about the Crown, how business in London had been, all of the social happenings about town, and the general talk of the day. The lighthearted tone of the conversation was nice and made everyone feel at ease.

Finally, after tea and coffee, it seemed time for a more robust topic of conversation. I stood, and the gentlemen did so in turn, and then walked some small steps toward the stone railings of the terrace. The men regained their seats. Charles knew that I stood a lot so it was natural for him to sit down. The others simply followed after him.

"Master Smith, last time we met, you said that you had heard tales of strange things meant to keep children in line?"

"Ma'am, I meant no offense, as I said."

"Relax, Master Smith. I'm not offended in any fashion. I would like to hear these fantastic tales of yours."

"What's that, then?"

"Could you please relay to me some of the tales of your youth? The ones told by your ancestors. I would much like to hear them. I might glean some new insight about my English family."

I turned and smiled broadly at the old veterinarian, and my reworked smile shown brightly in the summer sunlight. The teeth still felt strange, but they looked human. My shiny ivories made Master

Smith come around to the sarcasm in my words. He snickered to himself. It was lost on the other two, which I thought was strange.

"Yes, ma'am, I'd be pleased to tell a tale about your kin. It's a tale passed down from many grandfathers past when young Mistress Grey was overseeing your estate."

The old vet began to speak in a low, tranquil tone that suggested a happy tale. It was the story of a young girl with strange ways who had the weight of the world on her shoulders. She was an only child, who had been left to lead a company and keep up lands in different parts of the isle.

The young girl had a house full of well-mannered staff and an assistant who acted as her go-between on many occasions. The girl seemed to possess all that one could want. Nevertheless, she seemed constantly melancholy. She would be up at many odd hours, walking the grounds and out about the woods and doing all manner of strange things. Her assistant claimed that she had been stricken by some strange malady and could not handle the light of day.

Her staff came to suspect that she was unnatural. Many rumors circulated the halls of her great house that she was actually a vampire, though no one that his ancestor knew of ever sought out proof.

"Was it ever said that those rumors spread beyond the halls of her great house?"

"Not to my knowledge, Lady Gibbs. Young Lady Grey was reported to be a kind and goodly person. All the staff was reported to be perfectly content and happy in her employ."

"That is nice to hear, Master Smith."

The vet continued on a bit longer with his tale, telling us about young Sara Grey and her struggles in the world. His stories ended in a somewhat neutral fashion. It seemed a good omen. I had actually been waiting for worse. I wondered if he had toned down the stories for my hearing, but I didn't stop to ask.

Once finished with the storytelling, he returned to his position in the chair and surveyed the three of us. The storytelling was a part of his craft and a useful tool.

"I have to say, Master Smith, they all seem fairly accurate, as tales go. I truly don't remember being constantly melancholy, though I was upon occasion."

"I had always thought them to be just stories."

"And they are just that, Master Smith. They just happen to be basically factual. That's how history is made, you know. You take the basic truth and let it simmer until it has the right amount of fascination in it. Then you have history. This is no different. They all knew by the way."

"The staff?"

"Yes, sir. I openly confided in the staff when I was younger. It seemed an easier way to live, less suspicion and back hall talk. They all appeared amenable to the arrangement."

"I have to say that I am still having trouble coming to believe it all."

"I would actually appreciate it if you didn't manage to get all the way around to belief."

"I can understand that perfectly well, Lady Gibbs. I am not sure that I would like it if I were the one we were conversing about."

"I appreciate your objectivity, sir."

I looked around at the ensemble gathered on the terrace, Charles was unconcerned and just taking it all in; Fletcher was intent but confused that I was having such an open conversation; and Master Smith was pleased. I was content that the folklore of the day had not put me in a bad light with history.

The fact that the whole of our conversation had been overheard by another party had not made me happy. But there was no overreacting in my own home.

I let the conversation continue on a little longer. When midday had finally come to the terrace, it was time for the men from London to return from whence they had come. I rose from my chair, and the gentlemen followed suit. I thanked them for coming, and then each of us excused ourselves in turn. I asked Charles to go and find the servant girl who had been listening to our talk and bring her back to my study before she could spread her tale.

Moments later, Charles came back through the doors of the study with a young servant girl firmly in his grasp. She seemed terrified and objectified at the same time. In a different setting, she most likely would have fought back, but she did not do so then. The two of them came to a hovering stop in front of my overstuffed, leather chair. Charles released his grip, and the girl rubbed her arm and stared at me in wide-eyed disbelief.

"First, young miss, I do not appreciate people listening to my conversations uninvited."

"I ... I did not mean to, ma'am. I did not want to disturb, but you all continued to talk."

"Normally, that would be fine enough, but you stood off in the shadows for more than an hour. That is not the same thing. You were listening and doing it intently."

"I ... I ... "

The girl's focus sharpened as she realized that I had had my back to her the whole time. The realization of strange things was always interesting to observe.

"That was you he was talking about?"

"Very good, young lady."

Charles looked at me with a confused expression.

"What will happen to me now?"

"You will go back to your tasks as if it were any other day. Keep in mind ... "

"Julia, Lady Gibbs."

"Keep in mind, Julia, that the only person who would potentially talk about anything you overheard is you. So I suggest you learn the fine art of sealed lips, or the consequences will be dire."

"Yes, Lady Gibbs. I am quiet. There will be no gossip coming from me."

"Very good, Julia. Now, why don't you return to your tasks before you're missed?"

"Yes, Lady Gibbs, right away, ma'am."

The young girl curtsied in the fashion of the staff and quickly left the room. Charles stood to the side, unsure of what to say.

"Yes?"

"Are you sure that was wise?"

"People are people, Charles. It's no different today than it was two hundred years ago. You treat people well, and they will do the same to you. Besides, I always like a member of the staff to know the truth. It makes some things easier for all of us."

"That's what I'm for, isn't it?"

"Yes, but I'm a young girl and like the company of other young girls from time to time. It keeps me from sounding like the men."

"And if she isn't steadfast and true?"

"Then she's food."

Charles found the realism in the words and understood it all. He took a seat next to me, and we continued on as if it were any other day in the world.

# chapter 35

The remainder of July passed at the Grey Estate in a pleasant fashion. Then finally, the time had come. I was glad; confrontation was one of the things I didn't like to dwell on. That only made the field more rightly set for the competition.

For the first time in many trips to Court, on my appearance of August 1, 1837, I was prompt. Normally, I was as fashionably late to Court as I was able to be, since no one questioned the travels of a lady. That day I wanted to be almost early. America had taught me to head in and get things done early. In the royal setting, the new trait made me look American.

I was ready. I had been planning things out to cover all the details. I was emotionally ready for what was to come. I must say that I hoped that the new Queen of England was a levelheaded lady, or it could all go badly.

My main backup plan was the amulet. I really did not want to go down that road unless all else failed. She had a talent for excess. I didn't want her to kill them all, but, if that was necessary, then so be it. The problem was that that would require me to escape from the British Empire, never to return. I really didn't want to banish myself from the island, because it was my home. That was a last resort.

That day, Charles and I made our way through the grand gates of Buckingham Palace to be promptly received by the Beefeaters. Queen Victoria was the first monarch to take up residence in Buckingham Palace. She had actually been born in Kensington Palace. I guess she had thought a change of residence necessary. I looked up on the way in and caught sight of the Queen's colors. Her flag flew high in the clear blue sky. She was there, all right.

I was helped from my ornate carriage by the steward on station. From the entrance, I proceeded straight on to the Queen's meeting hall. It was a brash move, but hell, I was American. I marched down the middle of the grand hallway with a smooth, ladylike cadence.

I had chosen an ensemble for the occasion that hopefully set me apart from the remainder of the crowd. That day, I wore a discreet (read: floor-length), light blue, silk gown with delicate blue, lace fringes. I wore sturdy-heeled boots that had thick cloth covers nailed over the soles to quiet the sound on the stone floors. Dainty white, lace gloves and a small golden chain bracelet complemented it all. It made me look young and beautiful. That was the plan.

I made my way straight down the hallway and to the stewards stationed at the opulent hallway doors located at the far end. The steward in charge gave me a quizzical look as I came to a smooth stop in front of him.

"Good sir, I am Lady Allison Gibbs, Earl of Northwick. Could you please inform the Queen that I have come, as requested?"

The steward laughed. Apparently, he had never been directed by a child before. It was a planned approach. It allowed him to become comfortable with me.

"Young Lady Gibbs, Her Majesty must meet with the dukes first. She will meet the earls and so forth on down the line."

"Oh, I am sorry. I did not mean to be rude. Actually, I have never done this before, so I wanted to seem competent."

"And a very fine job, young Lady Gibbs. Please, let me escort you over to the outer hall. There you can be comfortable until such time as things commence."

I smiled happily. My clear, green eyes sparkled slightly as I did so. That made the steward relax completely. He seemed fully taken with the young lady before him. That was good. The stewards were not easily swayed, because they saw all sorts of strange occurrences.

"That would be grand."

I smiled, and the steward escorted me two doors back down the hallway to another set of ornate and oversize doors. There, he motioned me inside.

"Thank you very much, kind sir."

"You are quite welcome, Lady Gibbs. I say, you will do fine at Court today."

"Thank you."

I smiled again, and the steward did the same. Then, he promptly turned and headed back to his station at the far end of the hallway.

The waiting chamber that I had been escorted to was an ornate and comfortable affair. It was well lit by large windows down the length of the exterior wall. There were numerous people already waiting in the room. They were nobility of my own level and below. Many of the earls, counts, and knighted landlords of the Crown were in the room. They milled about talking to each other about whatever was the conversation of the day.

I moved slowly to take in the scene and observe the players. Charles took up a seat by the door. He wanted a good view of what was going on. Much more of a sentry, I supposed, than an attendant. That was fine; many other attendants were doing the same thing. It was good caution.

I made my way to the center of the room and introduced myself to a middle-aged couple who were gazing out the ornate windows. He turned out to be Count Monroe, from someplace. He seemed the old, military type, and his frumpy wife seemed the indoor type. They were well intentioned and allowed me to pass the time. Apparently, from the looks in the room, an earl wasn't supposed to casually converse with a count. I explained to the count that, being from America, I was not completely in tune with the social norms in England.

That opening made the count proclaim that he would be happy to introduce me to the other nobility in the room. It was a grand gesture, and I smiled broadly, my clear eyes big in acceptance. He smiled back; his wife did not. She seemed unimpressed with his doting over a lady of higher station, but she said nothing. Saying something objectionable would have been wrong.

Slowly, the three of us made our way about the room. I met two more earls, several counts, and about a dozen well-intentioned knights. They were all quite kind and well mannered toward the young American earl. I smiled continuously and talked openly about whatever the conversation of the moment happened to be. I presented every image possible of a young noble excited to be in such a setting.

The contentment of the impromptu affair was interrupted by the sound of music. It was the royal anthem, "God Save the Queen." It rang through the building and announced the presence of Queen Victoria. It seemed the day had officially begun.

I assumed, as was standard practice, that she would hear the roll of Parliament and then inspect the dukes and other high nobility. Then she would call on the middle nobility and others in lower lines. If things fell in that order, I should have to wait until about midday for my own introduction to Court and the start of it all.

It did take until about midday for the steward to start announcing the appearances of the earls, but when my turn should have come, he continued on past me to the next one in line. That was a bad sign. The nobility went by a well-structured ladder.

By the time the steward started in on the knights, I was sitting a corner chair next to Charles. The knights filtered out in quick succession, and soon enough, the two of us were alone. Something was definitely out of sorts. Things were simply not done that way at Court. The deviation made me worried. Maybe, whoever this new Brenfield man was, he had some real power in his title.

I sat and worried. Charles sat and worried. The amulet, on the other hand, began drawing in the deep, black magicks at her command. She was preparing for war. The power flowing from the crystal was making it hard for me to think. I could tell it was also affecting Charles's sensibilities. He was almost catatonic. *Stop,* I thought to myself. *Please stop now. This is not the way. We have a good plan. Please stop now.*

Finally, the amulet began to relent. That brought Charles back to the here and now and allowed me to think clearly. I could easily see how she could overwhelm the more easily turned minds of men.

The calm had no more than returned to the pair of us when the steward entered the room once more and requested our presence. I stood and quietly proceeded to a small side table where I could retrieve a glass of water. The steward was about to protest, because they do not like to be kept from their tasks, but he quickly realized my intentions and simply smiled patiently. I took a large drink of water and placed the glass back on the small table. Turning to face the steward, I waited for Charles to find his feet and ready himself, and then we were ready to be off.

"Is it my turn to see the Queen?"

"Yes, Lady Gibbs. If you could please follow me, I will make your entrance announcement."

I smiled. The steward was a nice man. He was as nice as he had been at the beginning of the day. That said a lot about him. The stewards had so many rude people to deal with; I was happy that he could manage to keep some sense of humor.

We proceeded back down to the end of the hallway. I had sat, wondering why I had been made to wait so long to be seen. I had been waiting most of the day. The sun was tipping its hat to the day and heading off the side of the world. I couldn't see the point of it all.

What I had not noticed was the orientation of the palace. The queen's meeting hall in the palace was on the west side and apparently was composed of many large glass windows that filled the room in radiant glow.

When the steward opened the door, I was staring into the sun. I could see the outline of the Queen's throne and two aisles of people, but everything else was a fiery wash of sunlight. The steward casually tilted his head toward the floor. I would offer no such satisfaction. I squinted tightly and headed straight in toward the Queen. On a mark appropriate for my station, I stopped and curtsied properly. The steward backed away gracefully, and I was alone.

The Queen raised her hand, and draperies dropped to cover the large windows. They stopped at a point that allowed the room to be well lit but not overwhelmed. My vision refocused, and I noticed the Queen wave her hand a second time so I might stand.

Until that point, I had never actually met Queen Victoria. She was of medium height and possessed that European beauty that was both simple and elegant at the same time. She would find a good husband, of that I was sure.

"Lady Allison Gibbs, Earl of Northwick, you hail from America, yes?"

"Yes, Majesty. I was born and raised in New York City until it was time to return to England." I kept my head tilted slightly, but my bright eyes were obvious to all. The vision of a young, bright-eyed girl automatically captivated the crowd, as I had known it would.

"That is a lovely dress, Lady Gibbs, where did you come by it?"

"In New York, Majesty. My mother retained a seamstress that the family utilized for all elegant occasions. I could get her information for you, if you desire, Majesty."

The Queen laughed. She seemed pleased by the statement. That was a good thing. We were bonding.

"That's quite fine, Lady Gibbs. I have enough seamstresses already. So tell me the status of your holdings."

"The lands of Brimme House and its surround are all quite well and prosperous. The area produces a quality not matched by other areas of its size, I believe, Majesty."

The Queen looked around the room at all the dukes and viscounts.

"And much more than some bigger ones as well."

She had done her homework. That was excellent. Money always talked quite loudly in that room. The statement put the dukes noticeably on edge. That was not good.

"Yes, Lady Gibbs, your dominion does quite well. I assume that it is your plan to continue on in that fashion?"

"Absolutely, Majesty."

"Good, it's always nice to know that the Crown has support from the nobility."

"Yes, Majesty."

"Now, about your title."

"Majesty?"

"You are the seventh Earl of Northwick and current holder of that status?"

"That is my understanding of my lineage, Majesty."

"It is an interesting state that all the recent Earls of Northwick have been female, don't you think?"

"I don't understand, Majesty."

"There have been no male heirs to your title."

"Apparently, my family is better at making women, Majesty."

A hush fell over the room. Apparently, I had upset the powerful dukes in the room again. The Queen smiled broadly. She seemed impressed by the sarcasm. I could not do that too often.

"It would seem so. Apparently, it would also seem that one of your forebears was a good friend to the Crown, since your title is *ad infinitum*."

"Majesty?" I kept a quizzical look on my face to suggest that I didn't understand. It was a lie.

"Your title cannot be taken away."

"Oh, that's quite nice, Majesty." I smiled broadly, and so did the Queen. I tried to seem excited by the news, even though I had been there when it had happened the first time.

"Yes, it is nice to have one's family thought well of. It would seem that the affairs of state are now concluded. Now, there is another in the room who has a few questions for you."

"Majesty?"

"William."

The grand duke, William Bennett of Stratford, stepped out from a row of high nobles and walked confidently to one side of the raised, throne platform. That was just great. The new leader of the Brenfield Society was a grand duke. I was in real trouble.

I could feel the power of the amulet start to buzz inside my head. She was obviously inclined to skip the foreplay and head straight to fighting. That was wrong. We could not attack. I quickly calmed my mind and thought, *Please stop. Please stop. Please stop. This won't help yet.*

It must have been the "yet" that grabbed her attention, for she stopped immediately. I could feel the impulse of attack swimming in my mind as the power ebbed. I had no more than regained complete focus when the grand duke began to speak.

"Lady Gibbs, I am the council chairman for a group called the Brenfield Society. We study odd occurrences in the world, and it is our observation that you are indeed a vampire."

There was an expelling of air in the room. I was sure that no such thing had ever been spoken in Court before.

"I beg your pardon?"

"That is 'Your Grace,' Lady Gibbs."

"I don't give a damn what your station is if you plan to stand there and insult my virtue."

"Is it not true that your true name is Sara Anne Grey? You have been around for two hundred years, and you hold possession of the lands of your family. The reason all your line is composed of women is because they are all you in disguise."

"That's just idiotic. If I were two hundred years old, then I would be two hundred years old. Do I look two hundred years old to you? I would probably have to check, but I would imagine that a woman of fifteen and one of two hundred would not be easily mistaken."

"That's 'Your Grace.'"

"Prat was more the title I was thinking of." Everyone in the room laughed loudly, save for the duke. However, it was becoming obvious that the Queen wanted decorum back in the room. "I apologize, Your Majesty. I will address the grand duke appropriately during the remainder of our interactions." I curtsied once more, and the Queen visibly relaxed. "I confess, I have not read many tales of fiction, Your Grace, but as I remember, vampires are not daytime creatures. They are said to abhor the light of day."

"That is true."

I raised an eyebrow and let my clear, green eyes sparkle in the fading light of the day. The look was not lost on the members in attendance.

"It is well known that you possess an amulet that gives you unique abilities that other vampires do not possess. Please pull out the chain around your neck and show all the fine people here your power source."

I slid my hand to my neck and put a finger under the golden hoop chain around my neck. I wasn't sure I wanted to pull out the chain. It seemed like I was giving in somehow.

"Majesty, is this really necessary?"

"Please do as the grand duke requests, Lady Gibbs."

I nodded and slowly pulled the finger all the way around the chain. The feeling of building excitement was evident in the crowd. The grand duke seemed pleased that I would be forced to show my secrets. I slowly pulled it out, letting the excitement build. The charm on the end caught on my corset and a small tug was required to free it from the corset strings. The movement of my breast gained the eye of almost every single, male noble in the crowd. *Great, more problems to deal with*, I thought to myself. I gave one last, small tug and a small, stylish, golden cross popped out from under the blue silk and came to rest in my palm. I gently settled it on the front of my gown and let its shiny surface shimmer in the fading rays of the sun.

The Queen gave a small wave of her hand, and the steward who had escorted me into the hall returned once more. He visually examined the cross and then asked politely if he could touch it. I removed it from my breast and allowed him to hold it in his hand. He did so for a mere second and then let it go once more.

"It is a real cross, Your Majesty."

"Of course it's a real cross, as I was raised to be a proper girl, Majesty."

The Queen began to glare at the grand duke, who was sweating, even though it was quite comfortable in the hall.

"As I remember, Your Grace, vampires do not take to the trappings of Christendom."

"That is true."

"Then, let's see. I also remember something about them not having a reflection. Is that also true?"

"That is true. They lack the ability to project an image."

"Well, let's see. Lord Mills, the thirteenth Earl of Brighton, has been admiring my posterior since my arrival. I am sure that he would be able to identify it as the same one in the mirror behind me."

The earl blanched and then nodded slowly. He, like everyone else in the room, had been eyeing up potential conquest.

"I can report that she produces a fine reflection, Majesty." He blanched once more. The statement came out a bit more lurid than he had intended. That was fine; he had done his part.

"Duke."

"Yes, Your Majesty." He was really beginning to sweat. The duke removed a small pin from his pocket, strode over to me, and stuck me in the exposed skin of my arm. The pain of the sticking made me react without thinking. I kicked the grand duke hard in the space between his legs. He crumpled to the floor in a heap. A trickle of blood ran from the hole that the pin had made. I let out a few tears as well, just enough to make it look believable.

"If this is the famous British hospitality, then I will promptly be returning to America."

"I am also rapidly becoming irritated by your show, Duke."

The Queen picked up a delicate piece of glassware, which was positioned next to her, and threw it at the duke. Another mass expelling of air came from the crowd. The glass bounced off the duke's head as he tried to right himself.

"You are just about out of rope, Duke. Do you understand me?"

"Absolutely, Your Majesty. I don't understand how she can cry and bleed. But surely there is one easy way to finish this examination. Vampires are dead, so they have no heat in their body. She will be cold to the touch."

"You attempt to touch me, and next time, you won't get up from the floor, Duke."

The Queen laughed. She was well on my side by that point. She was a friend to the House of Brimme, as many before had been.

"He will not, Lady Gibbs."

"Perhaps, Majesty, you would accept the words of Baron Shaw, seventeenth Earl of Yorkshire and member of the House of Commons?" At the time, he seemed as likely a choice as anyone else in the room.

"The baron will do fine, Lady Gibbs."

"Lord Shaw, if you please."

"Yes, Majesty." The baron separated himself from the crowd and made his way to where I was standing. I removed a lace glove and politely extended my hand so that he might take it. He seemed apprehensive after the show with the duke, but I smiled politely and calmed his anxiety. My adolescent gaze has had that effect on many occasions.

The baron took my hand in his and held it gently. He seemed a nicer man up close than what I had gathered from his place in the crowd.

"Young Lady Gibbs is quite warm to the touch, your Majesty. I would say the same temperature as myself."

"Thank you."

The Queen waved him off, and he nodded respectfully.

"You have a lovely smile, Lady Gibbs. I am truly sorry for your trouble."

Lord Shaw spoke quietly as he moved back to his place in the crowd. Yes, he was a nice man. I would remember the Earls of Yorkshire.

"Duke!"

The Queen was rapidly losing patience.

"Your Majesty, I am at a loss to explain the outcome. I have one last request, Majesty. A vampire has fangs that she uses to draw blood from her victims. She will not be able to hide such weapons from physical inspection."

"Lady Gibbs, do you possess fangs?"

"No, Majesty, and frankly, I find the whole affair to be in poor taste. That is, begging your pardon, Majesty."

"I find it the same way."

"Make her open her mouth. She will have fangs, my Queen."

"Your Highness, might I suggest that his grace, the ninth Duke of Kent and noted mathematician, Jonathon Mitchell, handle that request? My inquisitor doesn't seem to believe the words of earls; maybe another duke will make him happy.'

"Duke Mitchell, would you been so kind?"

"I would be happy to serve in any fashion you desire, Highness."

"Very well, then."

The old and handsome Duke of Kent made his way confidently out to where I was standing. I smiled and bowed my head, then I opened my mouth wide enough so he might inspect my teeth. The duke looked at each one in turn, from several angles and elevations. Confident of what he was seeing, he stepped away and straightened himself back to his full six feet of height.

"You have fine teeth and a sweet and refreshing fragrance, Lady Gibbs." He smiled as he spoke. He was obviously taken with the fresh-faced, young earl before him.

"Thank you, your grace. I brush my teeth every day. I find mint leaves help keep my breath fresh. Young men do not like unkempt young ladies, not even titled ones." I smiled and he returned the gesture. He also seemed a better man up close than I had figured him to be in the crowd. Being a man of math and science also made him objective. He was a good final choice.

"Her teeth are no different than my own teeth, Your Majesty. There are no fangs to be found amongst the young lady's teeth."

"Thank you, Your Grace, you may return to the procession."

The duke nodded to both the Queen and me and then walked back toward where he had been observing things. The Queen waited for him to regain his position before leveling her stern gaze on my inquisitor.

"I have to say, Duke Bennett. You have managed to do nothing but make me and everyone else in this room look absolutely idiotic. That is not to be put above the fact that you outright disgraced and objectified the young Earl Gibbs here.

"I am completely convinced that the only person of any danger to be found in this gathering is you. This Brenfield Society that you supposedly represent will, from this moment forth, be disbanded under order of the Crown. If I hear of anyone in my empire using that name or any other associated with it, they will be put to the noose. Am I perfectly clear, Mr. Bennett?"

"Majesty?"

"Do I make myself perfectly clear to you?"

"Yes, Your Majesty, perfectly clear."

"Now, Lady Gibbs, seeing how you are the one being wronged here, how would you like the duke to pay for his transgressions?"

"I'm inclined to approve of that trip to the noose you were discussing earlier, if that would also please Your Majesty."

The duke blanched. I don't really think he had considered the consequences of losing up until that point. The Queen turned and stared down the duke for several seconds.

"I think I can arrange that for you, Lady Gibbs."

The Queen clapped her hands loudly, and the Royal Guard appeared as if out of thin air. The sturdy, military men quickly and efficiently took possession of the grand duke and dragged him from the great hall. He kicked and spouted some silliness as the door slammed shut on his plea.

Seemingly satisfied that the calamity had finally passed, the Queen turned her attention back to me. I was still standing in the middle of the great hall alone, hands behind my back with my head slightly bent. She inspected me for several more seconds, apparently wondering what to make of me.

"It seems I am going to be short a duke in the near future. Would you like to be a duke, Lady Gibbs?"

"Is it possible to decline such a magnificent gift from a favorable Crown?"

"It is possible, but might I inquire as to the cause?"

"Your Majesty, I am only coming to terms with the implications of being an earl. I think being a duchess more than I could safely manage, considering the lands and good people I already have in my charge. I would not want to seem a poor choice at a later date. Plus, I have no desire for grand military deeds or conquest. That would seem a better place for men, Majesty. However, if you feel it absolutely necessary, I would not object to your desire."

"That was a wonderfully tactful answer, Lady Gibbs. For now, I will accept your answer. However, I may look differently upon it in the future. If I change my mind, I'll be sure to notify you."

"Yes, Majesty."

I nodded in acceptance of her kind words and curtsied in approval. I was hoping that that was going to be the end of it all.

"Well, now I would call this day done. Everyone, please feel free to take your leave."

The Queen stood and made her way from the room, escorted by her Royal Guard. The ornate double doors that we had entered through opened once more so the contents of the great hall could empty out as well.

When it was my turn, I collected Charles and headed straight for the carriage. Fortunately, it was ready and waiting for us. As soon as we were aboard, our conveyance was on the move and headed directly out the palace gates. I didn't want anyone changing their minds and trying to stop us. I wanted out; Charles wanted out; and the amulet still wanted to fight, so we left.

The ride across the city was quiet as we escaped London proper and headed out toward the estate. It was the part of the ride that I enjoyed the most. It wasn't the city, but it also wasn't the country.

"So you could have been Duchess Gibbs? Your father would be proud of that."

"So would yours, I think, and all the others behind him. I really didn't want to be a duchess. Titles can sometimes be a problem for people like me. A middle-of-the-pack title is good enough, Charles."

"Sara, could you please do me a favor?"

"Certainly."

"Remove that dreadful amulet from my pocket. And if you don't mind, never force me to carry it again. It makes me feel ways that I don't want to feel."

I reached into the pocket of his stylish jacket and extracted the amulet. The surfaces of the jewel glimmered brightly in the early night air.

"She does the same thing to me, from time to time."

The surfaces of the jewel pulsed with a bright blue moonlight. I slipped the chain around my neck and let the amulet fall next to the cross, which had been hanging out of my dress all that time.

"One more question?"

"Certainly."

"What's with the cross? I mean, where did you come by it?"

"It was a present from my father on my tenth birthday. I have carried it with me ever since. I had it deconsecrated by a shaman in the Americas long before you were born. I wanted to wear it once more. I used to wear it every day when I was human. Now, it reminds me of my family."

"And gets you out of sticky spots."

"Yes, that too."

The horses ran along the road toward the estate. I closed my eyes and listened to the sounds of the English night. They were soothing sounds that calmed my nerves. It had been a really long day.

# chapter 36

The sun rose early and bright on August 2, 1837. It was as if the world was trying to partake of my little victory. The birds outside my window sang songs to the sun, and a light breeze blew the fragrance of the thickets into the house. Yes, life was better that day than it had been the day before.

I had risen from my bed and dressed in the utter blackness of the predawn hours. By the time the sun decided to join me, I was sitting on the study terrace, waiting patiently. I liked to take in the essence of the early summer mornings. It all made me so pleased that I didn't hear the butler come out on the terrace to find me.

"Lady Gibbs, ma'am."

I jumped. His voice was loud. I had retuned my ears to the small sounds of the earth, and the new sounds of speaking were harsh on them. My startled reaction seemed to frighten the butler as well.

"Apologies, Lady Gibbs, I didn't mean to startle you."

"It's fine. I just didn't think anyone was about the manor yet."

"I'm an early riser. I like the quiet of the morning, before the demands of the day begin."

"I'm the same way."

"Would you like a nice cup of tea, ma'am? Perhaps some breakfast?"

"Not now, I guess. When the remainder of the house comes to life, they can accomplish such tasks. For now, why don't you sit and enjoy the quiet with me."

"That really isn't my place, ma'am."

"At the end of the day, people are people, and also at the beginning, I think. Please sit with me."

He sat and the two of us quietly enjoyed the morning terrace scene for some time. As with all things, the quiet was finally done in, that time by Charles lumbering out onto the terrace. He appeared with a young girl who carried a large silver tray of stuff. And that soon, the quiet was gone for the day, just as the butler had said.

I had sat there in that spot on hundreds of occasions. My companion on that morning had not done it nearly so long, but he seemed to appreciate it as much. The two of us would have to do that more often. Maybe I could make a new friend.

My nice butler and the young girl who had brought the tray faded back into the house as Charles settled into his usual chair and planted the large cup of black coffee down in front of him.

"If I didn't know you better, I would almost say you were happy."

"I am happy, Charles." I smiled, and he nodded. Then I looked off, back toward the meadows and the thicket.

"It's a very welcome change, I must say."

"I am happy enough quite often. The melancholy look that it's accompanied by is just the issues of the day."

"The young should always smile, I think."

"That is extra funny, coming from you."

We both laughed. It was nice to be thought of as young.

As one last side note, I have never really thought of myself as old. I know that I'm not young anymore, but that doesn't mean that I am old. At some point, I just became me, I guess. I'm not sure when that happened, but it was a long time ago.

Charles and I sat and laughed for some time. The sun climbed high above the trees and splashed the meadows with the colors of the day. I was happy. It seemed that everyone was happy. That was good. I really wanted to keep it that way, though even then, I knew it was fleeting.

The previous night, I had found myself too twisted up to sleep properly, so I had sat and composed a letter to young Jeremy Worthington back in New York City. He was the one member of the Brenfield Society I actually liked. I knew that the society was severely wounded but by no means put down. Their kind didn't bow to convention, even from the Crown. They would resurface. Hopefully, I had a few decades of peace before that happened.

Into the quiet of night had come thoughts of Jeremy. Even if he was the enemy, Charles was correct; we had both lied to each other. He was doing what he did. The part he did with me, I wanted to continue. So, as was my way, I sent a correspondence. It was fairly concise.

*Jeremy,*

*It would seem that your employer has been dissolved by the Crown. I would like this to not affect our previous arrangement. If this is acceptable to you, then I will look for you when I return to America once more.*

*If it is not, that is fine as well; we will just let it all pass by. If you choose not to, however, our relationship will meet a short end.*

*Be well.*

*Abbigail*

I wrapped the piece of parchment in a fine, heavy envelope and sealed it with the Grey family seal. He would understand the implications of both decisions. I hoped he would see things my way. As Charles finished his coffee, I handed him the envelope.

"Could you be a dear and see that onto the next ship headed for New York City?" Charles looked at the name and then flipped it over to inspect the family seal. He seemed perplexed.

"You mean to keep on with that Worthington fellow?"

"He's very good at the things we do together. If he chose to continue, then so would I. That's if we ever get back to New York in his lifetime. Besides, you told me he wasn't married."

We laughed some more. It was meant to be funny. *We need much more laughter at the estate*, I thought to myself.

It was about that time that the butler returned with a correspondence. He looked unhappy to be holding it. When Charles took the note from him, the look of displeasure transferred occupants. That wasn't good at all. It seemed that the happy was gone once more.

Charles handed over the envelope, which was sealed by the large red seal of the Brenfield Society. I had assumed that they wouldn't give up, but this was not what I had planned for. I figured on at least a decade. *Oh, hell,* I thought to myself, *I might as well just get it over with.* I slid a fingernail under the seal and across, until the seal was gone. Their message, too, was concise.

*Lady Grey,*

> *The Brenfield Society would like to concede, with regard to our previous terms of interaction. The society will no longer be interjecting itself in your affairs, in any fashion. Hopefully, somewhere in the future, neutral ground might be an option. Until such time, we leave you to your own path.*

The declaration of surrender was signed by nine knights, three earls, and two dukes. It seemed that the board of governors wasn't in a warring mood anymore. That was actually the best news that I had heard all day. The note was proof that I had done it. I was free of them, at least for some time to come.

I tossed the note down in front of Charles. He quickly read it twice, without lifting it from the glass tabletop. He looked up and beamed with approval. I agreed with his appraisal. We three, Charles, the amulet, and myself, had all gone against our basic nature, and the end result was victory, of a sort. Anyway, it would be quiet for a while.

"Do me a favor and deliver that to your brother. I am sure that he would also find it interesting."

"Will do."

"Thank you, Charles."

We stood and headed off in our own directions. Charles headed for the glass doors of the study, and I went down the steps to the well-kept lawns of the estate. Charles stopped short of the doors and turned back to look at me. I paused about two steps down and waited.

"Sara, I really am pleased that it all worked out well for you."

"Thank you, Charles. I, too, for all our sakes."

"I'll be off to see Fletcher."

"Be safe."

With that, he was gone through the glass doors of the study once more. I continued down the steps and out onto the lawns. I stopped briefly to examine the entrance to the maze. No, I had a happier place in mind. I had good news, and the dead always appreciated good news. I wanted to share my good news with my friends. I wondered what they would all think of my tale. I was sure that they would find it audacious, at best. The dead always liked that sort of thing.

I turned off the lawns and headed for the hedgerows that protected the path leading up to the family plots. I could walk it blindfolded by that point, but I always looked about curiously. I like the meadows and the wild spaces outside the manicured lawns of the manor.

When I was done with the dead, maybe I would go on vacation. I could have a new ship built and then go somewhere. Maybe, I would just get in my carriage, head north, and see what Zoey was up to in the Highlands. No, maybe I would just cross the city and see if Antonio was still being an arse.

Well, I could figure that out later. The day was nice, and I needed to enjoy it while it lasted.

# about the author

Aaron Brownell works as a field engineer for a large, United States-based environmental remediation company. He holds a bachelor of arts degree in physics from Potsdam College. When not traveling, he resides at his home in Potsdam, New York.